Worlds Unraveled:

The McAllister Saga

Jacob Salvia

Copyright © 2025 Jacob Salvia
All rights reserved.

Published by Makwa Press

No part of this publication may be reproduced, stored in a retrieval system, or transmitted in any form or by any means — electronic, mechanical, photocopying, recording, or otherwise — without the prior written permission of the copyright owner, except in the case of brief quotations embodied in critical articles or reviews.

This is a work of fiction. Names, characters, places, and incidents are either the product of the author's imagination or used fictitiously. Any resemblance to actual persons, living or dead, events, or locales is purely coincidental.

Printed in The United States.
ISBN: 979-8-9989451-0-6

DEDICATION

This is for my grandmother, a fellow writer, and the kindest person I know. She was always happy to see anyone who walked through her door. I love you and miss you, Mema.

CONTENTS

	Acknowledgments	i
1	When My World Unraveled	1
2	The Price of the Ring	6
3	Rune and Ruin	10
4	Echoes of a Vanished World	14
5	The Castle's Heart	19
6	Hollow Shades and Hollow Voices	26
7	Gravel and Ghosts	42
8	Hunger's Hollow	53
9	Claws of the Past	61
10	Whispers in the Water	69
11	Myth Made Flesh	76
12	Breath of the Forest	84
13	Roar of the Ruins	99
14	Breath of the Broken	106
15	Shadows of the Hollow	113
16	Bones of the Beast	118
17	Forest Reborn	128
18	Road to Ruin	134
19	Portal's Last Pulse	151
20	Echoes of the Empty	155
21	Blood on the Logbook	163
22	Highway to Haven	174
23	Rest Area Respite	183
24	Neon and Nightmares	194
25	Fur and Fury	208
26	Prayer on the Pavement	219
27	Curse in the Candlelight	230
28	The Bleeding Veil	238
29	Malakar's Mantle	245
30	Axel's Awakening	253
31	Scream in the Stone	263
32	Blood on the Blade	273
33	Scream Through the Stones	279
34	The Glow Against the Hollow	285

DEDICATION

This is for my grandmother, a fellow writer, and the kindest person I know. She was always happy to see anyone who walked through her door. I love you and miss you, Mema.

CONTENTS

	Acknowledgments	i
1	When My World Unraveled	1
2	The Price of the Ring	6
3	Rune and Ruin	10
4	Echoes of a Vanished World	14
5	The Castle's Heart	19
6	Hollow Shades and Hollow Voices	26
7	Gravel and Ghosts	42
8	Hunger's Hollow	53
9	Claws of the Past	61
10	Whispers in the Water	69
11	Myth Made Flesh	76
12	Breath of the Forest	84
13	Roar of the Ruins	99
14	Breath of the Broken	106
15	Shadows of the Hollow	113
16	Bones of the Beast	118
17	Forest Reborn	128
18	Road to Ruin	134
19	Portal's Last Pulse	151
20	Echoes of the Empty	155
21	Blood on the Logbook	163
22	Highway to Haven	174
23	Rest Area Respite	183
24	Neon and Nightmares	194
25	Fur and Fury	208
26	Prayer on the Pavement	219
27	Curse in the Candlelight	230
28	The Bleeding Veil	238
29	Malakar's Mantle	245
30	Axel's Awakening	253
31	Scream in the Stone	263
32	Blood on the Blade	273
33	Scream Through the Stones	279
34	The Glow Against the Hollow	285

ACKNOWLEDGMENTS

Bringing this book to life has been a journey I could not have completed alone. I am deeply grateful to the people who stood beside me, offering their unwavering support, guidance, and belief in my work.

First and foremost, I want to thank my mother. Her dedication to helping me research, navigate the complexities of publishing, and her constant financial and emotional support have been invaluable. She has always been my strongest advocate, ensuring that I had the tools and encouragement needed to follow my dreams.

To my fiancée, thank you for always pushing me to be better – as a writer, as a person, and as a partner. Your belief in me, your constant motivation, and the way you inspire me to grow every day have been a driving force behind this book.

Without your love, patience, and relentless support, this story would have remained a dream. Because of you, it is now a reality.

1 WHEN MY WORLD UNRAVELED

The day Earth started stitching itself into Ashvalen was ordinary enough. I'd just punched out from my shift at the supermarket, a soul-deadening gig that smelled of stale bread and desperation, barely keeping the lights on in our sagging Florida bungalow even with the bullshit 20% disability pay.

"Catch you tomorrow, Deb," I muttered, shoving through the rusted employee exit into the parking lot. The air hit me humid, thick with the tang of asphalt and a subtle whiff of ozone, like rain brewing too long. That's when I caught it: a blue orb, fist-sized, flickering like a dying ember near my Jeep. It pulsed once, twice, casting jagged shadows across the cracked pavement, then winked out. I rubbed my eyes, still gritty and raw from too many sleepless nights, and chalked it up to exhaustion. Shrugging it off, I climbed into the beat-up rig that'd rattled me through life since the army, its olive drab paint chipped like old scars.

The radio hummed static over my classic rock as I drove, tires thumping over potholes. Zeppelin's riffs fought the white noise until a voice sliced through, crisp and clipped, "Unexplained energy spikes detected globally, stay indoors," before fuzz swallowed it whole. I snorted, picturing some intern at the station fumbling the board. Someone's getting fired for that, I thought, then I remembered when I was in South Korea, there was some interference in our early warning system. We thought World War 3 happened, turns out the E2 in charge checking everything skipped a few steps. We were all chewed out for that. A smile came to my face, remembering the good old days. Then I started to plan dinner.

Mom counted on me to cook since her hands started trembling last year, and my stomach growled at the thought of spaghetti, simple, easy, and quick. Then the Emergency Alert System kicked in, three gut-punching beeps that vibrated through the Jeep's frame.

"Stay home. Unknown phenomenon reported," it droned, looping like a broken record. I tapped the dial; every station was dead air, just hissing silence. My phone buzzed on the passenger seat, Sara's name flashing. I hit the speaker, expecting her usual Michigan check-in, all brisk cheer and small-town gossip.

"Jake, something's wrong," she said, voice tight, frayed at the edges.

"People with red eyes, they're breaking in!" A crash exploded through the line, glass shattering, then her scream high, primal, before static ate the call. I swerved, tires kissing the guardrail with a metallic screech, and redialed. Busy signal. "Sara!" I barked, slamming the dash with a fist. Michigan was 1,400 miles North, a world away, but that call lit a fuse in my chest. I had to get to her, logic be damned.

I rolled into the driveway, gravel crunching under the Jeep's bald tires, and found Mom perched on the couch, staring at the TV. The news was chaos, dragons flying over New York, their scales glinting like oil slicks against the smoggy skyline; elves with bone-white hair and orcs with tusks like butcher knives storming Times Square like a geek's fever dream gone live. The anchor's voice cracked, sweat beading on his brow:

"Reports from every major city, stay indoors, the military's mobilizing." Mom's knitting needles clacked in her lap, a frantic rhythm, her eyes wide and lost behind thick glasses. The living room smelled of dust and her lavender soap, a subtle comfort against the madness. "What's happening, Jake?" she asked, voice small, like she was twelve again, not sixty-two.

"No clue," I said, glued to the screen, jaw tight. Dragons. Actual damn dragons, leathery wings cutting the air, fire blooming in their throats. But Sara's scream rang louder than any broadcast, echoing in my skull. She'd moved to Michigan with Mark and their kid, Lily, five years old, all pigtails and giggles chasing seasons, she'd laughed over FaceTime, all snow and cider and a good life. Now? Red-eyed freaks smashing through her door didn't fit that picture. "I need to get Sara," I said, breaking for the stairs.

Mom's needles froze mid-stitch, yarn dangling like a lifeline cut short. "What? You can't, she's too far, and this," she waved a trembling hand at the TV, helpless, the glow painting her face in flickering blues. "She called, Mom. She's in trouble. I'm not sitting here while my sister …" I stopped, my throat closing around the words. The army had taken everything else, friends, faith, half my hearing in one ear; family was all I had left. I wasn't losing her, not like this. Not again.

Upstairs, I dragged out my gear from under the bed, kit I'd "lost" on discharge, still smelling of gun oil and desert dust, plus camping junk I'd hoarded since. Battle belt with its frayed webbing, chest rig heavy with mag pouches, a backpack stuffed with a hammock, MREs, med kits, and my rifle, an AR-15, matte black and scratched from drills. Overkill, sure, but I'd seen what "underprepared" looked like: graves in the sand, names I couldn't forget. Packed quickly, muscle memory on autopilot, boots thudding on the creaky floorboards as I headed down. Mom caught me halfway, eyes tracing the gear. I looked like a cut-rate action hero, tactical vest over a tee that said Fueled by

Caffeine and Hate. To be fair, it was the only comfortable shirt that was clean. And jeans patched at the knees with reinforced knee pads; her frown called it out, deep lines carving her face.

"What are you doing?" she asked, steady but firm, hands clasped tight.

"Camping," I said, faking a grin that didn't reach my eyes. We both knew it was a lie, thin as the air between us.

"Stay home. The government will handle this." Calm, firm like she could, like she'd willed Dad's cancer into remission before it took him anyway.

I laughed, bitter and jagged, tasting bile. "You think they give a damn? I've seen men die for suits who'd sell us out in a heartbeat, bled out in dirt while brass sipped coffee." It spilled out like a glass vial with cracks, years of scars bleeding through, raw and unfiltered. Her face twisted with anger, sadness, something new, maybe fear. I'd never snapped at her like that, not since I came home hollowed out.

"You don't know that," she said, gently, stepping closer. "They'll fix it."

"They won't," I shot back, heat rising, pulse hammering. "I'm not letting Sara and Lily die because you trust some desk jockey who's never held a gun." Time was slipping, I felt it in my bones, a ticking clock. Then a knock slow, heavy, too deliberate hit the door, rattling the frame. Outside, the wind stilled, the silence thicker than it should've been. Like something from a horror movie, the Supernatural nature is just out of place and wrong.

"Don't!" I barked as Mom moved for it, hand on the knob, curiosity overriding sense. My body moved before I could react. Training took over instincts I couldn't bury, forged in firefights and sleepless nights. Shadows loomed beyond the frosted glass, tall, too angular, too still. Rifle up, safety off, I fired as the door swung open. Two shots, center mass, the crack echoing off peeling wallpaper. The figures dropped gangbangers from the outskirts, I thought at first, clad in mismatched leather and hoodies, but their eyes glowed red, faint even in death. I quickly switched to the other two targets. Each one got two shots. Then I saw Mom.

She was down, crumpled against the wall, a jagged hole in the front of her chest, blood pooling dark on the linoleum. My knees hit the floor, rifle clattering beside me. "No, no, no," I pressed the wound, hands shaking, slick with red, like I could shove the life back into her. Her eyes were blank, staring past me, gone. Rage and grief tore at me, silent but choking, a scream I couldn't let out. A groan snapped back, one of those things still twitched, its fingers curling like spiders, clawing at the floor.

I stood, cold as a lonely winter night, and used my boot to get it over. Humanoid, but wrong skin grayish, veins black under the

Jacob Salvia

surface, eyes fading from red to dull glass. It spoke with a guttural rasp, syllables grinding like stones, nothing from Europe or the Middle East. Not even Spanish, which is common around these parts, just something interesting I noticed but didn't care enough to figure out why. I crushed its chest with my boot, felt the ribs snap like dry twigs, and put a bullet between its eyes.

I found the other two lying nearby, same deal, dispatched with shots that rang in my ears. The air reeked of smoke, copper, and something sour I couldn't place. Mom's body was there, small, broken, her knitting spilled across the floor like a child's toy. I slid my arms under her, lighter than she should've been, fragile as ash, and whispered, "I'm sorry," again and again, voice hoarse. It didn't fix shit.

Outside, the night stung, cold and raw, the wind carrying distant screams and the crackle of fire. No shovel, no time. I clawed a grave with my hands in the backyard, nails splitting on roots and rocks, dirt staining red with her blood and mine. Laid her in, draped her old wool coat over her face, couldn't face those blank eyes staring up. Patted it down with numb hands, mumbled something about peace that sounded hollow even to me. My voice cracked, a sob I choked back, knowing that wouldn't help, I felt the old me coming back from the sandbox. The house gaped behind me, door wide, fire fading in the hearth, bodies festering on the floor. I could've burned it, torched the memories with the trash. I didn't. I couldn't.

Gear slung in the Jeep, I dialed Sara, busy signal again. "Stay put," I muttered a prayer to no one, the engine rumbling to life. Roads out of Florida were empty, unnaturally still, streetlights flickering like they knew what was coming. I hit Jacksonville in ninety minutes, pedal pinned, the skyline ahead glowing orange flames chewing through buildings, something huge overhead spitting fire like a living furnace. A dragon. Took a second to sink in, the sheer size of its wings blotting stars, tail whipping like a storm. Out of my depth, but I'd manage. Took a back road, weaving through abandoned cars and debris, tires crunching glass.

A call cut through an unknown number buzzing the dash. "Hello, this is about your car's warranty" I hung up, pissed, knuckles white on the wheel. Spam in an apocalypse, but Sara's line was dead. That inconsistency had me distracted. I was about to start venting all the pressure I've been under. Then a roar ahead stopped me cold, deep, resonant, shaking the air. Brakes locked, tires squealing, I prayed it wasn't that dragon. No dice. It stood there in the road, horse-sized, smaller than the city burner but no less deadly, wings clawed and tattered, skull glinting metallic in my headlights. Sparks flicked in its jaws, ember-bright, scales shimmering like wet tar.

"What's that?" I started, then gunned it as fire flared a jet of heat grazing the hood. It looked like I was just driving into a bonfire. The

Jeep slammed its head on, metal and bone crunching, the impact jarring my teeth. I stopped hard, got out, and the bumper was ok. Thankfully, it was one of those reinforced ones for moving cars off the road. The dragon's head cracked open, leaking silver ichor onto the pavement. Smaller up close, maybe ten feet wingtip to wingtip, but dead. That's when I checked the engine, thankfully it was coughing but alive, good enough.

A scream sliced through the stillness, sharp enough to cut past the dull ringing in my ears. "Help!" It was distant, ragged, pleading somewhere off the road. "Not my problem," I muttered under my breath, dragging a sleeve across my sweat-streaked face, smearing the grime deeper into my skin. I didn't need this. Not now. My boots stayed planted for a moment, heavy as lead, every muscle screaming to keep moving the other way away from trouble, away from more ghosts. Mom's blood still clung to my hands in memory, sticky and warm; Sara was gone, Lily's laugh a knife twisting in my skull. I didn't have room for someone else's mess.

But the scream came again, weaker, and damn it, my feet shifted. Gravel crunched under my reluctant steps, each one a curse I didn't bother voicing. Rifle up, more out of habit than intent, I trudged toward the sound, jaw tight, anger smoldering like a coal I couldn't stamp out. The darkness closed in, and I let it, half-hoping it'd swallow me before I got there.

2 THE PRICE OF THE RING

It didn't take long to find the source of that scream, a campsite tucked in the woods, glowing softly under torchlight that danced like liquid amber across the pines. The air smelled of sap, smoke, a coppery tang I knew too well. Green-skinned figures moved around it, all muscle and leather, their silhouettes hulking against the flickering flames. Orcs, I guessed, piecing it together from the news footage I'd seen back home, broad shoulders, jagged tusks glinting in the light, like they'd walked off a bodybuilding stage into a medieval reenactment gone feral. A dozen of them, maybe more, their heavy boots crunching pine needles as they paced. In the center, a group of suits, business types, ties loose and faces pale as moonlight, sat tied up, trembling on the dirt.

Briefcases and shredded suit jackets littered the ground near them, relics of a world that didn't exist anymore. Every few minutes, one got dragged out by a meaty green fist, forced to square off with the biggest orc in a makeshift ring of logs and stones. Didn't end well for the suit's bones cracked, blood sprayed, and the crowd roared with guttural cheers.

I crept closer, rifle ready, the cold steel slick against my palms as I wove between trees, keeping low. My breath fogged in the crisp night air, heart pounding like a war drum. Tried to muster some swagger, fake it 'til you make it, but it was a thin shield. Walking away wasn't an option, not after Mom's blood soaking my hands, not with Sara's voice still rattling in my skull, piercing and desperate. Confidence was a lie, but it'd have to do. A shadow shifted ahead, too quiet, and my grip tightened. I stepped into the open, boots snapping a twig loud enough to turn heads.

"Hey!" I barked, voice carrying over the crackle of the fire. "Stop whatever the hell you're doing."

One of them turned a wiry orc with a scar splitting his brow, laughed deep and guttural, the sound bouncing off the trees, and nodded to the big guy in the center. The chief, probably taller than the rest, maybe seven feet, his leather armor studded with rusted iron plates, a necklace of what looked like finger bones clattering against his chest. He stepped forward, tossing me a ring that glinted dull silver in the torchlight. It hit the ground near my feet with a quiet thud.

He gestured, short, brisk, to put it on. I bent down slowly, keeping my eyes locked on him, muscles tense, didn't trust him not to rush me while I blinked. Slipped it on; it was cold, plain metal, heavier than it looked. Instantly, their grunts and growls turned to English in my head, clear as a radio signal cutting through static. Magic. Great. Just what I needed, more weird shit in a world already unraveling.

"Oh good, you understand me now," the chief said, smirking, his tusks catching the firelight. His voice was gravelly, like rocks grinding together, with a hint of amusement. "I'm Gorzod, leader of the Gin tribe. The ring's a translator, handy, huh?" He scratched at a patchy beard, his yellow eyes sizing me up like I was meat on a scale. "Yeah, real handy," I said, grip tightening on my rifle 'til my knuckles ached. "So what's this? Dinner and a show?" I jerked my chin toward the captives, the bitter tang of their fear-sweat mixing with the woodsmoke in the air.

He glanced at the suits, bound with coarse rope that bit into their wrists, their polished shoes scuffed and useless in the dirt.

"They begged for protection. Offered nothing, no tribute, no skills. Useless mouths." He laughed again, louder, a sound that rattled my ribs. "You know what a 'businessman' is?" He spat the word like it tasted sour, kicking a cracked leather briefcase into the fire. It flared briefly, spitting embers.

"Talkers who talk to other talkers," I said, keeping it simple, my voice steady despite the churn in my gut. "Not much else push paper, cash checks, die soft."

Gorzod's grin widened, splitting his face like a cracked melon. "Punching bags, then. Perfect." He waved at the suits like they were props in some twisted play, his tribe chuckling low behind him, rumbles of approval. I nodded toward the women in the group, three of them, huddled tight, their mascara-streaked faces pale under the grime, dresses torn at the hems. My stomach turned, bile rising. "And them?"

"Wives," he said, casual as hell, shrugging like he was discussing livestock. "Willing or not, they'll serve the tribe, cook, mend, and breed. Stronger stock than these weaklings." He nudged a groaning suit with his boot, the man curling tighter into himself. Of course. Should've walked away right then. I didn't need this fight, didn't need more blood on my ledger. But Sara's scream clawed at me, Mom's blank eyes stared from the dark corners of my mind, they wouldn't let me turn back.

"What if I challenge you?" I asked, voice flat, locking eyes with him. Part of me still wanted to bolt, to peel out in the Jeep and chase Sara's ghost north. Gorzod blinked, surprised, then laughed full-bellied, head thrown back, the bone necklace jangling.

"You? An outsider? It's to the death, and I've got nothing to gain. My daughter's the prize, but what've you got worth that?" He crossed his arms, biceps bulging under scarred green skin, waiting for me to back down.

I jerked my thumb back toward the road, where the dragon's corpse still steamed faintly in the night. "Killed a dragon out there. Meat's yours if you want its scales, bones, whatever you butcher types value." The only thing I had that might mean something to them, a gamble on their pride or hunger. His jaw dropped literally, mouth hanging open, tusks framing a stunned gape.

"You killed a dragon?" he sputtered, eyes wide, yellow irises catching the fire like twin suns. "And you're offering it?" His tribe muttered behind him, a ripple of disbelief and awe passing through them, words like "draka" and "slayer" filtering through the ring's magic.

"Don't want your daughter," I said, shedding my pack with a thud, clipping the bayonet to my rifle with a sharp click. "Want the captives. Deal?"

I rolled my shoulders, feeling the weight of the gear settle, the ache in my bones from the Jeep crash waking up. He recovered fast, smirking again, wiping a hand across his mouth.

"Let's see you try to refuse her. She's a beauty, worth ten of you." He grabbed a short spear from a rack near the fire, iron-tipped, haft wrapped in leather, and twirled it with a flourish, the blade whistling. "You first, dragon killer."

I eyed my rifle, its scratched barrel steady in my hands. He'd never seen that one spear versus gun wasn't a fair fight, but he was too smug to care, too rooted in his world of muscle and steel. I didn't bother explaining it to him. I'll let him learn the hard way. Raised the barrel, aimed for his chest, and squeezed.

The shot cracked like thunder, splitting the night; he moved too fast, unnatural, a blur of green, and it grazed his shoulder instead, tearing leather and drawing a thin line of green blood. He charged, spear flashing, and I barely sidestepped, the air hissing past my ear as the tip grazed my jacket.

Instincts took over years of drills, nights in the sandbox dodging shrapnel. I swung the bayonet, aiming for his gut; he blocked with the spear haft, wood splintering under the force, grinning like a kid at a game.

"Nice trick, spear and bow in one. Clever!" he said mid-fight, voice bright, like we were sparring buddies trading tips. I yanked the blade free, spotting a discarded club nearby forearm-length, carved from dark wood, heavy at the tip with a knob of polished stone. Dropped the rifle, but I had my sling, so it stayed with me. Grabbing it, melee was my ground now, close and dirty.

"Good choice," Gorzod taunted, circling me, spear loose in his grip. "Die with something proper, not your thunder stick."

He swung; I dodged late, catching the blow on the club instead of my skull. My hands stung, bones vibrating, didn't know you're supposed to sidestep, not block, not against a freight train like him. His hits kept coming, relentless, a storm of muscle and intent spear haft cracking against the club, then a fist to my ribs that stole my breath.

My grip faltered; one hard strike sent the club flying, spinning into the dark beyond the firelight. He loomed over me, chest heaving, eyes almost sad, like he didn't want to finish it, like I'd disappointed him by breaking too fast.

Screw that. I kicked his knee, hard, felt the joint buckle; he stumbled with a grunt. Lunged up, fists hammering his face, rage from Mom's death, from Sara's silence, from every betrayal I'd swallowed pouring out in a flurry of blows. Skin split under my knuckles, his tusks scraping my hands raw. He shielded himself, grunting, then kicked me back, right in the gut, a mule's kick that sent me sprawling.

I hit the dirt, wind gone, tasting blood and pine needles, cursing myself. Dumbass, helping people who'd spit on me yesterday, suits who'd fire me for a nickel.

He pinned me, knee crushing my chest, the stink of sweat and iron rolling off him. I fumbled for my bushcraft knife, six inches of battered steel strapped to my thigh, drew it blind, and thrust up with a snarl. The blade sank deep, just under his ribs; warm blood splashed my face, thick and coppery, running into my mouth. His eyes met mine, wide, yellow fading to gray, a flicker of something—respect, maybe— before they dulled.

Jake watched the light fade from his eyes. Not rage. Not victory. Just... exhaustion.

"You picked the wrong fight," he whispered, unsure who he meant it for.

I shoved him off; he slumped sideways, heavy as a felled tree, peaceful like he'd just nodded off mid-sentence. Dead.

Silence screamed louder than the fight, deafening, oppressive. The tribe watched, frozen, torchlight painting their faces in stark relief, waiting for him to get up, to laugh it off with that bone-rattling chuckle. He didn't. His blood pooled green and black in the dirt, steam curling up in the cold air.

3 RUNE AND RUIN

The chief Gorzod lay still, blood pooling under him in a dark, glistening stain, soaking into the pine-strewn dirt. His smug grin was gone for good, replaced by a slack-jawed emptiness that didn't match the fire in his eyes minutes ago. The tribe's shouting hit me like a wall, their guttural tongue buzzing through the translator ring. Anger, confusion, maybe grief, words like "kresh" and "thul" flickering into meaning: betrayal, loss.

I braced, expecting spears to fly, my rifle still warm in my hands, Gorzod's blood dripping from the bushcraft knife clutched in my other fist. Chest heaving, I scanned the crowd, green faces taut, yellow eyes glinting in the torchlight, but no one moved. They just stared, frozen, like they couldn't believe he was down. Neither could I, the weight of it sinking in slow, heavy as the night air thick with smoke and copper. A spear shifted in someone's grip, metal catching the firelight, and my finger twitched on the trigger.

The captives didn't waste time; ropes hit the dirt with dull thuds as they bolted, scattering into the woods like startled deer. Their polished shoes crunched over twigs, ties flapping uselessly, disappearing into the shadows without a second thought. Smart. Selfish, maybe, but I'd have done the same run first, figure out the guilt later.

My eyes flicked back to the tribe, waiting for the backlash, muscles coiled tight, when a green-skinned woman, shorter than the rest, leaner, built like a coiled spring, stepped out from the milling crowd. Her leather tunic was patched with fur, and a short cape of wolf pelts swayed at her back. She knelt by Gorzod, her movements deliberate, and picked up his club, dark wood slick with his blood. Pressed it to her forehead, eyes closed, lips moving in a silent murmur. A ritual, I figured, something sacred in their world. Daughter, probably, same sharp jaw, same crimson eyes that locked on me as she stood, piercing through the haze. My gut tightened, a cold knot forming.

She walked over, stopping an arm's length away, boots silent on the earth. Up close, her skin shimmered gently, a sheen like wet stone, and purple symbols, jagged runes, crawled up her left arm, pulsing dimly under the torchlight. She handed me a rag, coarse, stained, carrying a trace of sweat and herbs. Blood still streaked my face, warm

10

and tacky, mixing with dirt and his ichor; from the fight, splattered across her cheek.

"Thanks," I muttered, wiping it off, the cloth coming away green, black, and red. Her ring matched mine, glowing softly on her finger, and those symbols on her arm flared brighter for a heartbeat. Magic again. Fantastic, just what I needed, more rules I didn't understand in a world gone sideways.

"I am Mithis of the Gin tribe," she said, voice low, trembling just enough to notice like a blade held steady by will alone. "I'm your wife now." Her crimson eyes didn't waver, but her hands shook slightly at her sides, betraying the calm she wore. My brain stalled, gears grinding to a halt.

"Wait, what?" I said, louder than I meant, voice cracking through the quiet. "I told him I didn't want that, the deal was for the captives, not a damn bride." I gestured back toward the road, half expecting Gorzod to sit up and call it a joke.

She didn't flinch, didn't blink, just held my gaze. "You killed my father. Our law binds me to you. Victor takes the burden." Her tone steadied, hardening, but her fingers twitched, curling into fists. "Refuse, and they'll kill me. A chief's daughter without a protector will see it as bad luck. And it will taint the tribe." She tilted her head toward the others, their muttering growing sharper, eyes darting between us.

I sucked in a breath, holding it 'til my chest burned. Bullshit law, some archaic trap I'd stumbled into, but her life hung on it, red eyes or not, she wasn't lying. Mom's face flashed blood pooling on the linoleum, her body light in my arms, my fault for pulling that trigger not fast enough. Couldn't let that happen again, not even to a stranger who'd watched me gut her dad. That's when it clicked. He saw me risk everything for people I don't know, so he knew I can't walk away from this if it means her death. What a clever bastard.

"Fine," I said, exhaling harshly, the word tasting like ash. "You're with me. But I'm not leading this circus, right? No throne, no tribe bullshit?"

Mithis glanced at the tribe; some cheered, fists pounding chests, others muttered low, spears shifting in their grips. "Only if you claim it. Father's death gives you the right, not the duty. Blood's your key, not your chain." Her voice softened, just a fraction, like she was testing me.

"No thanks," I said fast, shaking my head. "Got enough on my plate."

She nodded, quick and decisive, and before I could blink, she lunged and hugged me, tight and quick, her arms wiry but strong. Caught me off guard; I stiffened, breath hitching, then relaxed as the scent of leather and pine hit me. The tribe erupted with yells, fists thrust skyward, a chant rising in their tongue that the ring turned into "Blood bound! Blood bound!" Celebrating. Weird as hell, considering I'd just gutted their leader, his body still cooling ten feet away. "Thanks," she whispered, pulling back, her breath warm against my ear.

I nodded, that's when I remembered why I am on this trip, I don't have time for this. Sara was out there, clock ticking, her scream looping in my head. That's when a commotion broke the chant, weapons drawn, steel rasping, Mithis tensing beside me, her hand dropping to an axe at her hip. I followed her gaze, and my blood ran cold, a shiver clawing up my spine.

The dead were walking. Slow, shambling straight out of a cheap horror flick I'd watched with Sara on late-night cable, when we were much too young to be watching those movies, making sure we were quiet and did not disturb Mom. Dozens of them, rotting faces lit by torchlight, flesh peeling in gray strips, eyes milky and blind. They stumbled from the treeline, dragging broken limbs, jaws working silently, some in suits, others in rags, all reeking of decay that hit me even from yards away.

"There is trouble!" I snapped, raising my rifle, the barrel shaking slightly in my grip. Popped the first few headshots, clean, brains splattering black against the pines, but they kept coming, relentless, their groans a low hum under the crack of gunfire. Burned through half my mag, brass clinking at my feet, before switching to my pistol, Glock 17, worn but reliable, a police trade that I got a while ago, modified it to my liking, dropping more with tight, controlled shots.

Beside me, Mithis swung her axe, small, glowing purple along the edge, runes flaring with each strike, cleaving skulls with precision, bone crunching wetly. The tribe fought too, clubs and spears smashing through rotten flesh, green muscle flexing under torchlight, a chaos of roars and splatter.

Adrenaline crashed hard after the last one fell, a crumpled heap twitching once before going still. I leaned on a tree, bark rough against my shoulder, shaking like a leaf in a storm, pistol hot in my hand, barrel smoking subtly. Corpses littered the ground, piles of rot and ruin, flies already buzzing in the damp air. My chest heaved, lungs burning, the acrid sting of gunsmoke mixing with the stench of death. Mithis stepped up beside me, breathing steadily despite the gore streaking her arms, her axe dripping black sludge onto the dirt. "We need to go," she said, voice firm, urgent.

"Necromancer's close. These are his grunts... scouts, weak fodder."

"Necro what?" I rasped, head spinning, throat raw from shouting. The word landed like a punch more fantasy crap I didn't have time to process.

"Dead raiser," she said, grabbing my arm, her grip iron-tight, pulling me toward where I stumbled out of. Her eyes flicked to the shadows, searching, and I let her lead, boots dragging as my brain caught up slowly. I think she'd said something mid-fight, but I wasn't listening, since I was in fight mode and cut everything out that was not important. Fell back on my training.

We hit the Jeep, gravel crunching underfoot, and I froze. A flicker blue, like that orb back in the parking lot, danced near the hood, pulsing once, twice, then vanishing into the dark. My pulse spiked, a jolt of dread cutting through the fog. "Now!" I barked, shoving Mithis toward the passenger side, my voice rougher than I meant. She fumbled the handle, hands slick with blood, axe still clutched tight, and I leaned over, yanked it open with a creak of rusted hinges. "In!" She slid inside, leather creaking against the torn seat, axe resting across her lap as I gunned the engine. The Jeep roared to life, coughing once before settling into a growl, and I peeled out, tires spitting dirt and pine needles. A distant roar chased us deep, pissed, and not human rumbling through the trees, vibrating the steering wheel in my hands. I floored it, headlights slicing the night, Mithis silent beside me, her crimson eyes fixed on the road ahead.

4 ECHOES OF A VANISHED WORLD

As we were between cities, driving toward my sister's place, something was itching at the back of my mind, not quite there, but annoying enough to chew on. That's when it clicked: I hadn't removed the dragon from the front of my vehicle. Or... had I? Where did this dead dragon go?

I shot a glance at my passenger. "Hey... Missy... no... Mythol... no... I'm sorry, what's your name again?"

She turned her head slowly. "Mm... Mithis... where are the horses pulling this cart?" Her tone was flat, like someone who'd just noticed a hole in the boat they'd already sailed out on.

"Mithis... Mithis, Mithis," I chanted, letting it bounce around like a spell. "Is that how you say it?"

"Yes," she said, "and can you tell me where the horses went?"

I frowned, her words sinking in. "What horses? This is a car."

"Ohh, this is a car," she said with a tone of a person who finally got to see something that they had heard about, but now gets to see it. And the original question was lost with the confusion and distance. Then I had the thought that she needs some gear.

So we rolled up to the survival store in silence, the Jeep's engine humming low, a steady growl that vibrated through the cracked dashboard. The place loomed ahead, dark, windows blank as dead eyes, not a soul around. The sign overhead hung crooked, "Outdoor Edge" in peeling red letters, swaying slightly in the night breeze.

The door was unlocked, though, hanging ajar like someone bailed mid-shift, leaving a subtle whiff of gun oil and dust trailing out. I killed the headlights so I didn't advertise that we are here and stepped out, boots crunching on gravel, rifle up and ready, the weight of it grounding me. Mithis followed, her axe in hand, her eyes scanning the shadows, glinting like embers in the dimness. Her breath fogged in the cool air, quick and shallow.

"Clear," I muttered, pushing inside, the door creaking on rusted hinges.

The store was a hollow shell of shelves, half-stocked, their metal frames glinting dimly under a flickering fluorescent bulb that buzzed like a dying fly. Ammo cans lined one wall, some toppled with spilled brass; racks of clothes hung limp, camo and flannel swaying as we passed; tools, hatchets, knives, a dented shovel scattered across a countertop. I grabbed what I could carry: a box of 5.56 rounds, heavy and cold, the green metal ammo can rattling as I shoved it into my pack; a spare mag, scratched but solid, its spring still tight; a med kit with gauze and tape spilling out of its ripped pouch, the faded red cross peeling at the edges. I was starting to wonder why this looked so disheveled; it is like no one has been here for years. But it has only been a few hours.

My pack was already straining, straps digging into my shoulders, but Mithis needed gear, her leather scraps, patched with fur and that tiny glowing axe wouldn't cut it long-term in this mess. She stood near the entrance, axe still in hand, crimson eyes flicking over the store like she was sizing up prey.

Waved her over to the clothing racks, the air thick with dust and the subtle musk of mildew. "You're not running with me half-naked and armed with a museum piece," I said, digging through a pile. Found her a jacket, olive drab, a hooded tactical number with a waterproof liner, stiff from sitting on the shelf too long. The sleeves were a touch long, but it'd keep her dry and warm. She slipped it on, rolling her shoulders, then she fiddled with the zipper, trying to figure it out, and then gave up. Next, cargo pants black, heavy-duty, a size too big but adjustable with drawstrings at the waist. They hung loose on her lean frame, the multiple pockets sagging empty for now, scuffed knees hinting they'd been returned once. She cinched the belt. I tossed her a wide nylon strap with a steel buckle, matte gray and scratched from use, tightening it until it hugged her hips, the excess strap dangling like a tail.

She moved to the tools, her boots scuffing the linoleum, and I followed, eyeballing the weapons. Her axe was fierce but short-range, fine for skull-splitting, but she'd need something with reach. She paused at a rack of machetes, fingers brushing the handles, then hefted one, blade broad and slightly curved, about eighteen inches of dull steel, scratched from display but sturdy. The handle was wrapped in worn black cord, fraying at the edges, with a slight heft that balanced it in her grip. She swung it once, a slow arc that whistled quietly, testing its weight, her runes pulsing purple along her arm as if approving.

"This'll do," she said, voice low, nodding crisp and decisive. I grabbed a sheath from a bin, black plastic, cracked but functional, and handed it to her. She strapped it to her thigh over the cargo pants, the machete sliding in with a satisfying click.

Anything else?" I asked, scanning the shelves.

Her eyes landed on a row of work-grade gloves, leather palms with reinforced knuckles, dark brown and scuffed. She picked a pair, slipping them on; they fit snug, the leather creaking as she flexed her hands, the backs ventilated with mesh that'd keep her from sweating too much.

"Good for gripping," she muttered, clenching a fist, the gloves darkening slightly with her sweat.

Then she snatched a red bandana, folded into a tight square on the shelf, unfurling it with a flick and tying it around her neck, the fabric stark against her green skin. "Keeps blood off," she said, matter-of-fact, like she'd done it a hundred times. I didn't ask whose blood she meant.

I rifled through a bin of odds and ends, pulling out a small flint striker, steel loop, and rod, scratched but sparking when I tested it against my knife.

"Fire's your friend out there," I said, tossing it to her.

She caught it one-handed, tucking it into a cargo pocket with a grunt. Last, I spotted a canteen aluminum, dented on one side, with a screw cap and a faded camouflage sleeve. Filled it from a jug of water near the counter, the liquid sloshing cold against the metal, and handed it over.

"Stay hydrated. You're no use to me passing out." She slung it over her shoulder by the strap, adjusting it so it hung beside her machete, the weight settling against her hip. She stood there, geared up, jacket unzipped, pants loose but belted, machete sheathed, gloves and bandana adding a rough edge to her look. Still orcish, with those crimson eyes and runes, but less like she'd walked out of a fantasy raid and more like she could survive this hell with me.

"Ready," she said, hefting her axe in one hand, machete in the other, a subtle smirk tugging her lips like she was daring the world to throw more at her.

I nodded, slinging my pack higher, and we loaded the Jeep, gear rattling in the back, metal clanking against metal as we piled it in. Moved out fast, eyes peeled for a place to crash, the road stretching dark and empty ahead, the weight of her new kit a quiet promise she'd hold her own.

A motel popped up a mile down, neon sign dead, its "Vacancy" letters cracked and unlit, casting jagged shadows across the lot. Empty, not a single car, tire tracks faded into dust. Too quiet for a city this size, Jacksonville's outskirts should've been chaos, even now. My gut twisted, a slow churn like bad coffee gone cold; should've been stragglers, looters, screams something.

"This ain't right," I said, parking under a busted streetlight, its glass shattered, pole leaning like a drunk. The Jeep's engine ticked as it cooled, a subtle counterpoint to the silence pressing in. Mithis tilted her head, axe still out, the purple glow along its edge pulsing faintly.

"No one's good, yeah?" she said, frowning, her voice rough with that clipped orcish cadence. "Less to fight." Her cape of wolf pelts rustled softly.

"Not when it's this empty," I shot back, voice low, tense. "A city doesn't just vanish, no struggle, no bodies, no trash. Like they walked off into thin air."

My fingers tightened on the rifle's grip, the metal cool against my palm. She tensed beside me, catching my drift, her grip whitening on the axe handle. We grabbed the gear packs slung over our shoulders, clinking quietly, and hit the office, a squat box of chipped paint and smeared windows. Inside, keys hung on hooks behind a counter littered with stale cigarette butts and a cracked coffee mug. Easy pickings snagged one labeled Room 12, the ring cold in my hand. Lights still flickered on inside the room, a dull yellow glow seeping under the door. Small mercies in a world that didn't owe us any.

I dropped my pack by the door with a heavy thud, the weight of the day crashing into my shoulders, and nodded to the bathroom dingy tile, a rust-streaked sink, a shower stall with a stained curtain.

"Shower's yours first. Hot water, if it works."

I didn't think she started stripping right there, leather and fabric hitting the floor with quiet thumps, cape pooling like a shadow.

"Whoa, hold up!" I barked, turning fast, heat creeping up my neck despite the exhaustion. "Not in front of me."

Mithis froze, half out of her gear, tunic dangling from one arm, brow furrowed over those crimson eyes. "In Gin, we clean together after battle," she said, voice flat, confused, not flirty, just a matter-of-fact. "Bonds the pact, blood and water shared." Her head tilted, studying me like I was the odd one.

"Yeah, well, here we don't," I said, keeping my eyes locked on the wall peeling wallpaper, a faded palm tree pattern, anything but her.

"Shower alone. I'll go after." My tone was crisper than I meant, frayed by the day. She grunted half-annoyed, half-resigned, grabbed the new clothes in a bundle, and headed in, bare feet slapping the tile. The door clicked shut, water hissed on, an uneven sputter that echoed through the thin walls. I sank onto the bed, springs creaking under me, and rubbed my face, palms grinding into my eyes. Mom's blood still stained my hands in memory, Sara's scream looped in my skull, that damn dragon's roar lingered in my ears the past twelve hours were a meat grinder, shredding what little I had left. And now I had a green-skinned battle buddy who didn't get doors or privacy, her axe propped against the bathroom wall like a sentinel. Figured Earth falls apart, and I'm stuck playing guide to an orc who thinks I'm her husband.

She called out, voice cutting through the drone of the water, sharp and annoyed: "How does this work?"

I sighed, hauled myself up, legs leaden, boots scuffing the carpet, and cracked the door, keeping my gaze high, fixed on the chipped ceiling. Steam billowed out, thick and warm, fogging the air with a subtle chlorine tang.

"Turn the left knob for hot, right for cold," I said, pointing at the rusted faucets jutting from the wall. "Soap's there, bar on the ledge, rub it on when you're wet."

She stood there, water streaming down her back, glaring at the faucet like it'd insulted her lineage, her muscled frame taut with frustration. Then she waved me off with a flick of her hand, water dripping from her fingers.

"Got it," she muttered, voice low, almost a growl. "Your world's strange, too many rules for simple things."

I shut the door, leaned against it, the wood cool against my spine. Strange didn't cover it, empty cities silent as graves, walking dead clawing from the shadows, and me stuck with her, a stranger bound by a law I didn't ask for. Needed rest, needed a plan. Sara was out there, Lily too, Michigan a distant beacon through the haze. Couldn't stop now, not with their voices pulling me north, but my body screamed for a pause, a breath. The water cut off with a groan of pipes, and I straightened, steeling myself for whatever came next in this unraveling nightmare.

5 THE CASTLE'S HEART

After a night of rest and a cleanish shower, we piled into the Jeep and headed off. The highway stretched north-west, cracked asphalt tangled with glowing vines, Ashvalen's fingerprints all over it, shimmering subtly green under the morning light. Mithis sat shotgun, her eyes fixed on the horizon, her axe resting across her lap. I gripped the wheel, knuckles white, mind locked on Sara and Lily every mile closer to Michigan, every mile deeper into this twisted mess.

The world was shifting too fast; grass spiked tall overnight, knee-high and razor-edged, swaying in unnatural breezes; trees punched through concrete, their bark glistening wet and black, roots cracking the road like skeletal hands. This wasn't abandonment, this was invasion, something ancient and alive stitching itself into Earth's bones.

Then I saw it, a castle. Jutting up from the flat, featureless land, no mountain, no sense. Stone spires clawed the sky, jagged and moss-slick, ancient and wrong, like it'd been dropped here from some medieval nightmare. No castles in America, not real ones, not built of weathered granite blocks the size of my Jeep, their edges worn but sharp. I pulled over, tires crunching gravel, and stared, breath fogging the windshield. Turrets loomed, tipped with iron spikes, and faint green light pulsed through cracks in the stone.

This shouldn't be," I muttered, voice low, a chill crawling up my spine.

Mithis sucked in a breath, quick and rare, her first sign of anything close to fear.

"We need to leave," she whispered, voice tight, leaning forward, her wolf pelt cape rustling softly against the seat. Her runes flared brighter, casting dim shadows across her green face.

"Road's gone?!," I said, glancing back through the rearview. Where asphalt once ran, dense forest loomed, trees too even, too perfect, trunks straight as spears and woven tight, their leaves glowing gently like the vines. Magic, no question, thick and oppressive, pressing against the Jeep's frame.

I killed the engine, the sudden silence deafening, and grabbed my gear rifle slung over my shoulder, ammo cans clanking, pack heavy

Jacob Salvia

with the weight of survival.

"We're on foot. Grab what you can."

She nodded, axe in hand, and slid out, her new machete bouncing against her thigh, canteen sloshing quietly. We pushed into the woods, boots crunching brittle leaves that crackled like glass underfoot. No birds, no wind, just an eerie stillness, the air damp and heavy, smelling of rot and ozone. Then a rattle bones clacking, sharp and rhythmic, like a science class skeleton gone rogue, echoing through the trees. Mithis froze mid-step, her axe rising; I raised my rifle, heart kicking hard. A figure shambled out from the shadows, skeletal, eyeless sockets black as pitch, ribs exposed under scraps of decayed cloth, lurching straight for us with jerky, relentless intent.

"Shit," I hissed, firing.

The bullet cracked its skull, bone shattering in a spray of dust, and it dropped, but more came, rattling from the shadows, ten, twelve, closing fast, their jaws clicking in silent hunger. Mithis swung her axe, purple glow slicing through bone clean as a guillotine, shards flying. "Necromancer," she said between swings, voice steady despite the strain. "These are scouts, weak, but they are near watching."

"Same one from the camp?" I asked, popping another, aiming for the joints' knee cracked, it stumbled but kept coming, trying to slow them down.

"Maybe," she grunted, cleaving two at once, their spines snapping with a wet crunch. "Or worse, a world-ender. Gin tales warn of one merging realm for power, pulling lands together like thread."

Her axe and machete whirled, a blur of purple light and grey iron. I emptied my mag into the swarm, thinning them, brass hitting the ground, switching to my pistol when the rifle clicked dry. We fought through a brutal rhythm of gunfire and steel until the trees parted, revealing the castle closer now, stone walls pulsing sickly green, towering over us like a predator waiting to strike.

"Trap," I said, ducking behind a boulder, its surface slick with moss and cold against my back. "Every path loops back here; woods are herding us."

My breath came in short bursts, sweat stinging my eyes. Mithis crouched beside me, eyes narrow, scanning the wall.

"Who's inside is controlling the dead. Kill them, we break this." Her voice was low, certain, her runes glowing brighter as if sensing the threat.

"No front door, bullshit," I said, tracing the wall with my gaze too high, too smooth for climbing, the stone slick with damp moss that glowed muted green in the dim morning light. Mithis pointed a seam, subtle, near the base, barely a hairline crack in the granite, hidden by a tangle of thorny vines that pulsed like veins.

Hidden door. I pried at it with my knife, the blade scraping against stone with a high, grating whine, sparks flickering briefly until rusted hinges groaned deep and protesting, echoing into the woods behind us. The door swung inward slowly, reluctant, releasing a gust of cold, stale air thick with mildew, rot, and something sour, like spilled wine gone bad. We slipped inside, the passage swallowing us whole, the dim light from Mithis's glowing runes casting jagged shadows as the door thudded shut behind us, sealing us in.

The tunnel was damp and narrow, walls pressing close, rough-hewn stone dripping with condensation that glistened in the purple glow from her arm. I desired to turn on my helmet light. The light was on the back of my helmet, facing towards the ceiling. What that does is the Light hits the ceiling, bounces down, and acts like a normally lit room. A trick I picked up from some SF buddies I had. Then we began to move. My boots scraped over uneven flagstones, slick with slime and littered with brittle bones, small, splintered, maybe rats or something worse, crunching underfoot.

The air hung heavy, clinging to my skin, tasting of earth and decay, every breath a reminder we were trespassing somewhere old and alive. Carvings lined the walls jagged, spiraling symbols etched deep into the stone, wriggling if you stared too long, like worms burrowing under flesh. I caught glimpses fanged skulls, clawed hands, eyes with no pupils shifting as we passed, a silent warning written in a language I didn't need to read to feel.

"Gift from my father," Mithis muttered when I glanced at her arm, her voice low, clipped, almost defensive as the runes flared brighter, illuminating a puddle of black water ahead.

The passage twisted abruptly, doubling back on itself, a labyrinth carved by something that didn't think in straight lines. The ceiling dipped low, brushing my head, forcing me to hunch, my pack scraping against jagged outcrops that snagged at the straps. Mithis moved smoother, her shorter frame ducking effortlessly, her axe held loose but ready, the purple glow reflecting off beads of moisture clinging to the stone. No sound but our breathing, mine ragged, hers steady, and the quiet drip of water somewhere deeper, a slow, maddening rhythm. Then a clatter of bones rattling ahead, faint but growing, a dry, staccato clicked like dice rolling across a table.

"Patrol," Mithis whispered, flattening against the wall, her cape blending with the shadows. I pressed beside her and quickly shut off the light, rifle up, the barrel cold against my cheek, peering into the gloom.

Two skeletons shuffled into view, taller than the scouts outside, their frames wrapped in rusted chainmail that clinked with each step, scraps of decayed leather flapping loose. One gripped a notched shortsword, the blade pitted but sharp; the other dragged a flail, its spiked ball scraping the floor, leaving subtle gouges. Eyeless sockets gleamed faintly, green, locked on nothing but moving with purpose, straight for us. Mithis signaled thumb across her throat and slid forward, silent as a ghost, axe raised.

I followed, clumsy, boots scuffing despite my effort, heart pounding loud enough, I swore they'd hear it. She struck first, axe flashing purple, cleaving the sword-bearer's spine in a spray of dust, the body collapsing before it could swing. I lunged at the second, rifle butt slamming its skull bone cracked, but it turned, flail whipping toward me. Dodged late, the spikes grazing my thigh, a dull sting through my jeans. Finished it with a shot pistol barked, head shattered, and it dropped, chainmail rattling like loose change.

"Quiet," Mithis hissed, wiping her axe on her sleeve, her runes dimming briefly as if catching their breath.

I nodded, reloading slowly, hands steadying as adrenaline ebbed. The passage forked ahead, left sloped down, air growing colder, wetter; right climbed slightly, the carvings denser, more frantic, claw marks joining the runes like something tried to escape.

"Down," she said, pointing left, her voice barely a breath. "Chanting's stronger there, closer to it."

I heard it now, low and guttural, a chant rolling up from the depths, vibrating through the stone into my boots, a rhythm that clawed at my chest like a second pulse.

"Ritual," she added, eyes narrowing. "Interrupt it, it will be vulnerable, caught mid-spell."

We moved fast, the tunnel sloping steeper, walls slicker, my hand brushed stone, came away coated in slime that stank of sulfur and rot. The air thickened, pressing harder, laced with a subtle metallic tang like blood spilled days ago. Another patrol loomed, three this time, broader, clad in dented breastplates, one wielding a spear with a barbed tip that gleamed wet in the rune light. Mithis took point, darted low, axe slicing the spearman's legs out, bone snapping like dry twigs while I fired on the second, bullet punching through its chestplate, staggering it. The third swung a rusted axe at me, blocked with my rifle, metal clanging, then kicked its shin, toppling it. Mithis finished it, her blade splitting its skull clean through, dust billowing.

"Too many," she muttered, breathing harder now, a subtle sheen of sweat on her green brow. "It knows we're here."

The passageway widened, walls pulling back into a cavernous stretch, ragged tapestries hung limp, their faded threads depicting horned figures tearing at flesh, threads unraveling into the damp air. A side chamber gaped to the right, rusted chains dangled from bolts in the ceiling, swaying gently, a wooden rack stained dark with old blood dominating the center. A rack of weapons lined one wall: spears, a cracked shield, and a short sword glowing subtly, its blade etched with spiraling runes that shimmered gold against steel. Some thing was tell me to take it. So I grabbed it, sheathed it at my hip, light as hell, barely heavier than my knife, the steel solid and warm to the touch, humming quietly like it was alive.

"Useful," I said, testing its balance with a quick swing, the glow flaring briefly. Mithis nodded, her eyes flicking to the chains something dark flickered in them, a memory maybe, but she shook it off.

The chanting grew louder, harsher words I couldn't catch, guttural and wet, bouncing off the stone like a chorus of throats gargling blood. The air pulsed with it, heavy and electric, raising the hairs on my arms. The passage curved one last time, a final twist dumping us into the massive chamber, vaulted ceiling lost in shadow, walls slick with green slime that pulsed in sync with the castle's heartbeat, the witch waiting at its core. We'd made it, but the underground had marked us, sweat and slime on my skin, the weight of that sword a new anchor, and Mithis's runes glowing like a warning as we stepped into the fight.

. It was a woman with a long flowing dress and a pointed hat. She looks like the Wicked Witch of the West. I was so surprised at something so similar but different. Yes, she had the green skin, but it wasn't a vibrant life green but a rotten green. Eyes sunken in, nose protruding outwards, and her frame almost skeletal, with bony fingers, with the skin sagging on her. Oh, and she was floating too. Her eyes, black pits, bottomless, locked on me, and a grin split her bony face, teeth sharp and yellowed.

"You," she rasped, voice like breaking glass, jagged and sharp. "The one who reeks of failure, blood on your hands, guilt in your bones."

"Shut it," I snapped, raising my rifle, finger itching on the trigger.

Mithis charged, axe blazing purple, but the witch flicked a wrist, undead surged from the shadows, not scouts now, bigger, armored in rusted plates, swords sharp despite the decay. Six of them, fast, splitting us with mechanical precision. I fired, clipped one's shoulder, metal sparking, it spun, swung at me. Dodged late, blade nicking my arm, a hot sting of blood welling under my sleeve.

"Focus on the runes!" Mithis yelled, axe smashing a skeleton's helm, steel crumpling like foil. I aimed, popped a glowing rune orbiting the witch, green energy flickered, dimmed, then ducked as another lunged, its sword grazing my pack, tearing a strap. Too close. Drew the new blade, glow flared bright, cut through its arm like butter, bone parting clean. It staggered; I finished it with a thrust to the chest, dust billowing as it collapsed.

Mithis danced through two, axe-splitting ribs with wet cracks, but a third grabbed her from behind, clawed arm around her throat, squeezing. She snarled, elbowed free with a quick jab, and beheaded it in a spray of bone shards. Green bolts flew with the witch's magic, scorching stone where we'd stood, leaving black char marks and a smell like burnt wire.

"She's waking more!" Mithis shouted, nodding to shadows birthing fresh undead, eight now, shambling up, some with shields, others with spiked clubs, bigger than the scouts. The air thickened, heavy with rot and power.

"Cover me!" I barked, sprinting for the circle of runes on the floor, etched into stone, glowing green, pulsing faster.

A skeleton intercepted a tall, spiked mace swinging in a brutal arc. Blocked with the sword glow pulsed, held firm against the impact, my arm jarring, then kicked its knee, bone crunching with a crisp snap, then I stabbed its chest where there was a crystal core. It crumbled into a heap. Reached the runes, fired point-blank three, shattered, with sparks flying like a firework went off, then a high-pitched whine splitting the air. The witch screeched, a sound that clawed at my skull, hurling a bolt straight at me green fire. I dove, heat singeing my back, jacket smoking as I hit the stone hard.

Mithis took a hit of green blast to her side, searing through her jacket. She grunted, stumbled, but kept swinging, axe carving a path through another skeleton, its head rolling across the floor.

"Finish it!" she roared, voice raw, blood trickling dark from her ribs.

I emptied my pistol into the last rune circle, and then it exploded, shockwave knocking me flat, ears ringing, dust choking the air. The witch flickered, skeletal hands clawing at nothing, robes billowing like ink in water.

"You can't save them," she hissed, voice digging into me, sharp and personal. "Your mother bled out by your hand, your sister's next, screaming in the dark. I curse you, Jake, every life you touch will rot, every hope will crumble!"

Her words punched deep, Mom's blank eyes staring up, Sara's scream echoing, Lily's laugh fading, she knew, saw my failures like they were carved into me. I froze, guts twisting, bile rising, until Mithis leaped, axe sank into the witch's neck with a wet thunk, head tumbling, body dissolving to ash in a swirl of green sparks. Silence hit hard, sudden and heavy, the air clearing, the oppressive weight lifting like a storm passing.

Mithis staggered over, clutching her side, blood seeping through her fingers, staining the olive jacket dark.

"It's done," she panted, breath ragged, leaning on her axe for support, its glow dimming. "Yeah," I said, voice rough, hauling myself up, boots scraping stone. "But she knew me, the curse feels personal, not some generic hex."

Blood dripped from my arm, a slow trickle I ignored, the sting fading under adrenaline's echo. Outside, the forest withered trees collapsing into dust, vines shriveling the road reappeared, asphalt cracked but open, the castle gone like it'd never been.

"Let's find Sara," I added, jaw tight, the witch's words gnawing at me. She'd seen my failures, named them, meant this wasn't random, meant something bigger was hunting me. I'd beat it anyway, break that curse with my hands if I had to, Mithis at my side or not.

6 HOLLOW SHADES AND HOLLOW VOICES

The witch's ash settled slowly, gray flecks drifting like snow in the cavern's stale air, catching the faint purple glow of Mithis's runes. My knees ached from the stone floor, rifle still warm against my thigh, the sword's hum fading in my grip. Her curse clawed at me, "Every life you touch will rot," a jagged hook in my gut, twisting Mom's blood and Sara's scream into something I couldn't shake. I spat, tasting copper and dust, and forced myself up, legs shaky but moving. No time for ghosts, not yet.

Mithis leaned on her axe, blood oozing dark from her side, soaking the ranger jacket I'd scavenged for her.

"We need to get out," she rasped, voice rough but steady, her crimson eyes flicking to the ceiling.

Cracks spiderwebbed overhead, stone groaning like it was ready to bury us. The witch's death had snapped something of her magic holding this place together, maybe, and now it was coming down.

"Yeah," I said, slinging the rifle over my shoulder, the strap biting into my neck. "Exit's that way back through the tunnel."

I grabbed her arm, steadying her as she staggered, her weight solid despite the wince she hid.

"Move fast, or we're gravel." We hauled ass, boots slipping on slime-slick flagstones, the air thick with rot and the subtle tang of sulfur. Bones crunched underfoot, rats, prisoners, didn't care, scattering as we ran. The tunnel shuddered, dust raining down, a deep rumble rolling through the walls. Mithis stumbled, caught herself on the stone, her runes flaring bright enough to light the path ahead. Thankfully, I didn't have time to turn on my flashlight.

"Faster!" she barked, shoving me forward, her axe clanking against her hip.

The hidden door loomed rusted iron, vines pulsing dimly green around it. I slammed into it, shoulder first, hinges screaming as it gave. Cold night air hit like a slap, crisp with pine and smoke, the forest stretching dark and warped beyond. We spilled out, Mithis right behind, and the castle roared a deep, gut-shaking collapse, stone crashing into stone, swallowing the chamber we'd left. Dust billowed past us, gritty in my lungs, and I coughed, dragging her clear as the ground settled.

The Jeep sat where we'd left it, headlights off, a shadow under twisted oaks. "Still got wheels," I muttered, catching my breath, the ache in my chest spreading Mom, Sara, now this damn curse. Mithis slumped against a tree, hand pressed to her side, blood seeping through her fingers.

"Patch me up," she said, voice clipped, peeling the jacket back. A gash ran along her ribs, shallow but ugly, green-tinged from the witch's bolt, skin raw around it. I dug into my pack, med kit rattling gauze, tape, a half-empty bottle of antiseptic sloshing cold in my hand. Poured it over the wound; she hissed, hissingly and low, runes flickering as the liquid bubbled. "Stings," she grunted, glaring at me like it was personal.

"Better than rotting," I said, wrapping gauze tight, tape sticking to my sweaty fingers. "Hold still, don't need you bleeding out before we hit Michigan." Her eyes met mine hard, but she nodded, a flicker of something like trust, maybe something more behind that warrior honor.

"Let's find my sister," I said, determination hardening my voice.

"And then?" Mithis asked.

"I don't know." I exhaled, still trying to recover, trying to make sense of this new world. As we reached the Jeep, I turned to look back at the castle.

It was gone.

Vanished. As if it had never existed.

Mithis and I got into the vehicle in silence, still processing everything that had just happened. The road stretched ahead, a surreal tapestry of what Earth used to be, invaded by the strange oddities of Ashvalen. The cracked asphalt was overgrown with wild grass and bioluminescent flora that pulsed with an eerie glow.

Mithis stared out the window, her crimson eyes darting across the changing landscape. She hadn't said much since the castle. Maybe it was exhaustion, or maybe it was the witch's curse weighing on her mind. I tightened my grip on the wheel, the hum of the engine filling the silence. The simple act of driving felt like the last shred of normalcy I had left in this warped reality. "You've been quiet," I said, glancing at her briefly.

She turned to me, her expression unreadable. "I'm thinking about what the witch said." I nodded. That curse, her venomous last words, had been gnawing at the back of my mind, too. "Curses are... tricky," Mithis continued. "They don't always work the way they're intended, but they always have consequences."

"Great," I muttered. "Just what I need. Consequences on top of everything else."

She gave a small smile, though it didn't reach her eyes. "You're handling this situation better than most would. Few people could face what we just did and still have the strength to keep going."

"Strength? No. Stubbornness, maybe." I sighed, tapping the dashboard. "But thanks..." "And what about you?" I asked, studying her. "You've adapted to all this pretty quickly, too."

Mithis hesitated, as if recalling something long buried. "We've had travelers tell us about a world... about machines, weapons, and things that resemble what I've been seeing here." Her voice was distant, like she was reciting an old legend. "I never thought I would see anything from those stories."

"What are you talking about? What stories?" I asked, confused.

"This machine," she said, motioning toward the Jeep. "A vehicle that moves on its power."

"Wait, wait... how old do you think this machine is?" I asked, still trying to wrap my head around one new thing after another.

"The stories go back several hundred years," she said, her tone utterly sincere. "So, I would say 200 years old, give or take a century."

I stared at her. Then, I mumbled to myself, "So, you've had stories from my world for centuries?"

Mithis turned to me, intrigued. "So what does that mean?"

I looked at her, frozen in place, mind racing. "Just another mystery, I guess?"

The miles ticked by, and the scenery grew stranger. Massive trees with trunks as wide as buildings loomed over the road, their branches reaching out like skeletal hands. Occasionally, I spotted figures in the distance, shadowy humanoid shapes that vanished the moment I looked directly at them.

Mithis noticed them too. Her hand rested on her axe, her posture tense.

"Do you know what they are?" I asked.

"Spirits," she said. "Or echoes of what used to be. They won't harm us unless provoked." "Good to know."

The gas gauge caught my eye, and a wave of frustration hit me. "We're running low on fuel. We need to find a stop soon." The next town we came across was eerily quiet. Broken streetlights flickered weakly, and abandoned cars lined the streets. The convenience store I pulled into was half-buried under a twisted tree, but its gas pumps looked intact.

"Stay here," I said, grabbing my rifle.

Mithis raised an eyebrow. "You think I'll let you go alone?"

I didn't argue. She grabbed her axe and followed me out. The air was still as we approached the pumps. I scanned the area for any movement, human, undead, or otherwise. Nothing. Mithis stood guard, her keen eyes darting around. I moved to the store, hoping to scavenge some supplies.

Inside, the shelves were ransacked, but I managed to find some canned food and bottled water. Mithis wandered to the back of the store and emerged holding a strange artifact, a small orb that glowed dimly blue.

"What's that?" I asked.

"Magic," she said simply. "Not strong, but it might be useful."

"Take it," I said, not questioning her judgment.

I couldn't shake the feeling that something was staring at us. Every so often, I caught glimpses of movement in the distance, shadows darting just out of sight.

Mithis noticed my unease. "What is it?"

"Probably nothing," I said, though I didn't believe it.

Her hand tightened around her weapon. "Nothing doesn't move like that."

The sun dipped below the horizon, casting the world into an eerie twilight. The light from the store barely cut through the encroaching darkness, and the shadows in the distance seemed to grow bolder.

"We'll keep driving," I said, looking around the area. "Whatever it is, it's not catching us tonight."

Mithis nodded, her expression hardening. "Agreed. But we should be ready."

"Alright, give me a second so I can unlock the gas pump, then we can get moving," I said seriously. I ran behind the cashier desk, pressed the button for the gas pump, and motioned for Mithis to head outside. "I'll be right behind you."

The convenience store's old gas pump clanked as I slid the nozzle into the car. The digital display on the machine was dead, but the subtle smell of fuel reassured me there was still something left in the tank.

"Let's hope this works," I muttered, cranking the lever.

Mithis stood beside me, her axe in hand, her eyes scanning the dark streets. The shadows danced strangely under the flickering streetlights, making the already tense atmosphere worse.

"Is it always this... dead?" she asked, her voice low.

"Small towns can be quiet, but not like this," I replied, glancing over my shoulder. "Even when people leave, animals move in. But here? Nothing. No sound, no life, like the whole place just gave up."

The pump sputtered to life, a slow trickle of gas flowing into the car's tank. I watched the nozzle, feeling the seconds drag on as if the pump itself were testing my patience. Mithis tightened her grip on her axe. "We're not alone."

I froze, my heart skipping a beat. "What do you mean?"

She nodded toward the far side of the lot, where the darkness seemed to ripple. At first, I thought it was a trick of the light, but then I saw it, a dim, humanoid figure, almost translucent, standing perfectly still.

"Spirits?" I asked quietly.

"Not just spirits," she said, her voice tense. "Hunters. They're drawn to magic or people like me."

I frowned, gripping the nozzle tighter. "And what do they do when they find you?"

She didn't answer immediately, her gaze fixed on the figure. "We don't want to find out."

The pump clicked, signaling the tank was full. I yanked the nozzle out, capped the gas tank, and slammed the car door shut.

"Get in!" I barked, but Mithis didn't move.

The figure began to drift closer, followed by another, then another. They emerged from the shadows like smoke coalescing into shapes, thin, gaunt, glowing dimly with a sickly green hue.

"Mithis!" I shouted.

She snapped out of her trance and climbed into the car just as I hit the gas. The tires screeched against the cracked pavement, and the car lurched forward, speeding away from the store and the encroaching figures.

"Those things back there," I said, trying to catch my breath. "What were they?"

"Hollow Shades," she said, gripping the door handle. "They're remnants of people whose souls were stripped away. They're empty, nothing but hunger and instinct. If we'd stayed, they would've drained us dry."

I shuddered, the image of their skeletal forms etched into my mind. "Why didn't they follow us?"

"They can't stray far from places steeped in death. That town must've been cursed long before Ashvalen merged with your world."

The road stretched ahead, the eerie glow of the dashboard illuminating Mithis's determined expression.

"We'll need to be more careful," she said. "There's worse out there than the Shades."

I tightened my grip on the wheel. "Great. Just what I wanted to hear."

As the car sped down the desolate highway, the lingering unease of the Hollow Shades hung over us. But with a full tank of gas and a clear road ahead, we had at least bought ourselves some time. For now. The headlights cut through the thickening darkness as we sped down the cracked, overgrown highway. The adrenaline from our escape was starting to wear off, and exhaustion was creeping in. The gas tank was full, but I knew we couldn't keep going without rest.

"We need to stop," I said, breaking the silence.

Mithis glanced at me, her crimson eyes still keen despite the fatigue etched on her face. "Do you trust stopping? After what we just saw?"

I didn't, not really. But driving in this twisted world while half asleep seemed like a worse idea. "We'll stop somewhere defensible. Just for the night."

She didn't respond but nodded, gripping her axe like it was her lifeline. The road led us to the outskirts of what must have been a small town once, though the warped reality of Ashvalen and Earth's fusion had twisted it into something unfamiliar. Eventually, we spotted a faded sign with "MOTEL" in flickering neon, the rest of the letters too dim to read. The building was a single-story L-shape, its cracked stucco walls lined with doors that looked more fragile than the plywood they were likely made of. A single car sat in the lot, rusted and covered in vines.

"Looks... promising," I said dryly, pulling into the lot.

She squinted at the dilapidated structure. "It doesn't look safe."

"Nothing is safe anymore," I muttered, stepping out of the car. "But we need sleep."

The front office door was unlocked, the bell above it jingling as we stepped inside. The air was stale, heavy with mildew. A faded calendar on the wall was frozen in a year long past. Behind the desk, a key rack still held several room keys, their tags coated in dust.

"No one's here," I said, grabbing a key at random. Room 7.

Mithis picked up a pen from the counter and turned it over in her fingers like it was a relic of a forgotten age. "Your world is strange."

"Tell me about it," I said, gesturing toward the door.

Room 7 was as depressing as I'd expected: a sagging bed, peeling wallpaper, and a single flickering light overhead. At least the door had a lock, though it looked like it would barely hold up against a stiff breeze, let alone any monsters. Mithis set her axe within arm's reach and began inspecting the room, her warrior instincts refusing to let her relax. "Oh, there is another one? I thought you said this is for cheap stays," she asked, pointing to the bathroom.

"Well, ya," I said. "All places have one for each room. People want their privacy even when it is cheap."

She looked at me like I'd spoken another language. "Amazing."

"You're covered in blood and dirt," I said, sitting on the edge of the bed. "I'll jump in after."

With that, she disappeared into the bathroom. I used the time to check my rifle and ammo, making sure everything was in working order. The sound of water running was oddly soothing, a brief reminder of normalcy in this shattered world. When Mithis finally emerged, her damp hair hung loose around her face, and she wore one of the oversized shirts I'd packed. "It's... strange, but I feel better," she admitted.

I smirked. "Thought you might."

She sat on the floor, her axe within reach, and leaned back against the bed. "You should get some sleep. I'll keep watch."

"No," I said firmly. "You need rest, too. We'll take turns."

Her eyes narrowed. "You're stubborn."

"Thank the army for that," I replied, lying down on the creaking mattress.

The room fell silent, save for the dim hum of the light and the occasional groan of the wind outside. For the first time in what felt like days, I let my eyes close, though sleep didn't come easily. My mind kept replaying the witch's curse, the Hollow Shades, and the impossible task of finding my sister and her family in a world gone mad.

But as I drifted off, the sound of Mithis sharpening her axe nearby was oddly comforting. Whatever came next, we'd face it together. The creak of the bed springs woke me before my body was ready to move. For a moment, I thought it was just the wind outside, but then there was a noise. A knock at the door.

Three quiet taps.

I sat upright, my hand already reaching for the rifle leaning against the nightstand. Mithis stirred on the floor, her eyes snapping open as though she hadn't been asleep at all. Another knock.

"Who is it?" I called out, keeping my voice steady.

A reply came, soft and muffled but eerily familiar. "Help me... please..."

It was a woman's voice. Young. Desperate. Mithis immediately stood, her axe in hand. "Don't open it," she hissed.

I wasn't planning to. Because this is straight out of a horror movie. Accepted, I have a gun and Mithis has an axe, so there is that.

Who are you?" I called again, my grip tightening on the rifle.

The voice wavered, trembling with fear. "I... I'm lost. Something's chasing me. Please, let me in."

I exchanged a glance with Mithis, and her expression told me everything I needed to know. This wasn't right. The voice continued, becoming more frantic.

"Please! It's right behind me! I'm not going to make it!"

"Stay calm," I said, motioning for Mithis to stay back as I crept toward the window. I peeked through the edge of the curtain, careful not to expose myself. The lot outside was empty. Nothing moved.

"Do you see anyone?" Mithis whispered.

"No," I replied quietly, stepping back. "Nothing's out there."

The knocking turned to pounding. "Let me in!" The voice screamed now, its pitch fluctuating unnaturally.

Mithis's grip on her axe tightened. "It's not human," she said, her voice steady but low.

"Yeah, I'm getting that vibe too," I muttered. The pounding

stopped, replaced by an eerie silence. For a moment, I thought it was over, but then I heard something that made my blood run cold.

"Please, brother, let me in," the voice said.

It was my sister's voice.

I froze, my mind racing. It sounded exactly like her down to the inflection, the way she used to call me when we were kids.

Don't listen," Mithis said sharply, stepping between me and the door. "It's trying to trick you."

The voice outside changed again, gentler now, pleading. "I'm scared. It's me. Please don't leave me out here."

I shook my head, trying to focus. "You're not her," I said firmly.

A low growl came from the other side of the door, guttural and inhuman. The thing began scraping against the wood, its claws dragging slowly, deliberately, as if savoring the moment. "I can smell you," it whispered, its voice a twisted amalgamation of different tones. "You smell... afraid."

The door groaned as the thing pressed against it. The flimsy lock wouldn't hold if it decided to come in.

"What is it?" I asked Mithis, my voice tight.

She didn't answer right away, her gaze locked on the door. Finally, she said, "I don't know. I don't know of any creature that can change its voice."

That almost scared me more than the voice outside.

I steadied my rifle, aiming it at the door. "What's the plan?"

"Don't let it in."

"Yeah, I wasn't gonna let it in," I said, trying my best to add a little humor into a stressful situation so we both could think clearly.

The scraping stopped abruptly, and for a moment, there was only silence. Then it spoke again, its voice calm, confident.

"You can't stop me," it said, perfectly mimicking my voice.

I freaked out. I fired a single round through the door without thinking about what would happen next.

The creature howled, a deafening, otherworldly sound that shook the walls. The door splintered as something massive slammed against it, but it didn't break through.

"Shoot again!" Mithis yelled, raising her axe.

I fired twice more, the shots tearing through the wood. The thing screeched, and then there was a heavy thud as its body hit the ground outside.

Silence!

Mithis and I stood frozen, waiting for any sign of movement. When none came, she stepped forward cautiously, peeping through the shattered door.

"It's gone," she said finally, though her grip on the axe didn't loosen.

I exhaled slowly, my hands trembling as I lowered the rifle. "Let's not stay here any longer."

Mithis nodded. "Agreed. The witch's ash settled slowly, gray flecks drifting like snow in the cavern's stale air, catching the faint purple glow of Mithis's runes. My knees ached from the stone floor, rifle still warm against my thigh, the sword's hum fading in my grip. Her curse clawed at me, "Every life you touch will rot," a jagged hook in my gut, twisting Mom's blood and Sara's scream into something I couldn't shake. I spat, tasting copper and dust, and forced myself up, legs shaky but moving. No time for ghosts, not yet.

Mithis leaned on her axe, blood oozing dark from her side, soaking the ranger jacket I'd scavenged for her.

"We need to get out," she rasped, voice rough but steady, her crimson eyes flicking to the ceiling.

Cracks spiderwebbed overhead, stone groaning like it was ready to bury us. The witch's death had snapped something of her magic holding this place together, maybe, and now it was coming down.

"Yeah," I said, slinging the rifle over my shoulder, the strap biting into my neck. "Exit's that way back through the tunnel."

I grabbed her arm, steadying her as she staggered, her weight solid despite the wince she hid.

"Move fast, or we're gravel." We hauled ass, boots slipping on slime-slick flagstones, the air thick with rot and the subtle tang of sulfur. Bones crunched underfoot, rats, prisoners, didn't care, scattering as we ran. The tunnel shuddered, dust raining down, a deep rumble rolling through the walls. Mithis stumbled, caught herself on the stone, her runes flaring bright enough to light the path ahead. Thankfully, I didn't have time to turn on my flashlight.

"Faster!" she barked, shoving me forward, her axe clanking against her hip.

The hidden door loomed rusted iron, vines pulsing dimly green around it. I slammed into it, shoulder first, hinges screaming as it gave. Cold night air hit like a slap, crisp with pine and smoke, the forest stretching dark and warped beyond. We spilled out, Mithis right behind, and the castle roared a deep, gut-shaking collapse, stone crashing into stone, swallowing the chamber we'd left. Dust billowed past us, gritty in my lungs, and I coughed, dragging her clear as the ground settled.

The Jeep sat where we'd left it, headlights off, a shadow under twisted oaks. "Still got wheels," I muttered, catching my breath, the ache in my chest spreading Mom, Sara, now this damn curse. Mithis slumped against a tree, hand pressed to her side, blood seeping through her fingers.

"Patch me up," she said, voice clipped, peeling the jacket back. A gash ran along her ribs, shallow but ugly, green-tinged from the witch's bolt, skin raw around it. I dug into my pack, med kit rattling gauze, tape, a half-empty bottle of antiseptic sloshing cold in my hand. Poured it over the wound; she hissed, hissingly and low, runes flickering as the liquid bubbled. "Stings," she grunted, glaring at me like it was personal.

"Better than rotting," I said, wrapping gauze tight, tape sticking to my sweaty fingers. "Hold still, don't need you bleeding out before we hit Michigan." Her eyes met mine hard, but she nodded, a flicker of something like trust, maybe something more behind that warrior honor.

"Let's find my sister," I said, determination hardening my voice.

"And then?" Mithis asked.

"I don't know." I exhaled, still trying to recover, trying to make sense of this new world. As we reached the Jeep, I turned to look back at the castle.

It was gone.

Vanished. As if it had never existed.

Mithis and I got into the vehicle in silence, still processing everything that had just happened. The road stretched ahead, a surreal tapestry of what Earth used to be, invaded by the strange oddities of Ashvalen. The cracked asphalt was overgrown with wild grass and bioluminescent flora that pulsed with an eerie glow.

Mithis stared out the window, her crimson eyes darting across the changing landscape. She hadn't said much since the castle. Maybe it was exhaustion, or maybe it was the witch's curse weighing on her mind. I tightened my grip on the wheel, the hum of the engine filling the silence. The simple act of driving felt like the last shred of normalcy I had left in this warped reality. "You've been quiet," I said, glancing at her briefly.

She turned to me, her expression unreadable. "I'm thinking about what the witch said." I nodded. That curse, her venomous last words, had been gnawing at the back of my mind, too. "Curses are... tricky," Mithis continued. "They don't always work the way they're intended, but they always have consequences."

"Great," I muttered. "Just what I need. Consequences on top of everything else."

She gave a small smile, though it didn't reach her eyes. "You're handling this situation better than most would. Few people could face what we just did and still have the strength to keep going."

"Strength? No. Stubbornness, maybe." I sighed, tapping the dashboard. "But thanks..." "And what about you?" I asked, studying her. "You've adapted to all this pretty quickly, too."

Mithis hesitated, as if recalling something long buried. "We've had travelers tell us about a world... about machines, weapons, and things that resemble what I've been seeing here." Her voice was distant, like she was reciting an old legend. "I never thought I would see anything from those stories."

"What are you talking about? What stories?" I asked, confused.

"This machine," she said, motioning toward the Jeep. "A vehicle that moves on its power."

"Wait, wait... how old do you think this machine is?" I asked, still trying to wrap my head around one new thing after another.

"The stories go back several hundred years," she said, her tone utterly sincere. "So, I would say 200 years old, give or take a century."

I stared at her. Then, I mumbled to myself, "So, you've had stories from my world for centuries?"

Mithis turned to me, intrigued. "So what does that mean?"

I looked at her, frozen in place, mind racing. "Just another mystery, I guess?"

The miles ticked by, and the scenery grew stranger. Massive trees with trunks as wide as buildings loomed over the road, their branches reaching out like skeletal hands. Occasionally, I spotted figures in the distance, shadowy humanoid shapes that vanished the moment I looked directly at them.

Mithis noticed them too. Her hand rested on her axe, her posture tense.

"Do you know what they are?" I asked.

"Spirits," she said. "Or echoes of what used to be. They won't harm us unless provoked."

"Good to know."

The gas gauge caught my eye, and a wave of frustration hit me. "We're running low on fuel. We need to find a stop soon." The next town we came across was eerily quiet. Broken streetlights flickered weakly, and abandoned cars lined the streets. The convenience store I pulled into was half-buried under a twisted tree, but its gas pumps looked intact.

"Stay here," I said, grabbing my rifle.

Mithis raised an eyebrow. "You think I'll let you go alone?"

I didn't argue. She grabbed her axe and followed me out. The air was still as we approached the pumps. I scanned the area for any movement, human, undead, or otherwise. Nothing. Mithis stood guard, her keen eyes darting around. I moved to the store, hoping to scavenge some supplies.

Inside, the shelves were ransacked, but I managed to find some canned food and bottled water. Mithis wandered to the back of the store and emerged holding a strange artifact, a small orb that glowed dimly blue.

"What's that?" I asked.

"Magic," she said simply. "Not strong, but it might be useful."

"Take it," I said, not questioning her judgment.

I couldn't shake the feeling that something was staring at us. Every so often, I caught glimpses of movement in the distance, shadows darting just out of sight.

Mithis noticed my unease. "What is it?"

"Probably nothing," I said, though I didn't believe it.

Her hand tightened around her weapon. "Nothing doesn't move like that."

The sun dipped below the horizon, casting the world into an eerie twilight. The light from the store barely cut through the encroaching darkness, and the shadows in the distance seemed to grow bolder.

"We'll keep driving," I said, looking around the area. "Whatever it is, it's not catching us tonight."

Mithis nodded, her expression hardening. "Agreed. But we should be ready."

"Alright, give me a second so I can unlock the gas pump, then we can get moving," I said seriously. I ran behind the cashier desk, pressed the button for the gas pump, and motioned for Mithis to head outside. "I'll be right behind you."

The convenience store's old gas pump clanked as I slid the nozzle into the car. The digital display on the machine was dead, but the subtle smell of fuel reassured me there was still something left in the tank.

"Let's hope this works," I muttered, cranking the lever.

Mithis stood beside me, her axe in hand, her eyes scanning the dark streets. The shadows danced strangely under the flickering streetlights, making the already tense atmosphere worse.

"Is it always this... dead?" she asked, her voice low.

"Small towns can be quiet, but not like this," I replied, glancing over my shoulder. "Even when people leave, animals move in. But here? Nothing. No sound, no life, like the whole place just gave up."

The pump sputtered to life, a slow trickle of gas flowing into the car's tank. I watched the nozzle, feeling the seconds drag on as if the pump itself were testing my patience. Mithis tightened her grip on her axe. "We're not alone."

I froze, my heart skipping a beat. "What do you mean?"

She nodded toward the far side of the lot, where the darkness seemed to ripple. At first, I thought it was a trick of the light, but then I saw it, a dim, humanoid figure, almost translucent, standing perfectly still.

"Spirits?" I asked quietly.

"Not just spirits," she said, her voice tense. " maybe hunters. They're drawn to magic or people like me."

I frowned, gripping the nozzle tighter. "And what do they do when they find you?"

She didn't answer immediately, her gaze fixed on the figure. "We don't want to find out."

The pump clicked, signaling the tank was full. I yanked the nozzle out, capped the gas tank, and slammed the car door shut.

"Get in!" I barked, but Mithis didn't move.

The figure began to drift closer, followed by another, then another. They emerged from the shadows like smoke coalescing into shapes, thin, gaunt, glowing dimly with a sickly green hue.

"Mithis!" I shouted.

She snapped out of her trance and climbed into the car just as I hit the gas. The tires screeched against the cracked pavement, and the car lurched forward, speeding away from the store and the encroaching figures.

"Those things back there," I said, trying to catch my breath. "What were they?"

"Hollow Shades," she said, gripping the door handle. "They're remnants of people whose souls were stripped away. They're empty, nothing but hunger and instinct. If we'd stayed, they would've drained us dry."

I shuddered, the image of their skeletal forms etched into my mind. "Why didn't they follow us?"

"They can't stray far from places steeped in death. That town must've been cursed long before Ashvalen merged with your world."

The road stretched ahead, the eerie glow of the dashboard illuminating Mithis's determined expression.

"We'll need to be more careful," she said. "There's worse out there than the Shades."

I tightened my grip on the wheel. "Great. Just what I wanted to hear."

As the car sped down the desolate highway, the lingering unease of the Hollow Shades hung over us. But with a full tank of gas and a clear road ahead, we had at least bought ourselves some time. For now. The headlights cut through the thickening darkness as we sped down the cracked, overgrown highway. The adrenaline from our escape was starting to wear off, and exhaustion was creeping in. The gas tank was full, but I knew we couldn't keep going without rest.

"We need to stop," I said, breaking the silence.

Mithis glanced at me, her crimson eyes still keen despite the fatigue etched on her face. "Do you trust stopping? After what we just saw?"

I didn't, not really. But driving in this twisted world while half asleep seemed like a worse idea. "We'll stop somewhere defensible. Just for the night."

She didn't respond but nodded, gripping her axe like it was her lifeline. The road led us to the outskirts of what must have been a small town once, though the warped reality of Ashvalen and Earth's fusion had twisted it into something unfamiliar. Eventually, we spotted a faded sign with "MOTEL" in flickering neon, the rest of the letters too dim to read. The building was a single-story L-shape, its cracked stucco walls lined with doors that looked more fragile than the plywood they were likely made of. A single car sat in the lot, rusted and covered in vines.

"Looks... promising," I said dryly, pulling into the lot.

She squinted at the dilapidated structure. "It doesn't look safe."

"Nothing is safe anymore," I muttered, stepping out of the car. "But we need sleep."

The front office door was unlocked, the bell above it jingling as we stepped inside. The air was stale, heavy with mildew. A faded calendar on the wall was frozen in a year long past. Behind the desk, a key rack still held several room keys, their tags coated in dust.

"No one's here," I said, grabbing a key at random. Room 7.

Mithis picked up a pen from the counter and turned it over in her fingers like it was a relic of a forgotten age. "Your world is strange."

"Tell me about it," I said, gesturing toward the door.

Room 7 was as depressing as I'd expected: a sagging bed, peeling wallpaper, and a single flickering light overhead. At least the door had a lock, though it looked like it would barely hold up against a stiff breeze, let alone any monsters. Mithis set her axe within arm's reach and began inspecting the room, her warrior instincts refusing to let her relax. "Oh, there is another one?," she asked, pointing to the bathroom.

"Well, ya," I said. "All places have one for each room. People want their privacy even when it is cheap."

She looked at me like I'd spoken another language. "Amazing."

"You're covered in blood and dirt," I said, sitting on the edge of the bed. "I'll jump in after."

With that, she disappeared into the bathroom. I used the time to check my rifle and ammo, making sure everything was in working order. The sound of water running was oddly soothing, a brief reminder of normalcy in this shattered world. When Mithis finally emerged, her damp hair hung loose around her face, and she wore one of the oversized shirts I'd packed. "It's... strange, but I feel better," she admitted.

I smirked. "Thought you might."

She sat on the floor, her axe within reach, and leaned back against the bed. "You should get some sleep. I'll keep watch."

"No," I said firmly. "You need rest, too. We'll take turns."

Her eyes narrowed. "You're stubborn."

"Thank the army for that," I replied, lying down on the creaking mattress.

The room fell silent, save for the dim hum of the light and the occasional groan of the wind outside. For the first time in what felt like days, I let my eyes close, though sleep didn't come easily. My mind kept replaying the witch's curse, the Hollow Shades, and the impossible task of finding my sister and her family in a world gone mad.

But as I drifted off, the sound of Mithis sharpening her axe nearby was oddly comforting. Whatever came next, we'd face it together. The creak of the bed springs woke me before my body was ready to move. For a moment, I thought it was just the wind outside, but then there was a noise. A knock at the door.

Three quiet taps.

I sat upright, my hand already reaching for the rifle leaning against the nightstand. Mithis stirred on the floor, her eyes snapping open as though she hadn't been asleep at all. Another knock.

"Who is it?" I called out, keeping my voice steady.

A reply came, soft and muffled but eerily familiar. "Help me... please..."

It was a woman's voice. Young. Desperate. Mithis immediately stood, her axe in hand. "Don't open it," she hissed.

I wasn't planning to. Because this is straight out of a horror movie. Except, I have a gun and Mithis has an axe, so there is that.

Who are you?" I called again, my grip tightening on the rifle.

The voice wavered, trembling with fear. "I... I'm lost. Something's chasing me. Please, let me in."

I exchanged a glance with Mithis, and her expression told me everything I needed to know. This wasn't right. The voice continued, becoming more frantic.

"Please! It's right behind me! I'm not going to make it!"

"Stay calm," I said, motioning for Mithis to stay back as I crept toward the window. I peeked through the edge of the curtain, careful not to expose myself. The lot outside was empty. Nothing moved.

"Do you see anyone?" Mithis whispered.

"No," I replied quietly, stepping back. "Nothing's out there."

The knocking turned to pounding. "Let me in!" The voice screamed now, its pitch fluctuating unnaturally.

Mithis's grip on her axe tightened. "It's not human," she said, her voice steady but low.

"Yeah, I'm getting that vibe too," I muttered. The pounding stopped, replaced by an eerie silence. For a moment, I thought it was over, but then I heard something that made my blood run cold.

"Please, brother, let me in," the voice said.

It was my sister's voice.

I froze, my mind racing. It sounded exactly like her down to the inflection, the way she used to call me when we were kids.

Don't listen," Mithis said sharply, stepping between me and the door. "It's trying to trick you."

The voice outside changed again, gentler now, pleading. "I'm scared. It's me. Please don't leave me out here."

I shook my head, trying to focus. "You're not her," I said firmly.

A low growl came from the other side of the door, guttural and inhuman. The thing began scraping against the wood, its claws dragging slowly, deliberately, as if savoring the moment. "I can smell you," it whispered, its voice a twisted amalgamation of different tones. "You smell... afraid."

The door groaned as the thing pressed against it. The flimsy lock wouldn't hold if it decided to come in.

"What is it?" I asked Mithis, my voice tight.

She didn't answer right away, her gaze locked on the door. Finally, she said, "I don't know. I don't know of any creature that can change its voice."

That almost scared me more than the voice outside.

I steadied my rifle, aiming it at the door. "What's the plan?"

"Don't let it in."

"Yeah, I wasn't gonna let it in," I said, trying my best to add a little humor into a stressful situation so we both could think clearly.

The scraping stopped abruptly, and for a moment, there was only silence. Then it spoke again, its voice calm, confident.

"You can't stop me," it said, perfectly mimicking my voice.

I freaked out. I fired a single round through the door without thinking about what would happen next.

The creature howled, a deafening, otherworldly sound that shook the walls. The door splintered as something massive slammed against it, but it didn't break through.

"Shoot again!" Mithis yelled, raising her axe.

I fired twice more, the shots tearing through the wood. The thing screeched, and then there was a heavy thud as its body hit the ground outside.

Silence!

Mithis and I stood frozen, waiting for any sign of movement. When none came, she stepped forward cautiously, peeping through the shattered door.

"It's gone," she said finally, though her grip on the axe didn't loosen.

I exhaled slowly, my hands trembling as I lowered the rifle. "Let's not stay here any longer."

Mithis nodded. "Agreed."

7 GRAVEL AND GHOSTS

We grabbed our gear and headed for the car, the eerie quiet of the night pressing down like a wet blanket. The motel lot was a graveyard of rust and shadows, that lone car in the corner swallowed by vines so thick they looked like they'd grown overnight. Whatever that thing at the door had been, its howl still rattled in my skull, a sound like nails on glass, twisted with my voice and Sara's plea. I knew it wouldn't be the last bastard trying to stop us; this world was too far gone.

The Jeep roared to life, a guttural snarl that cut through the silence, and I peeled out of the parking lot fast, tires spitting gravel like shrapnel. The shattered door of Room 7 shrank in the rearview, jagged wood glowing faintly under the busted neon a reminder of how close we'd come to being another stain on this twisted mess.

Mithis sat beside me, her axe resting on her lap, blade still flecked with dried blood that caught the dashboard's green glow. She stared out the window, crimson eyes slicing through the dark, hunting for movement. Her wolf pelt cape bunched against the seat, damp from the shower and streaked with dirt, a subtle musk of leather and pine clinging to her. Adrenaline still burned through me, a hot wire under my skin, but exhaustion was creeping in my hands shook on the wheel, knuckles split and raw from too many fights, too little sleep. The air in the Jeep was thick, smelling of gun oil, sweat, and the trace sulfur tang of whatever hell we'd left behind.

"What do you think that thing came from?" I asked, breaking the tense silence, my voice rough as gravel, scraping past the lump in my throat.

"Nothing from my world can do what it did," Mithis replied, steady but low, her words clipped like she was chewing them over. She shifted, the axe haft creaking under her grip, and her eyes flicked to me, sharp as a blade.

"I noticed the last voice that creature got the strongest reaction out of you. Who was it?"

"It used my sister's voice," I muttered, fingers tightening on the wheel 'til the leather groaned.

Sara's scream from that phone call looped in my head, now layered with that thing's mimicry, soft, pleading, then guttural and wrong.

"Great. Just what we need, monsters that can mimic the voices of the people we love." The sarcasm came out bitter, tasting like the bile I'd swallowed back at the motel.

Mithis gave a small nod, a tight jerk of her chin, but said nothing. Her silence was heavy, not empty. Her mind was turning, same as mine, picking at the edges of what we'd seen. The road stretched ahead, lit only by the dim glow of the headlights, cutting a shaky path through the black. The highway twisted and warped like it was alive, asphalt buckling under Ashvalen's grip, cracks spiderwebbed with glowing vines, pulsing faint green like veins.

Trees loomed on either side, taller and more gnarled the farther we went, their bark slick and black, branches clawing at the sky like skeletal hands frozen mid-grab. Every so often, I caught movement in the shadows, fleeting shapes, too quick to pin down, gone when I squinted. My gut churned; this wasn't just woods anymore; this was a trap waiting.

"Do you think it'll come back?" I asked, keeping my eyes on the road, the Jeep's hum a thin lifeline against the quiet pressing in.

Mithis shook her head, slow and deliberate, her cape rustling softly against the seat.

"No. You hurt it, drove it off. The longer we stay in these woods, the more dangerous it becomes." Her voice was flat, matter-of-fact, but her hand stayed tight on the axe, runes glowing faintly purple under her sleeve like they were listening too.

I glanced at her, brow furrowing under the grime caked on my face. "These woods?"

She hesitated, jaw tightening, like she was weighing how much to say. "The witch's magic must've infected this place much more deeply than we realize. Some of these areas feel like they hold power much older than our world's merging." Her eyes flicked to the trees, narrowing as a branch scraped the Jeep's roof with a high, grating whine.

"What? Like magic from my world?" I pressed, my voice edging sharp, disbelief cutting through the fog in my head.

"Yes i think it must be magic from your world. That's the only explanation that makes sense, even after the merge." She turned to me fully now, her gaze steady, unyielding, like she'd just laid down a fact I couldn't dodge.

I looked at her like she'd told me the Earth was flat, my mouth half open, words stuck somewhere between a laugh and a curse.

"Look, there's never been magic in this world. Ever." My voice cracked, rough with exhaustion and the absurdity of it, dragons, orcs, witches, sure, but Earth magic? That was a bridge too far, even now. Mom's old fairy tales flickered in my head, woods that ate people, voices in the dark, but those were just stories, not this.

The road twisted like a serpent, weaving through dense woods that seemed to stretch endlessly, swallowing the horizon. The forest's unnerving quiet pressed on us, a weight I could feel in my chest, broken only by the Jeep's low growl and the occasional rustle of leaves in a wind I couldn't feel. The air filtering through the cracked window smelled damp and sour, like rot left to fester too long, undercut with a slight metallic tang that stung my nose. My hands ached on the wheel, split knuckles throbbing with every bump, Sara's face flashing behind my eyes, scared, screaming, needing me. I'd lost Mom to my damn trigger finger; I wasn't losing her too.

"Look," Mithis said suddenly, pointing through the windshield, her voice snapping me out of the spiral.

In the distance, just beyond the forest's edge, a dim glow flickered warm, like torchlight, cutting through the dark like a lifeline. I slowed the Jeep, knuckles tight on the wheel, the engine's rumble dropping to a low purr. As we crept closer, the trees parted into a clearing, and there it was: a medieval village nestled in the shadow of the gnarled woods. Timber houses with steep, thatched roofs huddled in a rough circle, their walls patched with mud and stone, weathered like they'd stood for centuries. A crumbling stone wall ringed the place, moss-stuck and riddled with cracks, its gates yawning wide, flanked by torches spitting flame into the night. The sight was surreal, like we'd driven straight into one of those old books Sara used to read me, all knights and dragons, except this wasn't ink on a page. This was real, and it stank of smoke and sweat.

"Do you think they're hostile?" I asked, glancing at Mithis, my rifle resting heavy against my thigh.

She shook her head, crimson eyes narrowing as she studied the scene, her axe shifting in her lap.

"It doesn't feel like an ambush, but this village... it feels out of place. Be cautious." Her voice was low, edged with that quiet steel I was starting to lean on, her runes pulsing dimly like they sensed it too.

I parked the Jeep a safe distance from the gates, under a sprawling oak with branches twisted like they'd been caught mid-scream. Camouflaged it with leaves and branches I yanked from the underbrush, their sap sticking to my hands, bitter and cold. "Let's go in on foot," I said, grabbing my rifle, the weight of it grounding me as I slung my pack over one shoulder, its straps digging into my neck. Mithis nodded, her axe slung across her back, the machete at her thigh clinking softly as she moved, her boots crunching the brittle grass.

The air inside the village was thick with tension, heavy with the smell of woodsmoke, damp straw, and the slight sourness of unwashed bodies. People scurried between homes and stalls, their movements jerky, eyes darting toward the forest like it might lunge at them. Worn cloaks hung off bony shoulders, faces gaunt under hoods and scarves, hands clutching baskets or tools with white-knuckled grips. A group of guards stood near the gate, chainmail rattling quietly under patched tunics, halberds propped against the wall, their tips notched and dulled. They watched us approach, suspicion carving deep lines into their weathered faces, a nervous twitch flickering in their hands.

"Halt!" one barked, voice steady but brittle, like he was holding it together by will alone. His grip tightened on his halberd, the wood creaking, his eyes darting over us, dirty jeans, blood-streaked jacket, rifle, and landing on Mithis, hard and wary.

"State your business!"

I raised my hands slowly, palms out, trying to look less like the guy who'd just shot a door to splinters. "We're travelers. Looking for supplies and information." My voice came out rough, scraped raw from shouting, but I kept it even, watching his stance, tense, ready to swing if I blinked wrong.

His eyes flicked to Mithis, narrowing at her green skin, the axe slung over her shoulder, the runes glowing muted under her sleeve.

"You travel with an orc?" The word spat out like a curse, his lips curling, hand twitching toward the halberd.

Mithis stiffened, a low growl rumbling in her throat, but I stepped forward, cutting her off. "She's not what you think. We're not here to cause trouble." My tone stayed firm, a soldier's edge slipping in don't push me, pal, I've had a shitty night.

The guard hesitated, jaw working like he was chewing on his next move, then lowered the halberd an inch, the tip scraping the dirt.

"If you mean no harm, speak with the Elder. He'll decide what to do with you." He jerked his head toward a larger building at the village's heart: a modest hall, timber walls stained dark with age, a wooden sign swinging above the door, carved with an oak tree that looked like it'd been hacked out with a dull blade.

Inside, the hall smelled of old wood and tallow, the air thick and warm from a hearth spitting smoke into the rafters. A man with a long white beard sat at a heavy wooden table, his robe simple but stitched with faded embroidery swirls and knots that might've meant something to someone else. His eyes were keen, cutting through the dimness, belying the age in his hunched frame. Two advisors flanked him, one a grizzled warrior, face scarred under a graying beard, leather armor creaking as he shifted; the other in a robe marked with arcane symbols, gentle blue lines glowing against the fabric, his hands bony and restless.

The Elder rose as we entered, slow but deliberate, his voice deep and commanding, rolling out like thunder over a quiet field.

"Travelers in these times are rare," he said, eyeing my rifle, Mithis's axe like he was sizing up a threat. "I am Aldred, Elder of Kalden. What brings you to our village?"

I stepped forward, boots scuffing the worn planks, the weight of the day heavy in my chest. "We're on a haul north looking for my sister. Ran into some shit in the forest back there a witch stirring up dead things. Figured you might know something about what's bleeding into this place." My voice rasped, every word dragging Sara's scream with it, the witch's curse a burr under my skin.

Aldred listened, his face darkening with every detail, lines deepening around his mouth like cracks in old stone. "You have survived much," he said finally, voice dropping low, heavy with something I couldn't pin regret, maybe. "And your arrival may not be a coincidence. Kalden has been beset by troubles of its own."

"What kind of troubles?" Mithis asked, her tone crisp, cutting through the smoky air like a blade.

Aldred sighed, a sound like wind through dead branches, and gestured for us to sit on a bench that creaked under our weight.

"The forest. It has been encroaching on our land, its trees growing unnaturally fast, and the creatures within growing bolder. Our hunters and woodcutters disappear, and the village is running low on resources. To make matters worse, we believe there is a malevolent force at work, a creature that has claimed dominion over the woods." His hands clenched on the table, knuckles whitening, the wood groaning quietly under the pressure.

"What kind of creature?" I asked, my grip tightening on the rifle, the cold steel grounding me as my pulse kicked up.

"The stories differ," Aldred admitted, leaning back, his beard brushing the table's edge. "Some say it is a spirit of the forest, angered by our presence, whispers on the wind, shadows that choke the life from men. Others claim it is a beast summoned by dark magic, all claws and hunger, tearing through flesh like parchment. Whatever it is, it drives the forest to consume us. If we cannot push it back, Kalden will fall." His voice cracked, just once, a fracture in his calm I felt in my bones.

Mithis exchanged a look with me, her crimson eyes glinting in the firelight. "This sounds like the witch's work," she said, voice low, deliberate. "Her magic could have spread farther than we thought."

"Possibly," I replied, rubbing my jaw, stubble rough against my palm. "Or something worse." The curse gnawed at me every life you touch, and now this village, teetering on the edge. Coincidence felt like a lie.

The Elder leaned forward, his eyes piercing, cutting through the haze of smoke and doubt. "You are armed and skilled. If you help us rid the forest of this evil, we will reward you with whatever we can spare: food, supplies, and safe shelter. Please, for the sake of my people, consider it." His voice carried weight, a plea wrapped in command, his hands splaying on the table like he could hold the village together by force of will.

I looked at Mithis. She gave a small nod, her expression resolute, the axe haft creaking as she shifted it.

"We'll help," I said, voice firm despite the ache in my chest. "But we'll need more information about this creature and your forest."

Aldred's advisors stepped up, the warrior's boots thudding heavily on the planks. He unrolled a crude map of yellowed parchment, edges curling, ink smudged from sweaty hands, spreading it across the table.

"Our hunters reported seeing the creature near the old stone circle, deep in the woods," he said, pointing to a marked spot with a scarred finger, the nail chipped and black.

"But none who have gone there have returned." His voice was gruff, worn thin by loss, his eyes flicking to the map like it was a grave.

The robed figure chimed in, his voice reedy, fingers tracing the arcane symbols on his sleeve.

"There is ancient magic in that part of the forest. I can provide you with charms to ward off some of the forest's influence, but they will only offer limited protection." He pulled two small pouches from his leather robe, stained dark, rattling quietly with whatever was inside, offering them like they were gold.

"Better than nothing," I said, taking one, the leather cool and rough against my palm. "We'll head out at first light. But before that, I do not help for free." My tone hardened, soldier's instinct kicking in, give me something to work with, or I'm out.

Aldred's face sharpened, eyes narrowing under bushy brows. "We cannot offer too much." His voice was tight, like he was bartering with the last scraps of his pride.

"All I ask for is some coin. We can negotiate the price afterwards," I said, keeping it simple, my gaze locked on his. Needed something tangible; food and shelter were fine, but coin meant options, and I wasn't betting Sara's life on charity.

Thankfully, Mithis stayed beside me, silent, her presence a solid wall at my shoulder not contradicting, just there, her axe a quiet threat. Aldred studied us, then nodded, slow and grudging.

"Very well. There is an inn on the other side of the village. Go there, get some rest, and help us in the morning." His voice softened, just a hair, like he was handing us a lifeline he barely had himself.

I nodded confirmation and left the hall, the smoky air clinging to my jacket as we stepped out. A village guard approached, his chainmail clinking quietly under a patched cloak, motioning us to follow with a curt wave. The inn wasn't much, just another timber box like the rest, weathered and squat, except for a wooden sign creaking above the door, "INN" carved in blocky letters half chipped away. We walked in, and the emptiness hit me hard. Afternoon light should've meant noise, bodies, life. Instead, it was dead, the air stale with old ale and dust. The place doubled as a tavern with scarred tables scattered across the floor, chairs wobbling on uneven legs, a bar running along one wall, its wood stained dark with spills and time. A lone candle flickered on the counter, wax dripping slowly into a puddle, casting jagged shadows.

Mithis didn't hesitate, striding to the bar like she owned it, her boots thudding lightly on the planks. She leaned in, axe still slung over her shoulder, and asked for a room, voice low but firm. The barkeep, a wiry guy, face creased like old leather, apron smeared with grease, scoffed, a harsh bark of a laugh that grated on my nerves.

I clenched my jaw, stepping up beside her, the rifle heavy in my hands.

"Hey, buddy, we're here to help with your monster problem. If you don't want our help, we can leave and tell everyone we walked out because you decided to be a dickhead." My voice came out rough, edged with the night's bullshit, and I leaned in, letting him see the dirt and blood on me, proof I wasn't bluffing.

His smirk dropped fast, eyes widening a fraction, like he'd just clocked the axe, the rifle, the fact we weren't here to screw around. Maybe someone had warned him about us, or maybe he saw the edge in my stare; either way, he caved, his demeanor shifting like a switch flipped.

"Room's yours," he muttered, tossing a key across the bar, a dull clink as it landed.

Small victories. We got it without further fuss, and I led the way, the key cold and scratched in my hand. The room was small, just a two-person bed shoved against one wall, its frame sagging under threadbare blankets that smelled of a hint of mildew, a tight square of floor barely big enough to pace, and a single candle on the windowsill, its flame spitting weak light against warped glass. I looked around and smirked, the corner of my mouth twitching despite the weight in my chest. "I've heen worse." Army cots in the desert, sand in my teeth, gunfire for a lullaby that beat that, at least.

As I walked in, taking in the cramped space the peeling walls, the quiet creak of the floorboards I glanced at Mithis.

"At least we don't have to worry about anyone or anything knocking on the door at night." The words slipped out, dry and halfhearted, and I froze mid-step, heat creeping up my neck. Shit, that sounded awkward as hell, me fumbling like some kid who didn't know how to talk to a woman, let alone one who'd just saved my ass from a witch and a voice-stealing freak. This was our first real moment alone, no dead things clawing at us, no curses spitting venom, just the two of us in a quiet that felt too big after the nightmares of the past few days. My shoulders eased, tension bleeding out slowly as I set my pack down by the bed with a heavy thud, the rifle leaning against the wall, barrel scratched and cold. The simplicity of the space, a wooden bed frame groaning under its weight, blankets thin as paper, the candle's flicker painting shadows on the walls, felt oddly comforting, a breather from the madness outside. I kicked off my boots, the leather scuffed and caked with dirt, and stretched my legs, joints popping loudly in the stillness.

Mithis was already moving, casing the room like it might sprout claws. Her crimson eyes flicked to the window, the door, then landed on me, steady and unreadable. She set her axe within arm's reach of the bed, the blade catching the candlelight, purple runes glinting dimly against the steel.

"It's not much," she said, sitting on the bed's edge, the frame creaking under her weight, her voice low and rough, like she was testing the quiet.

"For now," I replied, pulling off my jacket, the fabric stiff with sweat and grime, and tossing it over my pack. "Quiet doesn't last long in places like this." I stretched again, feeling the ache in my ribs from the motel fight, Sara's voice fake but real, still echoing in my head.

She nodded, staring at the floor for a beat, her damp hair falling loose around her face, green skin catching the light in a way that made her look less alien, more human, or whatever passed for it now. I could tell she was deep in thought about the witch, the curse, maybe her ghosts, but I didn't press. Instead, I dug into my bag, pulled out a water bottle, plastic scratched and cloudy, half full, and offered it to her, the cap gritty in my hand.

"Drink. You look like you could use it." My voice came out softer than I meant, rough edges worn down by the day.

Mithis took it with a small smile, a flicker that didn't reach her eyes, her gloved fingers brushing mine cool, steady.

"Thanks," she said quietly, unscrewing the cap with a soft crack, taking a sip that left a bead of water on her lip. She handed it back, and I took a swig, the water cold and flat but cutting through the dust in my throat.

I leaned back against the wall, the wood cool and splintered against my spine, running a hand through my hair, greasy, matted with sweat.

"So... what now? We're stuck here till morning, and I don't think either of us can sleep." My voice rasped, the words dragging out the weight of the night, the witch, the Shades, that thing at the door.

Mithis tilted her head, considering, her cape rustling as she shifted.

"We should learn more about the village, the people here, what they know, what they're afraid of. If we're going to face that creature, we need every advantage we can get." Her tone was firm, practical, her eyes flicking to the door like she was already mapping the next move. I nodded, grabbing my jacket off the pack, the fabric heavy in my hands.

"Good idea. Let's see what we can find out." I slipped it on, the weight settling over my shoulders like armor, and checked my rifle mag full, safety off, ready for whatever this place threw at us.

We stepped out into the cool evening air, the village quiet save for the soft clatter of a hammer somewhere distant and the low murmur of voices drifting on the breeze. The streets were narrow, packed dirt rutted from cart wheels, lined with modest homes, timber walls patched with mud, roofs sagging under thatch that looked ready to rot. Workshops huddled between them, shutters cracked, thin smoke curling from chimneys into a sky bruising purple. Despite the peaceful shell, unease hung thick like the whole damn place was holding its breath, waiting for the axe to fall.

Our first stop was a small market square near the village's center, a cramped patch of dirt ringed by stalls, wooden frames leaning under their weight, canvas flaps tattered and flapping in the wind. A handful of merchants were packing up for the night, their movements hurried, wary, hands trembling as they bundled goods into burlap sacks. Mithis and I approached a woman selling herbs and dried flowers, her stall a mess of lavender bundles and wilted petals spilling over the edge. She was older, face creased like cracked earth, her cloak patched with rough stitches, hands clutching a bundle of lavender so tight the stems bent.

"Excuse me," I said, keeping my tone polite but firm. The soldier's habit of kicking in doesn't spook her, but she doesn't back down. "We're new here. What can you tell us about the forest and the creature that's been causing trouble?"

She froze, her grip whitening on the lavender, the slight scent sharp in the air. Her eyes darted around checking corners, shadows, like someone might overhear and snitch before she leaned in closer, her breath sour with fear.

"You mean the monster?" she whispered, voice thin as a reed, trembling like it might snap.

I nodded, leaning on the stall's edge, wood creaking under my weight. "Yeah. What do you know about it?"

She hesitated, swallowing hard, then lowered her voice further, barely audible over the wind.

"It comes at night. You hear its howl, and you know someone won't see it in the morning. It's been like this for weeks now. The forest is alive with its powerful roots growing where they shouldn't, trees twisting like they're alive. My cousin tried to hunt it once, but..." Her voice broke, eyes glistening wet in the torchlight. "He didn't come back." She clutched the lavender tighter, like it could shield her from the memory.

Mithis frowned, her axe shifting as she crossed her arms, the blade catching the light with a dull gleam.

"How do the people survive?" Her voice was low, cutting, and demanding an answer.

The woman's expression darkened, shadows pooling under her eyes. "Barely. We don't go into the forest anymore. The Elder says we'll find a way to stop it, but I think we're just waiting to die."

Her words hung heavy, a quiet despair that sank into my bones too close to my own thoughts about Sara, about Mom.

"Not if we can help it," I said firmly, straightening up, the rifle a cold weight against my thigh. "Thanks for telling us." My voice rasped, edged with a stubbornness I didn't feel, but I'd be damned if I let her see that.

She nodded stiffly, gaze darting back to the forest beyond the wall, its dark bulk pressing in like a predator waiting to strike. "Be careful out there," she murmured, turning away, her hands trembling as she stuffed the lavender into a sack.

Before heading back, Mithis jerked her head toward the tavern across the square, a squat timber box with a slanted roof, smoke curling thick from its chimney.

"We should stop there and gather more," she said, her voice low, practical, her eyes scanning the sparse crowd like a hawk. I nodded, the weight of the day settling heavier, Sara's voice, the witch's curse, now this village's doom. Needed every scrap we could get.

The tavern was dimly lit, a haze of smoke hanging low, stinging my eyes as we stepped in. The air was thick with stale ale, burnt wood, and the slight tang of sweat from the handful of patrons nursing drinks at scattered tables. Rough-hewn benches wobbled under their weight, tankards clinking dully against scarred wood, their faces shadowed under hoods or bent over their cups.

The hearth spat embers into the gloom, a soft crackle under the low hum of muttered talk. We took a seat at the bar, the wood sticky under my elbows, a thin ring of spilled ale marking where someone had been sloppy. The barkeep was a broad guy, shoulders hunched, face creased like old leather, polished a mug with a rag older than the building, gray and frayed, his eyes flicking to us, wary but dull 'til I ordered two drinks.

"You're the ones the Elder brought in," he said, pouring dark ale into wooden mugs, the liquid sloshing thick and bitter, foam spilling over the rims. His voice was flat, worn, like he'd seen too much to care.

"That's us," I said, taking a sip, bitter as hell but crisp, a kick that steadied my hands. "What do you know about the monster?"

His face darkened, shadows deepening under his brow as he set the jug down with a thud. "Enough to know you're better off running than fighting. That thing's not natural. It's a demon, plain and simple." His hands stilled on the mug, rag dangling limp, his eyes flicking to the door like it might barge in right then.

"Demons can be killed," Mithis said firmly, her hand resting on her axe, the haft creaking as she leaned forward, her voice cutting through the smoke like steel through flesh.

"Maybe," the barkeep muttered, voice dropping low, almost lost in the hearth's crackle. "But not by us." He scrubbed the mug harder, like he could wipe away the fear in his own words.

"Lucky for you, we're not some push overs," I said, finishing my drink in one long pull, the burn settling warm in my gut. I slid the empty mug back across the bar, the wood scraping loudly in the quiet. "Thanks for the warning." My voice came out rough, edged with a defiance I wasn't sure I had left, but it felt good to say like spitting in the face of the curse still clawing at me.

We stepped back into the night, the tavern's warmth fading fast against the chill seeping through my jacket. The village huddled silently around us, torchlight flickering dimly against the dark, the forest looming beyond the wall like a beast waiting to pounce. Sara was out there, somewhere north, and every second here felt like a delay, but this place, these people, they were a thread I couldn't cut. Not yet. The witch's words echoed "every life you touch" and I wondered if helping them would just damn them too. Didn't matter. I'd fight 'til it killed me, or I found them. No other way.

8 HUNGER'S HOLLOW

We trudged back to the inn under the cover of night, boots scuffing the packed dirt, the village so quiet it felt like a tomb. The air was sharp, biting at my sweat-slick skin, carrying the soft rustle of leaves in a wind that barely stirred the torch flames flickering along the wall. Shadows stretched long and jagged, pooling under the timber houses like spilled ink, and I couldn't shake the itch between my shoulder blades like eyes were boring into me from the dark. My rifle hung heavy in my hands, barrel still warm from the motel, Sara's voice fake but too damn real echoing in my skull, twisting with that thing's growl. The witch's curse gnawed deeper, "every life you touch will rot," and I wondered if it was watching too, waiting to prove her right.

Mithis felt it, same as me. Her hand hovered near her axe, fingers twitching on the shaft, her crimson eyes slicing through the gloom like a hawk's—sharp, unblinking, hunting the shadows as we walked. The wolf pelt cape swayed with her steps, damp and matted from the day's blood and dirt, a subtle whiff of pine and leather cutting through the village's stink of smoke and rot.

"Do you think the thing is watching us?" she asked quietly, voice low and rough, barely louder than the wind's whisper, but it carried that edge I'd come to lean on—steady, ready.

"Maybe," I said, my voice scraping out, hoarse from shouting and the dust still clogging my throat. "We'll know more tomorrow, when we finally face the creature." The words tasted like ash, heavy with Sara's scream and Mom's blood, promises I wasn't sure I could keep, but I'd be damned if I didn't try.

We ducked into the inn, the door creaking loudly in the stillness, and climbed the narrow stairs to our room. Warmth hit me as I pushed inside, cozy almost, the candle on the windowsill spitting a weak glow across the sagging bed and peeling walls. The air smelled of mildew and old straw, a slight sweetness from the wax melting into a puddle, but it was a small comfort, a breather from the shitstorm waiting outside. Small comfort for two idiots about to face something dangerous and deadly, something that'd probably chew us up and spit us out before breakfast. I dropped my gear by the bed with a dull thud, the rifle leaning against the wall, its scratched barrel catching the light of my lifeline in a world gone feral.

Tomorrow, the real battle will begin.

The next morning, Mithis and I set out, armed to the teeth and strung tight as tripwires. The sun hung low, a pale smear bleeding through the heavy fog that clung to Kalden like a shroud, its light barely cutting the gray. My boots crunched the frost-rimmed dirt, breath fogging in short, sharp bursts, the cold biting at my split knuckles and the cut on my arm from the witch's goons. Behind us, the villagers gathered at the gate, a ragged line of cloaks and hollow faces, their silence louder than screams. Some clasped their hands, fingers twisting like they were praying to gods who'd already checked out; others turned away, heads bowed, unable to watch us vanish into the woods. I couldn't blame them–no one had dared face whatever plagued this land, and the ones who'd tried weren't around to warn us off. Their fear stank, sour and thick, mixing with the smoke curling from chimneys into the still air.

The forest swallowed us quickly, towering trees closing in like a trap snapping shut, blotting out what little light the day offered. Their trunks loomed black and slick, bark glistening with damp that smelled of rot and wet earth, branches twisting overhead into a canopy so dense it choked the sky. An unnatural chill settled over us, seeping through my jacket, prickling my skin like needles, and the air grew thick, muffling our footsteps, pressing down like a hand on my chest. Mithis walked ahead, her eyes scanning the shadows, battle axe slung over one shoulder, its runes glowing faint purple against the steel, pulsing like a heartbeat in this cursed place. Her cape dragged through the underbrush, snagging on thorns that gleamed wet in the dimness, her breath a steady fog cutting the haze.

"This isn't normal," Mithis muttered, voice low, rough as gravel, her sharp gaze darting to a patch of brambles that seemed to shift as we passed–tendrils curling slowly, deliberately, like they were tasting the air.

"The forest is watching us."

I nodded, gripping my rifle tight, the cold steel biting into my palms, steadying the shake I wouldn't admit to. The weapon was sturdy, reliable, my old Army lifeline–but it felt small, a kid's toy against the malevolence hanging thick around us, a weight I could taste, sour and metallic.

"Let it watch," I said, forcing the words out, though my voice cracked, lacking the brass I'd aimed for. Sara's face flashed–scared, screaming--and I shoved it down, focusing on the crunch of my boots, the ache in my legs. Couldn't let the fear win, not yet.

The deeper we went, the more the silence pressed, oppressive as a fist around my throat. No birdsong, no rustling leaves–just an eerie stillness, broken only by the snap of twigs underfoot and the soft drip of water somewhere ahead, slow and maddening. Then the whispers started-faint, indistinct, a murmur slithering through the trees, growing louder as we pressed on. A cacophony of voices, overlapping, clawing at my ears-pleas, warnings, threats-echoing from everywhere and nowhere, like the forest itself was muttering secrets it didn't want me to hear. My skin crawled, a cold sweat beading under my collar, the witch's curse clawing louder, "every hope will crumble."

Mithis stopped abruptly, holding up a hand, her cape swaying as she froze. "Do you hear that?" Her voice cut through, low and urgent, her runes flaring brighter, casting jagged shadows on the gnarled trunks.

I strained to listen, breath hitching, the rifle's weight grounding me as my pulse hammered. Among the whispers, I caught fragments of words like "run," "please," "flesh," sharp and fleeting, impossible to pin down. Couldn't tell if they were real, spilling from the trees, or just my damn head screwing with me, Mom's blank eyes and Sara's scream bleeding into the noise.

"Keep moving," I said, throat tight, unease coiling in my chest like barbed wire.

Finally, we broke through the dense undergrowth, thorns snagging at my jeans, tearing free with a sting, and stumbled into a clearing. The sight hit like a punch, stealing the air from my lungs.

The stone circle loomed ahead, ancient and weathered, its monolithic slabs jutting from the earth like broken teeth, each one taller than me, their surfaces pocked and moss slick. Glowing runes crawled across them, jagged, green, pulsing with an otherworldly light that flickers like a dying pulse, casting the clearing in a sickly sheen. The ground was scorched black, barren as a blast site-a stark contrast to the vibrant, twisted forest ringing it-grass and vines curling back like they'd been burned away by something unholy. Mist curled around the stones, thick and clammy, coiling like grasping fingers, the air heavy with the stink of decay and damp earth, sharp enough to sting my nose.

At the center stood the creature.

It towered over us, damn near ten feet of nightmare stitched together-wood, bone, and shadow twisting into a shape that didn't belong. Antlers branched from its head, gnarled like a stag's but draped with moss and bone fragments, clattering quietly as it shifted. Its limbs were long and warped, knotted like old roots, clawed hands dragging the ground, talons scraping gouges in the dirt with a sound like nails on slate. The creature's glowing green eyes locked onto mine, bright and piercing, cutting through the fog, and for a split second, I felt it see me-straight through the sweat, the blood, the guilt, right into the hollow part of my heart where Mom and Sara lived. My stomach dropped, a cold jolt spiking down my spine.

"Mortals," it growled, voice a deep, guttural rumble that shook the

Jacob Salvia

ground under my boots, vibrating up my legs like a quake. "You dare trespass in my domain?" The words rolled out slowly, thick with ancient malice, dripping like sap from a wound.

I raised my rifle, forcing a smirk despite the fear gnawing at my resolve, jaw tight enough to ache. "Yeah," I said, leveling the barrel at its chest, the sight trembling just a hair. "We're not great at staying out of trouble." Sarcasm was all I had left, a thin shield against the thing's stare, Sara's scream pushing me to keep my hands steady.

The creature loomed over the stone circle, antlers brushing the low-hanging clouds gray, heavy, pressing down like a lid on this hell. Its glowing green eyes fixed on us with an unnatural smarts, eerie against the gnarled, skeletal frame beneath–wood and bone woven tight, shadow filling the gaps like tar. Every step it took sent tremors through the dirt, a dull thud I felt in my chest, its voice growling from the forest itself, ancient and pissed, a sound that scraped my nerves raw.

Mithis darted at it again, axe slicing through the mist in a blur of purple light, aiming for its leg. The enchanted blade hit with a thunderous crack, a jolt that echoed off the stones, but the creature barely flinched–like she'd swung at a damn boulder. The impact sent her sprawling, boots skidding across the scorched earth, her axe clattering from her grip as she hit the ground hard, a grunt punching out of her.

I raised my rifle, letting loose a controlled burst of three shots, crisp and loud, cracking the air. The rounds struck true, punching into its chest, but they flattened against its hide, dropping to the dirt like spent coins, useless. It snarled, a sound that rolled through the clearing, thick with a mocking edge, amused, like I'd tickled it. "This isn't working!" I shouted, retreating to Mithis's side, my boots slipping on the slick ground. I grabbed her arm, hauling her up, her weight heavy but solid, her breath rasping hot against my neck.

"We can't give up!" she snapped, crimson eyes blazing, fierce as the fire in her glare. She shook me off, gripping her axe tight with a growl of defiance, and swung again, this time aiming high, the blade arcing for its head, purple runes flaring bright.

The monster moved fast, inhuman–sidestepping her strike like a shadow, fluid and wrong, then slamming a massive clawed hand into the ground. The earth bucked, a shockwave knocking me back a step, and vines erupted–thick, green, snaking toward us with a speed that turned my gut cold. One coiled around Mithis's leg, tight as a noose, dragging her toward the beast with a force that jerked her off her feet, her axe skidding free.

"Mithis!" I yelled, lunging forward, knife out–six inches of battered steel, scratched and dull but sharp enough. I hacked at the vine, blade biting deep into the living wood, sap spurting sticky and bitter across my hands. It fought back, twisting like it was alive, writhing under the cuts, but I slashed frantically–once, twice–'til it gave, snapping with a wet crack. Mithis scrambled free, breath coming in harsh gasps, her cape tangled with dirt and thorns as she rolled to her knees.

The creature's glowing eyes narrowed, voice rumbling deep from the forest's gut. "You are nothing but prey," it growled, slow and deliberate, each word a weight that sank into my bones. "Leave this place, or the woods will consume you whole." The threat hung there, heavy as the fog, promising a death I could already taste–rot and cold and silence.

"We need to go!" I shouted, gripping Mithis's arm, my fingers digging into the damp leather of her jacket, slick with sweat and sap.

She hesitated, frustration burning in her gaze, fierce as a cornered animal. "I'm not leaving without a fight," she muttered, gripping her axe tight, knuckles whitening under her gloves, the runes pulsing like they were pissed too.

The monster didn't wait. Its clawed hand swept through the air, a blur of shadow and bone, missing her head by inches. The force sent shockwaves through the dirt, a boom that knocked us both off balance, my boots sliding as I caught myself on one knee.

"Mithis, now!" I bellowed, voice cutting through her stubbornness, raw and desperate.

Reluctantly, she nodded, jaw tight with rage, teeth gritted hard enough I could hear it. "Fine, but this isn't over," she spat out, the words sharp as her blade.

We turned and ran, dodging roots and vines that lashed out like whips, the forest itself clawing at us–thorns snagging my jeans, tearing skin with a sting I ignored, branches raking my arms. The creature stood still, a dark silhouette against the stormy sky, but its eyes tracked us, green and unblinking, a hunter letting prey tire itself out. It roared again, louder, a sound that shook the air and sank into my bones, slowing every step with its weight, a promise of hunger and ruin.

We hit the clearing's edge, the ground shifting under us–a low rumble swelling, dirt trembling like it was about to split. We stumbled, barely upright, my rifle banging against my hip, Mithis's axe clanking as she caught herself. The forest ahead darkened, unnatural trees warping, twisting tighter, their bark glistening wet and black, shadows flickering at the corners of my eyes, darting shapes whispering threats I couldn't catch.

"Mithis," I said, breathless, chest burning, "I don't think it's letting us leave so easily."

She glanced back, face pale but resolute, sweat streaking the grime on her green skin. "Then it will regret that decision." Her voice was steel, low and fierce, her axe rising like she'd carve her way out if it

Jacob Salvia

killed her.

The creature's roar hit again, words riding it this time: "Run, little prey. The forest hungers, and you will not escape it." The sound burrowed into me, a chill that locked my knees for a split second, Sara's scream echoing under it, Mom's blood staining it red. Branches reached down–skeletal, black, clawing at us, splintered tips scraping my jacket, snagging the fabric. Vines erupted ahead, thick and green, forcing us to duck and weave–my knife hacked through the smaller ones, sap spraying sticky across my face, Mithis's axe cleaving the bigger ones in wet, crunching halves, her grunts sharp in the quiet. Relentless, like the forest knew we'd dared to strike its king.

A sudden clearing broke ahead, bathed in pale, silvery light, impossibly clean, untouched by the dark pressing in, glowing soft against the twisted trees. It felt wrong, a trap maybe, but Mithis grabbed my arm, her grip iron through my sleeve. "There!" she shouted, voice raw, dragging me toward it.

We sprinted, hearts pounding, boots slamming the dirt, the forest closing behind us–vines snapping, branches creaking loudly as they bent to grab. The creature's growls echoed, a promise this wasn't done, rolling through the trees like thunder chasing us. We burst into the clearing, the oppressive weight lifting suddenly, air hitting my lungs cold and clean, but we didn't stop, legs pumping 'til the trees thinned, the village gates looming ahead through the fog.

By the time we staggered through, my legs were lead, each step a fire in my thighs, chest burning with every ragged breath. The guards at the gate jolted, hands gripping halberds tight, their chainmail rattling as they stepped forward, faces pale under dented helmet.

"What happened?" one asked, voice high, cracking like he'd expected us back in pieces.

"We found your monster," I said grimly, leaning against the wall, the rough stone cold against my shoulder, catching my breath in short, sharp gasps. "But nothing we did even scratched it." My voice rasped, throat raw, the rifle heavy in my hands, useless against that thing, a toy in a war I didn't sign up for.

The guard paled, skin going gray under the grime, but before he could sputter, Aldred emerged from the village, his robe dragging through the dirt, face etched deep with concern-lines like cracks in old wood, eyes sharp despite the weight in them.

"Come inside," he said, voice low, urgent, waving us toward the hall with a hand that trembled just a hair. "You must tell me everything."

Inside, the hall's smoky warmth hit like a wall, thick with tallow and the slight sourness of old ale, the hearth spitting embers into the haze. Mithis and I slumped onto a bench, wood creaking under us, my pack thudding to the floor, rifle propped beside me, barrel scratched and cold. We recounted the fight–every snarl, every swing, the way bullets flattened and vines grabbed-my voice rough and clipped, Mithis's steady but tight, her hand resting on her axe like it might leap up and finish the story. Aldred listened, stroking his beard slowly, thoughtful, his fingers knotting in the white strands as he weighed our words.

"A creature immune to your weapons, commanding the forest itself," he murmured, voice dropping low, heavy with dread that sank into the room. "This is worse than I feared."

"It's worse than that," I said, pulling out my phone, screen cracked, battery flickering weak in the corner. "I think I know what we're dealing with." My hands shook, sweat slick as I fumbled it, the weight of the day pressing down on-Sara, Mom, the curse, now this.

Aldred and his advisors leaned in, eyes narrowing at the device-alien to them, a relic of my world glowing dimly in the firelight. My connection was spotty, bars dropping to nothing, then back, but it pulled up scraps of old forums, folklore sites, and myths I'd laughed at as a kid. I scrolled through, fingers smudging the screen, searching for anything that matched-antlers, hunger, forest- and stopped cold. "Here," I said, holding it up, the dim glow catching their faces. "This thing... it matches the description of a Wendigo."

"A Wendigo?" Mithis repeated, frowning, her voice rough, tilting her head like she was testing the word, her cape rustling as she leaned closer.

"It's a creature from my myths," I explained, throat tight, the words dragging out Sara's old bedtime stories-tales she'd whisper to scare me, her grin wide in the dark. "Supposedly a spirit of hunger and greed, tied to the cold wilderness. It's said to be a cannibal cursed into a monstrous form, with an insatiable hunger. They're practically indestructible, but there's a way to kill them." My voice rasped, raw with the memory of Sara's laugh, Mom's voice calling us to bed-now twisted into this.

"What way?" Aldred asked, leaning forward, his beard brushing the table, eyes piercing through the smoke, hungry for a shred of hope.

"White ash," I said, locking on him, the phone trembling in my grip. "According to the stories, a weapon coated in white ash can pierce its skin and end it." The words felt thin, a long shot from some old tale-it's all I had and all this village had too.

The robed advisor nodded slowly-his bony fingers tracing the glowing symbols on his sleeve, voice reedy but sure. "White ash is known in our world as a powerful ward against dark magic. If this creature is indeed tied to your myths, the remedy may be the same." His eyes flicked to Aldred, a flicker of something- relief, maybe-under the grim.

"But where do we find white ash?" Mithis asked, frustration cracking her voice, her axe shifting as she crossed her arms, the runes pulsing faint under the strain.

Aldred stroked his beard, thoughtful, the motion slow and deliberate, like he was pulling the answer from the smoke. "Our forest once had ash trees, but they've become rare with the spreading of corruption. However, there is an old grove on the far side of the village. If the trees still stand, you may find what you need." His voice carried a quiet weight, a lifeline dangled over a cliff, his eyes meeting mine, sharp, steady, daring me to grab it.

I nodded, the phone slipping back into my pocket, its cracked screen dark against my thigh. Sara was out there, Lily too, and this thing, this Wendigo, was a wall between me and them. The curse whispered, "Every life you touch..." but I shoved it down, focusing on the ache in my hands, the rifle's cold steel. We'd find the ash, kill the bastard, or die trying. No other way.

9 CLAWS OF THE PAST

Mithis and I didn't waste time. Dawn was barely a bruise on the sky when we hauled ass out of the inn, the village's creaky walls shrinking behind us. We'd grabbed what we could from Aldred's stash: stale bread that crumbled in my hands, a dented canteen sloshing half full,, and confirmed directions to the grove, his scribbled map stuffed into my pack, edges already fraying.

The villagers watched us pass, their eyes keen under hoods and scarves, cautious, like we were ghosts already, hope flickering weak behind the fear etched deep in their gaunt faces. A kid clutched his mom's cloak, staring at my rifle 'til she yanked him back, muttering something I didn't catch. Couldn't blame them that Wendigo had chewed up their lives, and we were the fools walking back into its jaws.

"We'll get it this time," I said, gripping my rifle tight, the cold steel biting my palms, split knuckles throbbing under the strain. "White ash is the key." My voice rasped, rough from too little sleep and too much dust, Sara's scream looping in my head, scared, pleading, pushing me forward.

Mithis nodded, her resolve hardening like steel cooling fast, her crimson eyes glinting in the gray light. "We'll make it pay for what it's done to this forest." Her words came out low, edged with a growl, her axe slung over her shoulder, runes pulsing faint purple against the blade, alive, angry, and ready. Her wolf pelt cape swayed as she moved, matted with dirt and blood, a subtle whiff of pine cutting through the village's stink of smoke and rot.

As the forest closed in again, swallowing us in its damp, twisted grip, I couldn't shake the weight of what was ahead. The Wendigo wasn't just a monster; it was a predator, a hulking bastard that owned these woods, and we were marching straight into its den, ants picking a fight with a sledgehammer. My boots crunched the frost-rimmed dirt, breath fogging quick in the chill, the witch's curse clawing deeper "every life you touch will rot." Sara's face flashing behind my eyes, Mom's blood staining my hands. But this time, we had a plan, white ash, a long shot from some old tale, and we'd bury that nightmare for good with any luck. Luck hadn't been my friend lately, but I'd take what I could get.

Jacob Salvia

Dawn broke over Kalden's crumbling husk, a pale smear bleeding through the fog, thick with tension that hung like wet cloth. We'd barely slept snatches of shut-eye on that sagging bed, the candle's flicker taunting me with shadows that looked too much like Mom, and now we were geared up, heading east toward what Aldred called the "Shifting Glade." A place where reality bent like a bad dream, where the ash we needed our ticket against the Wendigo and maybe that damn curse lay waiting, if it was there at all.

His warnings rattled in my skull: "The Glade is alive. It bends paths, distorts time, and tests resolve. If the ash is there, it won't be freely given." Sounded like a trap, but traps were old news. Sara was out there, and I wasn't stopping.

We loaded the Jeep with Kalden's scraps of bread that tasted like dust, a canteen that sloshed cold against my thigh, a couple strips of dried meat tough as leather, smelling slightly of salt and smoke. Mithis sat shotgun, silent, her crimson eyes locked on the road ahead, Aldred's map spread across her lap, parchment yellowed and smudged, lines twisting like veins. Her cape bunched against the seat, damp from last night's muck, the air in the cab thick with gun oil, sweat, and the trace sulfur tang still clinging from the witch's lair.

"You're certain this white ash is worth the risk?" she asked, breaking the heavy quiet, her voice rough, testing me like she was weighing the odds herself.

"No... but that is all we have, so it must," I replied, hands tight on the wheel, the leather creaking under my grip.

"Well, white ash can repel certain types of magic. If the curse the witch laid on us starts tightening, this might be our best shot to fight back. So we need it even if it doesn't work on the wendigo." My voice scraped out, raw and clipped, Sara's scream and Mom's blank eyes pushing the words needed this to work, needed something to claw back control from this screwed-up world.

Mithis nodded, slow and deliberate, but unease flickered in her eyes, a shadow under the steel. "Then let us hope this forest doesn't devour us first." Her tone was flat, practical, but her hand stayed on her axe, runes glowing dimly like they were listening too.

The road east was a bastard crack in the asphalt yawning wide, jagged enough to snap an axle, whole chunks swallowed by Ashvalen's grip. Trees arched overhead, their leaves shimmering crystalline, crisp, catching the weak sun in refracted bursts, throwing eerie patterns across the Jeep's hood that danced like broken glass. Vines curled along the ground, soft green tendrils glowing, pulsing like they had a heartbeat, weaving through the pavement's ruins, cracked slabs jutting up like bones from a grave. Wildflowers dotted the edges, petals vibrating with a low hum when the wind brushed them, a sound that crawled under my skin, unnatural as hell. The air smelled damp and sour, undercut with a metallic tang that stung my nose, clung to my throat, Earth rotting under Ashvalen's weight, or maybe the other way around.

We stopped at a husk of a sedan, its frame rusted to a skeleton, tires flat and sinking into the dirt like it'd been abandoned for decades, though it'd only been days since this mess started. Corrosion ate the metal, flaking off in red dust under my gloves time screwing with us again, fast-forwarding decay like a bad joke.

The deeper we pushed, the worse the woods got, trees pressing close, their shimmering leaves casting dappled light that flickered dizzy across the Jeep's windshield, like a strobe in a nightmare. The air thickened, heavy with that cloying metallic bite, sticking in my lungs, making every breath a chore. By midday, the forest had eaten the highway, no asphalt left, just a narrow path choked with roots and glowing vines, forcing me to slow the Jeep to a crawl, tires grinding over uneven dirt. My hands ached on the wheel, split knuckles pulsing, Sara's face flashing scared, needing me, driving me through the haze.

Then it hit a low, guttural growl, vibrating through the ground, rattling the Jeep's frame. Mithis froze mid-step as we climbed out to scout, her hand darting to her axe, runes flaring bright purple. I raised my rifle, the familiar weight cold and steady, but it felt like a toy against the threat I couldn't see yet, heart hammering, sweat beading cold under my collar. From the shadowy underbrush, it emerged a hulking beast, half-hidden in the gloom, a nightmare stitched from rot and rage.

It was a wolf, but far worse. Matted fur glistened sickly, slick with oil or something darker, shimmering wet in the dim light. Glowing green eyes burned through the haze, piercing with a smarts that didn't belong, locked on us like we were meat already. Thick black ichor dripped from oversized fangs, jagged, yellowed, longer than my hand, sizzling quietly as it hit the ground, a crisp hiss cutting the quiet, the stink of burnt earth rising fast. Its frame was massive, shoulders hunched, claws digging ruts in the dirt with every shift, a predator built to rend.

"Darkwood Warg," Mithis said grimly, stepping forward without a flinch, her axe swinging free, blade catching the light with a dull gleam. "A predator of the cursed woods." Her voice was steady, rough with a warrior's edge, her cape swaying as she planted her boots.

The beast snarled, ears flattening, muscles coiling tight, ichor pooling under its jaw, ready to charge a spring wound to snap.

"Mithis," I hissed, keeping my rifle trained, sight locked on those glowing eyes, finger itching on the trigger. "Tell me it can die like anything else."

Her lips curved into a grim smile, tight and fierce, her grip whitening on the axe haft. "Oh, it can die. But it won't make it easy." The words were a promise, edged with a fire that matched her glare.

The warg leapt, a blur of fur and fangs, air rushing past with a snarl that shook my bones. I fired three shots, thunder cracking the suffocating silence, bullets tearing into its hide with dull thuds. It barely staggered, shrugging off the hits like flies, green eyes blazing hotter. Mithis surged forward, meeting it midair, her axe cleaving its front leg in a spray of ichor, black and sticky, splattering the dirt with a wet slap. The beast twisted, violent and fast, its bulk slamming into her, sending her sprawling, boots skidding, axe clattering as she hit the ground hard, a grunt punching out of her.

The fight was a brutal, close, no room for clean shots. My bullets slowed it, punching holes that oozed slowly, but the warg kept coming, tenacious as hell, claws raking the dirt inches from my boots. Mithis rolled to her feet, relentless axe swinging, tearing into its flank, ichor spraying hot across her cape, staining the wolf pelt black. Its green eyes burned, fury driving it even as it weakened, snarling through the pain.

Finally, it collapsed with a ragged howl, legs buckling, ichor pooling thick under its bulk, dead, but not before more howls echoed through the trees, distant but closing fast. "They hunt in packs," Mithis warned, wiping ichor from her face with a bloodied sleeve, her voice tight, urgent, breath heaving. "We need to move." Her runes pulsed, dim purple flickering through the grime.

I glanced at the Jeep, parked a dozen yards back, its frame scratched and dented from the road. "We can't outrun them on foot. Get in!" My voice cracked, raw and crisp, adrenaline spiking as I bolted for the driver's seat.

We barely made it, doors slamming, engine roaring, before the pack burst from the shadows, glowing eyes, a sickly green blur in the underbrush, snarls tearing the air. I floored the gas, the Jeep lurching wildly along the overgrown path, tires spitting dirt and roots. The wargs gave chase, claws thudding the ground, closing fast. Mithis leaned out the window, axe dripping ichor, swinging at snapping jaws and glowing tendrils that lunged too close, severing them with wet crunches. Ahead, a tight bend loomed, a massive fallen tree, its crystalline branches blocking the way, glittering brightly in the dim light.

"Hang on!" I yelled, veering off the path, the Jeep jolting hard as it tore into the forest undergrowth, snapping under the tires, branches screeching shrill against the sides, a sound like nails on glass. The wargs kept coming, howls piercing the trees, relentless green eyes flashing through the haze. Then, as suddenly as a switch flipped, they stopped howling, fading fast, retreating 'til only the soft hum of the flora buzzed in the quiet.

Mithis straightened in her seat, axe heavy in her lap, ichor streaking her gloves. "Why did they stop?" she asked, low and wary, her eyes darting to the trees shimmering, still, too damn still.

I shook my head, gripping the wheel tight, knuckles pulsing under cracked skin. "Maybe we crossed into something worse." My gaze flicked between the towering trunks, their leaves frozen in the dim light, no wind to stir them, silence screaming louder than the pack ever could.

The forest pulsed as we crossed into the Shifting Glade, a rhythm I felt in my chest, slow and heavy like a heartbeat under the dirt. Trees stretched impossibly tall, their pale, silvery bark glowing faintly from within, reflecting shards of light that danced dizzy across the Jeep's hood. Shadows shifted without a source, long, jagged, slithering over the ground, and the air shimmered, thick as a mirage, bending the edges of everything I saw. The ground turned spongy under the tires, moss breathing with every roll, a soft squelch rising as I cut the engine. We'd go on foot from here, no choice.

Mithis stopped suddenly as we climbed out, her crimson eyes narrowing, cape swaying in the still air. "Do you feel it?" she asked, voice almost reverent, low and rough, her axe shifting in her grip.

I nodded, slinging my rifle over my shoulder, the weight cold against my back. "It's like the forest is watching us." The words rasped out, Sara's scream echoing under them, the witch's curse a burr in my gut every step heavier, like the Glade knew what I carried.

She gestured to a cluster of massive trees ahead, their silvery trunks arching into what looked like a tunnel, branches weaving tightly, leaves glinting brightly in the dimness. "The path is there, but it won't stay for long. We need to move." Her tone was clipped, urgent, her runes flaring brighter as she stepped forward.

We grabbed what we could pack, bottles, rifle, axe, and ventured in, leaving the Jeep behind, its dented frame swallowed fast by the haze. The deeper we pushed into the Glade, the more the world blurred paths twisting, vanishing under our boots, reappearing yards off like taunts. Rocks and trees we'd passed loomed again ahead, warped and wrong, like we were looping through a funhouse from hell, my stomach churning, head spinning, Sara's face flickering in the corners of my eyes.

"It's like the place is alive," I muttered, breath fogging in the chill, the rifle's strap digging into my neck.

"It is alive," Mithis said, voice tense, her axe swinging low as she scanned the shifting trees. "This is no ordinary forest. It was likely enchanted centuries ago, meant to protect something or keep something hidden. The Glade bends reality to confuse intruders." Her words were steady, but her grip tightened, runes pulsing like they ached to cut through the lie.

"Great," I said dryly, sarcasm scraping past the lump in my throat, "a sentient maze. How do we beat it?" My boots sank into the moss, a soft suck pulling at each step, the air thick with a damp, sweet rot that clung to my lungs.

"We don't," Mithis replied, eyes flicking to a path that shimmered then faded. "We survive it. And we prove we're worthy." Her voice hardened, a warrior's edge cutting the unease she'd faced worse, and I'd damn well keep up.

Whispers started faint murmurs on the wind, so quiet they blended with the rustling leaves, a hum I couldn't shake. We traded a glance, her crimson eyes piercing, mine narrowed under the grime. I kept moving, rifle ready, Mithis a step ahead. Deeper in, the voices cleared, striking chords I knew too well: Mom's gentle disappointment, Sara's scared plea, my squad leader's bark from a desert I'd left behind. Each one dug up shit I'd buried, claws in my chest I couldn't pull out.

"You left her behind," one whispered, hauntingly familiar, gentle as Mom's voice before the shot.

Another cut, colder, sharper. "She's probably already dead. You're too late." Sara's tone, twisted, accusing.

I stumbled, boots catching on a root, rifle grip whitening under my hands, heart hammering, my breath short. The voices weren't whispers now, they were knives, slicing open old wounds, Mom's eyes, blank and staring, Sara's scream on that call, my squad's blood on the sand. Mithis spun sharply ahead, her voice firm but laced with unease. "Don't listen to them. They're not real." Her axe swung low, runes flaring, like she'd cut the sound itself if she could. "Easy for you to say," I muttered, shaking my head to clear it, sweat stinging my eyes, but the voices stuck, looping louder, relentless.

The trees came alive, shadows peeling off trunks, taking shape slowly and deliberately, ghostly figures forming in the haze. One stepped forward, Mom's silhouette, her face just like I remembered, hair tangled, eyes hollow with disappointment I'd carried since the trigger pull. "Why do you always run away?" she asked, voice trembling, frail as the day she'd begged me not to enlist. "Why weren't you there when we needed you?" It was her every line, every tone, stepping out of my head into the Glade.

I froze, heart slamming my ribs, a cold sweat breaking across my back, couldn't move, couldn't breathe, just stared as she stood there, real and wrong. Behind me, Mithis cursed in her tongue, crisp and guttural, swinging her axe at shadows creeping her way, faceless, hollow voids where eyes should've been, moving with a purpose that turned my gut. Her blade cut through one, smoke wisping off in tendrils, but two more rose, relentless, her grunts harsh in the quiet.

"They're illusions," she shouted, voice cutting through my fog, "they want you to hesitate, to doubt yourself. Fight it!"

But how? This wasn't just some trick it was me, everything I'd screwed up, given claws and a voice.

"You always run," Mom's figure repeated, echoing unnaturally, bouncing off the trees. "What makes this time any different?" She lunged, shadowy hands reaching for my throat fast, too fast. I raised my rifle, instinct kicking hard, and fired a burst, loud and crisp, bullets ripping through her, leaving no mark. She recoiled, the sound driving her back, a flicker of smoke where her face should've cracked.

Mithis fought behind me, her axe glowing fiercely, cutting shadows to ribbons, but they doubled, swarming her like flies on a corpse. "Focus!" she shouted, voice raw, runes pulsing as she hacked another down. "They're feeding on your guilt! Don't let them control you!"

I forced a step, breaking the freeze, but the ground shifted turned thick, black muck, viscous as tar, clinging to my boots, sucking me down slowly. "Mithis!" I called, struggling, the rifle slipping in my sweaty grip, heart racing, legs burning as I fought the pull.

She turned, crimson eyes wide, axe mid-swing. "It's the Glade," she said, cutting through another shadow, smoke curling off her blade. "It's trying to trap you!" Her voice cracked, urgent, as the shadows circled tighter, whispers rising to a roar.

"You'll fail them," one hissed, crisp and close to Sara's, twisted.

"You're nothing without your rifle," another sneered, a squad leader's bark.

"They'll all die because of you," a third Sara again, gentle and final, a knife in my gut.

The muck deepened, dragging me to my knees, arms aching as I tried to lift the rifle, the whispers drowning everything, overwhelming Mom, Sara, and the blood I couldn't wash off. I was done sinking, losing when Mithis barreled into me, axe swinging wide, a purple arc that scattered the shadows like ash. She grabbed my arm, hauling me out with a strength that jolted my bones, her grip iron through my jacket. "Get up!" she commanded, voice snapping at me loose, sharp as a slap.

I stumbled up, legs shaking, heart pounding. "Thanks," I muttered, gripping my rifle, the steel hot and real under my hands.

"We're not done yet," she said, gaze locked on the shadows regrouping, her axe steady, runes flaring brighter.

She raised it high, the glow pulsing fiercely brighter than before, a light that shoved the shadows back, forcing them to retreat, wisps curling off into the haze. "Mithis," I said, an idea clawing through the fog, "they're feeding on our emotions, right?"

She nodded, breath heaving, ichor streaking her face, "Yes. The more fear and guilt you feel, the stronger they become."

"Then what happens if we starve them?" My voice rasped, rough but steadying, Sara's scream fading as I latched onto the thought.

Her eyes narrowed, piercing and curious. "What are you suggesting?"

I took a deep breath, forcing the shakes down, steadying my nerve,s Mom's face, Sara's voice, the blood shoving it all into a box and locking it tight. "We don't give them anything to feed on. No fear, no guilt. Just focus on the mission." The words came out hard, and the soldier's instinct kicked in: strip it down, keep moving, and get the job done.

Mithis studied me a beat, then nodded slowly, her axe lowering a fraction. "Let's try it." Her voice was steel, ready, a lifeline I grabbed with both hands.

10 WHISPERS IN THE WATER

The shadows lunged, their whispers hitting a fever pitch, shrill, jagged, slicing through the Glade's haze like shrapnel. Each figure twisted and morphed, warping into ghosts I'd buried deep, my squadmates from the sandbox, faces burned and bloodied, my old man's hard stare under a whiskey haze, Sara trapped in shadows, her eyes wide and accusing.

Their voices wove a storm in my skull, guilt, doubt, a relentless howl of failure crashing over me: Mom's blood on my hands, Sara's scream on that call, the crack of my rifle too late to save anyone. My chest tightened, breath short and ragged, the rifle trembling in my grip.

But this time, I didn't retreat.

"They're not real," I whispered, voice scraping through the lump in my throat, grounding myself on Mithis's steady bulk beside me, green skin streaked with ichor, crimson eyes fierce through the gloom. "They're nothing." The words were a lifeline, thin but taut, pulling me from the edge.

Mithis raised her glowing axe, runes flaring purple, light swelling as she hacked through the first wave, shadows recoiling, their forms flickering like dying flames, smoke curling where steel met nothing. They didn't vanish, lingering jagged and stubborn, clawing at the air.

"You can't fight them with strength alone!" she shouted, voice cutting the chaos, raw and fierce over the whispers' drone. "They're feeding on you, not me. You have to reject them!" Her cape snapped as she swung again, a grunt punching out with the effort.

I forced my hands to lower the rifle, barrel dipping cold against my thigh, instinct screaming to shoot, but she was right. I shut my eyes, slamming the door on the twisting figures, Sara's trembling lip, Dad's sneer, the squad's blank stares, and locked onto my breath, steady and deliberate, in through the nose, out slow, counting beats like in the desert under fire. The air was thick, damp with rot and a subtle sweetness from the moss, grounding me as the whispers faltered, desperate hisses fading under my pulse.

"What are you doing?" one spat, voice cracking, frantic. "You'll never..."

"You're not real," I said, cutting it off, voice steadying, rough but solid like gravel under boots. "You're not real, and you don't control me." Each word hit harder, a hammer driving nails into their lie, the figures wavering, dissolving, smoke wisping off into the wind, Sara's face crumbling last, her scream fading to nothing.

Mithis pressed forward, axe slicing clean through the stragglers, their forms popping like blisters, gone as her runes flared hotter. The clearing fell silent, just the rustle of leaves and my ragged breathing, the weight in my chest lifting, a bruise fading. She turned to me, expression unreadable, sweat streaking the grime on her green skin, crimson eyes glinting in the dimness. "You did it."

"We did it," I corrected, wiping my brow with a shaky hand, the rifle's strap digging into my shoulder still here, still me.

She nodded, her gaze easing a fraction, a flicker behind the steel. "Come on. The Glade isn't finished with us yet." Her voice was low, edged with warning, her axe shifting as she straightened, always ready.

We kept walking, years dragging in the silence, boots crunching moss that squelched wet underfoot, eyes peeled for those bastards to slink back. The clearing pulsed alive in its quiet, no wind, no birds, just a stillness pressing down, watching. A pool of water spread ahead, flat and perfect like a mirror to some screwed-up world, reflecting the pale, twisted trees arching overhead, silvery bark glowing dim, branches clawing the sky. A bridge stretched across it, gnarled roots and twisted branches woven tight, fragile-looking, like it'd snap under a breath. But Mithis and I knew better that this wasn't just a path.

"The Bridge of Still Water," Mithis said, voice heavy, rough with something old, her cape swaying as she studied it, runes pulsing purple on her axe. "It's a trial. A test of resolve and courage."

I eyed it warily, the roots creaking in the quiet, black water lapping at the edges, too still, too deep. "If this is a trial, what happens if we fail?" My voice rasped, the rifle cold in my hands, Sara's scream echoing under the words.

Mithis met my gaze, crimson eyes unwavering, steady as stone. "You won't come back. The water consumes you, body and soul." Her tone was flat, matter-of-fact, but her grip tightened on her axe, knuckles whitening under the gloves.

"Good to know," I muttered, sarcasm scraping past the knot in my gut, tightening my grip on the rifle, an old friend, scratched and dented, all I had left of normal. "Any other advice?"

"Keep moving. Don't stop, no matter what you see or feel." Her voice was a blade, cutting through the haze, practical, clear, no room for doubt.

I took a deep breath, the air cold and damp, tasting of moss and something sour, and stepped onto the bridge. The roots shifted under my boots, creaking like old bones, a groan rising as my weight settled. Mithis followed close, her axe in hand, cape brushing the wood, her steps steady, her face grim with determination etched deep, like she'd walked worse and lived. The moment we were both on, the air thickened, pressing down like the forest held its breath, the water rippling, shimmering under an unseen touch.

"Don't look down," Mithis warned, voice low and tight, her boots thudding behind me. Of course, I looked down the soldier's habit, checked the threat, and scoped the field. At first, it was just the water, black and flat, mirroring the twisted trees and a sky bruising gray. Then the reflections shifted, blurred faces fading in, vivid, too real.

Sara came first, trapped in a cage of shadows, her voice echoing, trembling, "Why didn't you come sooner? You left me. You always leave me." Her eyes were wide, scared, the same as that call, cutting deep, a hammer to my chest, breath hitching as I stumbled, boots catching on a root.

"Keep moving!" Mithis barked, close, her hand brushing my pack, steady, pulling me forward.

I tore my eyes up, locked on the uneven path, gnarled wood slick with damp, roots twisting underfoot, but the water wouldn't let go. Mom's face rose next, pale and weary, hair tangled like the day I'd left. "You never listened," she said, voice breaking, frail as the last time she'd begged me to stay. "You always thought you knew better. Look where that's gotten us." Her stare pinned me, hollow and heavy, guilt clawing up my throat, my grip on the rifle faltering, the steel slipping in sweaty hands.

"Mithis," I said, voice shaking, raw and thin, "This... this isn't real, right?" Needed her to say it, needed the anchor.

"They're not real," she called back, steps steady, but her voice tight, fighting something too. "But they will feel real if you let them. Ignore them!" Clear, commanding, but I heard the strain; she wasn't untouched.

Easier said, Sara's scream, Mom's sigh looping, pulling me down like an anchor through mud. The water shifted under Mithis now, her steps growing heavier, boots scraping the roots, her grip on her axe whitening, runes flaring hot. I risked a glance at her reflection, a younger Mithis, green skin smooth, standing before a council of hulking figures, their faces stern, crimson eyes unyielding like hers. "You failed us," a deep, guttural voice boomed, rolling up from the depths. "You let your father die, and now you're nothing." It shook the bridge, a low rumble under my boots.

Her jaw clenched, teeth grinding, but she didn't slow, kept moving, axe steady despite the tremor in her shoulders. "Don't let them win, Mithis," I said, voice rough, hoping it'd hit her like hers had me.

She gave a single nod, crimson eyes blazing, alive. "I won't." Her words were steel, a vow spat into the dark.

We hit the center, and the water erupted, a massive, shadowy figure rising, writhing like smoke, formless but heavy, dripping black as it loomed. Dozens of glowing eyes dotted its face, green, yellow, shifting, tracking every flinch. Its voice roared, a deafening mess of screams, laughter, whispers crashing over us, shaking the bridge 'til roots cracked, splintering underfoot.

"You think you can cross my bridge?" it bellowed, mouths twisting into cruel grins, jagged and wet. "You carry your guilt like chains. You are unworthy."

The bridge bucked, a violent shudder. I braced, boots slipping, rifle banging my hip. "What is that?" I shouted, raising the barrel, sight trembling as I aimed at the mass.

"The Keeper of the Bridge," Mithis said, voice grim, axe glowing brighter as she stepped up, runes pulsing like a heartbeat. "It feeds on fear and doubt. If you show weakness, it will drag you into the water." Her cape snapped as she squared off, green skin stark against the black haze.

The creature lunged, amorphous limbs stretching, smoke and shadow clawing for us. I fired crisp bursts, thunder cracking the quiet, bullets punching through nothing, just wisps curling where they hit. "It's not working!" I shouted, voice hoarse, stepping back as the bridge groaned.

Mithis surged forward, axe flaring bright. "It's not meant to be fought with weapons. This is a battle of will." Her swing carved through its form, light slashing a gash, purple against black, the creature screeched, ear-splitting, recoiling but reforming, laughter rolling thick and mocking. "You can't win," it hissed, voices layering. "Your guilt is too great. Your doubts will consume you."

It turned its eyes on me, dozens, glowing, boring in, and a pressure slammed my chest, heavy as a fist. Sara trapped, Mom's stare, my squad's blood flashing, overwhelming.

"No," I whispered, shaking my head, boots scraping the roots, "You don't control me." The words clawed out, weak then stronger, a soldier's grunt against the weight.

The creature froze, form flickering, eyes narrowing, mouths twitching. I stepped forward, voice rising, "You're nothing but a shadow. You're not real." Rough, steady, pushing back, Mithis joined me, axe raised high, runes blazing, "We are more than our fears," she said, steady and defiant, her glare cutting through the haze.

It roared guttural, splintering, form cracking as we moved together, step by step toward the far side, roots steadying under us, water churning below. With a final scream, raw, shattering, it dissolved, sinking back into the black depths, smoke curling off in tendrils. The bridge held, the weight lifting, air cold and clean, hitting my lungs.

World's Unraveled: The McAllister Saga

We stepped off, boots hitting solid dirt, the trees here sparser, pale trunks rising like bones, air lighter but silent, too silent. Mithis leaned on her axe, chest heaving, eyes darting back to the bridge, roots trembling, recovering. "We survived," she said, quiet but firm, wiping sweat from her brow with a blood-streaked glove.

"By a thread," I muttered, glancing at the water, my reflection whole, steady, but the visions' weight lingered, a phantom ache in my ribs. My hands shook as I slung the rifle, Sara's voice whispering under my pulse.

Mithis turned, expression unreadable, sweat streaking the grime, cape matted with muck. "You did well back there." Her voice eased, a crack in the steel.

I let out a short, humorless laugh, dry, scraping. "Didn't feel like it. I almost let that thing pull me under." My boots scuffed the dirt, kicking up moss that smelled pungent and wet.

She shook her head, slow and sure. "You didn't. That's what matters." Her tone was steady, a lifeline I grabbed without thinking.

We moved to a clearing near a gnarled tree leaning over, roots thick with moss, a semblance of cover. I sank onto a rock, cold and damp through my jeans, wiping sweat from my brow, gritty, stinging my eyes, checking my rifle out of habit, mag full, barrel scratched but ready. Mithis stood a few paces off, back straight, axe planted firm in the dirt like a guard, rune Softeningnow, her shadow long in the dim light. Silence stretched, heavy but not empty, the Glade's hum faint under our breathing.

"What did you see in the water?" she asked, low and sudden, catching me off guard, my hands tightening on the rifle, metal cold under split knuckles.

I hesitated, throat tight. "It doesn't matter. It's in the past." My voice rasped, deflecting, eyes on the dirt, black and wet, flecked with silvery leaves.

"It does matter," she said, stepping closer, tone insistent but not harsh, an edge that pinned me. "The Glade tests your soul. What you saw lingers. Ignoring it won't make it go away." Her boots thudded, cape swaying, her shadow falling over me.

I sighed, staring at the ground, roots twisting like veins. "I saw my sister. She was... trapped. Scared. She said I was too late, that I always leave people behind." The words dragged out, rough and heavy, Sara's wide eyes, her voice trembling, cutting deeper than the witch's curse.

Mithis crouched, crimson eyes locking mine, steady, unflinching. "And do you believe that?" Low, direct, her gloved hand resting on her knee, ichor staining the leather.

I swallowed hard, throat raw. "Sometimes. I wasn't there when my squad needed me. I wasn't there for my sister when all this started. Maybe I am always too late." The confession burned, Mom's blood flashing red, Sara's scream looping, truth I'd dodged too long.

She studied me, then clapped a hand on my shoulder, firm, grounding, her grip warm through my jacket. "The Glade preys on doubt, twisting it 'til you believe it's the truth. But doubt isn't weakness. It's a reminder to act, to prove the shadows wrong." Her words hung heavy, a weight I could lean on, practical, real.

"What about you?" I asked, meeting her gaze, pushing back. "What did you see?" Needed to know, needed her to crack too.

Her mask slipped, a flicker, eyes darting away, hand tightening on her axe haft 'til the wood creaked. "I saw my tribe. My father. They told me I'd failed them, that I'd brought nothing but dishonor." Her voice dropped, rough and distant, vulnerable, raw in a way I hadn't heard.

"You don't believe that, do you?" I pressed, watching her green skin stark against the pale trees, shoulders stiff.

She hesitated. "I've spent my life trying to prove myself to them, to me. Some days, I wonder if it will ever be enough." Quiet, almost lost in the silence, her axe dipping a fraction, a crack in the steel I hadn't expected.

"Hey," I said, standing, clapping a hand on her arm, firm, steady, her muscle solid under my grip. "You've saved my life more times than I can count in just a few days. If that doesn't prove your worth, I don't know what does." Rough, honest, her eyes flicked to mine, searching.

A smile tugged her mouth, real. "You're stubborn, you know that?" Her voice lightened, a spark behind the crimson.

"Yeah, I've been told," I replied, shrugging, the ache in my chest easing. "But seriously, we've got stuff we're carrying. Maybe that's why we're still standing. Because we carry it together." The words landed solid, a truth I hadn't seen till now.

Her smile grew, small, genuine. "Perhaps you're right. For a human, you're not entirely hopeless." A tease, dry and warm, cutting the tension.

I laughed short, real, breaking the Glade's weight. "I'll take that as a compliment." The sound echoed, swallowed fast by the trees.

The levity faded, not gone, just lighter, the burden on our shoulders less cutting. Mithis glanced back at the bridge, roots still, water flat, her axe shifting as she straightened. "The Glade will keep testing us," she said, voice firm again, steel sliding back. "But we're stronger than we think."

I nodded, gripping my rifle, cold, scratched, steady. "Let it try. We'll show what we're made of." Rough, defiant, Sara's scream was quieter now, a flicker I could fight.

We stepped onto the winding path, side by side, the Glade's shadows retreating a hair, silence giving way to rustling leaves, crisp. For the first time in this cursed mess, hope flickered small, stubborn, but alive. The air grew colder with every step, a bite that stung my face, the dim glow dimming to a murky twilight, trees thinning, their silvery bark glinting less, like candles burning out.

Ahead, the path split into a wide clearing bathed in silver light, gentle and cold, cutting the gloom. A massive tree loomed at its center, bark shimmering like frost, branches stretching high, leaves glowing white, like moonlight on snow. "The white ash," Mithis whispered, voice low, reverent, her axe dipping a fraction, runes pulsing.

I nodded, eyes locked on it, our shot, our weapon, but my gut twisted as something moved around its roots. Hard to see at first a writhing mass, scales glinting in the light, then it slid into view, clear and real. A hulking, serpentine beast towered over the tree, body coiling tight, multiple heads snapping at the air, jagged horns crowning each one, scales shimmering silver like the ash itself. Glowing eyes, yellow, green darted wild, dozens of them, tracking us through the haze.

"What is that?" Mithis asked, voice tight, axe rising, runes flaring brighter, her cape snapping as she braced.

I froze, mind racing, the image impossible, a nightmare ripped from old pages, myths Sara used to read me under the covers, torchlight on her grin, voice low with the thrill. I'd seen this thing before, not real, not till now, but in books, in whispers, a name clawing up from the dark.

My breath hitched, rifle trembling. "Hydra," I rasped, the word rough, heavy, Sara's giggle fading under the beast's hiss.

11 MYTH MADE FLESH

Mithis spun, confusion carving sharp lines into her green face, sweat cutting muddy streaks through the grime. Her crimson eyes narrowed under a tangle of damp hair plastered to her brow like wet moss. "A what?" Her voice scraped low, rough, and guttural, probing like I'd lost it in the Glade's choking haze. Her axe haft creaked as her grip tightened, calloused fingers flexing, purple runes flickering faint against the scarred steel.

"A hydra," I said, swallowing hard. A cold shard sank in my chest, panic twisting like a blade in my gut. "From an old story. Greek mythology. Fiction. Cut off a head, two grow back." The words rasped dry, Sara's giggle echoing soft under my skull, Hercules slaying heads in her thrilled whisper, torchlight on her grin. Now it was here, venom dripping thick from jagged jaws, yellow eyes glowing like hellfires through the fog.

Her gaze flicked from me to the beast, axe steady but runes pulsing dim, doubt flashing behind her iron resolve. "So another mess from your world's... reality now?" Her tone cut crisp, disbelief clashing with reality, heads coiling slowly, scales glinting silver in the Glade's sickly glow, casting warped shadows over moss-slick ground.

I shook my head, shoving panic down, hands trembling on the rifle, split knuckles throbbing under cracked skin. "Yeah, looks like it." My voice cracked raw, Mom's blood staining my palms in memory, Sara's scream shoving me forward. Myth or not, it was flesh and fury, and I'd kill it or die. No other way.

The hydra's heads whipped around, glowing eyes locking on yellow, green, too damn many piercing the haze like lanterns through fog, alive with hunger that turned my stomach cold. A guttural hiss tore from its throat, layered and jagged, vibrating the clearing until the dirt quaked under my boots, rattling my teeth. Sulfur and rot slammed thick, sour and hot, clogging my lungs, stinging my eyes. Its scales shimmered silver, catching the Glade's twisted light like honed blades gleaming in the murk.

"How do we kill it?" Mithis asked, voice steady but fear sparking in her eyes. Her wolf-pelt cape swayed damp as she squared up, runes flaring brighter, purple light casting jagged shadows over her blood-streaked arms.

I gritted my teeth, jaw aching, skull pounding, racking my brain for scraps of Sara's old tales, flashlight cutting the dark, her laugh bright. "In the myths, they burned the stumps after cutting heads to stop regrowth. No fire big enough here." I stared at the coiling mass, heads snapping, tails thrashing, scales rippling like liquid metal. "The heart. We hit the heart. Only way." My voice rasped, soldier's instinct kicking in, strip it down, strike the core, Sara's scream driving it deep.

Mithis nodded, grip whitening on her axe, runes blazing purple, slicing the gloom. "No choice. I'll find the heart. You distract the heads." Her tone was steel, fierce, crimson eyes locking mine, steady as bedrock, a lifeline I grabbed tight.

I hesitated, thoughts racing, heart slamming my ribs, fiction turned flesh, a kid's story now a towering bastard dripping venom in my face. Used to be Sara giggling safe under covers; now it was real, scales glinting wet, fangs cruel. I had to fight, not gawk. My hands shook, Mom's blank eyes flashing, Sara's plea cutting through static, the witch's curse clawing deep "every life you touch will rot."

"You with me?" Mithis's voice punched through, crisp and close, crimson eyes boring in, axe raised, cape matted with muck and blood.

I sucked in a breath cold, damp, rotting lungs burning as I raised my rifle, barrel trembling, venom burns stinging my wrist. "Yeah. Let's kill it." Rough, defiant, Sara's giggle drowned by the hydra's hiss, my hands steadying on steel, locking fear down tight.

The hydra reared, heads rising like scaled malice, glowing eyes fixed, each moving solo, coiling slowly then snapping fast, jaws gaping for blood. Venom dripped in sizzling strands, hitting moss with a quiet hiss, steam curling acrid. The ground quaked, roots cracking under my boots as its bulk twisted, a roar exploding, cries overlapping in a guttural chorus, shaking the clearing until my chest ached. Sulfur hit harder, mixed with decay, burning my nose, coating my tongue raw, scales shimmering wet steel under twisted branches.

"Worse than I thought," I muttered, gripping my rifle, cold metal biting my palms, grounding the shake. Breath fogged quick, venom burns searing my skin.

"The multiple heads, or are they still breathing?" Mithis shot back, tone dry despite the tension, axe glinting as she shifted, boots sinking into moss with a wet squelch, runes pulsing like embers.

"Both," I snapped, sarcasm cutting fear, soldier's habit holding the line, pulse hammering, Sara's scream soft under the hiss.

A head lashed out, jaws gaping, fangs dripping venom, a blur of silver hate ripping through the haze. I dove, hitting dirt hard, moss slick under boots, rifle banging my hip. Teeth slammed inches from my leg, gouging furrows, spraying damp earth and roots that stung my face. Venom crashed in, pungent as acid, sour, churning my gut, burning my eyes until they watered, its hiss vibrating my ribs.

"Move!" Mithis shouted, circling fast, boots pounding muck, cape snapping wet as she flanked, axe glowing fierce purple, slashing shadows.

I rolled up, knees sinking into damp, rifle snapping to my shoulder, sight locking a head, squeezing fast. Crack split the air, bullet striking scales with a spark that flared and died, ricocheting off like I'd hit steel. The hydra didn't flinch, heads whipping toward me, venom dripping thicker, pooling black and steaming. One gaped, wide bassi, jagged teeth gleaming, a hiss rolling sulfur-hot. I threw myself back, boots slipping as it lunged, jaws snapping where my chest had been, ground shaking, roots popping free.

"Bullets aren't working!" I yelled, scrambling up, heart wild, dirt caked on my palms, panic spiking under the soldier's calm, venom splashing my arm, searing through my sleeve like fire.

"Hit it where it hurts!" Mithis called, charging its side, axe raised, runes blazing purple, slashing shadows as she closed in.

A head swung for her, venom spraying in a glistening arc. I fired, crack loud, black ichor bursting from an eye socket, thick and sticky. The head jerked back, screeching high, splattering tar-like ichor, its others narrowing, glowing hotter. "Keep them distracted!" Mithis shouted, darting under its bulk, cape trailing, boots slipping but steady, vanishing into its shadow.

"Sure, no problem," I muttered, sarcasm bitter, heart hammering, three heads locking on, hissing loudly, drowning the Glade's hum.

The hydra lunged, heads snapping like vipers, a blur of scales and fangs. I ducked one, its jaws grazing my pack, tearing a strap, then sidestepped another, fangs inches from my arm, venom sizzling moss. Rifle up, I fired, bullet pinging off scales, sparking into darkness. Two lunged at once, one high, one low, jaws gaping. I dove left, boots skidding, ground quaking as they slammed down, spraying dirt and venom burning my cheek, hot and raw. A third coiled back, hissing low, venom steaming on moss.

Mithis hit its side, axe biting deep with a raw cry, steel crunching scales, wet and grating. The hydra roared, tails thrashing, slamming the ground, cracking roots, ichor spraying hot across her cape, staining the wolf pelt black. She hacked again, scales splintering under purple runes, hydra's roar spiking, one head swinging for her. I fired, clipping its jaw, bullet sparking, ichor leaking slowly, giving her space. Another lunged low, fangs scraping dirt, she leapt aside, axe grazing its neck, drawing a steaming black line.

She climbed its back, hands gripping slick scales, heads thrashing as she moved, tails slamming shockwaves knocking me back, moss sticking to my jacket. "This thing's massive!" she shouted, voice strained, venom splashing her legs, sizzling quietly against armor.

"Yeah, I noticed!" I called, dodging a head slamming dirt, venom stinging my knuckles through my glove, searing hot, rifle firing blind, bullet sparking off a fang, hydra snarling.

Mithis climbed higher, axe free, swinging as a head lunged, eyes glowing hot. "Look out!" I yelled, shot ringing, bullet striking neck base, ichor spurting. She swung aside, axe arcing, blade sinking into its chest with a wet crunch. The hydra froze, heads snapping wild, ichor dripping from the gash, pooling dark, steaming.

"I found it!" Mithis shouted, pointing at a soft glow pulsing under scales, runes flaring as she clung, ichor streaking her face.

"Great!" I yelled, dodging jaws snapping, tail flailing, venom burning my shoulder through my jacket. "Now what?" Boots skidded, another lunged, tearing my sleeve, venom soaking my arm, searing deep.

"Get over here!" Her hand outstretched, green skin stark against silver, eyes blazing, axe swinging back, heads hissing, venom spraying.

I sprinted, boots pounding muck, weaving through snapping jaws, tails thrashing, one clipping my leg, pain jolting sharp. I reached her, grabbed her hand rough and steady, and she hauled me up onto its coiling bulk, scales slick and hot under boots. The hydra bucked, heads snapping blind, ichor pooling below, steaming.

"It's here," she said, pointing at the glow pulsing where her axe bit, ichor dripping thick, heads lunging close, venom sizzling her shoulder.

"Cover me," I said, drawing the sword, glowing faint purple, humming heavy in my hands, venom burns throbbing.

Mithis nodded, axe swinging wide, purple arcs slashing air, cutting recoiling heads, ichor spraying her face as she hacked. I raised the sword, breath deep, lungs screaming, and drove it into the glow, blade sinking with a grinding thud, piercing scales, hitting solid. The hydra roared, convulsing, heads thrashing, tails slamming, venom splashing my chest, searing skin, pain spiking raw.

"Not deep enough!" Mithis shouted, hacking a lunging head, ichor spraying, cape tearing, another coiling fast, fangs gaping.

Gripping the hilt, knuckles screaming, arms burning, I drove it deeper, blade cracking through muscle and bone, hitting hard. The hydra screamed deafeningly and finally, heads dropping limp, one slamming beside me, venom pooling. Glow swelled hot, blinding purple, then faded, its bulk shuddering, collapsing into silver ash swirling over dirt, dusting my boots.

The clearing went quiet, air hitting my lungs cold and clean, chest heaving, venom burns throbbing. Mithis climbed down, boots crunching ash, axe dripping ichor, cape torn, soaked with muck and blood, runes dimming slowly. "That was..." I started, voice rough, staring at the ash, sword heavy in hand.

Jacob Salvia

"Terrifying?" she offered, gentle smile tugging her lips, her eyes glinting soft, sweat cutting tracks through ichor, cape swaying as she straightened, venom burns red and raw on her arms Mithis spun, confusion carving sharp lines into her green face, sweat cutting muddy streaks through the grime. Her crimson eyes narrowed under a tangle of damp hair plastered to her brow like wet moss. "A what?" Her voice scraped low, rough, and guttural, probing like I'd lost it in the Glade's choking haze. Her axe haft creaked as her grip tightened, calloused fingers flexing, purple runes flickering faint against the scarred steel.

"A hydra," I said, swallowing hard. A cold shard sank in my chest, panic twisting like a blade in my gut. "From an old story. Greek mythology. Fiction. Cut off a head, two grow back." The words rasped dry, Sara's giggle echoing soft under my skull, Hercules slaying heads in her thrilled whisper, torchlight on her grin. Now it was here, venom dripping thick from jagged jaws, yellow eyes glowing like hellfires through the fog.

Her gaze flicked from me to the beast, axe steady but runes pulsing dim, doubt flashing behind her iron resolve. "So another mess from your world's... reality now?" Her tone cut crisp, disbelief clashing with reality, heads coiling slowly, scales glinting silver in the Glade's sickly glow, casting warped shadows over moss-slick ground.

I shook my head, shoving panic down, hands trembling on the rifle, split knuckles throbbing under cracked skin. "Yeah, looks like it." My voice cracked raw, Mom's blood staining my palms in memory, Sara's scream shoving me forward. Myth or not, it was flesh and fury, and I'd kill it or die. No other way.

The hydra's heads whipped around, glowing eyes locking on yellow, green, too damn many piercing the haze like lanterns through fog, alive with hunger that turned my stomach cold. A guttural hiss tore from its throat, layered and jagged, vibrating the clearing until the dirt quaked under my boots, rattling my teeth. Sulfur and rot slammed thick, sour and hot, clogging my lungs, stinging my eyes. Its scales shimmered silver, catching the Glade's twisted light like honed blades gleaming in the murk.

"How do we kill it?" Mithis asked, voice steady but fear sparking in her eyes. Her wolf-pelt cape swayed damp as she squared up, runes flaring brighter, purple light casting jagged shadows over her blood-streaked arms.

I gritted my teeth, jaw aching, skull pounding, racking my brain for scraps of Sara's old tales, flashlight cutting the dark, her laugh bright. "In the myths, they burned the stumps after cutting heads to stop regrowth. No fire big enough here." I stared at the coiling mass, heads snapping, tails thrashing, scales rippling like liquid metal. "The heart. We hit the heart. Only way." My voice rasped, soldier's instinct kicking in, strip it down, strike the core, Sara's scream driving it deep.

Mithis nodded, grip whitening on her axe, runes blazing purple, slicing the gloom. "No choice. I'll find the heart. You distract the heads." Her tone was steel, fierce, crimson eyes locking mine, steady as bedrock, a lifeline I grabbed tight.

I hesitated, thoughts racing, heart slamming my ribs, fiction turned flesh, a kid's story now a towering bastard dripping venom in my face. Used to be Sara giggling safe under covers; now it was real, scales glinting wet, fangs cruel. I had to fight, not gawk. My hands shook, Mom's blank eyes flashing, Sara's plea cutting through static, the witch's curse clawing deep "every life you touch will rot."

"You with me?" Mithis's voice punched through, crisp and close, crimson eyes boring in, axe raised, cape matted with muck and blood.

I sucked in a breath cold, damp, rotting lungs burning as I raised my rifle, barrel trembling, venom burns stinging my wrist. "Yeah. Let's kill it." Rough, defiant, Sara's giggle drowned by the hydra's hiss, my hands steadying on steel, locking fear down tight.

The hydra reared, heads rising like scaled malice, glowing eyes fixed, each moving solo, coiling slowly then snapping fast, jaws gaping for blood. Venom dripped in sizzling strands, hitting moss with a quiet hiss, steam curling acrid. The ground quaked, roots cracking under my boots as its bulk twisted, a roar exploding, cries overlapping in a guttural chorus, shaking the clearing until my chest ached. Sulfur hit harder, mixed with decay, burning my nose, coating my tongue raw, scales shimmering wet steel under twisted branches.

"Worse than I thought," I muttered, gripping my rifle, cold metal biting my palms, grounding the shake. Breath fogged quick, venom burns searing my skin.

"The multiple heads, or are they still breathing?" Mithis shot back, tone dry despite the tension, axe glinting as she shifted, boots sinking into moss with a wet squelch, runes pulsing like embers.

"Both," I snapped, sarcasm cutting fear, soldier's habit holding the line, pulse hammering, Sara's scream soft under the hiss.

A head lashed out, jaws gaping, fangs dripping venom, a blur of silver hate ripping through the haze. I dove, hitting dirt hard, moss slick under boots, rifle banging my hip. Teeth slammed inches from my leg, gouging furrows, spraying damp earth and roots that stung my face. Venom crashed in, pungent as acid, sour, churning my gut, burning my eyes until they watered, its hiss vibrating my ribs.

"Move!" Mithis shouted, circling fast, boots pounding muck, cape snapping wet as she flanked, axe glowing fierce purple, slashing shadows.

I rolled up, knees sinking into damp, rifle snapping to my shoulder, sight locking a head, squeezing fast. Crack split the air, bullet striking scales with a spark that flared and died, ricocheting off like I'd hit steel. The hydra didn't flinch, heads whipping toward me, venom dripping thicker, pooling black and steaming. One gaped, wide bassi, jagged teeth gleaming, a hiss rolling sulfur-hot. I threw myself back, boots slipping as it lunged, jaws snapping where my chest had been, ground shaking, roots popping free.

"Bullets aren't working!" I yelled, scrambling up, heart wild, dirt caked on my palms, panic spiking under the soldier's calm, venom splashing my arm, searing through my sleeve like fire.

"Hit it where it hurts!" Mithis called, charging its side, axe raised, runes blazing purple, slashing shadows as she closed in.

A head swung for her, venom spraying in a glistening arc. I fired, crack loud, black ichor bursting from an eye socket, thick and sticky. The head jerked back, screeching high, splattering tar-like ichor, its others narrowing, glowing hotter. "Keep them distracted!" Mithis shouted, darting under its bulk, cape trailing, boots slipping but steady, vanishing into its shadow.

"Sure, no problem," I muttered, sarcasm bitter, heart hammering, three heads locking on, hissing loudly, drowning the Glade's hum.

The hydra lunged, heads snapping like vipers, a blur of scales and fangs. I ducked one, its jaws grazing my pack, tearing a strap, then sidestepped another, fangs inches from my arm, venom sizzling moss near my boot. Rifle up, I fired, bullet pinging off scales, sparking into darkness. Two lunged at once, one high, one low, jaws gaping. I dove left, boots skidding, ground quaking as they slammed down, spraying dirt and venom burning my cheek, hot and raw. A third coiled back, hissing low, venom steaming on moss.

Mithis hit its side, axe biting deep with a raw cry, steel crunching scales, wet and grating. The hydra roared, tails thrashing, slamming the ground, cracking roots, ichor spraying hot across her cape, staining the wolf pelt black. She hacked again, scales splintering under purple runes, hydra's roar spiking, one head swinging for her. I fired, clipping its jaw, bullet sparking, ichor leaking slowly, giving her space. Another lunged low, fangs scraping dirt, she leapt aside, axe grazing its neck, drawing a steaming black line.

She climbed its back, hands gripping slick scales, heads thrashing as she moved, tails slamming shockwaves knocking me back, moss sticking to my jacket. "This thing's massive!" she shouted, voice strained, venom splashing her legs, sizzling quietly against armor.

"Yeah, I noticed!" I called, dodging a head slamming dirt, venom stinging my knuckles through my glove, searing hot, rifle firing blind, bullet sparking off a fang, hydra snarling.

Mithis climbed higher, axe free, swinging as a head lunged, eyes glowing hot. "Look out!" I yelled, shot ringing, bullet striking neck base, ichor spurting. She swung aside, axe arcing, blade sinking into its chest with a wet crunch. The hydra froze, heads snapping wild, ichor dripping from the gash, pooling dark, steaming.

"I found it!" Mithis shouted, pointing at a soft glow pulsing under scales, runes flaring as she clung, ichor streaking her face.

"Great!" I yelled, dodging jaws snapping, tail flailing, venom burning my shoulder through my jacket. "Now what?" Boots skidded, another lunged, tearing my sleeve, venom soaking my arm, searing deep.

"Get over here!" Her hand outstretched, green skin stark against silver, eyes blazing, axe swinging back, heads hissing, venom spraying.

I sprinted, boots pounding muck, weaving through snapping jaws, tails thrashing, one clipping my leg, pain jolting sharp. I reached her, grabbed her hand rough and steady, and she hauled me up onto its coiling bulk, scales slick and hot under boots. The hydra bucked, heads snapping blind, ichor pooling below, steaming.

"It's here," she said, pointing at the glow pulsing where her axe bit, ichor dripping thick, heads lunging close, venom sizzling her shoulder.

"Cover me," I said, drawing the sword, glowing faint purple, humming heavy in my hands, venom burns throbbing.

Mithis nodded, axe swinging wide, purple arcs slashing air, cutting recoiling heads, ichor spraying her face as she hacked. I raised the sword, breath deep, lungs screaming, and drove it into the glow, blade sinking with a grinding thud, piercing scales, hitting solid. The hydra roared, convulsing, heads thrashing, tails slamming, venom splashing my chest, searing skin, pain spiking raw.

"Not deep enough!" Mithis shouted, hacking a lunging head, ichor spraying, cape tearing, another coiling fast, fangs gaping.

Gripping the hilt, knuckles screaming, arms burning, I drove it deeper, blade cracking through muscle and bone, hitting hard. The hydra screamed deafeningly and finally, heads dropping limp, one slamming beside me, venom pooling. Glow swelled hot, blinding purple, then faded, its bulk shuddering, collapsing into silver ash swirling over dirt, dusting my boots.

The clearing went quiet, air hitting my lungs cold and clean, chest heaving, venom burns throbbing. Mithis climbed down, boots crunching ash, axe dripping ichor, cape torn, soaked with muck and blood, runes dimming slowly. "That was..." I started, voice rough, staring at the ash, sword heavy in hand.

"Terrifying?" she offered, gentle smile tugging her lips, her eyes glinting soft, sweat cutting tracks through ichor, cape swaying as she straightened, venom burns red and raw on her arms.

12 BREATH OF THE FOREST

I nodded, wiping sweat from my brow, hand shaking where venom burns stung raw red welts blistering under cracked skin. "Yeah. Let's go with that." My voice scraped rough, dry, chest aching like I'd been mule-kicked. The sword hung heavy against my thigh, cold steel grounding me, its faint purple glow a lifeline in the Glade's murk.

The white ash tree shimmered ahead, branches dipping slowly, bowing like it knew we'd earned it. Bark glinted frost-white, wrapped in a soft glow of moonlight on fresh snow, alive, humming faintly under the haze. Mithis stepped up, hand pressing its trunk, green skin stark against the pale light flaring around her.

A single branch snapped free, drifting gently into her hands, white as bone, edges sharp with frost, glowing soft but fierce, like it carried the Glade's soul. "This is it," she said, voice low, reverent, cradling it like gold. Her runes pulsed faint on her axe, crimson eyes softening a flicker of hope cutting through the steel. "With this, we can fight corruption. Maybe even lift that witch's curse off you."

I nodded, sweat stinging my eyes, chest throbbing, the witch's voice clawing deep "every life you touch will rot." The branch's glow sliced through, a thin thread to grab. "Let's get out before the forest throws more shit at us." My voice rasped, tired but edged, rifle slung heavy, boots crunching hydra ash as I turned. The Glade's hum faded under a quiet too thick, pressing my skull.

Mithis's lips twitched in subtle relief, determination sparking in her crimson eyes. Together, we stepped back onto the path, ash swirling slowly behind us, the clearing's weight slipping off like shed skin.

The trek to Kalden dragged along a path stretching long, the forest closing in tight. Trees loomed, gnarled branches retreating a hair, less hostile but still watching, shadows twisting at the corners of my eyes. The white ash branch glowed in Mithis's grip, casting jagged flickers over moss-slick roots and silvery bark, a beacon in the murk. My boots crunched brittle leaves, each step echoing loudly in the eerie silence, a stillness that sank into my bones. Rustles too quiet, too far hit my ears, heart pounding, nerves strung tight.

"Stay alert," Mithis said, voice low, rough, crimson eyes darting through the treeline. Her axe rested on her shoulder, runes dim but ready, cape swaying, damp, matted with ichor and dirt, pine cutting through the forest's rot.

I nodded, gripping my rifle, cold steel biting my palms, split knuckles throbbing, venom burns stinging sharply.

"Hope whatever's left knows we mean business." My voice scraped dry, Sara's scream looping soft, Mom's blood a shadow I couldn't shake. Exhaustion clawed my bones, heavy and cold, but I kept my eyes sharp, scanning the dark.

The silence thickened oppressively, broken only by our steps and those distant rustles. Branches creaked quietly, whispers I couldn't catch, pulse hammering with every flicker in the gloom. The hydra fight had drained my legs, ribs aching, but a soldier's habit kept me upright, rifle steady.

"You all right?" Mithis glanced over, crimson eyes catching the branch's glow, searching breath fogging dim in the chill.

"Yeah," I lied, voice rough, the weight of Sara, the curse, the hydra piling on. "You?" My hands tightened, rifle cold, grounding the shake I wouldn't admit.

She gave a gentle smile, glow softening her steel hair. "Been through worse. You held your own back there. More capable than you think." Her tone warmed, steady, cutting the cold a lifeline I didn't expect.

"Thanks," I said, heat flickering under the grime, chest easing a fraction. "Save the compliments 'til we're out." Rough, dry, rifle sling digging into my shoulder, a familiar ache.

Torchlight glimmered ahead, dim, warm, cutting the trees. Relief hit my gut as Kalden's gates loomed, wooden beams weathered and scarred, less imposing now. Guards stood stiff, eyes scanning the treeline, hands twitching on halberds pale under dented helmets. One spotted us, raised a hand, voice cracking crisp, "They've returned!" a jolt rippling through them.

Gates creaked loudly, wood groaning as they swung wide, guards stepping aside eyes wide, awe and disbelief mixing, chainmail rattling softly under patched cloaks. "You made it," one said, voice shocked, jaw slack. "We thought..."

"That we wouldn't?" Mithis cut in, tone biting, crimson eyes narrowing. Her axe propped easily, runes flickering, cape swaying as she squared up. "We don't fall that easily." Steel snapped in her words, the guard swallowing hard, gaze flicking to the glowing branch, white, alive.

"It's done," I said, stepping forward, boots scuffing dirt, voice rough but steady. "Where's the Elder? He needs to see this." Rifle hung heavy, exhaustion tugging, adrenaline holding me up.

The guard nodded fast, jerking his head toward the hall. Waiting inside. Go ahead." His voice trembled, eyes darting, torchlight catching sweat on his brow.

The Elder's hall hit familiar timber walls stained dark, smoky air thick with tallow and straw, but tension coiled tighter now, heavy in the haze. Aldred stood center, robe dragging the planks, flanked by his advisors, the warrior's scarred face grim, the mage's robes glowing muted with arcane lines. His keen eyes widened a hair as we stepped in, snapping to the white ash branch cutting the gloom. "You've succeeded," he said, voice rolling with deep relief and awe mixed. "I scarcely believed it." His hands clenched, knuckles whitening, the table behind littered with maps and runes, flickering vivid.

"Yeah, there was another monster, but we killed it," I said, sharper than I meant, rough with the day's blood. "A hydra, something from my world's myths, brought to life in the worst way." My tone bit, Sara's giggle twisting under the hydra's hiss, rifle cold against my thigh, chest aching where venom burned.

Aldred's face darkened, lines deepening, beard brushing the table. "A hydra... That confirms my fears. The corruption isn't just our world's merging, it's deeper. Ancient." His voice dropped, sinking into the room, eyes flicking to the branch, then me, piercing, weighing.

"What do you mean?" Mithis stepped up, axe propped, runes dim but alive, voice cutting the quiet, steady, edged, cape swaying damp, ichor-stained.

The mage spoke, voice low, deliberate, fingers tracing his robe's glowing lines. "The magic binding our worlds has awakened forces long buried; neither your world nor ours is ready for them. The hydra was just the start." His tone measured, eyes glinting, hands trembling.

I sighed, rubbing my nose, grime smearing under my fingers. "Great. So it's not over." My voice rasped, bitter Sara's scream looping, the witch's curse clawing "every hope will crumble."

"Far from it," Aldred said, nodding grimly. "But the white ash helps. It's magic can cleanse the forest's corruption and shield the village for a time." His voice steadied, eyes locking mine, a lifeline dangled over a drop.

"For a time?" Mithis repeated, tone biting, crimson eyes narrowing, axe shifting, runes flaring dim purple.

Aldred nodded, slowly, "The corruption returns unless the source is destroyed. And the Wendigo's still out there hungry, waiting. You've bought us a chance to rebuild, prepare." His hands splayed on the table, wood creaking, torchlight catching the lines in his face.

"The Wendigo?" I asked, gut sinking, rifle heavy. "Thought the ash was for that."

"It's a start," the mage said, voice deliberate. "The branch can wound it, white ash cuts through its hide where steel fails, but it's not enough alone. The Wendigo's tied to something bigger, deeper in the forest." His runes flared dim, eyes piercing.

Mithis frowned, gripping the branch tighter, its glow pulsing soft but fiercely, frost-white edges jagged, about two feet long, straight as a spear shaft but light, like it weighed nothing. Runes from the Glade etched its surface, faint, silvery, shimmering when she moved it, humming low like wind through ice. "Then we craft it into a weapon," she said, voice firm, practical. "Something to kill with."

Aldred nodded. "Our smith can shape it, forge it into a blade or spear tip. It's magic holds against dark forces: Wendigo, curse, whatever's stirring." His tone hardened, offering a threat.

The advisors moved, muttering low runes glowing brighter as they prepped the ash. A guard escorted us out, halberd clanking, leading us to the inn. The barkeep, the same bastard who'd scoffed, grinned nervously now, yellow teeth flashing, handed us a key fast, eyes darting to the branch. The room was a small sagging bed, peeling walls but after the hydra's stench and Glade's rot, it felt like a damn palace, candle spitting weak light, wax pooling on the sill.

Mithis set her axe within reach, propped against the chair, collapsing into it by the window, crimson eyes scanning the darkened street, cobblestones glinting under torchlight. Her cape bunched damp, ichor drying black.

"Think this'll hold them off?" she asked, voice rough, branch glow softening her steel.

"For now," I said, sitting on the bed's edge, the mattress creaking loudly. "But it's a band-aid. The Wendigo's still out there, whatever's feeding it too." My voice rasped, hands on my knees, rifle cold beside me, Sara's voice soft, the curse a burr in my gut.

She nodded, crimson eyes distant. "At least we gave them a shot." Her voice softened, axe resting on her knee, runes dim, steady.

Silence fell, heavy my mind replaying the hydra's jaws, scales glinting, the impossible weight of our worlds crashing, spitting nightmares out of god knows where. "Hydra and Wendigo both from my myths," I said, voice rough, cutting the quiet. "Think more'll show up?"

Mithis glanced at me, the branch glowing dim in her lap. "If our worlds keep colliding, yeah. Nightmares made real. Hope some aren't killers." Her tone was dry, crimson eyes glinting, practical, fierce.

A knock jerked me awake sharp, loud hand snapping to my rifle, cold steel under fingers, heart slamming my ribs. Three hours on my watch, enough for twelve more of hell. "Who is it?" I called, voice steady, rough, eyes flicking to Mithis already up, axe in hand, eyes piercing in the candle's flicker.

"Village guard," came the reply, tight, high. "Elder needs you now." His voice trembled, halberd thudding soft outside.

Mithis and I traded a glance, hers hard, mine tired. She grabbed her axe, runes flaring dim; I slung my rifle, boots scuffing as I opened the door. The guard stood pale, hands shaking, torchlight catching sweat on his face. "Something's happening in the forest," he said, voice tight, eyes darting. "Elder says it's urgent."

"We don't get a break, do we?" I muttered, gripping my rifle, split knuckles pulsing, Sara's scream looping soft, pushing me up.

He led us through the village in dim torchlight, flickering, shadows shifting on cobblestones. His steps hurried, uneven, halberd clanking, tension thickening the air every instinct screaming something watched from the dark.

"What's happening?" Mithis asked, voice steady, axe on her shoulder, runes glowing softly, cape swaying.

"The forest," he replied, glancing nervously at the treeline, black, still. "Elder says it's stirring again. Told us to bring you fast." His voice cracked, torch trembling.

I shot Mithis a knowing glance, her eyes glinting with the same thought. We quickened pace, rifle heavy, shadows twitching, rustles hitting my nerves, Sara's voice soft under the quiet. The hall loomed, the door swinging wide before we knocked. Aldred stood inside by a table, maps and runes glowing dim, advisors pale, faces tight. His keen eyes locked with us as we stepped in.

"You came quick," he said, voice grave. "Good. No time to waste." His robe dragged, torchlight catching weariness in his stance.

"What's going on?" I asked, voice rough, rifle slung over my shoulder. Mithis shut the door, wood thudding muted.

The mage pointed, robe glowing dimly. "Look." His voice was low, his hand was trembling, gesturing to the window.

I crossed, boots scuffing planks, peered out night black, forest a silhouette. Then a glow pulsed deep in the woods, sickly green, moving slow, alive. "What's that?" I asked, eyes narrowing, chest tightening flickering like fireflies gone wrong.

Aldred sighed. "Spirits. Wraiths. Stirred when you killed the hydra." His voice sank, eyes flicking to the branch, white, glowing, then to me.

I turned, gut sinking. "Killing the hydra made this worse?" My voice rasped, biting Sara's scream twisting under it, rifle cold.

"Not worse," the mage said, deliberately. "It's drawn the attention of something deeper. These aren't just spirits, harbingers of something greater. The Wendigo's out there, and it's pissed." His eyes glinted, runes flaring dim.

"Something greater?" Mithis asked, grip tightening, axe shifting, runes pulsing, voice cutting the quiet, steady.

Aldred nodded. "Villagers report shadows at the forest's edge. It's testing us, growing stronger." His tone hardened, eyes locking, her torchlight catching strain.

"What do you need?" I asked, voice firmer than I felt, rifle heavy, Sara pushing me, chest aching.

He pointed at the map on the table, lines twisting, runes glowing. "Wraiths circle an old ruin deep in the forest. Could be the corruption's source maybe what spawned the hydra, drives the Wendigo." His hand pressed, wood creaking voice urgent.

The warrior spoke, voice low and steady, cutting the smoky air. "If the source isn't destroyed, corruption spreads again, the ash won't hold forever. The ruin's gotta be cleansed, or we're done." His scarred face tightened, halberd propped nearby, dull blade notched from battles past.

"Of course," I muttered, glancing at Mithis, voice dry and worn. "Ever catch a break?" My rifle hung cold, exhaustion biting deep into my bones.

She smirked subtle, crimson eyes gleaming in the torchlight. "Rather wait for wraiths to hit us here?" Her tone teased, axe resting easily on her shoulder.

I sighed, rough and edged. "No. Just hope the ruins aren't hiding another hydra." Sara's voice flickered soft, pushing me forward despite the weight.

Aldred's hand slammed the table with a firm and crisp thud, echoing off the timber walls. "I won't send you alone. Two hunters, my best, will guide you to the ruin. They know the forest might dodge the traps." His voice rolled solemnly, eyes piercing, dangling a lifeline.

"Fine," I said, flicking my gaze to Mithis. "But if they slow us " My voice rasped, soldier's edge slicing through rifle ready in my grip.

"They won't," Aldred snapped, finally, hand still on the table, wood creaking under his weight.

A knock cut the tension, and the guard stepped aside. Two figures slipped in: Daven, tall and wiry, bow slung across his back, eyes calm, steady as stone. "I'm Daven," he said, voice low. "This is Corin." Younger, dark braid pulled tight twin swords at his hips, eyes hard and focused. "We'll guide you to the ruin," he added, blades catching dim torchlight, no-nonsense.

I sized them up quick, silent steps, precise, danger in their bones. "Fine. Sooner we start, the better." My voice scraped, boots scuffing the planks, Sara's echo driving me relentlessly.

The forest hit heavier, like wading through a dream, every step dragging slowly. Air thickened with a chill that sank deep, glowing lights dancing closer, pale, malevolent fireflies flickering between trees, always just out of reach. Daven led, bow in hand, silent as a ghost. Corin trailed behind us, blades ready. Mithis and I followed behind Daven, my rifle cradled tight, eyes scanning shadows twitching, rustles spiking my nerves, Sara looping soft under the quiet.

"What's the plan at the ruin?" I asked, voice low, breath fogging quick rifle cold against my chest.

"Scout first," Daven replied, eyes locked forward, voice steady. "If it's guarded, we go carefully." His bow shifted, boots silent on moss.

"And if it's not?" Mithis asked, axe propped, runes glowing dim, her voice cutting through the chill.

Daven paused, a beat too long. "That's worse. Means it doesn't need guards." His tone sank, weight slamming cold into my gut.

The words hung trees thickening, roots twisting underfoot, silence pressing my chest. Lights danced ahead, taunting. Corin whispered, "We're close. Air's colder, always a sign." His voice trembled, blades glinting, eyes piercing in the dark.

He was right the chill clawed my gut, doubting every step, rifle steadying me against the shake. Daven raised a fist, crouching low, peering through the gloom, motioning us down. Mithis and I traded a glance her crimson eyes glowing dim, stepping carefully, boots crunching quiet. The ruins loomed ahead crumbling stone swallowed by forest, ivy and moss clinging tight, greenish light pulsing within, air shimmering, warped like a mirage gone bad.

"Magic's here," Mithis murmured, grip tightening on her axe runes flaring softly, cape swaying damp.

Daven nodded. "Corin, circle right. I'll take the left. You two hold here, cover the entrance." His voice stayed low, bow shifting, he vanished into shadow. Corin gave a quick nod, melting into the dark blades glinting dim.

Mithis and I crouched at the clearing's edge, my rifle trained on the entrance green light pulsing like a heartbeat, alive, watching. "Feel that?" she whispered, crimson eyes flicking to me, axe steady.

"Feel what?" I asked, eyes locked ahead, breath fogging in the cold.

"The forest. It's breathing." Her voice tightened, runes glowing brighter, cape rustling lightly. I frowned, focusing wind still, but branches swayed slowly, in and out like lungs under the dirt. A shiver hit my spine, cold and piercing, rifle trembling a hair. Before I could answer, a scream tore through Corin's, high and raw, shattering the silence. Daven's voice barked, "It's a trap! Fall back!" panic spiking my gut hard.

Green light surged, spilling like liquid, shadows writhing within coalescing fast into tall, twisted forms, eyes glowing malevolent green. "Move!" Mithis shouted, yanking me up her grip iron through my jacket, boots skidding as I fired. The burst ripped through shadow, flickering, faltering, reforming, quick lunging again.

"Bullets don't work!" I yelled, scrambling back rifle barrel warm, Sara's scream loud under the chaos.

Mithis swung, axe blazing purple, cutting through shadow with a shriek, ichor splattering moss, black and steaming. "Magic works!"

she shouted, runes flaring hot, cape snapping as she spun.

Daven burst from the trees, arrow notched, glowing dim, loosed it fast, striking true, shadow wisping off in smoke. Corin stumbled in blood, staining his side, gasping, "Destroy the source! The light fuels them!" clutching his wound, eyes hard despite the pain.

I nodded, heart pounding. "Cover me!" Rifle up, Sara's telling me this is a waste of time. Daven and Mithis moved fast, attacks glowing, Corin leaning on a tree, blade raised, deflecting blood dripping slowly onto the moss.

I sprinted, green light pulsing harder, my mind screaming to turn back, boots pounding dirt, entrance yawning wide, air colder inside. Walls hummed, alive center glowing a massive crystal, green light throbbing symbols shifting, shadows surging tethered to it. Sara's scream rang loud "No time," I muttered, raising my rifle fired bullets sparking off, useless "Damn it!"

Mithis charged in "Keep them off me!" Voice commanding runes flaring fiercely. I turned, firing shadows closing, holding them back. Her roar echoed axe high purple light, blinding, cracking loud as it hit the crystal light, dimming, surging out force slamming me into the wall, hard shadows shrieking, dissolving dust settling. Mithis stood, axe glowing, smile weary but triumphant. "It's done."

"For now," I thought, grim ground quaking, a roar ripping through shadow blotting the canopy. A dragon landed crashing, deafening stones tumbling, emerald scales shimmering, smoke coiling from its jaws, amber eyes blazing fury. I nodded, wiping sweat from my brow, hand shaking where venom burns stung raw red welts blistering under cracked skin. "Yeah. Let's go with that." My voice scraped rough, dry, chest aching like I'd been mule-kicked. The sword hung heavy against my thigh, cold steel grounding me, its purple glow a lifeline in the Glade's murk.

The white ash tree shimmered ahead, branches dipping, bowing like it knew we'd earned it. Bark glinted frost-white, wrapped in a glow of moonlight on fresh snow, alive, humming under the haze. Mithis stepped up, hand pressing its trunk, green skin stark against the pale light flaring around her.

A single branch snapped free, drifting into her hands, white as bone, edges jagged with frost, glowing fierce, like it carried the Glade's soul. "This is it," she said, voice low, reverent, cradling it like gold. Her runes pulsed on her axe, crimson eyes easing with hope, cutting through the steel. "With this, we can fight corruption. Maybe even lift that witch's curse off you."

I nodded, sweat stinging my eyes, chest throbbing, the witch's voice clawing deep, "every life you touch will rot." The branch's glow sliced through, a thin thread to grab. "Let's get out before the forest throws more shit at us." My voice rasped, tired but edged, rifle slung

91

heavy, boots crunching hydra ash as I turned. The Glade's hum faded under a quiet too thick, pressing my skull.

Mithis's lips twitched in relief, determination sparking in her crimson eyes. Together, we stepped back onto the path, ash swirling behind us, the clearing's weight slipping off like shed skin.

The trek to Kalden dragged along a path stretching long, the forest closing in tight. Trees loomed, gnarled branches retreating a hair, less hostile but still watching, shadows twisting at the corners of my eyes. The white ash branch glowed in Mithis's grip, casting jagged flickers over moss-slick roots and silvery bark, a beacon in the murk. My boots crunched brittle leaves, each step echoing in the eerie silence, a stillness sinking into my bones. Rustles, distant, hit my ears, heart pounding, nerves strung tight.

"Stay alert," Mithis said, voice low, rough, crimson eyes darting through the treeline. Her axe rested on her shoulder, runes dim but ready, cape swaying, damp, matted with ichor and dirt, pine cutting through the forest's rot.

I nodded, gripping my rifle, cold steel biting my palms, split knuckles throbbing, venom burns stinging. "Hope whatever's left knows we mean business." My voice scraped dry, Sara's scream looping, Mom's blood a shadow I couldn't shake. Exhaustion clawed my bones, heavy and cold, but I kept my eyes fierce, scanning the dark.

The silence thickened, broken only by our steps and those distant rustles. Branches creaked, whispers I couldn't catch, pulse hammering with every flicker in the gloom. The hydra fight had drained my legs, ribs aching, but a soldier's habit kept me upright, rifle steady.

"You all right?" Mithis glanced over, crimson eyes catching the branch's glow, searching, breath fogging in the chill.

"Yeah," I lied, voice rough, the weight of Sara, the curse, the hydra piling on. "You?" My hands tightened, rifle cold, grounding the shake I wouldn't admit.

She gave a smile, easing her steel. "Been through worse. You held your own back there. More capable than you think." Her tone warmed, steady, cutting the cold, a lifeline I didn't expect.

"Thanks," I said, heat flickering under the grime, chest easing a fraction. " But save the compliments 'til we're out."Torchlight glimmered ahead, warm, cutting the trees. Relief hit my gut as Kalden's gates loomed, wooden beams weathered and scarred, less imposing now. Guards stood stiff, eyes scanning the treeline, hands twitching on halberds pale under dented helmets. One spotted us, raised a hand, voice cracking clear, "They've returned!" a jolt rippling through them.

Gates creaked, wood groaning as they swung wide, guards stepping aside, eyes wide, awe and disbelief mixing, chainmail rattling under patched cloaks. "You made it," one said, voice shocked, jaw slack. "We thought..."

"That we wouldn't?" Mithis cut in, tone biting, crimson eyes narrowing. Her axe propped easily, runes flickering, cape swaying as she squared up. "We don't fall that easily." Steel snapped in her words, the guard swallowing hard, gaze flicking to the glowing branch, white, alive.

"We got it," I said, stepping forward, boots scuffing dirt, voice rough but steady. "Where's the Elder? He needs to see this." Rifle hung heavy, exhaustion tugging, adrenaline holding me up.

The guard nodded fast, jerking his head toward the hall. "Waiting inside. Go ahead." His voice trembled, eyes darting, torchlight catching sweat on his brow.

The Elder's hall hit familiar timber walls stained dark, smoky air thick with tallow and straw, but tension coiled tighter now, heavy in the haze. Aldred stood center, robe dragging the planks, flanked by his advisors, the warrior's scarred face grim, the mage's robes glowing muted with arcane lines. His eyes widened a hair as we stepped in, snapping to the white ash branch cutting the gloom. "You've succeeded," he said, voice rolling with relief and awe mixed. "I dared not hope." His hands clenched, knuckles whitening, the table behind littered with maps and runes, flickering vivid.

"Yeah, there was another monster, but we killed it," I said, rougher than I meant, edged with the day's blood. "A hydra, something from my world's myths, brought to life in the worst way." My tone bit, Sara's giggle twisting under the hydra's hiss, rifle cold against my thigh, chest aching where venom burned.

Aldred's face darkened, lines deepening, beard brushing the table. "A hydra... That confirms my fears. The corruption isn't just our world's merging, it's deeper. Ancient." His voice dropped, sinking into the room, eyes flicking to the branch, then me, piercing, weighing.

"What do you mean?" Mithis stepped up, axe propped, runes dim but alive, voice cutting the quiet, steady, edged, cape swaying damp, ichor-stained.

The mage spoke, voice low, deliberate, fingers tracing his robe's glowing lines. "The magic binding our worlds has awakened forces long buried; neither your world nor ours is ready for them. The hydra was just the start." His tone measured, eyes glinting, hands trembling.

I sighed, rubbing my nose, grime smearing under my fingers. "Great. So it's not over." My voice rasped, bitter, Sara's scream looping, the witch's curse clawing, "every hope will crumble."

"Far from it," Aldred said, nodding grimly. "But the white ash helps. It's magic can cleanse the forest's corruption and shield the village for a time." His voice steadied, eyes locking mine, a lifeline dangled over a drop.

"For a time?" Mithis repeated, tone biting, crimson eyes narrowing, axe shifting, runes flaring purple.

Aldred nodded. "The corruption returns unless the source is destroyed. And the Wendigo's still out there hungry, waiting. You've bought us a chance to rebuild, prepare." His hands splayed on the table, wood creaking, torchlight catching the lines in his face.

"The Wendigo?" I asked, gut sinking, rifle heavy. "Thought the ash was for that."

"It's a start," the mage said, voice deliberate. "The branch can wound it, white ash cuts through its hide where steel fails, but it's not enough alone. The Wendigo's tied to something bigger, deeper in the forest." His runes flared, eyes piercing.

Mithis frowned, gripping the branch tighter, its glow pulsing fierce, frost-white edges jagged, about two feet long, straight as a spear shaft but light, like it weighed nothing. Runes from the Glade etched its surface, silvery, shimmering when she moved it, humming like wind through ice. "Then we craft it into a weapon," she said, voice firm, practical. "Something to kill with."

Aldred nodded. "Our smith can shape it, forge it into a blade or spear tip. It's magic holds against dark forces, Wendigo, curse, whatever's stirring." His tone hardened, offering a threat.

The advisors moved, muttering low, runes glowing brighter as they prepped the ash. A guard escorted us out, halberd clanking, leading us to the inn. The barkeep, the same bastard who'd scoffed, grinned nervously now, yellow teeth flashing, handed us a key fast, eyes darting to the branch. The room was a small sagging bed, peeling walls, but after the hydra's stench and Glade's rot, it felt like a damn palace, candle spitting weak light, wax pooling on the sill.

Mithis set her axe within reach, propped against the chair, collapsing into it by the window, crimson eyes scanning the darkened street, cobblestones glinting under torchlight. Her cape bunched damp, ichor drying black.

"Think this'll hold them off?" she asked, voice rough, branch glow easing her steel.

"For now," I said, sitting on the bed's edge, the mattress creaking. "But it's a band-aid. The Wendigo's still out there, whatever's feeding it too." My voice rasped, hands on my knees, rifle cold beside me, Sara's voice a burr in my gut.

She nodded, crimson eyes distant. "At least we gave them a shot." Her voice eased, axe resting on her knee, runes dim, steady.

Silence fell, heavy, my mind replaying the hydra's jaws, scales glinting, the impossible weight of our worlds crashing, spitting nightmares out of god knows where. "Hydra and Wendigo both from my myths," I said, voice rough, cutting the quiet. "Think more'll show up?"

Mithis glanced at me, the branch glowing in her lap. "If our worlds keep colliding, yeah. Nightmares made real. Hope some aren't killers." Her tone was dry, crimson eyes glinting, practical, fierce.

A knock jerked me awake, hand snapping to my rifle, cold steel under fingers, heart slamming my ribs. Three hours on my watch, enough for twelve more of hell. "Who is it?" I called, voice steady, rough, eyes flicking to Mithis, already up, axe in hand, eyes piercing in the candle's flicker.

"Village guard," came the reply, tight, high. "Elder needs you now." His voice trembled, halberd thudding outside.

Mithis and I traded a glance, hers hard, mine tired. She grabbed her axe, runes flaring; I slung my rifle, boots scuffing as I opened the door. The guard stood pale, hands shaking, torchlight catching sweat on his face. "Something's happening in the forest," he said, voice tight, eyes darting. "Elder says it's urgent."

"We don't get a break, do we?" I muttered, gripping my rifle, split knuckles pulsing, Sara's scream pushing me up.

He led us through the village in dim torchlight, flickering, shadows shifting on cobblestones. His steps hurried, uneven, halberd clanking, tension thickening the air, every instinct screaming something watched from the dark.

"What's happening?" Mithis asked, voice steady, axe on her shoulder, runes glowing, cape swaying.

"The forest," he replied, glancing nervously at the treeline, black, still. "Elder says it's stirring again. Told us to bring you fast." His voice cracked, torch trembling.

I shot Mithis a knowing glance, her eyes glinting with the same thought. We quickened pace, rifle heavy, shadows twitching, rustles hitting my nerves, Sara's voice under the quiet. The hall loomed, the door swinging wide before we knocked. Aldred stood inside by a table, maps and runes glowing, advisors pale, faces tight. His eyes locked with us as we stepped in.

"You came quick," he said, voice grave. "Good. No time to waste." His robe dragged, torchlight catching weariness in his stance.

"What's going on?" I asked, voice rough, rifle slung over my shoulder. Mithis shut the door, wood thudding muted.

The mage pointed, robe glowing. "Look." His voice was low, hand trembling, gesturing to the window.

I crossed, boots scuffing planks, peered out, night black, forest a silhouette. Then a glow pulsed deep in the woods, sickly green, moving slow, alive. "What's that?" I asked, eyes narrowing, chest tightening, flickering like fireflies gone wrong.

Aldred sighed. "Spirits. Wraiths. Stirred when you killed the hydra." His voice sank, eyes flicking to the branch, white, glowing, then to me.

I turned, gut sinking. "Killing the hydra made this worse?" My voice rasped, biting, Sara's scream twisting under it, rifle cold.

"Not worse," the mage said, deliberately. "It's drawn the attention of something deeper. These aren't just spirits, harbingers of something greater. The Wendigo's out there, and it's pissed." His eyes glinted, runes flaring.

"Something greater?" Mithis asked, grip tightening, axe shifting, runes pulsing, voice cutting the quiet, steady.

Aldred nodded. "Villagers report shadows at the forest's edge. It's testing us, growing stronger." His tone hardened, eyes locking, torchlight catching strain.

"What do you need?" I asked, voice firmer than I felt, rifle heavy, Sara pushing me, chest aching.

He pointed at the map on the table, lines twisting, runes glowing. "Wraiths circle an old ruin deep in the forest. Could be the corruption's source, maybe what spawned the hydra, drives the Wendigo." His hand pressed, wood creaking, voice urgent.

The warrior spoke, voice low and steady, cutting the smoky air. "If the source isn't destroyed, corruption spreads again. The ash won't hold forever. The ruin's gotta be cleansed, or we're done." His scarred face tightened, halberd propped nearby, dull blade notched from battles past.

"Of course," I muttered, glancing at Mithis, voice dry and worn. "Ever catch a break?" My rifle hung cold, exhaustion biting deep into my bones.

She smirked, crimson eyes gleaming in the torchlight. "Rather wait for wraiths to hit us here?" Her tone teased, axe resting easily on her shoulder.

I sighed, rough and edged. "No. Just hope the ruins aren't hiding another hydra." Sara's voice flickered, pushing me forward despite the weight.

Aldred's hand slammed the table with a clear thud, echoing off the timber walls. "I won't send you alone. Two hunters, my best, will guide you to the ruin. They know the forest might dodge the traps." His voice rolled solemn, eyes piercing, dangling a lifeline.

"Fine," I said, flicking my gaze to Mithis. "But if they slow us " My voice rasped, soldier's edge slicing through, rifle ready in my grip.

"They won't," Aldred snapped, hand still on the table, wood creaking under his weight.

A knock cut the tension, and the guard stepped aside. Two figures slipped in: Daven, tall and wiry, bow slung across his back, eyes calm, steady as stone. "I'm Daven," he said, voice low. "This is Corin." Younger, dark braid pulled tight, twin swords at his hips, eyes hard and focused. "We'll guide you to the ruin," he added, blades catching dim torchlight, no-nonsense.

I sized them up, quick, silent steps, precise, danger in their bones. "Fine. Sooner we start, the better." My voice scraped, boots scuffing the planks, Sara's echo driving me relentlessly.

The forest hit heavier, like wading through a dream, every step dragging. Air thickened with a chill that sank deep, glowing lights dancing closer, pale, malevolent fireflies flickering between trees, always just out of reach. Daven led, bow in hand, silent as a ghost. Corin trailed behind us, blades ready. Mithis and I followed behind Daven, my rifle cradled tight, eyes scanning shadows twitching, rustles spiking my nerves, Sara looping under the quiet.

"What's the plan at the ruin?" I asked, voice low, breath fogging, rifle cold against my chest.

"Scout first," Daven replied, eyes locked forward, voice steady. "If it's guarded, we go carefully." His bow shifted, boots silent on moss.

"And if it's not?" Mithis asked, axe propped, runes glowing, her voice cutting through the chill.

Daven paused, a beat too long. "That's worse. Means it doesn't need guards." His tone sank, weight slamming cold into my gut.

The words hung, trees thickening, roots twisting underfoot, silence pressing my chest. Lights danced ahead, taunting. Corin whispered, "We're close. Air's colder, always a sign." His voice trembled, blades glinting, eyes piercing in the dark.

He was right the chill clawed my gut, doubting every step, rifle steadying me against the shake. Daven raised a fist, crouching low, peering through the gloom, motioning us down. Mithis and I traded a glance, her crimson eyes glowing, stepping careful, boots crunching quiet. The ruins loomed ahead crumbling stone swallowed by forest, ivy and moss clinging tight, greenish light pulsing within, air shimmering, warped like a mirage gone bad.

"Magic's here," Mithis murmured, grip tightening on her axe, runes flaring, cape swaying damp.

Daven nodded. "Corin, circle right. I'll take the left. You two hold here, cover the entrance." His voice stayed low, bow shifting, he vanished into shadow. Corin gave a quick nod, melting into the dark, blades glinting.

Mithis and I crouched at the clearing's edge, my rifle trained on the entrance, green light pulsing like a heartbeat, alive, watching. "Feel that?" she whispered, crimson eyes flicking to me, axe steady.

"Feel what?" I asked, eyes locked ahead, breath fogging in the cold.

"The forest. It's breathing." Her voice tightened, runes glowing brighter, cape rustling. I frowned, focusing wind still, but branches swayed, in and out like lungs under the dirt. A shiver hit my spine, cold and piercing, rifle trembling a hair. Before I could answer, a scream tore through Corin's, high and raw, shattering the silence.

Daven's voice barked, "It's a trap! Run!" panic spiking my gut hard.

Green light surged, spilling like liquid, shadows writhing within, coalescing into tall, twisted forms, eyes glowing malevolent green. "Move!" Mithis shouted, yanking me up, her grip iron through my jacket, boots skidding as I fired. The burst ripped through shadow, flickering, faltering, reforming, lunging again.

"Bullets don't work!" I yelled, scrambling back, rifle barrel warm, Sara's scream loud under the chaos.

Mithis swung, axe blazing purple, cutting through shadow with a shriek, ichor splattering moss, black and steaming. "Magic works!" she shouted, runes flaring hot, cape snapping as she spun.

Daven burst from the trees, arrow notched, glowing, loosed it fast, striking true, shadow wisping off in smoke. Corin stumbled in, blood staining his side, gasping, "Destroy the source! The light fuels them!" clutching his wound, eyes hard despite the pain.

I nodded, heart pounding. "Cover me!" Rifle up, Sara's voice telling me this is a waste of time. Daven and Mithis moved fast, attacks glowing, Corin leaning on a tree, blade raised, deflecting, blood dripping onto the moss.

I sprinted, green light pulsing harder, my mind screaming to turn back, boots pounding dirt, entrance yawning wide, air colder inside. Walls hummed, alive, center glowing a massive crystal, green light throbbing, symbols shifting, shadows surging, tethered to it. Sara's scream rang, "No time," I muttered, raising my rifle, fired bullets that sparked off, useless. "Damn it!"

Mithis charged in. "Keep them off me!" Voice commanding, runes flaring fierce. I turned, firing, shadows closing, holding them back. Her roar echoed, axe high, purple light blinding, cracking as it hit the crystal, light dimming, surging out, force slamming me into the wall, hard, shadows shrieking, dissolving, dust settling. Mithis stood, axe glowing, smile weary but triumphant. "It's done."

"For now," I thought, grim, ground quaking, a roar ripping through, shadow blotting the canopy. A dragon landed, crashing, deafening, stones tumbling, emerald scales shimmering, smoke coiling from its jaws, amber eyes blazing fury.

13 ROAR OF THE RUINS

The dragon's roar ripped through the ruins, a deep grinding bellow that rattled my bones and buzzed in my teeth. Its emerald scales shimmered wet under the pulsing green glow from the shattered crystal, each plate as big as my chest, overlapping like jagged armor plating a fortress. Smoke poured thick from its jaws, curling around teeth long and sharp as swords, yellowed at the roots, glistening with an acrid sheen that hinted at venom or acid. Amber eyes burned with fury, twin suns piercing the haze, locking onto us with a predator's focus that promised charred bones and ash.

"You dare disrupt my magic?" it thundered, voice rolling like a landslide, shaking loose dust from the crumbling stone arches overhead. Embers spilled from its maw, glowing orange, sizzling as they hit the moss-slick ground, sending up thin curls of bitter smoke. The air slammed hot and heavy, sulfur and char clogged my lungs, searing my throat raw until every breath stung like swallowing glass shards.

"Move!" I shouted, diving hard to my left. My boots skidded on the rubble, moss-slick and uneven, kicking up damp grit that stuck to my jeans. Emerald flames erupted from its jaws, an inferno sweeping the clearing in a wide arc, a wall of green-tinged fire roaring ten feet high. Heat blistered my face even from a dozen yards away, forcing my eyes to squint against the glare. I hit the ground rolling, crashing behind a crumbled pillar, its stone warm and rough under my palms, scorching where the flames licked close. My rifle banged hard against my hip, strap digging into my shoulder, and the fire surged past, close enough to singe my pant leg. Venom burns from the hydra flared hotter under my sleeve, red welts throbbing like live coals pressed into my skin, a vivid reminder of the last fight's toll. I pressed my back to the pillar, chest heaving, peering around its edge. Flames still crackled, igniting patches of dry ivy clinging to the ruins, filling the air with a green stench that burned my nose.

Mithis leapt to her right, moving fast. Her axe blazed with purple light, runes carved into its steel head glowing bright as she twisted mid-air. Her wolf-pelt cape snapped wet behind her, heavy with muck from the forest trek, and the fire caught its edge, singeing the fur black in a quick flare that smoked before dying out. She landed in a crouch, boots sinking into damp dirt near a toppled statue, some old warrior's head half-buried in the soil, and rolled clear as the flames faded, leaving smoking streaks scorched into the ground.

Daven and Corin scattered too, splitting wide to avoid the blast. Daven sprinted left, bow already in hand, notching an arrow mid-run, its tip glowing with a village charm. He loosed it, the string twanging in the chaos, and it streaked through the haze, striking the dragon's flank with a dull spark that flared bright then died, grazing the scales, useless as a pebble against a tank. He ducked behind a jagged wall remnant, cursing low under his breath. Corin went right, clutching his bloody side where the wraiths had torn him, blood oozing dark through his fingers. His twin swords stayed drawn, steel glinting as he deflected falling embers with quick, precise flicks of his wrists. He stumbled behind a slab of cracked stone, grunting as he hit cover, face pale but eyes hard, refusing to buckle despite the pain.

The dragon reared up, towering fifteen feet at the shoulder, wings snapping wide with a rush of wind that sent dust and ash swirling, blotting out the canopy overhead, plunging us into deeper shadow beneath its bulk. Its claws, long and curved like butcher hooks, gouged the stone floor with a high-grating screech that clawed at my skull, each talon carving furrows a foot deep, spraying chips of rock that clattered around us. Its tail lashed out, thick as a tree trunk and spiked along the ridge with bony protrusions, slamming into a wall to my right. The impact shattered it, stone exploding outward in a cloud of debris that rained down like shrapnel, stinging my arms and neck where it grazed through my torn jacket.

"Wretched insects!" it snarled, amber eyes narrowing to slits, flames coiling visibly in its throat, a deep orange glow pulsing brighter with every heaving breath of its massive ribcage. My heart slammed into my ribs, Sara's scream lost under its roar, rifle trembling in my sweaty grip, split knuckles pulsing hot under cracked dirt-caked skin.

"Bullets won't dent it!" I yelled, popping up from behind the pillar. My rifle barked three crisp shots, cracks loud in the smoky air, brass casings clinking as they hit the ground beside me. The rounds struck its snout, sparking bright against the scales like I'd fired at a steel plate, ricocheting off into the dark with whines, leaving no mark, not even a scratch to show for it.

The dragon didn't flinch, just whipped its head toward me, jaws gaping wide enough to swallow me whole, fire surging fast up its throat in a churning ball of heat. I dropped low, scrambling back behind the pillar, flames roaring over its top, licking the stone black with soot, heat blasting my face and shoulders. My jacket smoked where it grazed too close, sweat stinging the venom burns on my arms, raw and pulsing under the strain, a searing ache that cut through adrenaline's focus.

Mithis charged from her angle, boots pounding the dirt with heavy thuds. "Keep it busy!" she shouted, voice slicing through the chaos like a blade, axe swinging high in both hands. The purple arc of its enchanted edge slashed through the air, aiming for its left flank where scales overlapped in tight rows. The blade bit shallow, steel meeting scales with a grating crunch that echoed off the ruins, splintering a few loose shards that fell glittering to the ground. Ichor dripped black and steaming where it seeped out, a thin trickle running down its side, staining the moss below with a hiss. The dragon snarled, a low guttural rumble shaking my boots through the earth, and swung its tail hard, cracking the ground where Mithis had stood a heartbeat before.

She dove low, rolling under the swing, boots skidding across damp moss as the tail passed overhead with a rush of air, cape trailing a smear of mud and ash behind her, axe still clutched tight in her fists.

I got back up, rifle snapping to my shoulder in one smooth motion. "Daven, Corin, flank it!" I barked, soldier's instinct kicking in, chest aching where the hydra's venom had burned through fabric a day ago, leaving scars that throbbed under pressure. Daven nodded, slipping out from cover, bow drawn taut, arrow glowing brighter with a village charm pulsing in the fletching. He aimed low, losing it with a twang that cut the roar, striking just under the dragon's left wing where the scales thinned near the joint. The arrow punched through with a crack, embedding an inch deep, ichor oozing, black and thick, dripping to the dirt below in heavy drops.

The dragon roared louder, wing sweeping down in a violent arc, wind rushing past, knocking Daven off his feet. He hit the ground hard, bow clattering free as he rolled into a pile of loose stones, grunting through gritted teeth, scrambling to grab it before it slid out of reach. Corin darted in from the right, blades flashing in tight arcs, slashing at its nearest claw. Steel scraped across scales with a shower of orange sparks, nicking the edge of one talon with a gouge. The dragon's head swung, jaws snapping fast, teeth gleaming wet in the firelight. He leapt clear, braid whipping as teeth grazed the air where he'd been, landing in a crouch near a pile of broken stone, knees sinking into the damp earth.

The white ash spear hung at Mithis's side, forged back in Kalden by their smith in a rush before we left, a weapon born from the Glade's frost-white branch. Two feet long, straight and light as a reed, its surface shimmered with silvery runes etched deep, etched by the same magic that had pulsed in the tree, glowing like moonlight trapped in ice. The spear tip, honed thin, gleamed with a cold edge, forged onto a steel haft, reinforced with leather grips worn smooth from the smith's hands, humming low with a power I could feel in my bones when I stood near it. She yanked it free from its sling, runes flaring silver against the dark wood, gripping it tight in her left hand while her axe stayed in her right, crimson eyes blazing with focus under her sweat-streaked brow.

"This'll pierce it!" she shouted, voice fierce and steady, dodging a claw swipe that raked the air, tearing up a chunk of mossy earth beside her that flew past in clumps. The spear glinted as she spun, catching the firelight in a quick flash that danced across its rune-etched length.

"Hit the throat!" I yelled, breaking into a sprint, rifle barking again, five shots this time, aimed tight at its snout. The rounds pinged off with bright sparks, drawing those amber eyes to me, jaws gaping wider, fire coiling hot and bright in its gullet like a furnace igniting. I dove left, flames scorching the stone where I'd stood, an arc of emerald heat blasting past, igniting a patch of dry vines clinging to a nearby arch. The fire crackled, spitting sparks into the air that floated down like tiny stars, heat slamming my back, jacket smoking as I rolled to my knees, venom burns throbbing raw under my sleeve, a sting cutting through the adrenaline pumping in my veins.

Mithis lunged from her angle, spear thrusting upward, aiming under its jaw where the scales parted into a narrow seam. White ash glowed fiercely, runes pulsing silver with every inch it moved, cutting through the haze like a beacon. The dragon twisted, faster than anything that size should manage, its right claw slashing down, catching her side with a glancing blow that tore through her jacket's leather. The spear grazed its scales, tip scraping along the edge of its neck with a spark, missing flesh, knocking her back hard. She hit the ground with a thud that shook the dirt, axe clattering free beside her, spear skidding a few feet across the rubble into a pile of broken bricks. She grunted as blood streaked her ribs, seeping dark through her torn jacket, cape tangling in the jagged stone beneath her, wolf pelt matting with dirt and ash under her weight.

"Mithis!" I barked, scrambling toward her, firing blind over my shoulder, bullets sparking off its snout and jaw, keeping its focus split between us. The dragon's head whipped toward me, tail thrashing wildly, slamming another wall with a crack that sent chunks flying, pelting my legs, bruising through my jeans with stings. She rolled to her knees, grimacing through the pain, grabbing the spear with a quick snatch, runes flaring brighter as her blood-slick gloves gripped tight, ichor from earlier fights staining the leather black, mixing with her red.

"It's too quick!" she shouted, voice raw but steady, dodging a burst of flames that swept low across the ground, spear held firm in her left hand. Her cape smoldered where embers caught the edges, sending up wisps of gray smoke that curled into the haze. "Need an opening!"

Daven hauled himself up from the dirt, bow shaking in his hands, arrow notched, glowing brighter with a charm that pulsed in the dark fletching. He aimed high, loosing it with a twang that cut through the roar, striking the dragon's left eye dead center. Ichor burst out, thick and black, steaming where it splattered the ground in wet globs, the dragon screeching high and shrill, head rearing back, blinded on one side, thrashing wildly in a spray of dust and ash. "Now!" he yelled, voice hoarse, bow trembling as he notched another, breath heaving in short gasps.

I sprinted to Mithis's side, grabbing her fallen axe, purple runes warm under my palms, a heavy, balanced weight that felt alive in my grip. I hurled it hard, blade spinning through the air, a blur of glowing steel crunching into the dragon's chest just below its throat, where scales overlapped thinner in a narrow band. Steel bit deep, splintering a plate with a snap, ichor spraying hot and black across the moss in a wide arc, the dragon roaring, staggering back a step, claws gouging the dirt in jagged ruts that kicked up clods of earth.

"Go!" I shouted, rifle snapping up, firing tight bursts, three shots clipping its jaw, bullets sparking off bone, keeping those amber eyes locked on me, buying her precious seconds.

Mithis charged, spear raised high in both hands, runes blazing silver, leaping over a pile of rubble, boots slamming stone for leverage as she vaulted upward. She drove it deep, white ash piercing under its throat where the axe had weakened the scales, tip sinking into flesh with a wet visceral crunch, cutting through muscle and sinew in a spray of black ichor. The dragon froze mid-roar, sound choking off abruptly, ichor gushing from the wound, steaming as it pooled dark on the ground in a spreading puddle. Its head thrashed wildly, wings beating hard, wind slamming us back, a gust that kicked up ash and grit into my eyes. Ground quaked under my boots as it bucked, claws slashing air blindly, tail whipping in desperate arcs that cracked stone and uprooted vines.

"Hold it!" I yelled, lunging forward, grabbing the spear shaft just below her hands, muscles burning as I added my weight, driving it deeper into the beast's flesh. The runes flared hot, silver light pulsing up the wood into my palms, dragon's scream splitting the air, deafening and raw, claws slashing wild. One raked my left arm, tearing through my sleeve in a quick slash, venom burns searing under fresh blood, a jolt of pain rocking my grip. I gritted my teeth, holding firm, sweat stinging my eyes, legs braced against the trembling earth under its thrashing weight.

Mithis joined in, her hands sliding over mine, green skin stark against the white ash, pushing hard, muscles straining under her torn jacket as blood dripped from her side onto the dirt. The spear ground deeper, wood creaking under the force, hitting something solid inside, heart or bone, a dull thud reverberating up my arms like a hammer strike. The dragon convulsed hard, flames spitting weak from its jaws in a fading sputter, emerald scales dulling to a lifeless sheen, amber eyes dimming fast, pupils shrinking to slits in the haze. Its massive body shuddered once more, wings folding limp against its sides, then slammed into the dirt with a shockwave that knocked us flat, dust and ichor choking the air, thick and sour in my lungs as it settled over us.

Silence fell, sudden and heavy, ruins smoldering around us, patches of stone glowing red where fire had bitten deep into the surface. The dragon's bulk sprawled still, ichor pooling black under its emerald hide in a spreading stain, smoke curling from its slack jaws where embers had died out. I lay there sprawled on my back, chest heaving, lungs burning from the heat and smoke, venom burns throbbing hot on my arm, rifle lying in the ash beside me.

Sara's scream faded under ragged, uneven breaths, a distant echo in my skull. Mithis pushed up slowly, spear still glowing, runes dimming to a pulse, blood streaking her side where the claw had torn her open. Her cape hung charred black and in tatters, crimson eyes glinting with weary triumph as she planted the spear's haft into the dirt for support, leaning on it to stand.

"Dead?" I rasped, hauling myself up, boots crunching ash and broken stone, hands shaking as I brushed grit from my face. Sara's voice lingered, the witch's curse clawing at my gut, "Every life you touch will rot."

"Dead," she said, voice rough and low, spear standing firm, ichor dripping from the tip, pooling dark at her feet below the haft. "For now." Her gaze flicked to the forest beyond the ruins, dark and still, trees looming like sentinels, the Wendigo out there somewhere, its hunger unanswered, coiled tight in the shadows beyond our sight.

Daven staggered over, bow dangling loose in one hand, the other clutching his ribs where the wing had struck him, face smeared with dirt and sweat, breath hitching in short gasps as he stared at the dragon's corpse. "That was..." he started, words trailing off, voice hoarse and unsteady in the quiet.

Corin limped up behind him, blood soaking his side, dark and sticky down his leg, swords sheathed at his hips, leaning heavy on a chunk of rubble for balance. His eyes stayed hard and focused despite the pain etched deep in his clenched jaw, sweat beading on his pale forehead.

"Hell, I finished him," voice dry and cracked, rifle heavy in my grip, glancing at the dragon's dull scales, smoke fading thin from its jaws into the smoky air. "But we're still standing."

Mithis nodded, a smile tugging her lips, half-hidden under the grime. "Just." Her tone steadied, spear firm in her grip, runes glowing against the dark wood, cape a ragged mess, blood and ash matting the wolf pelt, her green skin streaked with grime and ichor from the fight.

The ruins smoked around us, air thick with char and the sour tang of rot, cracked stone walls glowing where flames had seared them, ivy burned to crisp black threads that crumbled at a touch. The forest loomed beyond, silent but alive, its shadows shifting subtly under the canopy, the Wendigo's presence a weight I could feel in my chest, waiting, watching from the dark. I gripped my rifle tighter, split knuckles screaming under the strain, fresh blood mixing with venom burns in a sticky mess down my arm. Sara's voice pushed me north, the curse a burr sinking deeper into my gut with every beat of my heart. "Let's get back," I said, rough and low, boots scuffing ash as I straightened on shaky legs. "Before something else crawls out of this damn place."

Mithis clapped my shoulder, firm and warm through my torn jacket, crimson eyes steady, cutting through the weariness with a glint of steel. "Together," she said, steel threading her voice, a lifeline I grabbed with both hands, holding tight against the ache.

14 BREATH OF THE BROKEN

Corin tilted his head toward the shattered ceiling of the ruins, his dark braid swinging against his blood-streaked tunic. His face was grim, eyes shadowed under the grime caking his brow. "We need to get out of these ruins before nightfall. This place feels... wrong. Even without the dragon." His voice was tight, rasping from pain, his hand clutching his side where the wraiths had torn him open, blood seeping dark through the hasty bandages.

He wasn't wrong. The air hung thick, sour with char and the dragon's lingering rot, sulfur, and burnt moss clotting my lungs. Crumbled stone arches loomed like broken ribs overhead, their edges glowing red where emerald flames had bitten deep. Shadows clung too long in the corners, twitching when I blinked, like the ruins were holding their breath, waiting for us to slip. My chest ached where claws had raked me, venom burns throbbing under torn fabric, a dull fire pulsing with every heartbeat.

I stood, slinging my rifle over my shoulder, the strap digging into my neck where sweat and ash had caked into a gritty paste. "Alright, let's move. Mithis, you and I take point. Daven, lean on Corin if you need to."

Daven snorted, a dry rasp that turned into a wince as he shifted his weight, his bow dangling loose in one hand. "We're all one wrong step from being dragon chow anyway. I'll manage." His leg trembled under him, ribs cracked from the dragon's wing swipe, his face pale under a smear of dirt and sweat.

Mithis nodded, her axe slung over her back, the purple runes etched into its blade flickering in the dim light. She moved stiffly, favoring her left side where the dragon's claw had gouged her, blood crusting dark along her torn olive jacket. Her wolf-pelt cape hung in tatters, charred black at the edges, swaying as she straightened. "Let's go," she said, voice low and rough, crimson eyes scanning the treeline beyond the ruins.

We limped out into the forest, the oppressive silence slamming down like a wet blanket, broken only by our ragged breaths and the crunch of brittle leaves underfoot. Towering trees stretched above, their gnarled branches weaving a canopy so thick it choked out the last smears of evening light, bruising the sky gray. Every shadow felt alive, slithering at the edges of my vision, and every rustle jerked my hands tighter on the rifle, cold steel biting my split knuckles, grounding the shake I wouldn't admit to.

"We can't make it back to Kalden tonight," I said after a while, voice scraping past the dust in my throat, breaking the uneasy quiet. Sara's scream looped in my head, pushing me north, but my legs were lead, each step a grind through pain and exhaustion. "We need somewhere safe to crash."

Mithis nodded, her axe haft creaking as she adjusted it, her green skin stark against the fading glow of her runes. "Agreed. These woods at night are a death wish." Her tone was clipped, practical, but her eyes darted, hunting the dark like a predator cornered.

Corin winced, shifting his pack with a grunt, his twin swords clinking at his hips. "I hate to say it, but I'm holding it together by a thread. One wrong step, and I'm done." Blood stained his fingers where he pressed his ribs, his face pale under the grime, eyes hard despite the strain.

Daven forced a laugh, strained and thin, leaning against a tree to steady his limp. "We're all one step from being a snack. Let's find cover before something else smells the blood." His bowstring twanged as he flexed it, testing his grip, sweat cutting tracks through the ash on his face.

I scanned the forest, eyes catching on a rocky outcrop a hundred yards off, jagged stone jutting from the earth, half-swallowed by twisted roots and glowing vines pulsing green under Ashvalen's touch. "There," I said, pointing with the rifle barrel. "Not a damn fortress, but it'll shield us for the night."

We moved slowly, every step a test of grit. Corin's boots scuffing the dirt, Daven's limp dragging us, Mithis's cape snagging on thorns that gleamed wet in the dimness. My chest burned where the dragon's claw had torn me, blood mixing with venom burns in a sticky mess under my shredded t shirt. When we hit the outcrop, I dropped my pack with a thud that echoed too loud, the rifle clanking against stone as I cleared debris, broken twigs, and moss that smelled of rot and damp earth.

"Corin, help me with a fire," I said, digging out the flint striker from my pack, its steel loop scratched and cold in my hand, kindling spilling from a ripped pouch.

He glanced at the dark treeline, nervous, his braid swaying as he shifted. "You sure that's smart? Light's a beacon out here." His voice trembled a hair, blades glinting at his hips.

"We need warmth and light," I shot back, striking the flint, sparks spitting into the kindling with a crackle. "Anything hunting us'll find us, fire or not. At least this way, we see the bastard coming." My tone was rough, edged with exhaustion, Sara's voice whispering under the words, "keep going, don't stop."

He nodded, reluctant, and gathered dry, splintered branches, snapping as he stacked them. Minutes later, a small flame flickered alive, casting jagged shadows across the rocky shelter, the smell of smoke cutting through the forest's sour tang. Mithis finally sat, leaning heavily against the stone. A bruise bloomed dark purple across her side, spreading under her green skin like ink, blood crusting a gash above her eye.

"Dragon did a number on us," she muttered, swigging from the canteen, water sloshing cold against the dented metal.

"You need to clean that," I said, pointing at the gash, grabbing a rag from my pack, coarse, stained with sweat and herbs, and a half-empty water bottle, its plastic scratched and cloudy.

She rolled her crimson eyes but didn't fight me, tilting her head as I stepped close. "Fine. Don't make fuss, though." Her voice was firm, but she held still, breath fogging in the chill.

"Wouldn't dream of it," I said, smirking despite the ache in my chest, dabbing the wound. Blood washed away in thin streaks, her green skin warm under the rag, runes on her arm pulsing purple as I worked.

Daven reclined against a tree, stretching his leg out, the bow resting across his lap. "We're lucky to be breathing," he said, quieter now, voice strained from the ribs he kept clutching. "That dragon could've torched us without breaking a sweat."

"Luck didn't save us," Mithis replied, tone cutting like her axe, sure and precise. "We fought like hell." She flexed her gloved hand, ichor still staining the leather black from the dragon's hide.

"And you drove that spear through its throat," Corin added, easing down near the fire, his swords propped beside him. Flames danced in his hard eyes, easing the pain etched deep in his jaw.

Mithis shrugged, her expression thawing a fraction, crimson eyes glinting in the firelight. "We all pulled our weight. Without that, we'd be ash." Her cape bunched against the stone, wolf pelt matted with dirt and blood, a warrior's trophy turned rag.

I nodded, settling beside the fire, the heat stinging my venom burns but easing the chill in my bones. "Let's just survive the night. One step at a time." My voice rasped, Sara's scream hovering, the witch's curse clawing at my gut, "Every life you touch will rot." I shoved it down, focusing on the crackle of the flames.

The night dragged on, restless, and none of us slept deeply. The forest buzzed alive with unseen threats, every rustle or snap spiking my hand to the rifle, cold steel slick with sweat. A low growl rolled through the trees, distant but close enough to kick my pulse, the fire spitting embers into the dark. Mithis's eyes snapped open, axe in her grip, before I could blink, her runes flaring purple. "Something's out there," she whispered, voice steel, crouching low.

Then it came a shadow loomed beyond the firelight, ten feet of nightmare stitched from wood and bone, antlers branching wide, rattling with fragments that clacked like dry twigs. Glowing green eyes pierced the gloom, fierce with hunger that turned my stomach cold, its growl rumbling the dirt under my boots. The Wendigo. My breath hitched, rifle snapping up, barrel trembling as I aimed center mass, the weight grounding me against the dread, anchoring my knees.

"Shit," I hissed, finger itching on the trigger. "Not now."

Mithis stood, axe raised, runes blazing brighter, her cape swaying as she squared off. "Stay back," she barked, voice steady but tight, crimson eyes locked on those green orbs. "It's testing us."

The Wendigo stepped closer, claws dragging gouges in the earth, a low snarl vibrating my ribs ancient, pissed, promising ruin. "Prey," it growled, voice thick like sap from a wound, shaking the outcrop's stone. My gut twisted, Sara's scream drowning under it, Mom's blood staining my hands red in memory. I fired a crisp burst, three shots cracking the silence, bullets slamming its chest, flattening useless against gnarled hide, dropping like spent coins.

It didn't flinch, just tilted its head, antlers scraping a branch overhead with a shrill whine. Mithis lunged, axe swinging a purple arc, blade biting shallow into its leg, ichor spraying black, steaming, but it swatted her back with a claw, fast as a whip. She hit the rock hard, a grunt punching out, axe clattering as the fire flared wild from the impact.

"Move!" I shouted, diving for her, grabbing her arm, green skin slick with sweat and ichor, hauling her up as the Wendigo loomed, claws slashing air where we'd been. Daven notched an arrow, glowing with a charm, loosing it into its shoulder, ichor oozing, but it snarled louder, unfazed. Corin staggered up, blades flashing, slashing its claw a spark, a nick, nothing more before it kicked him back, tumbling into the dirt with a cry.

"Fall back!" I yelled, dragging Mithis behind the outcrop, rifle barking blind to keep it at bay, bullets sparking off bone. It roared, a sound that sank into my bones, slowing every step, but then it stopped, eyes narrowing, turning slow, melting into the dark like smoke, its growl fading to a whisper on the wind.

We slumped against the stone, chests heaving, firelight flickering weakly against the night. "It's gone," Mithis rasped, wiping blood from her lip, axe trembling in her grip, runes dimming. "For now."

"Not gone," I muttered, rifle heavy, Sara's voice clear in my skull. "Just toying with us." My hands shook, venom burns searing under fresh cuts, the curse a burr sinking deeper.

Dawn broke pale, filtering through the canopy, a reprieve I didn't trust. We packed fast too damn uneasy to linger boots scuffing dirt, the Wendigo's growl echoing in my head. The forest shifted in daylight, less oppressive but no less warped, trees twisted into deliberate patterns, branches glistening black and wet, an energy thrumming like a heartbeat refusing to quit. The green glow from the dragon's reign was gone, but the air buzzed, alive with something ancient, pissed we'd dared to breathe here.

By midday, the strain hit hard. Daven's limp worsened, his leg dragging with every step, his bow clutched like a lifeline. Corin grimaced, hand clutching his ribs, blood soaking through his bandages anew, his face pale as ash. Mithis stayed quiet, but her grip on her axe whitened, her green skin paler under the bruises, exhaustion carving lines around her crimson eyes.

"Stop here," I said, hitting a small clearing black dirt ringed by gnarled trunks, moss breathing underfoot. "We rest here before we push on."

Corin dropped onto a fallen log with a groan, swords clanking. "Not arguing."

Daven eased against a tree, leg trembling, bow resting across his lap. "Any chance this cursed forest has food?" His voice was thin, strained, sweat beading on his brow.

I rummaged my pack, pulling out ration bars, scratched wrappers, stale as hell, tossing one to him. "Not fresh, but it'll keep us going." I lobbed another to Corin, who caught it, turning it over like I'd handed him a damn relic.

"What... is this?" he asked, frowning, his hard eyes narrowing at the bar like it might bite back.

I stared, blank for a beat, then it clicked medieval folks, no clue about MREs. "It's food," I said, unwrapping mine, the smell of burnt oats hitting me. "Compact. Built to last."

Corin wrinkled his nose, sniffing it like it was poison. "This is food? Looks like horse fodder."

"It's not that bad," I said, half-lying, biting into mine, gritty, dry, sticking to my teeth.

"It smells like burnt bread," he muttered, holding it like a live grenade.

Daven tore into his, shrugging. "Beats starving. Chew fast, don't think about it." Crumbs stuck to his stubble, his smirk real.

Corin eyed him suspiciously. "You're eating it like it's normal."

"Two years marching through war zones, you'll eat worse," he said, swallowing hard. "Trust me, this is gourmet."

He raised an eyebrow, taking a tentative bite, his face twisting instantly, like he'd sucked a lemon. "Gourmet? Daven, what in the Nine Hells have you been eating?"

I chuckled, rough and low, the sound scraping my throat. "It grows on you."

"No," he said, waving the bar like a flag. "It's growing in me, and it's gonna kill me."

Mithis broke her silence, sharpening her axe with slow, deliberate strokes across a whetstone, the rasp cutting the quiet. "Complaining won't make it taste better." Her voice was distant, crimson eyes fixed on the blade, runes glinting purple.

"Won't make it worse, either," Corin shot back, forcing another bite, grimacing through it.

I sat beside Mithis, leaning back against the log, the wood rough and damp through my jacket. "Think of it as fuel. Not supposed to be good, just keeps us alive 'til we hit real food."

"Then let's move faster," Corin said, wiping crumbs off his lips, his tone thick with longing. "I'd kill for a stew right now."

Daven snorted, chewing slowly. "I'd take stale bread and cheese."

Mithis glanced at the treeline, axe pausing mid-stroke, her grip tightening 'til the haft creaked. "Survive first. The forest isn't safe, even now." Her voice hardened, crimson eyes darting, the Wendigo's growl a ghost in her stare.

I nodded, unease coiling back into my chest, cold and tight. "Rest a bit, but stay alert. Corin, you're on first watch. Daven, you're next."

"What about you?" Corin asked, bar dangling in his hand.

"Last shift," I said, pulling the cracked map from my pack, Aldred's scribbled lines, edges fraying. "Need to figure out the best route."

Daven gave a humorless laugh, wincing as he shifted. "Best route? Only good ones are the ones that get us out alive."

No one argued. The forest groaned around us, wind stirring branches like a sigh of disapproval, warped trunks leaning closer, their bark glistening wet and black. Mithis was right, this place didn't want us. I just hoped it wouldn't act on it yet.

We left the clearing, the forest pressing in tighter, gnarled trees bending like they'd grab us, silence broken by the crunch of leaves under our boots. My rifle stayed ready, barrel cold against my chest, eyes scanning for movement, the Wendigo's eyes burned into my skull. Mithis walked beside me, axe on her shoulder, crimson eyes darting steadily, grounded, a rock in this mad world.

"We're close," she said after a stretch, voice a whisper, breath fogging.

I nodded, spotting torchlight flickering through the trees, warm, real. The warped trunks thinned, giving way to natural ones, the oppressive weight lifting a hair, though the air still thrummed with old magic, pissed and restless. Kalden's gates loomed ahead, wooden beams scarred and weathered, less a barrier than a plea.

Guards watched us limp in, halberds twitching in their grips, faces tense under dented helms 'til recognition hit. "You survived," one said, more shocked than glad, voice cracking high.

"Just," I replied, rifle heavy, chest aching where blood crusted my shirt. "Forest won't be your problem much longer." Sara's scream pushed me, clear and piercing, north, still calling.

15 SHADOWS OF THE HOLLOW

The gates of Kalden creaked shut behind us with a heavy thud, wood groaning like it was as tired as we were. Torchlight flickered across the dirt street, casting long, jagged shadows that danced over the guards' pale faces, their hollowed-out eyes wide like they'd seen ghosts stroll in instead of us. One gripped his halberd so tight the haft shivered, his breath fogging quick in the chill like he couldn't believe we'd crawled out of that forest alive.

The air stank of smoke and damp straw, a tang of rot drifting from the treeline beyond the wall, reminding me that safe was a damn lie here. My boots scuffed the packed earth, each step grinding pain up my legs, venom burns searing under my torn jacket where dragon claws had raked me raw. The rifle hung cold and heavy against my chest, a scratched-up anchor keeping me upright when all I wanted was to collapse.

Mithis limped beside me, her axe slung over her shoulder, runes glowing purple in the dimness like dying embers. Her green skin looked paler under the bruises blooming across her jaw, blood crusting a fresh cut above her eye where the Wendigo's swipe had caught her last night. Her wolf-pelt cape dragged, charred and matted with ichor, a shredded relic of every fight we'd survived.

She caught my glance, crimson eyes glinting through the exhaustion, and gave a small nod like she knew we weren't done bleeding yet. Daven trailed a step behind, his bow clutched loose in one hand, the other pressed to his cracked ribs, face tight with every hobbled step. Corin brought up the rear, his dark braid swinging stiff with dried blood, twin swords clanking at his hips as he favored his uninjured side, a wet stain spreading dark across his bandages.

"Elder's waiting," the guard muttered, jerking his head toward the hall. His voice was thin, frayed, like he'd been shouting into the dark too long. "Heard the dragon's roar from here. Thought it'd be the end of us all." He didn't look at me, just stared at the ground, halberd tip scraping a rut in the dirt.

"Tell him we're coming," I said, rougher than I meant, my throat raw from smoke and shouting. "And get someone to patch us up. We're no good to him dead." Sara's scream flickered in my skull, piercing and desperate, pushing me north even as my body begged to stop. The guard nodded fast, scampering off like a kicked dog, his chainmail rattling in the quiet.

The village was a ghost town at dusk, timber homes hunched silent, shutters cracked or boarded, no kids running, no voices. Just the wind rattling thatch and the distant clank of a hammer from somewhere deep in the square, a stubborn pulse against the stillness. My chest tightened, the witch's curse clawing deeper, "every life you touch will rot," and I wondered if dragging Kalden into this fight was just another grave I'd dig. I shoved it down, focusing on the ache in my hands, the cold steel of the rifle. Couldn't afford doubt, not with Sara out there, Lily's laugh an echo behind her scream.

We hit the hall, door swinging wide before I could knock, the smoky warmth slamming into me like a wall of tallow and old wood, thick enough to choke on. Aldred stood by the table, robe dragging the planks, his white beard tangled like he'd been tugging at it all night. His eyes snapped to us, narrowing at the blood and ash streaking our gear, then easing a hair as they landed on the white ash spear Mithis carried, its runes glowing silver, a lifeline forged from the Glade's frost-white branch.

The warrior advisor loomed at his left, scarred face grim under a graying beard, halberd propped nearby, its blade notched deep from fights I didn't want to imagine. The mage flanked his right, robes shimmering with arcane lines, bony hands twitching like he felt the forest's pulse through the floor.

"You're alive," Aldred said, voice rolling deep, relief cracking through the weight. "We heard the dragon, felt it, even here. The ground shook like the world was splitting." His hands clenched on the table, knuckles whitening, maps and runes glowing under his grip.

"Alive," I rasped, stepping in, boots scuffing the worn planks. "Killed the bastard, but it wasn't the end. Wendigo hit us last night, tested us, then backed off. Something's stirring deeper in that forest, and it's pissed we took its pet dragon out." My rifle thudded against my thigh, venom burns throbbing hot under my sleeve, Sara's scream looping louder now, north, always north.

Aldred's face darkened, lines carving deeper around his mouth, eyes flicking to the spear. "A dragon and the Wendigo both. This is worse than I thought." He leaned forward, beard brushing the table, voice dropping low. "The corruption's root is still out there, isn't it?"

"Yeah," Mithis said, stepping up beside me, her axe clanking as she shifted it, runes flaring a purple glow. "The dragon was guarding something, a crystal in the ruins, pulsing green, spitting wraiths. We smashed it, but the forest didn't settle. It's alive, Elder, and it's not done with us." Her tone was steel, crimson eyes steady despite the blood crusting her side, cape swaying damp with the day's muck.

The mage nodded slowly, fingers tracing his robe's glowing lines, voice reedy but sure. "That crystal was a conduit channeling power, feeding the corruption. Breaking it weakened the source, but didn't kill it. Something stronger lies beneath, driving the Wendigo, waking these beasts from your myths." His eyes glinted, locking on me like he saw the curse etched in my bones.

"Great," I muttered, rubbing my jaw, stubble rough under my palm, grime smearing my fingers. "So we've got a bigger bastard to bury. Where's it hiding?" My voice scraped, edged with exhaustion and a stubbornness I couldn't shake, Sara's voice, Lily's laugh, Mom's blood all shoving me forward.

Aldred pointed to the map, a yellowed parchment spread across the table, ink smudged from sweaty hands. His scarred finger tapped a spot deep in the forest, north of the ruins, a jagged circle marked with runes that pulsed red, like blood under skin. "Here. The Hollow, a pit older than Kalden, older than any tale we tell. Hunters avoid it; even the trees twist away. If the corruption has a heart, it's there." His voice sank, heavy with dread, eyes meeting mine, daring me to flinch.

"The Hollow," Daven echoed, limping in behind us, his bow clattering as he leaned on the wall, breath hitching from his cracked ribs. "Heard stories as a kid, whispers saying it swallows men whole, spits back shadows instead. Thought it was just scare-the-brats bullshit." His tone was dry, but his eyes flickered nervously, sweat cutting tracks through the ash on his face.

"It's real," Corin said, easing onto a bench with a grunt, his swords clanking as he sat, blood soaking his side fresh through the bandages. "Lost a cousin to that place years back. Went in chasing a deer, never came out. The next night, we heard his voice calling from the trees, wrong, twisted." His voice trembled, hard eyes glinting wet in the torchlight, pain and memory mixing raw.

Mithis frowned, gripping the spear tightly, its white ash haft glowing fiercely under her gloved hand, silvery runes shimmering like ice caught in moonlight. "Then that's where we go," she said, voice firm, practical, cutting through the gloom. "We hit the Hollow, kill whatever's festering there, Wendigo, curse, all of it." Her crimson eyes flicked to me, steady, a rock I leaned on without thinking.

I nodded, throat tight, rifle cold against my chest. "No choice. My sister's out there in Michigan, north of this hellhole. Every day we waste, she's closer to... " I stopped, words choking off, Sara's scream clear in my ears, Lily's giggle fading under it. The curse gnawed, "Every hope will crumble," but I shoved it down, focusing on the map, the red circle pulsing like a wound.

Aldred studied us, eyes piercing through the smoky haze, weighing our battered frames, blood, ash, and exhaustion carved deep. "You're in no shape to march now," he said, voice rolling stern, a father's command wrapped in gravel. "Rest here tonight. Our healer will patch you up, and the smith is finishing the spear, reinforcing it with what's left of the ash. Tomorrow, you head for the Hollow with my hunters." His hand slammed the table, a thud echoing off the timber walls, finality ringing clear.

"Tomorrow's too late," I snapped, fiercer than I meant, stepping forward, boots thudding the planks. "Sara's out there now, every hour, that thing gets stronger, and I'm not." My voice cracked, fists clenching, venom burns searing under my skin, Sara's scream drowning the room.

Mithis clapped my shoulder, firm and warm through my torn jacket, cutting my spiral short. "He's right, Jake," she said, low and steady, crimson eyes locking mine. "We're half-dead. Push now, and we're no good to her or anyone. One night. Then we continue with the journey." Her grip tightened, a lifeline I grabbed tight, her resolve bleeding into me, cooling the panic in my chest.

I exhaled hard, breath fogging in the warm air, nodding slow. "Fine. One night." My voice rasped, rough but steadying, rifle heavy in my hands, Sara's voice still there, but quieter, waiting.

Aldred waved the guard over, his chainmail clinking as he stepped in. "Take them to the inn. Get the healer there, now." His tone brooked no argument, eyes flicking to the spear, then back to me, daring me to argue again.

The inn wasn't far, a squat timber box like the rest, its sign creaking above the door, "INN" chipped and faded under torchlight. The barkeep didn't scoff this time, just tossed us a key fast, his yellow teeth flashing nervously in a grin that didn't reach his eyes. The room was the same, sagging bed, peeling walls, candle spitting weak light on the sill, but it felt tighter now, the air thick with the day's blood and ash. I dropped my pack with a thud, rifle leaning against the wall, its barrel scratched and cold, and sank onto the bed, springs groaning under my weight. Mithis set her axe within reach, propping it against the chair, and collapsed into it by the window, crimson eyes scanning the dark street, cobblestones glinting wet under torchlight, shadows twitching beyond.

"You think the Hollow's the end of this?" she asked, voice rough, breaking the quiet, her gloved hand resting on the spear, its white ash haft glowing, runes pulsing like a heartbeat.

I rubbed my face, palms grinding into my eyes, venom burns stinging under the grime. "Maybe. Or maybe it's just another damn layer. Dragon's dead, but the Wendigo's still out there, and whatever's pulling the strings... " I stopped, Sara's scream cutting through, Mom's blood staining my hands red in memory. "I just want Sara and Lily safe. After that, I don't care what's left." My voice scraped, raw and tired, the curse a burr sinking deeper.

She nodded, crimson eyes easing a fraction, the glow from the spear catching the steel in her gaze. "We'll get them. Hollow first, then north. Together." Her tone was firm, a vow wrapped in gravel, her cape bunched damp against the chair, wolf pelt matted with ichor, a warrior's weight.

A knock hit the door, quick. My hand snapped to the rifle, cold steel under my fingers, heart kicking my ribs. "Who is it?" I called, voice steady, rough, eyes flicking to Mithis, axe already in her grip, runes flaring purple.

"The villages Healer," came the reply, clear but muffled through the wood, a woman's voice. "Elder sent me."

I eased the door open, rifle dipping but ready. A woman stepped in, short, gray hair tied back tight, hands clutching a leather satchel stained dark with use. Her eyes flicked over us, blood, bruises, ash steady under a creased brow.

"You've been through hell," she said, voice dry, setting the satchel on the bed with a clink. "Sit. Let me work."

She didn't wait for us to argue, pulling out bandages, a clay jar of something green and pungent, and a needle that gleamed in the candlelight. I sat first, peeling off my jacket, venom burns red and raw under shredded fabric, blood crusting where claws had torn me. She dabbed the green stuff on, a sting cutting through the ache, and I hissed, teeth grinding.

"Stings less than dying," she muttered, threading the needle fast, stitching a gash on my arm with quick, practiced jabs, pain flaring hot, then dulling under her hands. She moved to Mithis next, cleaning the cut above her eye, then wrapping her ribs where the dragon's claw had gouged deep, blood seeping dark through the bandages, her green skin paling under the strain.

Daven and Corin got the same, her hands steady, no fuss, patching cracked ribs and torn flesh like she'd done it a thousand times. When she finished, she stood, wiping her hands on a rag, eyes glinting hard in the dimness. "Rest. You'll need it for whatever's coming." She didn't linger, satchel clanking as she slipped out, door thudding shut behind her.

Silence fell, heavy, my chest easing a hair under the bandages, but the weight of tomorrow pressing down. Mithis leaned back, spear glowing in her lap, crimson eyes distant. "She's right," she said, voice low, rough. "Tomorrow's the Hollow. We end it, or it ends us."

I nodded, lying back on the bed, springs creaking, rifle cold beside me. "Yeah. Together." My voice rasped, Sara's scream quieter now, a flicker I could fight; hope, small, stubborn, alive in the dark.

16 BONES OF THE BEAST

Morning crashed like a fist, pale dawn light clawing through the inn's splintered shutters, painting jagged streaks across walls where paint peeled in curling strips, yellowed by time and damp. My eyes snapped open, breath fogging in the biting chill, the bed's iron springs screeching as I hauled myself upright. The healer's work was a marvel, venom burns, once raw and searing, now dulled to a faint throb beneath crisp linen bandages, the deep gash on my forearm stitched tight with black thread, itching fiercely under scabbed skin. I flexed my hand, split knuckles cracking under tight scabs, the rifle beside me a cold, reassuring weight, its scratched stock worn smooth from years of grip. Damn near 100%, or as close as this cursed, rotting land would let me get. Sara's scream echoed sharply in my skull, a desperate cry from the north, pulling me like a lodestone, while Mom's blood lingered as a dark, indelible stain I couldn't scrub out. The witch's curse, her voice hissing "every life you touch will rot," sank claws into my chest, but I shoved it down, focusing on the familiar heft of my gear: the rifle's steel, the pack's straps, the sword at my belt.

Mithis was already up, her silhouette sharp in the flickering torchlight, buckling her war axe across her broad back. Its broad blade, etched with runes that pulsed a deep violet, seemed to hum with caged magic, the steel glinting coldly in the dimness. Her green skin, tough as boiled leather, gleamed faintly, the bruises from yesterday's fight faded to mere shadows under her jaw and cheekbones. A jagged cut above her left eye had scabbed neatly, a thin line of black against her emerald hide. The healer's bandages wrapped her ribs snugly, no trace of the blood that had soaked her yesterday, just a subtle bulge beneath her patched olive jacket, its frayed cuffs stained with old sweat. Her wolf-pelt cape, freshly scrubbed of ichor, hung heavy across her shoulders, the gray fur rippling as she moved steadily, deliberately, like she'd never taken a blow.

"You holding together?" she asked, crimson eyes flicking to me, their slit pupils narrowing slightly. Her voice was rough, warm, cutting through the quiet like a blade through fog.

"Good enough," I said, slinging my pack over one shoulder, the canvas straps digging into muscle that felt alive again, though sore. "How are you doing?" My boots cracked leather caked with dried mud thudded on the warped floorboards, the rifle snapping to my chest, its cold barrel a soldier's lifeline, scratched but unyielding.

She smirked, a flash of teeth, hefting her white ash spear. The weapon was a masterwork: two feet of frost-pale wood, its grain shimmering like frozen breath, carved with runes that glowed silver, faint as moonlight trapped in ice. The steel haft gleamed, its razor-thin tip honed to split bone. "Better than you, look," she said, her tone all steel and fire, crimson eyes glinting with a fierce, unyielding spark. "Ready to gut whatever's waiting in that Hollow." Her cape rustled as she squared her shoulders, the fur catching a stray beam of dawn light.

Daven and Corin shuffled in from the shadowed hall, their gear clanking softly, both patched up nearly as well as us by the healer's deft hands. Daven's limp was gone, his wiry frame steady as he adjusted the bow slung across his back, its curved limbs polished smooth, strung tight with sinew. His cropped hair, dusted with gray, framed eyes calm as river stones, unyielding under pressure. "Ribs don't even creak," he said, voice low and even, testing his draw. The bowstring twanged sharply, a low hum that set the glowing arrows in his quiver, each fletched with raven feathers and tipped with charmed steel rattling softly. Corin stood taller, his dark braid pulled taut, twin swords gleaming at his hips, their hilts wrapped in worn leather. Bloodstains were gone from his gray tunic, fresh bandages hidden beneath patched leather armor that creaked faintly as he moved. He rolled his shoulders, the blades catching torchlight in a brief, cold flash, his hard eyes steady despite the pain he'd carried yesterday. "Good as new," he said, voice clipped, a grin tugging one corner of his mouth, daring the world to hit him again.

The barkeep hovered by the door, his gaunt frame tense, yellowed teeth flashing in a nervous grimace as he thrust a coarse burlap sack toward us. It bulged with provisions: dense rye bread, hard cheese wrapped in wax, and water skins that clinked with the weight of full bladders. "Elder's orders," he muttered, his watery eyes darting to Mithis's spear, then skittering away as if we were specters he feared would linger. I nodded, slinging the sack alongside my pack, its weight a grounding promise of fuel for the long night ahead.

Aldred met us in the low-ceilinged hall, his heavy robe dragging across the splintered planks, eyes glinting like polished flint under the smoky haze of wall-mounted torches. Their light carved deep lines into his weathered face, betraying the strain of days without rest. A broad-shouldered and scarred warrior stood to his left, his halberd's notched blade resting on the floor, its shaft etched with faintly glowing runes. To his right, a mage in shimmering robes clutched a gnarled staff, its tip pulsing faintly blue. Maps lay strewn across a rough-hewn table, their edges curling, marked with ink and blood in chaotic swirls of strategy.

"Smith's done his work," Aldred said, his voice rolling deep, resonant, nodding to Mithis's spear. The weapon had been refined overnight, its white ash haft now reinforced with polished steel bands, the runes carved deeper, pulsing silver like a heartbeat caught in crystal. "It'll cut the Wendigo where mortal steel fails. The Hollow's your target, end it tonight, or it ends us all." His fist slammed the table, wood creaking under the blow, the finality of his words ringing like a war drum.

"Tonight?" I asked, voice rough, stepping forward, the rifle's cold stock pressed against my chest, Sara's scream spiking loud in my ears, sharp as a blade.

"We're on our last legs," the mage cut in, his voice reedy but firm, robes catching the torchlight in ripples of silver thread. "Wraiths struck the outskirts last night, shadows clawing at the gates, tearing planks to splinters. The Hollow knows you're coming." His bony hands twitched, eyes piercing mine, as if he could see the witch's curse etched into my bones, a dark lattice of doom.

Mithis tightened her grip on the spear, the runes flaring silver for a heartbeat, casting jagged shadows across her green face. "Then we hit it hard, straight through, no detours." Her tone was unyielding, crimson eyes locked on Aldred, her cape swaying, damp with the morning's clinging mist.

"Take the north trail," the warrior said, his voice low and steady, a scarred finger tracing a jagged line on the map, a path twisting past crumbling stone ruins, plunging deep into the warped forest where trees grew wrong. "Fastest route. Watch the trees, they move, and they hunger for flesh." his halberd thudded against the floor, her dark eyes glinting with the weight of battles fought and barely won.

I nodded, my gut coiling tight, the rifle's weight steady in my hands. "Let's move." Sara's voice surged north, relentless, the curse sinking deeper like thorns, but Mithis's solid presence at my side kept it caged, for now.

The forest swallowed us the moment we passed Kalden's gates, their iron hinges creaking shut, the town's torchlight fading to a flicker behind gnarled, glistening trunks. The north trail was a scar of black dirt, slick with frost, roots twisting underfoot like petrified serpents. Trees loomed close, their bark wet and unnaturally smooth, branches swaying without wind, as if breathing. The air buzzed, thick with ancient magic, Ashvalen's fingerprints pulsing green in the vines that choked every trunk, their leaves glistening with a sickly sheen. My boots crunched brittle leaves, each step sending a faint echo, the rifle up and steady, adrenaline scouring the last aches from my bones. Mithis took point, her spear's runes glowing faintly, axe slung ready across her back, crimson eyes scanning the shadows, her cape snagging on thorns that gleamed like wet obsidian. Daven flanked left, bow notched, a glowing arrow casting a pale halo, his steps silent, predator-quiet on the uneven earth. Corin held right, twin blades drawn, their steel glinting coldly, his braid swaying as he moved, eyes hard as chipped flint.

"Keep tight," I said, voice low, my breath fogging in the chill, the rifle's barrel cold against my cheek, eyes flicking for movement in the undergrowth. "Wendigo's waiting it won't roll out a damn welcome mat."

"Wraiths first," Mithis muttered, the spear's haft creaking in her iron grip, its runes pulsing silver. "Forest's too quiet means they're close." Her tone was clipped, crimson eyes narrowing, her cape catching another thorn that tore a faint rip in the fur.

She was right. The silence pressed like a weight on my chest, no birds, no wind, just the low hum of warped trees, their trunks leaning inward as if to clutch us. Then a rattle broke the stillness, dry bones clacking through the gloom, sharp and deliberate. Shadows twitched ahead, green eyes igniting in the dark, malevolent and unblinking. Wraiths spilled from the treeline, tall, emaciated, their gray flesh peeling in strips, claws scraping the earth with a sound like nails on slate. Twelve, maybe fifteen, moving fast, their jaws clicking with silent, ravenous hunger, eyeless sockets locked on us.

"Move!" I barked, rifle roaring three shots clean headshots, brains splattering black against warped bark, the stench of rot bursting free. Two dropped, their bodies crumbling to dust, kicking up clouds that stung my eyes, but the rest surged forward, relentless, claws gleaming wet. Mithis lunged, her spear a silver arc, thrusting through a wraith's chest, runes flaring bright as day, ichor spraying hot and steaming, the creature shrieking a sound like tearing metal before dissolving into acrid smoke. Daven loosed an arrow, its glowing charm streaking like a comet, striking true, another wraith collapsing into a curl of ash that drifted on the damp air. Corin spun into the fray, blades flashing in tight, precise arcs, severing two heads with wet crunches, his boots skidding on moss as he dodged a claw swipe that raked the air, leaving a faint hum of disturbed magic.

We fought in a brutal rhythm, gunfire cracking, steel singing, thinning the pack with grim efficiency. My magazine emptied, brass casings clinking at my feet, glinting dully in the faint light. I switched to my Glock, the pistol's grip warm from my hand, popping tight shots, each one dropping a wraith with a wet crunch of shattered bone. The last fell, its claws twitching once before stilling, and silence slammed back, oppressive, the air thick with the reek of gunsmoke and steaming corpses, flies already buzzing in the damp heat. My chest heaved, lungs burning, the pistol hot but steady, my pulse a hammer in my ears.

"Scouts," Mithis said, wiping ichor from her spear with a flick, the runes dimming to a soft pulse, her voice steady despite the fight, her cape swaying as she scanned the dark. "Hollow's close, that was just the welcome party."

"Great," Daven rasped, notching another arrow, his bow trembling faintly, his eyes glinting with a mix of adrenaline and strain, breath hitching fast. "Love a warm-up."

Corin sheathed his blades, wiping sweat from his brow with a sleeve streaked with wraith grime, his tunic splattered with dark stains, eyes clear but shadowed with fatigue. "Let's keep moving. Night's not waiting."

The trail twisted sharper, the trees growing denser, their roots clawing the dirt like skeletal hands, glistening with a slick, unnatural dew. The air turned colder, heavier, stinging my nose with sulfur and the sour tang of rot. The Hollow loomed ahead, a yawning pit carved into the earth, its edges jagged stone slick with green slime that pulsed like veins beneath living skin. No bottom was visible, just a void of swirling shadows, alive with faint whispers. A low, guttural chant rolled up from the depths, wet and rhythmic, vibrating through my boots like a second pulse, setting my teeth on edge. My gut twisted, the rifle trembling in my grip, Sara's scream now a deafening wail, the north pulling hard, the curse clawing deeper, "every hope will crumble."

"Trap," I said, crouching behind a gnarled trunk, its bark rough and wet under my palm, the rifle trained on the pit's edge, my breath fogging fast. "No way it's this open."

Mithis nodded, her spear glowing brighter, runes flaring silver, casting stark shadows across her green face, highlighting the sharp angles of her jaw. "Something's down there, watching, waiting." Her voice was low, certain, her axe shifting in its sling, the cape blending with the shadows as she crouched beside me.

Daven peered through the gloom, his bow steady, the glowing arrow casting a faint halo around his gaunt face, his eyes narrowing. "No guards up here means it's worse below." His tone sank, the weight of his words pressing my chest.

Corin edged closer, his blades half-drawn, their steel glinting faintly, his eyes hard but flickering with unease. "That chanting it's a ritual, summoning something." His voice trembled just a hair, his grip on the sword hilts steadying him.

"Down we go," I said, standing slowly, rifle up, boots scuffing the damp earth, Sara's scream pushing me forward, relentless. "Cover me." My voice rasped, a soldier's edge cutting through the fear, Mithis at my side, spear ready, Daven and Corin fanning out to guard the flanks.

The descent was a nightmare, the stone steps slick with green slime, carved unevenly into the pit's spiraling edge, each one threatening to pitch me forward. My boots slipped, the rifle banging my hip, my free hand brushing the wall, coming away coated in a foul, sticky rot that stank of decay and copper. Mithis's runes lit the way, their silver glow cutting through the oppressive dark, illuminating bones littering the steps, small, splintered, some still glistening with marrow, crunching underfoot with a sickening snap. The air grew thicker, pressing my lungs with the reek of blood and mold, electric with old magic that raised the hairs on my arms. Carvings writhed on the walls, etched deep into the stone,e fanged skulls, clawed hands, eyes that seemed to shift and follow, silent warnings that pulsed in my bones like a heartbeat.

A clatter echoed up from below, sharp and rhythmic bones rattling against stone. Two skeletons shambled into view, their rusted chainmail clinking, swords notched but gleaming with a wet, unnatural sheen. Mithis struck first, her spear flashing silver, cleaving one's spine in a spray of dust and bone shards, the remains collapsing in a heap. I fired, the Glock barking twice, the second skeleton's skull shattering into fragments, its body crumpling with a hollow rattle. "Too easy," I hissed, reloading with steady hands, the click of the magazine loud in the tight space, adrenaline pumping hot through my veins.

"Patrol," Mithis muttered, her spear dripping with dark ichor, the runes dimming for a heartbeat, her cape blending into the shadows as she stepped over the bones. "More's coming, stay sharp."

The pit widened abruptly, the walls pulling back into a vast cavern, its ceiling lost in darkness. Tattered tapestries hung limp from jagged outcrops, their faded threads depicting horned figures tearing flesh, the images rotting into the damp air, fraying at the edges. The chanting swelled, a guttural chorus of throats choking on blood, the air pulsing with a weight that made my skin crawl, every hair standing on end. At the cavern's heart, a figure loomed ten feet of nightmare, the Wendigo, its body a grotesque fusion of gnarled wood and bone, twisted into a mockery of life. Antlers branched wide, jagged and pale, tipped with points that gleamed like bone. Its green eyes glowed with a malevolent hunger, claws dragging gouges in the stone floor, each scrape a low, grating snarl. Its growl rumbled through my ribs, ancient, pissed, alive with a dark magic that tasted of ash and despair.

"Prey," it snarled, its voice thick and viscous, like sap oozing from a festering wound, the antlers rattling a shrill clack that shook dust loose in gritty clouds, stinging my eyes and coating my tongue. My rifle snapped up, instinct overriding fear, firing three crisp shots, the recoil sharp against my shoulder. The bullets slammed into its gnarled hide, flattening uselessly against bark-like armor, dropping to the stone with faint clinks, no blood, no mark, just a low growl that vibrated my bones, promising death.

Mithis charged, her spear a blazing arc, the white ash glowing fiercely, runes searing silver like trapped lightning. She aimed high, thrusting into its shoulder with a wet crunch, ichor spraying black and steaming, splattering the cavern floor, hissing where it burned into the slime-slick stone. The Wendigo roared, a deep bellow that buzzed my teeth, its claws slashing in a blur of jagged hooks, swatting her back. She hit the wall with a sickening crack, stone splintering under her weight, the spear clattering free with a sharp ring, a raw grunt punched from her lungs as she crumpled, her cape tangling in a shredded heap beneath her green frame, blood trickling from a split lip.

I lunged, drawing the runed sword from the ruins, its gold glow flaring warm in my grip, the blade humming with a faint, living pulse. I slashed low, aiming for its leg, the steel biting shallow through gnarled wood, ichor oozing thick as tar, dripping to pool dark at my boots, the stench sharp and sour. The beast twisted, faster than its bulk should allow, antlers swinging wide, cracking my ribs with a dull thud that stole my breath. Pain flared hot, a live wire searing through my chest, my legs buckling. I hit the ground hard, the sword bouncing once, scraping stone, my lungs burning as I gasped, vision blurring red at the edges, the cavern spinning.

Daven's arrow streaked through the haze, its glowing charm cutting the dark, sinking an inch into the Wendigo's chest with a crack, splintering bark but barely grazing flesh. Ichor trickled, black and steaming, as he notched another, his bow trembling in his grip, his face pale with strain. The second arrow grazed an antler, the charm sparking bright before fading, clattering uselessly into the shadows. "Damn it!" he hissed, voice hoarse, ducking a claw swipe that raked the air, diving behind a jagged boulder as stone chips sprayed like shrapnel, pelting his back.

Corin darted in, his twin blades flashing tight arcs, their steel glinting cold, nicking the Wendigo's claws with showers of orange sparks. He moved like a storm, slashing a shallow gash across its forearm, ichor beading before it swung back, claws catching his shoulder. Steel scraped bone as he twisted clear, his boots skidding on moss-slick stone, a grunt escaping him as blood welled dark through his tunic, staining his braid where it swung wild. "Too tough!" he shouted, rolling low under another swipe, his blades raised to deflect a clang that echoed off the cavern walls, sharp and metallic.

"Throat!" Mithis yelled, scrambling to her feet, her spear back in hand, runes flaring bright as she shook off the hit, blood dripping from her nose, streaking her green skin red. She dodged a claw that slashed stone, sparks flying where it gouged deep, lunging again, the spear aimed under its antlers, the white ash slicing air, grazing its neck with a hiss of steaming ichor. The Wendigo reared, its roar shaking the earth, its tail whipping out, thick and spiked, slamming a tapestry free. The rotted fabric billowed down, tangling my legs in a musty heap, the stench of mold choking my throat. I cursed, slashing it away with the sword, the gold glow cutting threads like butter, staggering to my feet, ribs screaming, each breath a knife twisting in my side.

The Wendigo charged me, claws raised, antlers lowered like a battering ram, its green eyes blazing with primal fury. I dove left, stone scraping my knees raw through torn jeans, the sword swinging wild, clipping its flank with a dull thud, ichor spraying hot across my face, sour and thick, burning my lips. The beast pivoted, its tail lashing, catching my pack and ripping a strap clean off, MREs and a spare magazine spilling across the floor in a clatter of foil and metal. I rolled clear, snatching my rifle, firing blind, five shots barking, the bullets sparking off its chest, useless as pebbles against steel, buying seconds, not damage, the recoil jarring my bruised ribs.

Mithis leapt, her spear held high in both hands, runes pulsing silver, a war cry ripping from her throat, fierce, guttural, echoing off the cavern walls. She drove the spear deep under the antlers, the white ash piercing flesh with a wet crunch, sinking past scales into sinew, ichor gushing hot, steaming dark in the torchlight, splattering her boots. The Wendigo froze mid-roar, its sound choking off, claws slashing blindly, raking air, the ground quaking as it thrashed, its antlers snapping another tapestry loose, dust choking the air thicker, stinging my eyes. Mithis held firm, her boots braced on uneven stone, muscles straining under her torn jacket, blood dripping from her nose, her green hands slick with grime, pushing with every ounce of strength, the runes pulsing like a dying star.

"Pin it!" I shouted, staggering up, the sword thrusting beside her, its gold glow sinking into the Wendigo's chest, hitting bone with a dull thud that rocked my arms, ichor splashing my hands, slick and burning against my scabbed knuckles. Daven sprinted closer, his bow dropped, drawing a dagger from his belt, its blade glowing with village charms, plunging it into the beast's flank with a quick jab, ichor bubbling hot around the steel. Corin joined, his blades slashing its legs in a relentless flurry, steel biting shallow but persistent, ichor streaking his arms, mixing with his blood from reopened cuts across his shoulder and forearm. The Wendigo bucked hard, its claws slashing wildly, catching my leg in a quick, shallow slash through jeans, blood welling hot, stinging against old venom scars. I gritted my teeth, shoving the sword deeper, the gold light flaring bright, grinding past bone into something soft, a wet squelch echoing in the cavern, the vibration humming through my arms.

Mithis twisted the spear, the runes searing silver-hot, driving it up through the Wendigo's throat, ichor spraying wide, steaming where it hit stone, her cape smoldering from splashed heat. "Fall, you bastard!" she snarled, her voice raw, her green hands slick with blood and grime, pushing with everything she had, the runes pulsing wildly. I leaned in, the sword grinding deeper, my arms burning, ribs throbbing, together forcing the beast back, step by brutal step, its claws scrabbling stone, gouging ruts that kicked up dust and pebbles, pelting my shins.

Daven abandoned his bow, sprinting closer, his dagger flashing as he jammed it into the Wendigo's thigh, the glowing charms sizzling against its hide, ichor oozing thick and black. Corin slashed its legs again, his blades carving shallow grooves, steel screeching against wood-like flesh, his braid whipping as he ducked a wild claw swipe that grazed his back, tearing leather with a sharp rip. The Wendigo shuddered, its green eyes shrinking to slits, a low groan rattling its antlers, shaking the bones overhead one last time, a shrill clack that sent a chill down my spine.

It convulsed violently, its body seizing, claws curling inward like a dying spider, the acrid smoke curling thick and choking. Mithis yanked the spear free, ichor gushing wider, steaming in a dark, glistening pool that reflected the torchlight in sickly greens. She swung again, the white ash cracking its antlers, splintering bone with a sharp snap that echoed like a gunshot. I pulled the sword out, its gold glow dimming, slick with black gore, thrusting once more, straight through its chest, hitting what passed for a heart, a dull thud rocking my shoulders, the blade sinking deep into something vital. The Wendigo's massive frame buckled, its legs folding limp, antlers crashing against the stone with a boom that split the ground beneath, cracks spiderwebbing out, ichor pooling black and thick, smoke drifting thin from its slack jaws, the green eyes fading to dull, lifeless gray.

Silence slammed down, deafening, the cavern smoldering, the air thick with rot, char, and the sour tang of ichor, clinging to my throat like oil. My chest heaved, ribs screaming with each breath, blood dripping warm down my leg, soaking into my boot, the sword trembling in my grip, heavy with gore. Sara's scream faded under ragged breaths, but the curse clawed loudly, "Every life you touch will rot," a venomous whisper that twisted my gut. Mithis sank to one knee, her spear's haft thudding against the stone, its runes dimming to a faint pulse, blood streaking her face, dripping from her nose onto the floor, her cape a charred, tattered rag behind her. Daven slumped against the cavern wall, his dagger clattering free, his breath hitching fast, ichor streaking his face in dark, glistening smears, his hands shaking as he clutched his bow. Corin leaned on his swords, their blades propped in the dirt, blood soaking his shoulder, seeping through his torn tunic, his eyes hard but flickering with bone-deep weariness in the wavering torchlight.

"Is it Dead?" Daven rasped, his voice cracking, his bow shaking as he gripped it, ichor glistening wet on his cheeks, his breath shallow and uneven.

"Yes, it is Dead," Mithis said, her spear's haft thudding again, the runes barely glowing, her voice rough but triumphant, a smirk tugging her bloodied lips, her crimson eyes glinting with defiance.

"I need to keep moving," I whispered, to no one, my voice cracking, the rifle cold in my lap, the curse alive and gnawing "every life you touch." Sara's scream drowned all else, the north burning bright through the haze, pulling me onward, relentless.

17 FOREST REBORN

The Wendigo's corpse sprawled across the Hollow's cavern floor, a grotesque monument of ruin, ten feet of twisted wood and bone, its antlers splintered into jagged shards, ichor pooling black and viscous beneath slack, gaping jaws. The steaming liquid hissed faintly in the damp, chill air, curling tendrils of acrid vapor that stung my nose. My knees slammed into the cold stone, breath rasping hot and ragged, each inhale a knife twisting in my bruised ribs where the beast's antlers had struck, a dull, throbbing pain radiating through my chest. Blood trickled warm down my leg, seeping from a jagged claw slash that tore through my jeans, the wound pulsing hot against the old venom burns, now scabbed but aching under fresh bandages. The runed sword trembled in my grip, its gold glow fading to a faint shimmer, the blade slick with thick, black gore that dripped onto the floor, pooling with the ichor. My rifle clanked beside me, cold and scratched, its stock worn smooth from years of use, a soldier's lifeline now heavy with the weight of the fight. Sara's scream echoed north, her voice piercing my skull, "Jake, something's wrong," sharp and desperate, drowning out the witch's curse that clawed my gut: "Every life you touch will rot." No proof, no scrap of her, just that relentless cry pulling me like a frayed rope, hope and dread knotted tight in my chest.

Mithis leaned heavily on her white ash spear, its haft glowing faintly, the carved runes pulsing silver like a faltering heartbeat, casting jagged shadows across her green face. Blood streaked her skin, a dark crimson trail dripping from her nose, splattering onto the cracked stone below, mingling with the cavern's grime. Her olive jacket hung in tatters, its seams split, stained with sweat and ichor, the wolf-pelt cape a charred, matted rag clinging to her shoulders, singed fur clotted with dirt and the beast's foul blood. Yet her crimson eyes glinted with unyielding fire, triumph cutting through the exhaustion etched into her sharp features. "We need to move," she said, her voice rough as gravel, hauling herself upright, the spear's haft thudding against the stone. Her boots scuffed the slime-slick floor, kicking up faint clouds of dust as she squared her broad shoulders, her presence a rock in the chaos.

"Yeah," I rasped, shoving to my feet, pain flaring hot through my ribs and leg, but soldier's grit locked my spine straight. I snapped the rifle to my shoulder, its cold barrel steady despite the tremor in my hands, the familiar weight grounding me. "Back to Kalden. Then north." My chest tightened, her scream looping louder, a raw edge of hope twisting with dread, no tag or clue to grip, just instinct burning bright, a flame I couldn't let die.

Daven staggered over, his bow dangling loose in one hand, its polished curve flecked with ichor that streaked his gaunt face in dark, glistening smears. His breath hitched, cracked ribs straining under his patched leather vest, yet he'd held through the fight, wiry frame unyielding. He wiped his dagger clean on his sleeve, the blade's glowing charm faded to dull steel, its edge scratched but sharp, tucking it back into his belt with a low grunt. "Forest'll be lighter without that bastard," he said, his voice thin but steady, his slate-gray eyes glinting hard as he scanned the pit's shadows, searching for threats that no longer stirred. Sweat cut tracks through the grime on his cheeks, his cropped hair matted with dust, but a faint smirk tugged his lips, relief breaking through.

Corin sheathed his twin swords, their blades streaked with black gore, the steel glinting faintly under the cavern's flickering torchlight. Blood soaked his shoulder, welling dark through his gray tunic where the Wendigo's claws had reopened old cuts, the fabric torn and crusted with dried sweat and rot. He leaned against a broken pillar, its stone chipped and pitted, his dark braid swinging stiff with grime, his face pale but his flint-steady eyes unyielding despite the strain carving lines around his mouth. "Let's hope it stays dead," he muttered, pushing off the pillar, his boots crunching over splintered bone shards scattered across the floor, his tunic clinging damply to his frame. His voice carried a dry edge, but his posture, shoulders back, blades ready, dared the darkness to try again.

We climbed out of the pit, the stone steps slick with green slime that clung to my boots, each step sending a jolt of pain up my spine, my leg pulsing hot beneath torn jeans, the wound's edges raw and stinging. Mithis's runes lit the way, their silver glow cutting through the oppressive dark, flickering over the cavern walls where carvings of fanged skulls, clawed hands, and writhing serpents seemed to fade, their sharp edges softening as if the Hollow's malevolent pulse had flatlined. The air lightened as we ascended, the heavy reek of sulfur and decay thinning, replaced by a faint breeze carrying the clean scent of damp earth and pine through the pit's gaping mouth. I clenched my fist, knuckles scabbing tight, nothing to hold but Sara's voice, north pulling me with relentless force, the curse a shadow I couldn't shake, its words "every hope will crumble" sinking deeper.

Stepping into the forest was like waking from a nightmare. Kalden's torchlight flickered through the trees, a warm beacon piercing the dawn's gray gloom. The oppressive buzz that had choked the air was gone, replaced by a quiet that felt alive, not dead. Vines, once pulsing green with Ashvalen's corruption, shrank back, their glossy sheen withering to dry, brittle brown, crunching like dead leaves underfoot. Warped trunks, slick and black, peeled away to reveal plain oak and pine, their bark rough and natural, the glistening wrongness fading. Branches untwisted, no longer clawing like skeletal hands, the canopy parting to let pale dawn light stab through, bruising the sky with streaks of silver and gold. Real birds, sparrows, finches chittered in the boughs, their calls sharp where silence had reigned. My chest eased a fraction, the rifle dipping lower, my breath fogging less thickly in the cool air, Ashvalen's grip unraveling like a thread cut clean.

"Forest's waking up," Mithis said, her spear resting on her shoulder, its runes dimming to a faint shimmer, crimson eyes scanning the trail with a predator's focus. Her voice was low, a smirk tugging her lips, revealing a flash of sharp teeth. Her wolf-pelt cape swayed cleaner now, shedding ichor like old skin, the gray fur brushing pine needles that fell naturally, no longer gleaming with unnatural venom. Her green skin stood stark against the dawn's gray light, blood crusting at her nose, but her posture was unbowed, a warrior forged in fire.

"' Bout damn time," Daven muttered, his bow slung loose across his back, his limp fading as he stepped onto flatter dirt, his boots scuffing earth that no longer clung like rot. His glowing arrows rattled less in their quiver, their charmed tips catching the dawn in faint glints. "Thought I'd never see normal trees again." His tone was dry, relief cracking through the exhaustion, sweat, and grime streaking his face, but his eyes softened, taking in the ordinary pines with a hunter's quiet reverence.

Corin flexed his shoulder, wincing as blood crusted dry under his tunic, his twin swords clinking faintly as he walked, their hilts worn from use. His eyes glinted hard, but a softer edge crept in, relief at the forest's shift. "Feels like the air's not trying to kill us," he said, his voice steady, boots scuffing moss that breathed green, vibrant, not the sickly rot of before. "Wendigo's death did it." His braid swung, stiff with dirt, but his steps were sure, the weight of the fight lifting slightly.

"Maybe," I said, rifle steady, eyes flicking to shadows that no longer twitched with menace, Sara's scream quieter but crystal clear, north burning like a beacon. "Or it's just catching its breath." The curse gnawed, its words "every hope will crumble" a burr in my chest, but the forest's return to normalcy was a small, stubborn win, a shield against the darkness. My leg throbbed, bandages damp with blood, but the pain dulled to an ache, adrenaline still humming in my veins.

The trail stretched clear, its black dirt smoothing into a flat, packed path, roots sinking back into the earth, no longer clawing like skeletal hands. Knee-high grass sprouted, swaying naturally in the breeze, its blades soft and green, not razor-edged or glowing with wrongness. A deer, real, brown, eyes wide with natural fear, darted across the path, hooves thudding softly, vanishing into a rustle of leaves that smelled of life, not decay. My gut unclenched a fraction, the rifle's barrel dipping lower, my breath steadying as the forest exhaled around us, alive and clean.

"Kalden's close," Mithis said, pointing with her spear, its runes pulsing faintly, as torchlight sharpened through thinning trees. The town's wooden gates loomed ahead, weathered planks scarred from wraith claws, standing less like a plea for safety and more like a defiant stand. Her cape rustled, the wolf pelt catching the breeze, her green skin stark against the dawn's silver light, a warrior carved from the fight.

We reached the gates, the guards snapping to attention, their halberds twitching upward, faces pale under dented iron helms until recognition hit like a spark. "You're back," one stammered, his voice cracking high, his torch trembling in a gauntleted hand, chainmail rattling as he stepped aside, awe and fear mingling in his wide eyes. "Thought the Hollow'd swallow you whole."

"Just about," I rasped, stepping through, the rifle heavy against my shoulder, my chest aching where blood crusted my torn shirt, Sara's scream pushing me forward, north, relentlessly. "Wendigo's dead, forest's turning normal. Tell Aldred." My voice scraped, rough but firm, carrying the weight of a flicker I could chase, a lead to Sara.

The guard nodded fast, bolting off, his boots pounding the uneven cobblestone, his torchlight bobbing wildly, casting jagged shadows on the town's wooden walls. Kalden stirred awake, shutters creaking open, wary faces peering from behind warped glass, children poking heads from doorways, their whispers breaking the dawn's quiet. The air smelled of straw, smoke, and baking bread, clean, real, free of the rot and magic that had choked it sour. My shoulders eased, the rifle slinging lower, pain a dull throb under bandages, Sara's scream a burr I could fight, north pulling like a tide.

The elder's hall loomed at the town's heart, its heavy oak door swinging wide, Aldred waiting inside, his robe dragging across the polished planks, eyes glinting like polished flint under the smoky haze of wall-mounted torches. Their light carved deep lines into his weathered face, relief softening the strain that had hardened him yesterday. The warrior stood to his left, her broad frame steady, halberd propped against the floor, its notched blade catching the torchlight, runes glowing faintly. The mage flanked his right, robes shimmering with silver thread, his bony hands still, no longer twitching with arcane tension. Maps lay scattered across a rough-hewn table, their edges curling, the frantic red runes marking wraith attacks now dim, lifeless ink.

"You did it," Aldred said, his voice rolling deep, resonant, relief cracking through the weight that had bowed him. His beard brushed the table as he leaned forward, hands braced on the wood. "The Forest is quiet now, wraiths are gone, shadows are dead at the gates. Kalden breathes again."

"You're welcome," I said, stepping into the hall, my boots scuffing dirt onto the planks, the rifle thudding against my thigh, Sara's scream burning north, the curse clawing at my edges. "Took everything, but your village has a chance now." My tone rasped, edged with exhaustion, the north pulling hard, a relentless current I couldn't fight.

Mithis nodded, her spear resting easily against her shoulder, its runes dim but steady, her cape swaying cleaner, the wolf pelt shedding the last of the ichor. "Wasn't just us," she said, her voice rough, a rock I leaned on without thinking. "Daven, Corin, they were all in. Whatever held this place, it's broken." Her crimson eyes held Aldred's steady despite the blood crusting her nose, her green skin stark in the torchlight, a warrior unbowed.

Aldred's face darkened, lines carving deeper into his brow, eyes narrowing at the empty air as if searching for a ghost of the threat. His hand clenched the table, the wood groaning under his grip. "The Hollow's grip is gone here," he said, his voice sinking low, grim, heavy with unspoken dread. "But you've spoken of going north to Michigan, there is deeper corruption that way. Something's still out there."

The mage stepped forward, his robes catching the torchlight in ripples, his voice reedy but sure, carrying a scholar's precision. "The corruption's root may stretch beyond this realm, merging worlds, waking myths older than Ashvalen. The Wendigo's death severed its hold here, but the north pulses with it alive, hungry." His eyes glinted, piercing mine, as if he could see the curse woven into my bones, a dark lattice of fate. His hands twitched, tracing faint arcane lines in the air, then stilled, his staff's blue glow dimming.

"North's next," I said, the rifle cold in my hands, my chest tight, Sara's voice driving me, relentless, a beacon through the haze. I turned to Mithis and whispered, "We rest here, then we move. She's out there, I hear her." My voice scraped, a soldier's edge cutting through the fear, the curse a burr in my chest, but hope alive, stubborn, burning under it all.

Daven slumped against the hall's wall, his bow clattering softly, his breath easing as he wiped ichor from his face, the dark smears drying to a dull crust. "Forest is normal now, I'm out," he said, his voice thin but firm, his slate-gray eyes glinting weary but resolute, a hunter's job done. "My Village needs me, but I thank you for the assistance you gave us." His smirk was faint, but his nod carried weight, a farewell forged in blood.

Corin nodded, his swords sheathed, blood crusting his shoulder, the red soaking through his tunic's tears. He leaned on a bench, his braid swinging, stiff with grime, his face pale but his eyes softening a hair. "My village comes first," he said, his tone steady, hard edges giving way to relief. "You've got this, Jake." His nod was sharp, sealing a bond, his boots scuffing the planks as he straightened, ready to guard what he'd fought for.

Aldred waved a hand, a guard stepping in, chainmail clinking softly, his young face pale but eager under a dented helm. "The Inn is yours, rest, eat, heal," Aldred said, his voice rolling like gravel, stern, a father's command wrapped in care. "Tomorrow, we'll give you some supplies, whatever's left in the stores." His eyes dared me to argue, but the weight of his relief was a tether, grounding me for a moment.

Mithis clapped my shoulder, her grip firm and warm through my torn jacket, her crimson eyes locking onto mine, cutting through the haze of pain and doubt. "One night, then we find her. Together." Her tone was iron, unyielding, her spear steady, its runes pulsing faintly, her cape swaying as she stood tall, a lifeline I grabbed without hesitation, her strength a shield against the curse.

I nodded, the rifle heavy, sinking onto a bench, the springs creaking under my weight, my leg throbbing, ribs aching, blood crusting my shirt. Sara's scream quieted to a whisper, a flicker I could chase, north burning bright through the exhaustion. The forest was normal, trees straight, air clean, birds singing, but the curse lingered, clear and piercing "every life you touch," her voice a lead I'd follow until it broke me, Mithis at my side, the only thing keeping the darkness at bay.

18 ROAD TO RUIN

"May the gods watch over you," Aldred said, his voice a deep, resonant rumble, like stones grinding in a riverbed. He bowed slightly, his heavy robe brushing the hall's worn oak planks, torchlight catching the silver threads fraying at its hem, glinting faintly in the smoky haze. His eyes, shadowed under tangled white hair, gleamed with a mix of hope and dread, as if he saw the road ahead and wasn't sure we'd reach its end. "And may your path lead to safety." His words hung heavy, a prayer more than a farewell, his weathered hands clenching briefly before relaxing at his sides.

I hefted the wooden chest he'd given us, its rough-hewn oak scarred with scratches and dents, the iron bands rusted but sturdy, heavier than it looked. Packed tight with rations in waxed paper and a battered map scratched with red ink, it thumped against my bruised ribs as I shifted its weight, the pain a sharp reminder of the Wendigo's antler strike. The chest's edges bit into my palms, grounding me against the ache clawing my bones, the venom burns throbbing faintly under fresh bandages. Mithis stood beside me, her green skin stark against the hall's dim glow, her wolf-pelt cape swaying as we stepped out into Kalden's dusk. The village sprawled under a bruised sunset, cobblestone streets slick with evening damp, long shadows stretching like skeletal fingers from timber homes with sagging roofs. Smoke curled from chimneys, blending with the crisp tang of pine drifting from the forest beyond, the air clean now, free of the Hollow's sour rot.

"What now?" Mithis asked, her voice steady gravel wrapped in calm, cutting through the chill that settled with the fading light. Her crimson eyes flickered thoughtfully, catching the last rays of sun, her spear resting easy on her shoulder, its white ash haft glowing faintly, runes shimmering silver like frost on the reinforced steel tip.

I glanced at her, her silhouette sharp against the horizon, then at the dirt road snaking out of Kalden, vanishing into the treeline where pines stood tall and normal, no longer twisted by Ashvalen's touch. "We keep going. My sister and her family are out there, north towards Michigan. I'm not stopping 'til I find her." My voice scraped rough, Sara's scream echoing clear in my skull, "Jake, something's wrong," a piercing, desperate cry that drove me relentlessly, drowning the witch's curse gnawing at my gut: "Every life you touch will rot." My hand tightened on the chest's handle, split knuckles creaking under scabs, the weight a small anchor against the dread.

Mithis nodded, her expression unreadable, a mask of steel over whatever churned beneath her emerald skin. "Then let's not waste time." Her boots crunched on the cobblestones, the axe slung across her back clinking faintly, its runes pulsing violet in the dimness, a quiet promise of violence held in check.

We trudged to the Jeep, parked crooked by the inn's sagging porch. I popped the tailgate, rusted hinges screeching in protest, and slid the chest in beside my pack, ammo cans rattling against the dented steel floor, the sound sharp in the quiet evening. Mithis tossed her spear in, its white ash haft clattering softly, the runes shimmering brighter for a moment, casting a silver glow across the Jeep's cargo bay, illuminating scuffed leather grips worn from her iron hold. Her cape brushed the tailgate, shedding a few singed wolf hairs, the fur cleaner now but still bearing the faint char of the Wendigo's ichor. I climbed into the driver's seat, keys jangling cold in my hand, the metal biting my palm as I turned the ignition. The engine coughed twice, spitting a cloud of exhaust that smelled of diesel and burnt oil, then rumbled alive, a low growl vibrating the cracked dashboard, the needle gauges flickering erratically before settling. Mithis slid into the shotgun seat, her axe across her lap, the blade's edge catching the dashboard's faint glow, her crimson eyes fixed on the forest's fading outline, thoughtful, distant, like she was seeing something beyond the trees.

"You okay?" I asked, voice low, glancing at her as I shifted into gear, the Jeep lurching forward, tires crunching gravel with a satisfying bite.

She turned, her expression easing a fraction, crimson softening to warm embers in the dim cab's light. "I am. It's just... this world's stranger than I imagined. Wendigo, Hydra, roads twisting alive, myths bleeding into reality. But I'm glad I'm not facing it alone." Her tone warmed, her gloved fingers flexing on the axe haft, the leather creaking softly, a small anchor in the chaos.

I gave a small smile, lips tugging stiff under three days' stubble and grime caked into my skin. "I am glad I am not facing it alone, too." Her steel steadied me, Sara's scream quieting for a beat, the curse a burden shoved down, locked tight behind the rumble of the engine and the road ahead.

The Jeep rolled out, Kalden shrinking in the rearview mirror, its torchlight fading to pinpricks behind gnarled pines, the village's wooden gates a final silhouette against the dusk. The twisted forest peeled back, warped trunks thinning, their black, wet bark flaking off like dead skin, revealing rough, natural oak and pine underneath, the glistening sheen gone. Vines, once pulsing green and jagged, withered to brittle brown, snapping under the Jeep's tires with sharp cracks that echoed in the quiet. Sunlight stabbed through the canopy, golden patches warming the road, glinting off the Jeep's scratched hood, the metal pocked with dents from debris in the Hollow. The air lost its sour weight, the ozone and rot fading to crisp earth and needle-sharp pine, a normalcy that hit my lungs like a lifeline after days of choking dread, though the curse lingered, a faint whisper in my bones.

"The road's... fixing itself?" Mithis said, her voice laced with disbelief, leaning forward, her breath fogging the streaked passenger window. She pressed a gloved hand to the glass, peering out as the cracked asphalt beneath us smoothed, jagged edges merging into a proper highway, potholes filling like old wounds healing over, the transformation subtle but undeniable.

I nodded, gripping the wheel tight, knuckles whitening under split scabs, the steering wheel's worn leather creaking under my palms. Looks that way. Maybe the Wendigo's death broke whatever was twisting this place. Something's letting go." My tone stayed wary, hope flickering like a candle in a storm, not trusting the change fully, the curse's whisper "every hope will crumble" keeping me on edge.

She glanced at me, crimson eyes thoughtful, glinting in the dashboard's faint green glow. "Your world... it feels like it's trying to fight back, pushing the chaos out, reclaiming itself." Her voice was low, almost reverent, her cape rustling as she settled back, the wolf pelt brushing the torn vinyl seat.

"Maybe," I said, jaw tight, eyes flicking to the side mirrors for shadows that didn't come, the road stretching clear under the Jeep's headlights. "But let's not get too comfortable. Normal doesn't mean safe." My leg throbbed where the claw slash had torn through, the bandages damp with blood, but the pain was a dull ache now.

The highway smoothed further, overgrown grass and magical flora vanishing, replaced by weathered ditches choked with dry, tangled weeds, their brittle stalks swaying in the evening breeze. Street signs emerged, rusted green metal bolted to bent poles leaning from years of wind and neglect, paint peeling but legible. One caught my eye: "HARRISON 5 MI," faded white letters glowing in the headlights, a promise of civilization dangling close, though I knew better than to trust it blindly. The Jeep's tires hummed steadily, the engine's low growl a familiar rattle grounding me against the ache in my ribs, the curse whispering low, Sara's scream pulling north like a tide.

"Looks like civilization," I said, glancing at Mithis, her profile steady against the dusk, the axe haft creaking under her grip, her crimson eyes narrowing at the faint yellow lights flickering ahead, piercing the gloom.

"Is that good or bad?" she asked, her voice edged with caution, gloved fingers tightening on the weapon, the runes pulsing faintly violet, her cape bunching as she leaned forward, wary.

"We'll find out soon enough," I muttered, easing off the gas, the Jeep slowing as Harrison's outskirts loomed, a fragile bubble of order in the dark.

Harrison wasn't the crumbled ruins we'd seen elsewhere, shells of towns swallowed by warped forest, but a living, breathing outpost, fragile yet defiant. A low hum droned, the buzz of generators cutting through the evening quiet, floodlights casting stark beams over sandbag barricades and concrete slabs stacked at the town's entrance, their surfaces pocked with bullet scars and other marks that looked like lightning strikes. A tattered American flag flapped limply above a checkpoint, its stars faded to gray, stripes stained with ash and mud, snapping in the sharp evening freeze. Soldiers in camo patrolled with disciplined precision, M4 rifles slung low, night-vision goggles perched on helmets, their tan Humvees parked hulking behind barriers, paint chipped and streaked with dried mud, machine guns mounted and gleaming under the lights.

"Military," I said under my breath, slowing the Jeep to a crawl, gravel crunching under the tires.

Mithis shifted uneasily, her cape rustling against the torn seat, crimson eyes darting across the checkpoint. "Your people?" Her voice was low, cautious, the axe shifting in her grip, runes flickering purple, her green skin a stark contrast to the Jeep's drab interior.

"Yeah," I said, keeping my tone steady, hands firm on the wheel. "Let me do the talking, they might not take kindly to an unknown variable." Her green skin, crimson eyes, and rune-etched axe screamed outsider in a way that could make trigger fingers itch. I didn't need them to be twitchy.

The soldiers snapped their rifles up as we rolled close, muzzles glinting in the floodlights, a sharp "Stop!" barking out, cutting the quiet. I braked, tires crunching gravel, rolling down the window, cool air hitting my face with a tang of diesel and gun oil. "Identify yourself!" one shouted, his voice commanding, clipped, boots planted firm on the muddy ground, a sergeant's stripes glinting on his sleeve, his helmet casting a shadow over a weathered face.

"Former Army," I called back, keeping my voice steady, eyes locked ahead, hands visible on the wheel. "Jake McAllister, 11th Airborne." My tone stayed calm, soldier's habit kicking in, Sara's scream shoved aside for the moment, though it lingered like a burr in my skull.

He stepped closer, rifle dipping a fraction, peering into the floodlight's glare, his face lined with fatigue, stubble gray under tired eyes that flicked over my torn jacket and blood-crusted bandages. His gaze landed on Mithis, narrowing fast, taking in her green skin, the axe across her lap, her crimson stare glowing faintly in the cab's dim light. "Who's she?" he asked, voice hardening, his finger hovering near the trigger guard, tension coiling in his shoulders.

"A friend," I said quickly, cutting off suspicion before it could take root. "Mithis, she's been helping me survive out there. Saved my ass more than once." True enough, and I kept my tone firm, leaving no room for doubt, my eyes meeting his steadily.

He hesitated, jaw ticking under the helmet's strap, then waved us out, his rifle still low but ready. "Park it here," he jerked his chin at a muddy patch beside a Humvee, its turret swiveling slightly, the gunner's silhouette dark against the floodlights. "You'll need decontamination before you're inside both of you."

"Decontamination?" Mithis asked, frowning, her voice low, the axe shifting in her grip, her cape bunching as she tensed, crimson eyes narrowing at the sergeant.

"Standard protocol," he said gruffly, stepping back, his boots squelching in the mud. "You've been in the wild could be carrying anything. We don't take chances, especially now." His tone was flat, professional, but his eyes lingered on Mithis, wary of her otherness.

I exchanged a glance with her, crimson meeting gray, her steel steadying me. "We'll cooperate," I said, cutting the engine, the keys clinking cold as I pulled them free, the Jeep settling into silence. "Let's go."

They escorted us to a tent, its canvas flapping in the evening breeze, floodlights glaring off white fabric stained with mud and ash, the stakes driven deep into the soft earth. Inside, a team in yellow hazmat suits waited, their plastic crinkling, faceless behind tinted visors, their movements precise as they ushered us to metal benches bolted to the ground, the steel cold through my damp jeans. The air stank of bleach and antiseptic, biting my nose, underscored by the steady hum of a portable generator droning outside, its vibration buzzing through the bench.

They ran us through the process, blood pricks stinging my arm, the needle sharp against my venom-scarred skin, scanners beeping shrill as they swept over my chest, their red lights flashing in the dim tent. A cold hose blast followed, soaking my jeans and tattered tee, chilling the bandages clinging to my wounds, icy rivulets snaking down my back, pooling at my boots. Mithis glared daggers, water plastering her dark hair flat, dripping green strands over her shoulders, her cape sagging wet, the wolf pelt matted and heavy. She muttered low in her native tongue, sharp syllables lost under the spray, adjusting her soaked tunic with a sharp tug, the runes on her axe flickering purple through the damp, defiant.

"This is humiliating," she hissed, her voice muffled over the hose's roar, her crimson eyes flashing as water streamed down her face, streaking the blood crusted at her nose.

"Better than being shot," I whispered back, shivering as the hose hit my back, the icy spray stinging my ribs, a grin tugging my lips despite the discomfort. "Just roll with it." My teeth chattered, but the soldier in me found the absurdity grounding, a moment of normalcy in the madness.

They cleared us, the hazmat team nodding curtly, their visors reflecting the tent's harsh lights as they handed back our gear, dripping wet, the axe haft slick in Mithis's grip, my rifle cold and heavy as I slung it over my shoulder, water dripping from the barrel. A soldier waved us into town, his boots squelching in the mud, the air thick with tension under the floodlights' glare. Harrison buzzed with life, its streets bustling despite the hour, families hauling crates of canned goods, their faces drawn and pale, soldiers hammering boards over busted windows, the nails screeching against warped wood. Medics in stained scrubs darted between tents, stretchers creaking under wounded, their shouts sharp over the hum of generators. Barricades loomed at every corner, sandbags stacked unevenly, barbed wire glinting like jagged teeth, holding a fragile bubble of order against the dark beyond. The chatter was low, hushed voices, a child's whimper, a woman's sob, a thin veneer over raw, gnawing fear.

They steered us to a command post, an old courthouse, its brick facade chipped and weathered, ivy curling around cracked columns that sagged under years of neglect. Inside, maps sprawled chaotically across walls, pinned with rusting tacks, red circles bleeding ink over faded counties, the air heavy with the bitter scent of coffee and sweat-soaked uniforms. A woman in a crisp olive drab uniform met us, her face stern but not unkind, lines carved deep around brown eyes that sized us up with a glance. Her hair was pulled tight under a cap, gray streaks glinting at her temples, her boots planted wide on creaking floorboards.

"Captain Reed," she said, her voice clipped, offering a firm nod, her posture rigid but her eyes curious. "You're the first travelers we've seen in days, most don't make it this far. What's your story?"

I gave her the rundown, short and scrubbed of magic, ex-Army grunt surviving the wild, looking for family, Mithis my backup, no mention of Ashvalen or rune-etched weapons. Her gaze stayed unreadable, her pen tapping a battered clipboard, listening as I skimmed the chaos from Florida to Kalden, ending with the forest turning back to normal. "Been through hell," I finished, my voice rough, Sara's scream urging me to move, the curse a low burr in my chest.

"You've got that right," Reed said, her tone easing a fraction, her eyes flicking over my torn jacket, the blood crusted on my bandages, then to Mithis's axe, its runes dim but unmistakable. "You're lucky to hit Harrison alive. We're one of the last safe zones around here, holding back the worst of what's out there. But it's not sustainable supplies, thin, morale thinner." Her jaw tightened, the clipboard clattering to the desk as she set it down.

"What's attacking you?" I asked, leaning forward, elbows on the scratched wooden desk, my rifle thudding against my thigh, the weight grounding me.

"Everything," she said grimly, her voice sinking, her fingers clenching briefly. "Undead first slow, shambling, manageable with headshots. Then mutants' horrible creatures, fast, twisted, claws and teeth that tear through Kevlar. Now it's worse creatures we can't name, shrugging off rounds like nothing, some flying, some armored. Military's coordinating where we can, but comms are spotty, most units cut off or gone." She paused, weighing her words, then added, "I'm getting spotty reports that the powers in charge fled somewhere."

I seized the moment, slipping into my best E4 Mafia tone, smooth and just shy of cocky. "Since we're not staying long, I can find out what's going on with the higher-ups, maybe show your soldiers how to fight these things better, and can we look through your Refugee names to see if my family's here?"

She saw through it, a knowing glint in her eye, her lips twitching faintly. "Yes, you can, and I'm assuming you want supplies for that other endeavor."

I flashed a sly smirk, leaning back. "That'd be much appreciated, ma'am. Thank you so much."

As I turned to leave, she called out, "Hey, McAllister, you can't trick a mustang that easily." Her tone was dry, but the warning was clear: don't push your luck.

I nodded, catching the unspoken boundary. "Understood, ma'am." We stepped out of the courthouse, the heavy door thudding shut, the air cooling fast as the sun dipped below the horizon, painting the sky a bloody orange, the chill biting through my damp jacket.

Mithis turned, her expression wary, her voice quiet under the hum of generators. "They fear me, don't they?" Her crimson eyes glinted, searching mine, her axe haft creaking as she adjusted her grip, the runes pulsing faintly.

"They don't know you," I said, meeting her gaze, my voice steady, her steel anchoring me. "But I do. That's enough." My hand brushed her shoulder briefly, a soldier's reassurance, grounding us both.

Her face softened, crimson glinting warm for a beat, a nod sealing the moment. "Let's go then."

The high school loomed ahead, a squat brick box, its windows boarded with splintered plywood, nails driven haphazardly, the facade weathered gray under the floodlights' harsh glare. Barbed wire coiled crudely around the perimeter, glinting like jagged thorns, overturned cars blocking the entrance, their windshields shattered, tires flat. Two soldiers manned the gate, rifles slung low, their faces etched with fatigue but alert under helmets streaked with mud, their breath fogging in the dusk chill. Voices leaked from the building murmurs, a child's laugh cut short, a baby's wail echoing through cracked walls, a fragile pulse of life.

"This must be the place," I said, pulling the Jeep into a gravel lot, tires crunching, killing the engine, the air settling still save for the distant generator drone. The lot was littered with debris, empty MRE wrappers, a broken flashlight, and a child's shoe caked in mud.

Mithis eyed the soldiers, her cape rustling as she climbed out, axe slung over her shoulder, her voice low. "Are all your people so... tense?" Her crimson eyes narrowed, scanning the barricades, the soldiers' fingers resting near their triggers.

I chuckled, rough and dry, grabbing my rifle, its cold weight grounding me as I slung it across my back. "Yeah, pretty much. War does that. Let me talk." My boots crunched gravel, the sound sharp in the quiet, my leg throbbing faintly under the bandages.

We approached, hands visible, boots scuffing the lot, floodlights glaring, casting our shadows long and jagged across the cracked asphalt. One soldier stepped forward, his face lined deep, eyes darting under a helmet too big, rifle dipping but ready, his breath fogging in the dusk chill. "State your business," he said, his voice firm but not unkind, his gloved hand tightening briefly on his M4.

"Looking for family," I said, keeping my tone steady, palms up to show empty hands. "Captain Reed said refugees might be here, got names to check." My eyes met his, soldier to soldier, my rifle slung low to signal no threat.

He glanced at Mithis, his eyes lingering on her green skin, the axe gleaming with faint violet runes, then back to me, nodding curtly. "Intake officers in the gym, down the hall, can't miss it. She'll help." He stepped aside, rifle easing, his boots crunching as he waved us through, his partner watching Mithis warily, finger near the trigger guard.

The school hummed with life, its hallways lined with cots shoved tight, blankets patched and threadbare, families huddled close under the dim buzz of flickering fluorescents. The air hung thick with sweat, stale soup simmering in a corner where a volunteer stirred a dented pot, and the faint rot of despair clinging to everything. Kids darted between legs, chasing a ball made of tied rags, their laughter brittle, parents whispering in low, strained tones, their faces hollowed by loss. Volunteers in faded Red Cross vests passed out water in scratched plastic bottles, their movements mechanical, eyes shadowed with exhaustion. Resilience flickered in a woman humming softly to a sleeping child, a man carving a stick into a toy, but it felt fragile, ready to snap under the weight of the world outside.

The gym was chaos, rows of folding tables buckling under stacks of battered notebooks, their pages torn and stained, soldiers and volunteers shouting over a line of refugees snaking across scuffed hardwood, their boots kicking up dust. Clipboards clattered, pens scratching furiously, voices overlapping "Name?" "Last seen where?" the air thick with desperation and the faint chalky scent of old gym mats. A fluorescent bulb flickered overhead, casting stuttering shadows, the basketball hoop above rusted and netless, swaying faintly from the commotion.

"Busy place," Mithis muttered, her axe haft creaking in her grip, crimson eyes scanning the crowd, her cape brushing a cot as she edged closer, the wolf pelt damp from the decon hose. Her presence drew stares, refugees shrinking back, a child pointing before his mother pulled him close.

"Yeah," I said, rifle slung tight, eyes raking faces, searching for Sara's dark hair, her sharp gray eyes, but finding only strangers, her scream a burr pushing me still. "Let's find the officer."

A voice cut through, familiar as a punch "Well, I'll be damned. Is that you, McAllister?" freezing me mid-step, my heart skipping hard, a jolt of recognition cutting through the haze.

I turned. Max Turner stood there, grinning cocky through a rugged face unchanged since Kandahar, his buzzed hair graying at the temples, his patched uniform hanging loose on a frame worn thin by this new war. His boots were scuffed to hell, caked with mud, his M4 slung casually over his shoulder, a few new scars crisscrossing his knuckles. His eyes glinted under the gym's harsh lights, a spark of the old troublemaker still burning.

"Turner?" I said, disbelief crashing with relief, my voice cracking as he clapped my shoulder hard, jarring my bruised ribs, his grip warm through my torn jacket. "Man, I thought you were long gone, figured you'd punched out somewhere south. What the hell are you doing out here?" His grin held, his eyes flicking to Mithis, brow lifting, grin twitching curiously.

"This is Mithis," I said, nodding her up, her crimson eyes steady, axe gleaming faintly purple. "She's... from the other side of this crap, Ashvalen, whatever's bleeding in. Saved my ass more times than I can count." My tone was firm, leaving no room for doubt, hoping to ease the tension her appearance sparked.

She dipped her head cautiously, her voice low. "Good to meet you." Her lips tugged slightly, crimson eyes glinting warmly, disarming the moment.

Turner chuckled, rough and deep, slapping my back again, the jolt stinging my ribs. "Good to meet you, too. But McAllister's trouble, but you've probably found that already."

"Yeah," she said, smirking, crimson softening. "Noticed."

He sobered, grin fading, voice dropping to a serious tone. "Listen, if you're hunting family, I can help. We've got logs of everyone who's rolled through. Not perfect, people slip through cracks, but it's a start."

"That'd mean a lot," I said, chest tightening, Sara's scream a burr under his words, hope flickering despite the curse clawing low. "Thanks, man."

"No sweat," he said, leading us to a side table where a soldier hunched over a notebook, pages torn and stained, pencil stub scratching faintly. "Names?"

"Sara Carter," I said, voice steadying, hope a fragile spark. "Her husband, Mark, and their kid, Lily, five, pigtails, all giggles, last I saw." My words caught, memories of Lily's laugh flashing sharp, the curse whispering beneath.

The soldier flipped pages, fingers smudged black, eyes scanning, then shook his head after a beat. "No Carters here, not in the log. Sorry, man." His tone was flat, worn from delivering bad news, his eyes barely lifting from the page.

My gut sank, but I nodded, shoving it down, jaw tight. "Thanks anyway."

Turner clapped my back, eyes softening, his grip steady. "Hey, don't lose it. People move fast out there, could've hit another camp, skipped us. Roads are a damn lottery."

"Yeah," I said, Sara's scream looping, pulling me north, relentless, the curse a low gnaw.

"Tell you what," he said, grin creeping back, lighter now. "Stick around a bit food's shit, but warm. Supplies too. I could use a hand. Like old times, just with more weird crap."

I glanced at Mithis, her nod quick, crimson eyes steadying me. "Alright, but just a bit. We've got ground to cover, north's calling."

"Good," Turner said, grinning full, elbowing me lightly, his M4 clinking. "Old times, McAllister, except now we're shooting nightmares instead of insurgents."

I laughed roughly, the sound foreign, the first in days, weight easing a fraction despite Sara's scream and the curse lurking low. Solid ground, small and temporary, felt damn good.

He led us out of the gym, the clamor fading to a hum, into Harrison's heart, military pulsing everywhere. Soldiers patrolled, boots thudding cracked pavement, rifles gleaming cold under floodlights, barricades rising jagged at corners, sandbags sagging wet from recent rain. Supply stations crammed into gutted storefronts, glass shattered, signs dangling "Joe's Hardware" faded to rust, "Mary's Diner" barely legible. Refugees huddled near tents, blankets patched thin, eyes hollow with loss, soldiers barking orders, tension buzzing electric, a storm brewing under the fragile order.

"You've got a setup," I said, walking beside him, rifle slung low, air thick with diesel, sweat, and the faint tang of gunpowder. "Feels like you're bracing hard."

Turner nodded, grim, jaw tight under stubble. "Not wrong. We're holding, but it's slipping." His voice was heavy, his M4 clinking as he adjusted its sling.

"Reinforcements?" I asked, eyes flicking to a watchtower where a soldier swept binoculars, floodlight glaring off his helmet, casting a long shadow across the barricades.

He sighed, breath fogging in the chill, rubbing his neck. "Contacts are patchy, leaves us scrapping solo, mostly." His tone was bitter, the weight of abandonment clear.

Mithis broke her silence, axe haft creaking, voice cutting low. "Your world wasn't ready for this, none of it." Her crimson eyes narrowed, scanning the barricades, the soldiers' tense postures, her cape rustling faintly.

"Nope," Turner admitted, eyes glinting hard, meeting hers. "Caught us flat-footed, still reeling. Adapting, though learning fast or dying." His words were blunt, a soldier's truth.

We hit a command tent in the old town square, canvas sagging under the weight of damp, maps pinned chaotically to walls, red X's bleeding over counties, radio static crackling like distant thunder. Officers clustered around a table, uniforms creased, voices barking "Shift third platoon east!" "Ammo's low!" faces drawn tight under flickering lanterns, their light casting harsh shadows. "This is where the magic happens," Turner said, wry grin twitching, nodding at the organized chaos.

Captain Reed looked at me and asked, "Did you find your family?"

I had to shake my head no with defeat, "No, we did not."

"Well, I hope you can still keep your word. Turner, brief them on what is happening north of the river," she barked, voice cutting through the chatter. "Reports of something new, big, fast, and lethal. Some Patrols aren't coming back."

"Understood," he said, grin gone, nodding, waving us out. Outside, he leaned in, voice dropping near my ear, drowned by the generator hum. "North of the river's bad, worst mutations yet. Shit's ugly."

"Noted," I said, eyes flicking north, the dark treeline looming past barricades, the river glinting sluggish under floodlights, its surface rippling with an unnatural sheen. "Refugees safe here?"

He shrugged, shoulders sagging, M4 clinking. "Safe's relative. Food's tight, water's rationed, and the perimeter holds for now. Morale's trash people lost everything. It feels like we're just delaying the fall." His voice was grim, the weight of command heavy.

We passed an infirmary, an old diner, windows boarded with splintered plywood, moans leaking through cracks, a medic in blood-streaked scrubs hunched over a soldier, gauze soaking red fast, the air thick with antiseptic and despair. "Patrols gone missing," Turner said, nodding at the chaos, his face tight. He led us to the perimeter's edge, barricades rising jagged, watchtowers looming skeletal under floodlight glare.

Beyond, the land sloped to the river, its waters dark and sluggish, rippling under a bruised sky, the surface glinting with an oily sheen. North of it, trees thickened, their branches twisting unnaturally, shadows shifting, alive, watching us. "That's north," Turner said, nodding grimly, his M4 steady in his grip. "Drones watched it, used to. Ain't coming back now, something's chewing them up."

"What's out there?" I asked, rifle heavy, gut knotting tight, Sara's scream flickering north, the curse clawing low.

"Don't know," he admitted, eyes glinting hard, fixed on the woods, his jaw tight. "Kills patrols closing in. We can't hold it forever, whatever it is."

Mithis stared, crimson glowing in the dark. "Any ideas?" I asked, voice rough, her steel a lifeline in the chaos.

She hesitated, axe haft creaking, her voice low, certain. "Something ancient beyond our worlds, merging. A power older than Ashvalen, stirring here." Her tone sank, heavy, her cape rustling as she squared her shoulders, the runes pulsing faintly.

"Great," Turner said dryly, rubbing his jaw, stubble rasping under his fingers. "Ancient powers, exactly what we need."

I looked north, the knot in my gut tightening, the forest looming dark, Harrison a fragile bubble teetering on collapse. Rest and resupply for now, but north of the river waited, Sara's scream pulling relentlessly, the curse whispering low, a shadow I couldn't outrun.

The day dragged tensely, Turner roping us into the command tent, prepping for the inevitable. Refugees huddled near the gym, their faces gaunt, soldiers checking rifles, bolts clacking sharply, the air buzzing electric, a calm before hell broke loose. Mithis and I sat by the tent flap, sharing the quiet, her axe propped close, its runes dim, my rifle across my lap, barrel scratched but cold and steady. Turner hunched over a radio, static crackling, his face tight as he twisted dials, searching for a signal.

Then it hit an explosion, deafening, ripping through the night, rattling the tent's frame, canvas flapping wildly. "What the hell?!" Turner barked, snatching his M4, the rifle gleaming cold, his eyes snapping wide, adrenaline flaring.

The radio crackled, and a panicked voice cut through the hiss: "Perimeter breach! North sector! Multiple contacts, big ones!" Gunfire popped behind the words, screams echoing shrilly, metal clanging as barricades buckled.

Turner cursed, breath hissing, rifle snapping up, his boots scuffing dirt. "McAllister, you're with me. Mithis, stay close."

We grabbed gear, my rifle locked and loaded, Mithis's axe flaring purple, runes blazing hot, sprinting north, chaos swelling, refugees wailing, soldiers shouting, boots pounding cracked pavement. Fire flickered ahead, orange glow licking the sky, floodlights stuttering, gunfire rattling in a staccato, bullets singing through the dark, their whine sharp in the cold air.

We crashed into the barricade, and I froze. Towering creatures loomed as hulking beasts, eight feet tall, their jagged chitinous armor gleaming in the firelight. Overlapping black plates, thick and scarred, shrugged off bullets. Their sinewy limbs, unnaturally long, ended in razor-thin claws that shredded sandbags like paper, slick with blood under the floodlights. Glowing yellow eyes, slits of fury, scanned us. Some sprouted tattered, leathery wings, blotting out the stars as they swooped low, their shrieks a grinding mix of metal and bone clawing at my skull.

"Open fire!" Turner roared, unloading his M4, rounds sparking off a beast's hide, slowing it very little, ricochets whining into the dark, pinging off concrete slabs.

I raised my rifle, sights locking on those glowing yellow eyes, my first burst hitting true, ichor spraying black from a socket, the beast stumbling, roaring in pain, claws slashing blindly, gouging ruts in the pavement. "Eyes are the weak points!" I yelled, reloading fast, brass clinking at my boots, Sara's scream drowned under the chaos, the curse clawing low in my gut.

Mithis dove in, her axe blazing purple, runes flaring hot, carving a smaller beast's neck clean through, the head rolling wet, ichor gushing, steaming onto cracked pavement. It howled, a guttural shriek that buzzed my teeth, its body twitching, then grotesquely knit back, flesh bubbling, reforming fast, the wound closing like a living nightmare.

"They regenerate!" she shouted, crimson eyes wide, axe swinging again, splitting its chest, ichor splashing her cape, steaming hot, the air thick with the sour tang of their blood.

"Great," Turner muttered, firing over his shoulder, rounds sparking uselessly off another beast's armor. "We're screwed."

A winged beast dove, claws tearing a soldier beside us, his chest ripping open, scream cut short as it hauled him skyward, blood trailing dark in the firelight. I fired, my burst cracking its skull, ichor spraying, the creature crumpling heavy to the dirt, too late for the soldier, his blood pooling dark under the floodlight's glare, soaking into the mud.

"Need heavier firepower!" Turner yelled, radio crackling as he barked, "Get the PSRL up now!"

Static spat back, a voice shouting, "On the way, hold the line!"

The line buckled, creatures pouring through the breach, soldiers falling back, regrouping frantically behind a second barricade, floodlights flickering, shadows dancing wildly across the pavement, the air thick with smoke and the coppery reek of blood.

"Mithis!" I called, reloading, barrel hot, another beast lunging, claws raking air inches from my chest. "Ideas?"

Her crimson eyes glowed, axe dripping ichor, cape smoldering from splashes, her voice cutting through the chaos. "Their power's tied to something feeding them a source. Find it, stop them, maybe that will work." Her words were sharp, certain, her boots skidding on blood-slick pavement as she dodged a claw swipe.

I swore, scanning the chaos, the beasts moving deliberately, their yellow eyes flicking north, the woods looming dark past the breach, shadows twisting unnaturally. "Forest?" I asked, rifle barking, dropping another, ichor steaming where it fell, the ground slick with it.

"Possible," she said, axe swinging, cleaving a claw, the beast howling, staggering back, its limb twitching on the ground. "Need more time."

Turner caught it, firing tight over his shoulder, rounds sparking off a beast's hide. "Got a plan, then use it! We can't hold forever!" His voice was raw, his face streaked with soot, M4 trembling in his grip.

I nodded, rifle tight, Sara pushing north, the curse clawing low. "Mithis and I will hit the forest and see what is happening; you hold 'em as long as you can."

He frowned, then nodded, jaw tight. "Better do something, or we're dead." His eyes met mine, soldier to soldier, a bond forged in blood.

We broke off contact, slipping through the chaos, gunfire popping all around us, screams fading as we hit the woods, silence slamming down all of a sudden, eerie and heavy. Trees loomed, twisted, their branches leaning close, alive, watching, the air chilling fast, thick with sap and ozone, the floodlight glow fading to pinpricks behind us. My breath fogged, rifle up, boots crunching pine needles, the forest breathing slowly, oppressively.

"This way," Mithis said, voice low, axe haft creaking, crimson eyes narrowing, cutting the dark. Her boots snapped underbrush, her cape brushing thorns that glinted wet, the runes on her axe pulsing brighter, casting a faint purple glow across gnarled trunks.

We pushed deeper, the forest's air heavier, colder, pressing my lungs, raising the hackles on my neck. Then it loomed a portal glowing midair, pulsing liquid fire, orange and green swirling wildly, edges rippling like water, tendrils of energy reaching out like skeletal hands, humming thick enough to buzz my teeth. Shadows danced jaggedly across warped trunks, the light searing my eyes, suffocating the quiet, the air electric with raw power that prickled my skin.

"This is it," Mithis said, voice firm, axe blazing purple, runes flaring, cape swaying as she squared her shoulders, her green skin stark in the portal's glow. "Where are they coming from?"

I raised my rifle, barrel trembling, scanning shadows, the forest still but alive around the portal, every branch seeming to lean closer. "Another witch?" My voice was rough, Sara's scream pulling north, the curse clawing clear, "every life you touch will rot."

She shook her head, crimson glinting sure. "No older, primal, a tear between worlds, ours merging. Something's holding it, keeping it alive." Her tone sank, heavy, her axe haft creaking, runes glowing brighter, casting stark shadows.

"Then we have to close it," I said, my jaw clenching, rifle steadying, cold in my grip, the portal's hum vibrating my bones. "Can we?"

"Maybe," she said, eyes meeting mine, her steel steadying me. "For both of us, it won't be easy. Something's guarding it."

Shadows shifted, a figure loomed towering, swirling black smoke cloaking its form, yellow eyes piercing through, glowing slits of fury cutting the haze, unblinking and malevolent. Its voice snarled gutturally, echoing unnaturally, "You dare trespass? This portal's mine convergence is inevitable." The words rattled my ribs, chilling my spine, the air thickening with its presence, sap and ozone turning sour.

"Yeah, here to shut it down," I said, rifle snapping up, sights locking those yellow eyes, finger itching the trigger, adrenaline spiking hot. "Step aside."

It laughed, bone-cold, shaking leaves loose overhead, a dry rustle like bones clattering. "Mortals, you can't undo this." Smoke billowed thicker, tendrils writhing alive, coiling toward us like snakes.

"Watch us," Mithis said, axe blazing, grip whitening, lunging fast, her cape snapping in the sudden gust from the portal.

It surged, smoke hardening to claws, jagged limbs slashing air, fast and sharp. I fired, rounds punching through, dispersing wisps, but it reformed fast, yellow eyes glaring unblinking, undeterred. Mithis's axe cleaved its arm, a purple arc slicing clean, the limb dissolving to smoke, the creature roaring, unfazed, claws swinging back, raking stone beside her, sparks flying hot, stinging my face.

"It is tied to the portal!" she shouted, dodging swift, axe-blazing, her voice cutting through the chaos, boots skidding on damp earth. "Weaken it, break the connection!"

"How?!" I yelled, ducking claws slashing close, my rifle barking, rounds sparking off its smoky chest, the smoke swirling thicker, choking the air.

She pointed, runes glowing on trees circling the portal, carved deep into warped bark, pulsing orange in sync with the portal's rhythm, their light casting eerie shadows. "Those are the anchors, destroy them!" Her axe swung, holding the creature back, ichor splashing her gloves, steaming as it burned through leather.

I nodded, sprinting, rifle up, firing, bullets cracking wood, splintering bark, the orange glow dying fast, the portal shuddering, its edges wavering on, and off, light dimming a hair, the hum faltering. The creature roared, storming me, smoke boiling wild, tendrils lashing like whips. Mithis leapt, her axe slicing its torso, the beast howling shrilly, its form flickering, buying me seconds, ichor spraying hot, steaming on the forest floor.

"Keep going!" she yelled, crimson blazing, axe whirling, holding it off, ichor streaking her cape, steaming as it burned holes through the wolf pelt, her boots braced against the earth, muscles straining under her torn jacket.

I sprinted to the next tree, rifle barking, bullets shattering the rune, wood splintering, the orange glow snuffing out, the portal's hum stuttering, its fiery swirl shrinking inward, tendrils recoiling. The creature shrieked, smoke forming fraying at the edges, yellow eyes flaring brighter, fury palpable. It lunged, claws grazing my pack, tearing canvas, a spare magazine clattering to the ground. I rolled, firing mid-motion, rounds punching through its chest, dispersing smoke, slowing it a heartbeat.

Mithis carved another arc, axe splitting its shoulder, ichor gushing, the creature staggering, its roar shaking the trees, leaves raining down. "One more!" she shouted, voice raw, dodging a claw swipe that gouged earth, dirt spraying like shrapnel, pelting my face.

I hit the last tree, rifle up, firing point-blank, the rune exploding in a shower of splinters, the orange glow vanishing, the integrity, the portal convulsing, its fiery swirl collapsing inward, the hum dying to a low whine. The creature screamed, smoke forming, unraveling, yellow eyes dimming, tendrils dissolving into the air, its final roar fading to a guttural wheeze as it collapsed, smoke pooling harmlessly on the ground, dissipating like fog in sunlight.

Silence slammed down, the forest still, the air lighter, sap and ozone fading to pine and earth, my breath fogging in the chill. My chest heaved, rifle trembling, leg throbbing where blood soaked my jeans, Sara's scream quieter but clear, north pulling relentlessly, the curse clawing "every life you touch will rot." Mithis sank to a knee, axe dimming, runes faint, her cape smoldering, ichor streaking her green face, blood dripping from her nose, her crimson eyes glinting triumphant despite exhaustion.

"We did it," she rasped, voice rough, axe haft thudding earth, her gloves scorched, hands steadying on the weapon.

"Yeah," I said, rifle lowering, pain flaring, but soldier's grit holding me up. "Portal's down for now." My voice scraped, eyes flicking to the north, Sara's voice a beacon, the curse a shadow I couldn't shake.

"Back to Harrison," Mithis said, hauling herself up, cape swaying, runes pulsing faintly, her boots scuffing pine needles. "They need to know."

I nodded, slinging the rifle, the weight grounding me, Sara pushing me forward, north burning bright. The forest felt alive again, birds stirring faintly, dawn bruising the sky, but the curse lingered, a burr in my bones, Sara's scream the only lead I'd chase, Mithis's steel the only thing keeping me whole.

19 PORTAL'S LAST PULSE

We trudged back, the forest quieter now, its twisted branches untwisting, bark peeling back to reveal rough, natural oak and pine, no longer wet and black with Ashvalen's corruption. Pine needles crunched underfoot, dry and normal, the air lightening to frost-clear clarity, washing out the sour rot that had clung to every breath. Dawn bruised the sky, pale gray streaks cutting through the canopy, casting long shadows that softened as the light grew, the forest waking with faint bird calls, sparrows, finches where silence had reigned. My leg throbbed, the claw slash seeping blood, but the pain dulled to an ache, adrenaline fading, leaving exhaustion in its wake.

Gunfire faded as we neared Harrison, floodlights flickering weakly, their harsh glare stuttering across charred barricades, smoke curling thick from smoldering sandbags and shattered concrete slabs. The battle's chaos had died to distant shouts and boots pounding cracked pavement, the air heavy with ash, diesel, and the coppery tang of blood. Soldiers and refugees gaped as we emerged, their faces streaked with soot and blood, eyes wide under dented helmets and patched coats, staring at us battered, my jeans torn and blood-crusted, Mithis's cape smoldering, her green skin stark against the dawn's pale wash, yet alive against the odds. A child pointed, whispering, his mother pulling him close, fear and awe mingling in their hollowed gazes.

Turner waited at the barricade, his M4 slung loose over his shoulder, uniform streaked with mud and soot, boots planted wide on cracked asphalt, floodlight glare catching the gray stubble on his jaw, deepening the lines carved around his eyes. His gaze flicked over us, narrowing for a beat, then widened, glinting with fierce relief, a soldier's respect cutting through fatigue.

"McAllister, you crazy bastard, what'd you do?" His voice was rough, a half-laugh, half-awe, his rifle clinking as he shifted, his breath fogging in the chill morning air.

"Closed the portal," I said, my voice scraping dry, rifle thudding my thigh. "Cut their support creatures bailed. Town's safe for now." My words were clipped, soldier's habit, but hope flickered beneath, a small win against the convergence's tide.

He stared, jaw ticking, then let out a low whistle, breath fogging thick. "You're full of surprises, always were." His grin twitched cocky, but tired, his eyes flicking to Mithis, her axe dripping black ichor onto cracked pavement, steaming faintly in the cold. "Both of you."

I glanced at her, crimson meeting gray, her tired smile satisfied, her green skin stark against the dawn's pale light, blood crusting her nose, cape hanging heavy with damp and ichor. "You have no idea," I said, voice easing a hair, her steel grounding me, Sara's scream quieter for a beat, the curse a shadow held at bay.

Harrison stood scarred, barricades scorched black, sandbags spilled open, their contents strewn across blood-slick cobblestones, windows shattered to jagged teeth in brick facades, floodlights buzzing, casting long, flickering shadows.

Hammers clanged, soldiers nailing splintered boards over busted storefronts, the wood screeching under nails, the sound sharp in the quiet dawn. Murmurs drifted low from refugees hauling debris, broken planks, twisted rebar, their faces drawn tight under soot-streaked caps, eyes hollow with loss. Kids kicked a rag ball between sagging tents, their laughter brittle, cut short by coughs, the air thick with ash, diesel, and the faint tang of sweat and blood pooling sticky in pavement cracks. The creatures had retreated when the portal snapped shut, their hulking forms dissolving into the north woods, but their scars lingered, burnt husks of Humvees steaming in the morning chill, blood congealing in ruts, a soldier's helmet lying cracked, abandoned in the mud.

Turner met us near the command tent, its canvas sagging damp, pegs bent from the night's chaos, his M4 slung low, a battered clipboard clutched in one hand, his face worn hollow, eyes red-rimmed under graying stubble. "McAllister," he said, voice gravel-rough, handing me a creased paper, ink smudged from sweaty fingers, the edges curling in the breeze. "Here is a supply list, the least we can do after you pulled our asses out of the fire. Captain's permission." His tone was clipped, but gratitude shone through, his shoulders slumping slightly, the weight of command heavy.

I scanned it short, scratched in haste: two ammo can of 5.56 rounds, three jerry cans of fuel sloshing heavy, a med kit spilling gauze, iodine, and a few morphine syrettes, MREs in faded brown packs, labeled "Beef Stew" and "Chili Mac," enough for days, not weeks. The list was practical, soldiers' fare, but it felt like gold in a world falling apart.

"Appreciate it, Turner," I said, voice rough, folding the paper into my jacket's torn pocket, the rifle clinking against my side, Sara's scream pulling north, relentless, the curse whispering low.

He smirked, the grin not reaching his eyes, creasing lines deep around his mouth. "Don't mention it seriously, don't. Wish you were sticking around, could use a lunatic like you holding this dump together." His boots scuffed mud, the rifle barrel glinting dull under the floodlight's spill, his posture weary but resolute.

I shook my head, chest tightening, Sara's scream looping louder, the curse clawing at my edges. "Can't. My sister's out there, Sara, Mark, Lily. Every day here's a day they might not have. North's calling, man." My voice sank, heavy with the weight of it, my eyes meeting his, soldier to soldier, the bond unspoken but ironclad.

He sighed, breath fogging thick in the chill, nodding heavily, his eyes glinting tired but sure. "I get it, family's all we got. Just watch yourself. The further north, the weirder it gets. Heard chatter of worse past the river, things that don't die easily." His words were grim, a warning carved from experience, his hand rubbing the back of his neck, stubble rasping.

Mithis stepped up, adjusting her axe strap, the leather creaking under her gloved grip, her cape swaying cleaner now, the wolf pelt brushing her boots, shedding ash and ichor. "We're used to strange dragons, wraiths, portals." Her voice cut dry, crimson eyes glinting fiercely, a smirk tugging her lips, sharp and defiant, her green skin stark in the dawn's light.

Turner chuckled roughly, rubbing his jaw, the sound rasping in the quiet. "Fair enough. You two are a damn pair." His grin was fleeting, respect lingering in his gaze as he sized her up, the axe's purple runes catching his eye.

We hit the supply depot, a gutted gas station, its pumps rusted dry, their nozzles dangling like broken limbs, the canopy sagging under cracked concrete, creaking in the morning breeze. Soldiers loaded the Jeep, their boots squelching in mud, ammo cans thudding heavily into the tailgate, the metal clanging sharply, fuel sloshing in scratched jerry cans, the air thick with oil, sweat, and a faint tang of burnt rubber from charred barricades nearby. Mithis wandered close, her crimson eyes tracing their gear, fascinated, her fingers brushing a Humvee's pitted hood, studying its bulk like a predator sizing prey, her axe gleaming purple, runes etched deep catching the dawn's weak glow, casting faint shadows across the dented metal.

I leaned against the Jeep's hood, the metal cold under my palms, chipped olive paint flaking, watching them stack MREs beside the oak chest, cardboard tearing, labels faded to smears but legible "Beef Stew," "Chili Mac" stale but solid, the kind of food that kept you moving, not happy. My leg throbbed, bandages damp with blood, but the med kit's gauze and iodine would hold me together, at least until the next fight. Mithis joined me, boots scuffing gravel, her cape rustling, crimson eyes scanning the horizon, north stretching dark beyond Harrison's jagged edge, the river glinting sluggish under a bruised sky, its surface rippling with an unnatural sheen.

"Where next?" she asked, voice low, steady, axe haft creaking in her grip, her green skin stark against the Jeep's drab olive, her presence a rock in the uncertainty.

I pulled Turner's map from my jacket, creased and stained with mud, red ink bleeding over faded counties, spreading it across the hood, corners curling in the breeze, the air chilling fast, smelling of frost and pine. My finger tapped a red circle, ink smudged but clear, marking a spot two towns over, near a river snaking through dense forest. "Here, Marquette, old mill town, big refugee camp north of the river. If Sara and her family are near, they might've hit the biggest hub up there." My voice was rough, a fragile spark, the curse clawing low, Sara's scream pulling relentlessly.

She nodded, leaning close, her cape brushing my arm, warm through my torn sleeve, the wolf pelt's faint musk mixing with pine. "And if they're not?" Her crimson eyes met mine, steady but searching, her tone quiet, bracing for the answer.

I sighed, folding the map, paper rasping, shoving it back into my jacket, the curse's whisper sharp "every hope will crumble." "Then we keep looking, town by town, 'til I find her or what's left." My tone sank, heavy with dread, but hope burned stubbornly, my eyes meeting hers, her steel steadying me, grounding the chaos.

Turner strode up, boots crunching gravel, holding a small envelope, yellowed paper creased and worn, handing it over, his M4 clinking softly. "One more thing, refugees pitched in, said you earned it. Not much, but it's yours." His voice eased, eyes glinting tired, a grin tugging his lips, faint but genuine.

I opened it, fingers brushing rough edges, finding a handful of crumpled bills, five bucks, ten, edges torn and faded, coins clinking dull quarters, dimes, tarnished nickels, scavenged from pockets and rubble, all they had left in a world where money meant nothing. Guilt stabbed, and my chest tightened, their faces flashing hollow-eyed mothers, kids in patched coats, but I nodded, throat tight. "Tell 'em thanks means more than they know." My voice was low, the weight of their trust heavy, Sara's scream pushing me forward.

He stepped back, snapping a mock salute, fingers brushing his brow, grin fading to grim resolve. "Good luck, McAllister. Try not to die out there, hate to hear you bought it after all this." His eyes held mine, soldier to soldier, the bond unspoken but iron.

"Same to you," I said, rifle heavy, Sara's scream north, the curse whispering low, climbing into the Jeep, the engine coughing alive, a guttural growl vibrating the cracked dash. Mithis slid into the shotgun seat, axe across her lap, runes pulsing faintly, her crimson eyes fixed on the horizon, steady and unyielding. Harrison shrank in the rearview, barricades fading to jagged silhouettes against the dawn, north stretching dark and wild ahead, the river a glinting scar under a bruised sky, Sara's scream a beacon I'd chase until it broke me, Mithis's steel the only thing keeping the curse at bay.

20 ECHOES OF THE EMPTY

The highway stretched ahead, its cracked asphalt buckled and split, jagged fissures snaking through the pavement like old scars, tufts of weeds clawing through like skeletal fingers, their tips glinting wet with dew under the Jeep's flickering headlights. Sunlight broke through heavy, slate-gray clouds, golden shafts stabbing long, wavering shadows across the road, shifting with the breeze, the air sharp with frost and pine, cutting through the diesel tang clinging to my torn jacket, its cuffs frayed and crusted with dried blood. The Jeep's engine growled low, a steady rumble vibrating the cracked dashboard, the needle gauges twitching faintly, fuel hovering just above a quarter tank, enough to reach the next town if luck held.

"We'll find them," Mithis said, her voice steady, a quiet blade slicing through the thick silence that had settled in the cab. Her crimson eyes glinted north through the gloom, sharp and unyielding, her green skin stark against the Jeep's drab olive interior, her breath fogging faintly in the morning chill, curling like smoke against the streaked passenger window.

I glanced at her sharp profile, the hard line of her jaw set firm, her axe haft creaking under her gloved grip, the leather pitted from ichor burns, runes pulsing faintly purple in the dim light. My eyes flicked back to the road, the asphalt blurring under the tires, its faded yellow lines barely visible beneath dirt and debris. "Yeah, we will." My tone scraped firm, raw from days of shouting over gunfire, Sara's scream looping relentlessly in my skull, "Jake, something's wrong," a piercing cry driving me forward, north burning like a beacon. The curse clawed low in my gut, its whisper a cold burr: "every life you touch will rot." Mithis's steel beside me held it at bay, her presence a rock against the dread, her crimson gaze a quiet anchor.

The Jeep rumbled on, Harrison shrinking to a smudge in the rearview mirror, its scorched barricades and sagging tents fading into the haze, a fragile outpost swallowed by the horizon. Supplies rattled in the back, ammo cans thudding against dented steel, their 5.56 rounds clinking faintly, jerry cans sloshing with fuel, MREs shifting in torn cardboard a small comfort against the weight on my shoulders, the ache in my ribs pulsing with every bump, bandages damp with blood from the claw slash on my leg. North burned clear, direction enough for now, Sara out there somewhere, hope flickering stubborn under the dread, the curse's shadow trailing close.

Fields sprawled wide on either side, overgrown grass swaying gold under patchy sunlight, their stalks bending in the breeze, dotted with rusting car husks, sedans and pickups, doors ajar, windshields spiderwebbed with cracks, tires sunken into crumbling asphalt, their rubber cracked and peeling. Faded billboards leaned crooked over the road, their warped frames groaning as wind whistled through rusted metal, "Visit Greenville!" peeling away in flakes, "Bob's Diner: Best Pie in the County," a ghost of a lost world, the colors bleached to gray, the promises empty. The quiet gnawed, oppressive, no birds yet, just the Jeep's growl and the dry skitter of leaves tumbling across the pavement, their edges curling like charred paper, caught in eddies of wind.

I twisted the radio knob, scratched and loose, clicking under my calloused fingers, the plastic worn smooth from use. Static crackled loudly, a harsh hiss filling the cab, then snapped clear, a woman's voice cutting through, calm but clipped, echoing off the Jeep's steel walls. "This is the National Emergency Response Network," she said, each word precise, carrying the weight of a world unraveling. "If you're listening, you're not alone. Stay tuned for updates on safe zones, military operations, and survival tips."

I shot Mithis a look, crimson meeting gray, her brow lifting slightly, a flicker of surprise in her sharp features as I turned up the volume, the knob creaking faintly. "This is Acting Commander Julia Harris, United States National Security Council," the voice continued, steady but strained, a thread of steel holding it together. "The merging of Earth and the other world, now identified as Ashvalen, has destabilized global infrastructure, introduced threats we're still working to understand. Power grids are failing, supply chains are severed, and communication networks are limited to shortwave and satellite relays."

Mithis leaned forward, her cape brushing my arm, warm through my torn sleeve, the wolf pelt's faint musk mixing with pine and diesel. "They're acknowledging it publicly?" she said, voice low, edged with surprise, her axe runes flickering faint purple, casting soft shadows across the torn vinyl seat, her green fingers tightening on the haft.

"They'd have to," I replied, gripping the wheel tighter, knuckles aching under split scabs, the asphalt blurring under the tires, a pothole jarring the Jeep, rattling my teeth. "Dragons in New York, zombies in suburbs shit's too real now." Sara's scream flared north, pulling hard, the curse whispering low, a cold weight in my chest.

Harris continued, her voice heavier now, each word measured, carrying the toll of countless losses. "Safe zones are established in major cities, Chicago, Denver, Atlanta, and citizens are urged to reach military checkpoints. Supplies are limited, and efforts are ongoing to maintain order amidst widespread panic." A pause, static hissing faintly, then her tone darkened, a warning etched in grit. "New threats identified beyond undead. Intelligent, aggressive creatures, mythological in appearance, humanoids with unknown capabilities, some armored, some airborne. Avoid contact at all costs. They are not human, and their motives are unclear."

My knuckles ached, eyes flicking the empty road, scanning for shadows that didn't come, the fields stretching desolate, their golden grass swaying like a sea under the wind. "Sounds like they've met dragons, wraiths, whatever else Ashvalen's throwing at us," I said, voice rough, the curse clawing low, Sara's scream a relentless pull.

Mithis nodded, her gaze distant, crimson eyes narrowing as she stared through the windshield, the horizon a dark line of trees under a bruised sky. "Your world's adapting slowly. It wasn't ready. None of this fits your rules, your machines, your cities." Her voice sank, heavy with the weight of worlds colliding, her axe steady in her grip, runes pulsing faintly, a quiet promise of violence held in check.

"No kidding," I muttered, jaw tight, static crackling faint as Harris's voice pushed on.

Her tone shifted, hope strained through grit, like a soldier rallying troops before a losing fight. "Travelers, stick to highways, avoid forests, abandoned zones, and areas with reported anomalies. Portals have been sighted. report them to any military outpost, but do not engage alone." A beat, then stronger, defiant: "To survivors, we're working to restore communications, provide aid, and understand this crisis. Stay strong, together we'll endure." Static surged, swallowing her words, fading to mournful piano notes, slow and haunting, as the broadcast looped, a fragile thread in the silence.

I turned the volume down, the Jeep's rumble filling the cab, its growl a steady pulse against the quiet, Sara's scream pushing north, Harris's voice lingering like a ghost, her words a frayed lifeline I couldn't fully trust. The road stretched clear, but the weight of her warnings clung, the curse whispering low, "Every hope will crumble."

"So," Mithis said after a long stretch, her crimson eyes meeting mine, steady and searching, breaking the silence. "Your people are fighting back, organizing, even if it's crumbling."

"Yeah," I said, staring ahead, voice rough, the asphalt blurring under the tires, a faded signpost leaning crooked, "Exit 47" barely legible under rust. "Long shot they're swinging at shadows, barely grasping what's hitting 'em, trying to hold a world that's not ours anymore." My leg throbbed, bandages damp, the claw slash a dull ache, but the pain kept me sharp.

She tilted her head, green skin catching a shaft of sunlight, glinting faintly, her cape brushing the seat, wolf pelt shedding a few singed hairs. "They are still moving forward. That's a strength, sometimes." Her tone softened, a rare warmth cutting through her steel, her crimson eyes holding mine, steadying me.

I chuckled, dry and stiff, lips tugging under stubble and grime. " ya, that gets you far 'til it buries you." The Jeep hit a bump, supplies rattling louder, a jerry can clanging against the tailgate, the sound sharp in the quiet.

Her gaze held, then flicked north, the horizon darkening as clouds thickened, swallowing the sun. "And you're stubborn enough to find Sara, no matter what?" Her voice was quiet, testing, but sure, her axe haft creaking under her grip.

"Yeah," I said, tires humming low, Sara's scream loud, the curse clawing at my edges, hope flickering like a candle in a storm. "Ain't stopping 'til she's safe or I'm done." My eyes met hers, gray to crimson, her steel a quiet anchor, grounding the chaos, the curse's whisper held at bay.

The sun climbed higher, golden light spilling over fields and rusting cars, their hulks glinting dully, trees shedding warped bark in the breeze, their trunks peeling back to rough, natural oak and pine. Ahead, figures sharpened on the roadside, a dozen or so, huddled near a chipped RV, its white paint streaked with mud and ash, tires flat, windows boarded with splintered plywood. They were gaunt and worn, clutching makeshift weapons: rusted pipes, a splintered baseball bat, a kitchen knife flashing dull in the sunlight, their tired, wary eyes tracking us as we rolled close, their faces hollowed by hunger and fear, clothes patched and threadbare, boots caked with mud.

"Refugees," I said, easing the Jeep to a stop, the engine idling low, gravel spitting faintly under the tires, the air biting with frost and the faint rust of abandoned metal.

Mithis tensed, her axe shifting in her grip, runes flickering purple, her cape bunching as she leaned forward, crimson eyes narrowing. "Could be dangerous, desperation turns people fast." Her voice was low, cautious, her green fingers tightening on the haft, ready for anything.

"Could be," I said, grabbing my rifle, its cold weight grounding me as I slung it low, keeping it non-threatening but ready. "Might know something worth a shot." My boots crunched gravel as I stepped out, the air sharp with frost and the faint decay of abandoned vehicles, Mithis following close, her axe gleaming, cape swaying clean now, the wolf pelt brushing her boots, shedding ash.

The group stiffened, a man in his fifties stepping forward, gray hair matted under a frayed trucker cap, a crowbar gripped tight in calloused hands, its rusted edge glinting faintly. His face was lined deep under gray stubble, eyes narrowing on Mithis's green skin and glowing axe, suspicion flaring, his posture braced like a man who'd seen too much.

"That's close enough," he called, voice gravel-rough, the crowbar twitching in his grip, his breath fogging in the chill, his patched jacket stained with grease and blood, sleeves frayed to threads.

"Travelers," I said, hand raised, palm open, rifle slung low to signal peace. "Not here for trouble, just passing through." My tone was steady, soldier's habit, eyes meeting his, gray to brown, searching for trust.

His jaw ticked, gaze flicking to Mithis again, lingering on her crimson eyes, the axe's runes pulsing faintly, the crowbar easing slightly but not dropping. "And her?" His voice hardened, the group behind him shifting, pipes and knives tightening in their grips, a woman clutching a child close, her eyes wide with fear.

"With me," I said firmly, stepping slightly in front of Mithis, cutting off suspicion before it could flare. "Mithis, she's saved my life more times than I can count. She's solid." My words were clipped, leaving no room for doubt, my hand resting lightly on my rifle, non-threatening but ready.

He hesitated, eyes searching mine, then hers, the crowbar lowering to his side, thudding softly against his mud-caked boot. "What do you want?" His tone softened, wary but open, the group relaxing a fraction, their weapons dipping.

"Info," I said, scanning their gaunt faces, eyes hollowed by loss, a teenager clutching a bent wrench, a woman with a scarf wrapped tight, her hands trembling. "Looking for family, Sara Carter, Mark, and their kid, Lily. Sara's my sister, mid-thirties, dark hair, gray eyes. Mark's her husband, tall, bearded. Lily's five pigtails, always giggling. Seen 'em?" My voice caught, hope flickering, Sara's scream a burr in my skull, the curse clawing low.

A woman stepped up, pale and thin, her kind face softened by grief, a threadbare blanket draped around her shoulders, its edges frayed and stained. "Haven't seen them, sorry," she said, her breath fogging, hands trembling under the blanket's frayed edges, her eyes meeting mine, gentle but heavy. "We're from the north, though, Marquette, a big camp. They might've passed through up there, lots of folks do." Her voice was soft, a flicker of hope offered, her scarf slipping to reveal a cross necklace, tarnished but gleaming faintly.

Disappointment stabbed, a cold weight in my chest, but I nodded, shoving it down. "Thanks. How long have you been out here?" My eyes flicked over their group, counting twelve, maybe thirteen, including two kids, their faces smudged with dirt, clutching rag dolls.

"Too damn long," the man said, bitter, the crowbar thudding his boot again, the sound dull in the quiet. "Headed for a safe zone down south, but roads are blocked, bridges down, trees twisted unnaturally.

Then we got hit by... things. Lost half our group, and they were ripped apart in the dark." His voice shook, eyes darkening, the woman wincing behind him, her hand tightening on the child's shoulder.

"What kind?" Mithis asked, voice calm, crimson glinting as she stepped forward, her axe resting easy but ready, runes pulsing faintly, her cape swaying in the breeze.

"Mutants," he spat, eyes flashing with fear and rage, his crowbar twitching. "Looked human, but weren't. Fast, too strong teeth and claws like knives, blood everywhere." His voice broke, the teenager with the wrench looking away, his jaw tight, the woman's face crumpling for a moment before she steadied herself.

I glanced at Mithis, her grim nod confirming it, her crimson eyes steady. "Wraiths, or worse Ashvalen's bleed," she said softly, her tone heavy, the axe haft creaking under her grip, runes flaring briefly purple.

"We got supplies," the woman said softly, eyes flicking to our gear, hope and desperation mingling in her gaze, her blanket slipping further, revealing a patched sweater, holes darned with mismatched thread. "Not much, but we could share some canned beans, a little water."

"Appreciate it," I said, meeting her eyes, her kindness a small light in the dark. "We're stocked, but what about you? You look like you're running thin." My gaze flicked to their RV, its cargo bay open, a few dented cans and a single water jug visible, barely enough for a day.

The man shook his head, jaw tight, pride and defeat warring in his face. "We'll manage, always have." His voice was gruff, but his eyes softened, lingering on the kids, their rag dolls clutched tight.

I ducked into the Jeep, the tailgate creaking as I popped it open, grabbing three MREs, scratched packs labeled "Beef Stew," their corners torn but intact, and tossed them to the man, the packs landing with a soft thud in his calloused hands. "Take these, you might need 'em more than us." My tone was firm, leaving no room for argument, the soldier in me knowing hunger could kill as fast as claws.

He caught them, staring at the packs, then muttered a grudging "Thanks," his eyes softening further, a flicker of gratitude breaking through his wariness. The woman nodded, her smile faint but warm, pulling the blanket tighter.

"Careful out there," she said, voice low, eyes flicking south, where the highway vanished into a haze of dust and twisted trees. "South gets worse roads clogged with wrecks, things hunting in the dark. Saw a glowing crack in the woods, like a tear in the air. Stay away. Lost two running from it, didn't even scream." Her voice trembled, the child at her side burying his face in her leg, the rag doll dangling limp.

"Learned that the hard way," I said, nodding, the memory of the portal's searing light flashing sharp, the creature's yellow eyes burning in my skull. "You stay safe, too, stick together, keep moving." My words were clipped, soldier's advice, my eyes meeting hers, then the man's, a shared understanding of survival's cost.

We climbed back into the Jeep, the engine coughing alive, a guttural growl vibrating the dash, the tailgate slamming shut with a clang. Their huddle shrank in the rearview, the man clutching the MREs, the woman waving faintly, her blanket fluttering in the breeze, the RV a battered silhouette against the golden fields, fading as we rolled north.

"Strong," Mithis said after a stretch, voice low, crimson eyes flicking to the mirror, then to me. "Making it this far beat to hell, but breathing." Her tone was quiet, respect threading through her steel, her axe resting across her lap, runes dim but steady.

"Yeah," I said, tires crunching gravel, the highway stretching clear again, fields giving way to denser trees, their branches shedding warped bark, peeling normally in the breeze. "Strength only gets you so far, then it's luck or grit." My voice was rough, Sara's scream pulling north, the curse clawing low, hope a stubborn spark refusing to die.

The highway rolled on, monotony clawing at the edges of my focus, rusted cars silent sentinels, their husks glinting dully in the noon sun, signposts leaning crooked, their green paint peeling, "Marquette 30 MI" barely legible under rust and grime. Ahead, a military checkpoint loomed, abandoned, its skeletal frame stark against the sky, rusted Humvees sagging on flat tires, sandbags stacked unevenly, their burlap torn and spilling dirt, tattered American flags fluttering faintly under the harsh glare, their stars faded to gray, stripes stained with ash and mud.

"Been a while since anyone's been here," I said, easing off the gas, the Jeep slowing, gravel spitting faintly under the tires, the engine's growl dropping to a low idle, the air heavy with rust and decay, a faint tang of blood lingering.

Mithis leaned forward, crimson eyes narrowing, her axe shifting in her grip, runes flickering purple, casting faint shadows across the dash. "I Feel there is something wrong here and it is still lingering. Watch out." Her voice was low, edged with caution, her green skin stark in the sunlight, her cape bunching as she scanned the checkpoint, every sense alert, a predator's instinct honed by Ashvalen's chaos.

I stopped the Jeep, engine idling, stepping out with my rifle, its cold weight grounding me as I slung it low, barrel pointed down but ready, my boots crunching gravel, the air biting with frost and the sour rot of abandoned gear. Mithis followed, her axe gleaming, runes pulsing brighter, her boots scuffing softly, her cape swaying. The checkpoint sprawled desolate papers fluttering across cracked asphalt, caught in eddies of wind, MRE wrappers and torn maps, their edges curling like charred leaves. Gear lay scattered: a dented helmet, a cracked magazine, a blood-crusted bayonet half-buried in mud. Blood stained the sandbags, crusted black, pooling in ruts under the Humvees, their tan paint chipped and streaked with ash, machine guns rusted silent, barrels drooping like broken limbs.

Inside the guard station, a plywood shack sagging under a warped roof, maps hung torn on splintered walls, pinned with rusted tacks, red ink bleeding over faded counties, marking patrol routes long abandoned. A smashed radio lay cracked on a folding table, its dials shattered, wires spilling like guts, a faint hiss of static leaking from its broken shell. A logbook sprawled open beside it, yellowed pages smudged with shaky ink, the handwriting jagged, frantic, stained with sweat and blood.

I flipped through, my finger tracing the scrawled entries, each one a snapshot of collapse. "Day 3 refugees steady, supplies low, morale holding. Day 7 creature reports, patrols gone, no contact. Day 10 portal sighted near woods, blue glow, screams at night, morale shot." My gut sank, the words tightening my chest, Sara's scream echoing north, the curse clawing low. "Day 12 attacked, night, creatures everywhere, claws and wings, lost six. Day 14 can't hold, falling back, may God help us all..." Blood speckled the last page, a smeared handprint smudging the ink, the pen lying broken beside it, its tip bent, the silence slamming down like a tomb, heavy and final.

Mithis stood close, her axe haft creaking, crimson eyes scanning the shack, then flicking outside, to the blood-stained sandbags, the scattered gear. "They fought hard," she said softly, her voice heavy, respect threading through her steel, her green fingers tightening on the axe, runes pulsing faintly purple. "But something broke."

"Yeah," I said, closing the logbook, its cover creaking, the weight of their final words settling in my gut, Sara's scream pulling north, relentless, the curse whispering low, "every life you touch will rot." "Whatever hit 'em, it's gone now or waiting." My eyes flicked to the woods beyond, their dark treeline looming, branches twisting faintly, unnatural, a faint shimmer of blue glinting deep within, barely visible, a warning I couldn't ignore.

21 BLOOD ON THE LOGBOOK

I set the logbook down, my jaw tightening as the yellowed pages crunched against the desk's chipped wood, its surface scarred with gouges and stained with dried coffee rings. "They knew what was coming but couldn't stop it." The words tasted bitter, like stale coffee gone cold, the checkpoint's silence pressing against my skull, heavy as the blood-crusted air. The scrawled entries, creature attacks, portals, screams in the night burned in my mind, a grim echo of the chaos we'd been fighting, Sara's scream looping north, relentless, the curse clawing low: "Every life you touch will rot."

Mithis stepped into the guard station, her boots scuffing the cracked linoleum, the sound sharp in the stillness, her cape swaying with a rustle of wolf pelts, their singed edges shedding faint ash. Her expression was grim, crimson eyes glinting dull under the flickering light of a single bulb dangling from a frayed cord, its weak glow casting jagged shadows across peeling walls. "Did they say what attacked them?" Her voice cut low, steady but laced with urgency, her green fingers tightening on her axe haft, runes pulsing a faint purple, reflecting off the station's rusted metal shelves.

"Creatures," I said, tapping the logbook with a calloused finger, the ink smudged from someone's sweaty grip, the paper curling at the edges. "And a portal near the woods blue glow, screams at night. Sounds like what we've been dealing with." The air hung heavy, thick with the tang of rust from scattered gear and mildew creeping from damp corners, the walls sagging under years of neglect, their faded green paint flaking like dead skin.

She nodded, her green skin catching the bulb's weak glow, runes on her axe pulsing brighter, casting stark violet shadows across her sharp features. "The convergence is spreading faster than we thought." Her tone sank, a quiet certainty threading through it, like she could feel the world unraveling in her bones, her crimson eyes flicking to the busted window, where shards of glass glinted in the frame, catching the dusk's dying light.

As we turned to leave, a noise snagged my attention: a low, rhythmic thudding, distant but swelling, rolling through the ground like a heartbeat waking up, vibrating faintly through the linoleum. I froze, raising my hand, palm rough with dirt and split scabs, signaling

Mithis to stop, my pulse kicking hard against my ribs. The station's busted window rattled, glass shards tinkling softly, the sound sharp in the oppressive quiet, a breeze whistling through the frame, carrying frost and the faint rot of decay.

"What is it?" she whispered, her breath fogging briefly in the cool air, axe haft creaking as her grip tightened, her cape bunching as she crouched slightly, crimson eyes narrowing, scanning the shadows beyond the station's peeling walls.

I listened, heart hammering, the sound growing thud-thud-thud closer now, paired with a tremor I could feel through my boots, the ground pulsing like a living thing. "Something's coming." My voice scraped low, adrenaline spiking hot, my rifle snapping up, stock cold against my cheek, the scratched stock slick under my palm as I scanned the road ahead, shadows shifting unnaturally among the pines.

We moved fast, ducking out the door, gravel crunching underfoot as we took cover behind a rusted Humvee, its tan paint flaked off in jagged patches, streaked with mud and crusted blood, the hood dented like someone had taken a sledgehammer to it, its windshield shattered into a spiderweb of cracks. I peeked over the edge, rifle steady, the air biting with frost and decay, a diesel tang lingering from the checkpoint's abandoned pumps, mixing with the sour rot of blood pooled in ruts under sandbags. Mithis crouched beside me, her cape brushing the Humvee's pitted wheel well, axe held low, runes pulsing brighter, casting a faint purple glow across the gravel.

Out of the tangled pines lumbered a massive figure, easily eight feet tall, emerging like a nightmare stitched from bone and shadow, its silhouette stark against the bruised sky. It was humanoid but grotesquely twisted, a patchwork of jagged, bone-like protrusions jutting from its shoulders and spine, sharp as broken glass, glinting wet in the fading sunlight. Its skin gleamed gray and slick, rippling with corded muscle beneath, stretched taut over an unnatural frame, veins pulsing faintly blue under the surface. Its eyes glowed an unnatural green, twin slits cutting through the dusk, unblinking and malevolent, set in a skull too angular, too predatory in the shape of a triangle. Each step shook the ground, heavy and deliberate, cracking the asphalt under clawed feet the size of hubcaps, their talons scraping sparks with every stride, leaving gouges in the pavement.

"What the hell is that?" I muttered, breath fogging as I gripped my rifle tighter, knuckles aching under scabs, the stock pressing hard into my shoulder, my pulse a drumbeat in my ears.

"An enforcer," Mithis said, voice tight, her crimson eyes narrowing, tracking its every move, her axe haft creaking under her gloved grip, runes flaring like a warning pulse. "A creature sent to guard their creator or destroy those who interfere with them. Strong, fast, hard to kill." Her tone was clipped, analytical, but her posture tensed, a warrior bracing for blood, her cape swaying faintly in the breeze.

The enforcer paused near the breached barricade, sandbags spilling their dirt onto the pavement, barbed wire glinting dull and twisted, tangled like thorns. Its glowing eyes swept the area, slow and methodical, a guttural growl rumbling from its chest deep, bone-rattling, vibrating the air like a storm rolling in, buzzing my teeth. Its head tilted, nostrils flaring wide, sniffing the wind, jagged teeth flashing yellow in a maw that could snap a man in half, saliva dripping in thick strands, steaming faintly on the cold asphalt.

"It hasn't seen us yet," I whispered, ducking lower, the Humvee's cold metal pressing into my shoulder, its rusted edge biting through my torn jacket. "We need to decide fight or hide?" My breath fogged, heart pounding, Sara's scream flickering north, the curse clawing low, urging me to move, to act.

Mithis gripped her axe, the blade's purple glow reflecting off her green knuckles, her expression resolute as forged steel, crimson eyes blazing with a fire I'd come to trust. "If we run, it'll follow our scent, hunt us down. We need to end this now." Her voice held no doubt, only the weight of inevitability, her cape swaying as she shifted her stance, boots grinding gravel, ready to spring.

I nodded, checking my rifle mag full, thirty rounds, safety off, the familiar weight grounding me against the dread knotting my gut. "Alright. I'll distract it if you go for the kill." My tone was clipped, soldier's habit, adrenaline sharpening my focus, the pain in my ribs and leg dulling to a background hum.

Mithis gave a curt nod, her crimson eyes steady, glinting with fierce determination, her gloves creaking as she adjusted her grip, the axe's runes flaring brighter, casting stark shadows across the Humvee's pitted hood.

Taking a deep breath, I stepped out from behind the Humvee, boots crunching loudly on the gravel, the sound sharp in the eerie quiet, my rifle snapping up, barrel trained on the enforcer's glowing eyes. I fired a single shot, cracked, deafening, the bullet sparking off its shoulder, ricocheting into the pines with a high-pitched whine, leaves rustling as it struck. A thin line of black ichor trickled from the hit, steaming faintly, but its armor-like skin held firm, the wound shallow, barely a scratch. The creature roared, a sound that clawed at my ears, a guttural shriek that rattled my skull, and spun toward me with terrifying speed, green eyes locking on like searchlights, burning with fury.

"Over here, you ugly bastard!" I shouted, voice raw, firing again as I backed toward the station, the bullet pinging uselessly off its chest, sparking against bone protrusions, the recoil jarring my bruised ribs. My pulse hammered, legs moving on instinct drilled from years in the sandbox, dodging through scattered crates and sandbags, their burlap torn and spilling dirt.

The enforcer charged, its massive frame barreling forward, asphalt splintering under its weight, claws gouging deep ruts in the pavement, sparks flying as talons scraped stone. I dove at the last second, rolling hard, gravel biting into my elbows, tearing through my jacket, the pain sharp but fleeting. Its bony arm swung, missing me by inches, the air hissing past my head, the claw smashing a crate to splinters, wood shards spraying like shrapnel, pelting my face. Mithis sprang from the shadows, her glowing axe slicing a brutal arc through its side, the blade biting deep, black ichor spraying hot and steaming onto the pavement, hissing like acid. The enforcer howled, a shrill, guttural sound that buzzed my teeth, its body staggering, green eyes flaring brighter, claws slashing wildly, gouging the Humvee's hood with a screech of metal.

"Keep it distracted!" Mithis shouted, dodging a wild swing of its massive arm, the claw whistling past her cape, tearing a shred of wolf pelt loose, the fur fluttering to the ground. She danced back, boots skidding on loose gravel, runes flaring bright along her axe, casting violet light across her green face, sweat streaking her brow, her crimson eyes fierce with focus.

I fired again, aiming for its glowing eyes, the rifle barking sharply, recoil jarring my shoulder. One bullet connected, punching through the left socket with a wet pop, ichor splashing dark and thick, steaming as it hit the asphalt. The creature staggered, clawing at its face, a guttural snarl bubbling from its throat, its remaining eye blazing green, fury undimmed. Mithis seized the gap, lunging forward, her axe driving deep into its chest with a sickening crunch, bone and flesh parting under the glowing blade, ichor gushing in a steaming torrent, soaking her gloves, pitting the leather further.

The enforcer let out a final, bone-rattling roar, its remaining eye flaring bright then dimming fast, body jerking as black smoke curled from its wounds, swirling upward like a dying fire. It collapsed hard, knees cracking the asphalt, shards flying, then slumped still, a steaming heap of jagged bone and gray flesh, the ground stained dark beneath it, ichor pooling in ruts, reflecting the dusk's weak light.

Breathing heavily, Mithis yanked her axe free, ichor dripping in thick globs from the blade, splattering her boots, steaming faintly in the cold air. "It's done," she rasped, chest heaving, her green brow slick with sweat, blood crusting her nose from the fight's strain, her crimson eyes dulled by exhaustion but burning with triumph.

I nodded, lowering my rifle, barrel hot in my hands, the metal stinging my palms, adrenaline still buzzing through me, my leg throbbing where blood soaked my jeans, Sara's scream flickering north, the curse clawing low, "every life you touch will rot." "For now," I said, voice rough, wiping sweat from my brow, smearing dirt and ichor across my face, the rifle's weight grounding me against the tremor in my hands.

We returned to the Jeep, glancing back at the silent checkpoint, its busted guard station gaping like a wound, the enforcer's corpse a dark smear against the cracked pavement, smoke curling into the dusk, dissipating in the breeze. Whatever had happened here, the fight was far from over, the convergence bleeding deeper, Ashvalen's grip tightening with every portal, every creature. The logbook's final words May God help us all hung heavy, a warning we couldn't ignore.

"Let's keep moving," I said, sliding into the driver's seat, the cracked vinyl creaking under me as I turned the key, the engine coughing alive, a low growl vibrating the dash, gauges flickering erratically before settling. "The next checkpoint might not be so empty."

Mithis climbed in beside me, her gaze lingering on the enforcer's corpse, crimson eyes thoughtful, axe resting across her lap, its glow dimming to a soft pulse. "The convergence won't stop unless we find the source." Her tone was quiet but firm, her cape brushing the torn seat with a scrape, wolf pelts shedding ash and ichor, her green fingers tightening on the haft, runes pulsing faintly purple.

"Then we'd better hurry," I said, steering the Jeep back onto the highway, tires humming over buckled asphalt, the road stretching into the unknown, jagged pines clawing the horizon, their branches twisting faintly, unnatural in the dusk's dying light. The weight of the fight pressed heavier with each mile, Sara's voice pulling relentlessly north, the curse a shadow I couldn't outrun, Mithis's steel the only thing keeping it at bay.

The next checkpoint appeared as we crested a low rise, its silhouette sharp against the bruised sky, the sun dipping low, spilling weak gold through patchy clouds, glinting off rusted metal and cracked concrete. It mirrored the last sandbags and rusted Humvees but stood in better shape, barricades intact, neatly stacked, the faded U.S. Army emblem stenciled on the guard station's chipped concrete wall, its edges flaking. Yet, something gnawed at me, no movement, no flicker of life, just an eerie stillness hanging thick as the frost-clear air, the only sound the wind whistling through tangled barbed wire, its barbs glinting like jagged teeth.

Mithis leaned forward, crimson eyes narrowing, her breath fogging the streaked windshield, her axe shifting in her grip, runes pulsing a warning glow. "It's too quiet." Her voice cut low, edged with caution, her green skin stark in the cab's dim light, her cape bunching as she scanned the checkpoint, every sense alert, a predator's instinct honed by Ashvalen's chaos.

"Yeah," I muttered, easing off the gas, gravel spitting faintly under the tires as I slowed the Jeep to a crawl, the engine's growl dropping to a low rumble. "Let's check it out." My gut twisted, a slow churn like bad rations settling, the checkpoint too clean, too still for a military post in this mess, the absence of chaos its kind of warning.

I parked just outside the perimeter, the engine ticking as it cooled, and grabbed my rifle, slinging it over my shoulder, the weight grounding me against the unease crawling up my spine, my leg throbbing faintly under damp bandages. Mithis followed, axe ready, its blade catching the dusk's dying light with a shimmer of purple, her boots scuffing softly, cape swaying, the wolf pelt brushing her calves. The air hung heavy, laced with burnt fuel and a metallic tang, papers fluttering across the ground, torn maps, supply lists, a faded photo of a smiling family, its edges curling like charred leaves.

We swept the area cautiously, rifles up, my barrel tracing the shadows between sandbags and busted crates, their wood splintered, spilling nails and rusted tools. The guard station door hung ajar, swaying on rusted hinges, creaking a mournful note in the breeze, its faded green paint peeling in strips. I nudged it open with my rifle, metal scraping concrete, the sound sharp in the quiet, and stepped inside, the air stale with dust and the faint rot of abandoned gear. The station was chaotic, maps and documents strewn across the floor, curling at the edges from damp air, chairs overturned, a chipped coffee mug shattered in a corner, its handle lying like a broken bone. A bloodstain smeared the far wall, dark and crusted, streaking down like a claw had dragged it there, pooling in a congealed puddle on the linoleum, its edges flaking dry.

"Looks like they left in a hurry," I said, voice low, stepping over a splintered clipboard, its papers fluttering under my boots, the ink smudged with sweat and blood, listing patrol schedules long abandoned.

Mithis followed, her gaze raking the room, crimson eyes glinting in the dimness, her axe held loose but ready, cape brushing a toppled stool with a dull thud. "Or something forced them to leave." Her tone was flat, certain, her green fingers tightening on the haft, runes pulsing brighter, casting faint purple shadows across the cluttered floor.

I crouched by a desk, rifling through the mess, most were routine: supply logs scratched in hasty pencil, tallying MREs and fuel cans; patrol schedules smudged with sweat, marking routes to nowhere; radio frequencies long gone static, their numbers faded to illegibility. Then one snagged my eye, bold red letters stamped across the top: "CLASSIFIED." The paper was creased, edges torn, ink bleeding from dampness, the weight of its words palpable even before I read them.

"What's this?" I murmured, picking it up, the rough texture scraping my fingers, my pulse quickening as I scanned the text, each line hitting like a punch.

The document was a cold, calculated gut-punch government order, stripped of pretense: "All essential personnel are to evacuate to secured facilities on the West Coast, effective immediately. Civilian refugee influx is to be restricted to prevent resource strain. Military units are authorized to use any means necessary to prevent unauthorized movement toward secured zones. Lethal force is approved if compliance cannot be achieved." My stomach tightened, a knot of anger coiling hot, the words sinking in like lead, each one a betrayal carved in ink.

I clenched the paper, jaw locking hard enough to ache, the edges crumpling in my fist. "They've abandoned the rest of the country." My voice came out bitter, raw, the station's stale air tasting sour on my tongue, the bloodstain on the wall looming like an accusation.

Mithis stepped closer, her shadow falling over me, expression unreadable under the glow of her runes, her cape rustling as she leaned in, green fingers brushing the desk's edge. "What do you mean?" Her voice was low, cautious, her crimson eyes flicking to the paper, narrowing as she sensed the weight of it.

I handed her the document, the paper crinkling in the quiet, its words a poison I couldn't hold alone. "The government fled to the West Coast. They're pulling the military back to defend themselves, VIPs, brass, whoever they deem 'essential', and leaving everyone else to fend for themselves. Worse, they're ordering the military to stop refugees from getting anywhere near them, 'any means necessary.' That's code for shoot on sight." The words burned coming out, Sara's scream flickering north, the curse clawing low, "every hope will crumble," my hands flexing against the rifle's scratched stock.

She scanned it, crimson eyes narrowed to slits, her gloves creaking as she gripped it tighter, the paper trembling faintly in her hands. "Your leaders would abandon their people?" Disbelief edged her voice, cold and sharp, like she couldn't fathom the betrayal stitched into those lines, her green face tightening, a flicker of disgust breaking through her steel.

"Looks like it," I said, tossing the paper onto the desk with a dull slap, standing fast enough to make my knees crack, the linoleum creaking under my boots. "I shouldn't be surprised the army taught me plenty about brass screwing the grunts, friends bleeding out in the sandbox while suits sipped coffee in D.C. But this? This is a whole country left to rot." My voice shook, anger simmering hot, the memory of Lily giggling over FaceTime, Sara's voice fraying on that call, "Jake, something's wrong," stabbing sharp, driving me north, relentless.

Mithis set the paper down, her gaze drifting to the bloodstain, thoughtful, her crimson eyes glinting in the dimness. "If they're consolidating power, they must feel the situation is truly hopeless. They've decided to save what they can, even if it costs countless lives." Her tone steadied, analytical, but that flicker of disgust lingered, her green fingers tightening on her axe, runes pulsing faintly purple.

"Yeah, well, that's not good enough," I said, voice rough, hands flexing against my rifle, the cold steel grounding me against the rage boiling in my chest. "They can hide all they want, but people like my sister are still out here, fighting to survive. They deserve better than this, Sara, Mark, Lily, all of them." The memory of Lily's pigtails bouncing, her laugh echoing through a grainy video call, hit like a blade, the curse clawing low, but hope burned stubborn, refusing to die.

We searched deeper, boots scuffing over debris, splintered wood, torn papers, a rusted canteen leaking stale water onto the floor. The station held more signs of retreat: crates of unopened MREs stacked haphazardly in a corner, their brown packs faded but intact, labeled "cheese tortellini" and "Beef goulash"; ammo cans spilling 5.56 rounds across a shelf, brass glinting dull under the bulb's weak glow; a generator humming in the corner, its diesel growl the only life left here, its fuel gauge hovering near empty, cables snaking across the floor, powering nothing. Whoever manned this post had bolted fast, leaving gear scattered like they thought they'd be back or didn't care who picked up the scraps, their haste etched in every overturned chair, every spilled can.

"They didn't even try to destroy their resources," Mithis said, running gloved fingers over a box of rations, the cardboard tearing under her touch, "Chicken Noodle" peeling off the label, her crimson eyes narrowing, thoughtful. "Careless or desperate."

"Probably thought they'd be back," I said grimly, hefting an ammo can, its weight clinking cold in my hands, the brass rattling faintly. "Or didn't care enough to make sure no one else could use it." The waste gnawed at me, refugees starving, bleeding, while this sat untouched, a lifeline abandoned in the chaos.

We loaded the Jeep food, water, ammo, piling it into the back, cans thudding against dented steel, jerry cans sloshing heavily, their scratched surfaces glinting in the dusk. The MREs stacked unevenly beside the oak chest, their corners tearing, labels smearing under my grip, the weight a small comfort against the betrayal burning in my gut. We stepped outside, the checkpoint looming still, sandbags sagging under their weight, the bloodstain's shadow stretching long across the pavement, the air heavy with frost and decay, the document's words a poison lingering like rot.

"What now?" Mithis asked, climbing into the passenger seat, her cape pooling dark against the torn vinyl, axe propped between her knees, runes pulsing faintly, her crimson eyes meeting mine, steady and searching.

I gripped the wheel, chipped paint flaking under my palms, staring down the empty road ahead, asphalt buckling under encroaching vines, their leaves shimmering faintly blue, unnatural in the dusk's weak light. "This doesn't change what we do, find Sara, keep moving north. But people will have to answer for this, one day." My voice scraped firm, Sara's scream pulling relentlessly, the curse whispering low, "every life you touch will rot," but hope flickered, stubborn, fueled by anger now, a fire I could use.

Mithis nodded, resolute, her crimson eyes glinting sure in the cab's dimness, her green fingers tightening on her axe, runes pulsing brighter. "Then let's not waste time." Her tone was steady, a warrior's resolve, her cape brushing the seat with a quiet scrape, wolf pelts shedding ash.

The Jeep roared back to life, engine growling low as I pulled onto the highway, tires humming over cracked pavement, the checkpoint shrinking in the rearview, its sandbags and bloodstains fading to silhouettes against the dusk. The government might think they could bunker down behind West Coast barricades, safe in their fortified hubs, but they couldn't outrun this chaos forever, not with Ashvalen bleeding in, not with enforcers and portals tearing the world apart, not with survivors like us still fighting, moving. Anger simmered hot under my skin, fuel for the miles ahead, Sara's scream a beacon I'd chase until it broke me.

The road stretched on, winding through a landscape twisting stranger by the minute, Earth and Ashvalen fusing in jagged patches. Fields dotted with glowing plants, their stalks shimmering blue under the fading sun, swaying like underwater reeds; clouds overhead rippling unnaturally, streaked with veins of violet, pulsing faintly as if alive; a deer-like creature with antlers of crystal darted across the road, its hooves clicking sharp, vanishing into the brush with a flash of light, leaving a faint shimmer in the air. Mithis and I drove in silence, the checkpoint's betrayal lingering heavy, the Jeep's rattle a steady pulse against it, supplies thudding faintly in the back, a reminder of what we'd scavenged from the wreckage.

Then, cresting a hill, a town came into view, not the hollowed-out husks we'd passed, their windows gaping like skulls, but alive, buzzing with purpose. People moved through the streets, some hauling crates of supplies, their boots squelching mud, others posted at fortified barricades of wood and scrap metal, their edges jagged, glinting under floodlights' harsh glare. At the center, a glowing dome of magical energy shimmered gold, encasing a cluster of brick buildings, old storefronts, a library, and a town hall, its surface rippling like water under a breeze, casting a warm wash over the cracked facades, softening their scars.

"Looks like they're doing more than just surviving," I said, easing off the gas, tires crunching gravel as we slowed, the Jeep's engine dropping to a low rumble, the town's hum of activity carrying on the breeze, a mix of voices, hammers, and the faint crackle of magic.

Mithis leaned forward, crimson eyes narrowing, her breath fogging the streaked windshield, her axe shifting in her grip, runes pulsing brighter, casting purple shadows across her green face. "There's magic here, strong magic, woven deep." Her voice was low, reverent, her cape rustling as she straightened, her senses attuned to the energy pulsing through the town, a warrior recognizing power.

As we rolled to the outskirts, two soldiers stepped onto the road, rifles snapping up, muzzles glinting cold under the dusk's last light, their camo streaked with mud and ash, helmets casting shadows over weathered faces. Behind them stood a figure in flowing, deep blue robes, tattered at the hems, stitched with silver threads that glimmered faintly, catching the floodlights' glare. One hand raised, traces of magical energy flickered around their fingertips, green sparks dancing like fireflies, crackling faintly in the quiet. A hood shadowed their face, but their stance screamed authority, shoulders squared, robes swaying in the breeze, the air around them humming with restrained power.

"Halt!" one soldier barked, voice clipped, boots planted wide on the cracked pavement, his M4 steady, finger hovering near the trigger guard, his partner's rifle trained on the Jeep, eyes narrowing under a helmet streaked with mud. "State your business."

I stopped the Jeep, engine idling low, and raised my hands, palms rough and scabbed in the floodlights' glare, my rifle slung low to signal peace. "We're travelers looking for supplies and information." My tone stayed even, soldier's habit kicking in, eyes locked on the soldier's, gray to brown, searching for trust, Sara's scream flickering north, the curse clawing low.

The robed figure stepped forward, robes swaying, their voice calm but edged with command, cutting through the air like a blade, resonant and clear despite the hood's shadow. "You travel with one of Ashvalen's kin." It wasn't a question, their hidden gaze fixed on Mithis, energy flickering brighter around their hand, green sparks flaring, crackling like static, the air tightening with their scrutiny.

Mithis tilted her head, crimson eyes steady, unyielding, her tone firm as forged steel, her axe resting loose in her grip, runes glowing but controlled, a quiet challenge in her posture. "I'm not a threat. I'm here to help, same as you, fighting what's bleeding through." Her voice was calm, resolute, her cape brushing the seat with a quiet scrape, wolf pelts shedding ash, her green skin stark in the floodlights' glare.

The figure studied her, a long beat of silence stretching tight, the air humming with tension, the soldiers' rifles steady, their fingers twitching near triggers. Then the figure nodded curtly, sparks fading from their fingers, the green light dimming, the air easing slightly. "You may enter. But be warned, violence will not be tolerated here." Their voice eased a hair, the threat lingering beneath like a coiled spring, their robes swaying as they stepped aside, the soldiers lowering their rifles, muzzles dipping toward the pavement.

"Understood," I said, easing the Jeep through the barricade, tires crunching over splintered planks and gravel, the wood creaking under the weight, the town's hum growing louder, a pulse of life in the chaos. The soldiers waved us through, their eyes tracking us, wary but disciplined, their boots scuffing mud as they returned to their posts.

Inside, the town thrummed differently, a fragile bubble of order carved from the madness. Military Humvees squatted beside wooden carts, their tan paint chipped and streaked with ash, tires caked with mud; soldiers patrolled in camo, M4s slung low, runes glowing gold along their barrels, etched deep, shimmering faintly in the dusk. Civilians worked alongside robed figures, mages, I clocked fast, their hands weaving light into cracked walls, golden threads sealing bricks with a soft hum, purifying water in dented barrels with a shimmer of blue, the liquid glowing briefly before settling clear. Others tended wounds with glowing palms, green light pulsing over bloodied bandages, knitting flesh with a faint crackle, the air buzzing electric, a mix of diesel, sweat, and ozone, the glowing dome casting a warm wash over brick facades and boarded windows, softening the town's scars.

"This is impressive," Mithis said as we parked near the town square, the Jeep's engine ticking cool, her boots thudding gravel as she stepped out, axe slung low, runes pulsing faintly, her crimson eyes scanning the bustling streets, the dome's golden light reflecting in her gaze, a warrior marveling at a new kind of battle.

"Yeah," I said, slinging my rifle, its weight grounding me, my leg throbbing faintly under damp bandages, Sara's scream pulling north, the curse whispering low, but hope flickering brighter here, in this town's defiance. "They're not just surviving, they're fighting back, building something." My voice was rough, the town's pulse a spark against the betrayal of the checkpoint, the government's abandonment, the weight of the convergence. We stepped into the square, the hum of magic and grit surrounding us, a new chapter in the chaos.

22 HIGHWAY TO HAVEN

A woman approached, striding confidently through the bustling town square, her uniform crisp despite the mud streaking her combat boots, their laces frayed but tightly knotted. Captain's bars gleamed dull on her olive drab jacket, catching the golden glow of the magical dome overhead, but her gear stood out body armor etched with glowing symbols, blue lines pulsing along the ceramic plates, humming faintly with latent energy, a sidearm at her hip radiating a soft aura, its holster etched with runes that shimmered green in the dusk. Her face was angular, brown eyes cutting through us like a blade, her dark hair pulled tight under a cap streaked with ash and dust, a faint scar tracing her jaw, pale against her weathered skin.

"I'm Captain Elena Carter," she said, extending a hand, her grip firm through worn leather gloves, calluses scraping against mine, her posture radiating command tempered by hard-won pragmatism. "Welcome to Haven. You're lucky to have found us." Her voice carried weight, steady but not unkind, lines carved deep around her mouth from too many hard days, her breath fogging faintly in the frost-clear air, mingling with the dome's warm glow.

"Jake McAllister," I replied, shaking her hand, my calluses rough from days gripping the Jeep's wheel and my rifle's stock, the ache in my ribs a dull pulse beneath my torn jacket. "This is Mithis. We're just passing through, trying to survive out there." My tone stayed even, soldier's habit, my eyes meeting hers, gray to brown, searching for trust, Sara's scream flickering north, the curse clawing low: every life you touch will rot.

Carter's gaze slid to Mithis, lingering on the glowing axe strapped across her back, its runes pulsing purple, casting stark shadows across her green skin, her crimson eyes glinting fiercely in the dome's light. "You've brought an interesting ally. We've been working closely with those who can wield magic, Ashvalen's kin, mages from their world. It's been... enlightening." Her tone warmed, a smirk tugging her lips, softening the hard edges of her face, a spark of curiosity in her eyes as she sized Mithis up, soldier to warrior.

"Looks like it's working out for you," I said, nodding toward the bustling streets, where a mage sealed a cracked brick wall with a flash of silver light, threads of energy weaving tight, a soldier hauling a crate stamped "MRE" past a glowing cart, its wooden frame etched with runes that hummed softly, fruits and bread piled high, untouched by rot. The air buzzed with purpose, diesel, sweat, and ozone mixing with the faint crackle of magic, the dome's golden wash softening the town's scars, its barricades of scrap metal and wood standing firm against the chaos beyond.

"It's not without its challenges," Carter admitted, crossing her arms, her armor creaking faintly, the blue runes pulsing brighter for a moment, reflecting off her cap's brim. "The convergence keeps throwing new threats, creatures, anomalies, and portals. But we've made progress. The mages have been helping us enhance our equipment, giving us an edge against whatever's out there." Her voice carried a soldier's grit, tempered by cautious hope, her eyes flicking to a pair of civilians patching a boarded window, their hammers clanging in rhythm with the town's pulse.

Mithis tilted her head, crimson eyes curious, her axe haft creaking in her gloved grip, the purple glow flaring briefly as she shifted her weight, her cape of wolf pelts rustling, shedding faint ash. "Enhancing your equipment? How?" Her voice cut clear, green fingers brushing the hilt of her machete, its blade strapped to her thigh, its own runes pulsing faintly in sync with her axe, a warrior's instinct drawn to the promise of new power.

Carter gestured with a gloved hand, beckoning us forward, her boots scuffing gravel as she turned. "Come. I'll show you." Her tone was brisk, commanding, but laced with a quiet pride, her cap casting a shadow across her brow as she led us through the square, weaving past soldiers hauling ammo cans and mages weaving light into dented water barrels, their blue glow purifying the liquid with a soft hum.

She guided us to a warehouse on the town's edge, its steel walls dented and patched with mismatched plates, rivets glinting in the dome's light, the massive doors groaning wide on rusted tracks, screeching as they parted to reveal a hive of activity within. Inside, chaos hummed soldiers and mages bent over long tables, tools clattering, the air thick with the sharp tang of oil, sweat, and a low hum of magic that buzzed my teeth, like standing too close to a live wire. A soldier test-fired a rifle at a makeshift range in the corner, glowing projectiles streaking blue across the room, punching through a steel plate with a crack, sparks flying, the impact echoing off the concrete floor. A mage adjusted runes on a set of body armor, its surface shimmering with protective energy, silver threads pulsing as they wove the spell tight, the air around it rippling faintly, like heat off asphalt. Another table held glowing stones, some green, some violet, pulsing in wooden crates, their light casting eerie shadows across the warehouse's high ceiling, where exposed beams sagged under years of neglect.

"We've been experimenting," Carter explained, her voice cutting through the din, gesturing to a workbench littered with gun parts, disassembled rifles, pistol slides, magazines, and glowing stones, their surfaces etched with runes that pulsed in rhythm with the mages' chants. "Combining our world's technology with Ashvalen's magic. It's not perfect, misfires, unstable runes, the occasional explosion, but it's giving us a fighting chance against creatures that shrug off standard rounds." Her tone was matter-of-fact, but her eyes glinted with fierce determination, her hand resting on her sidearm's grip, its runes flaring green under her touch.

Mithis picked up a modified sidearm from a crate, its sleek barrel etched with runes that shimmered green, pulsing as she turned it in her gloved hands, the metal warm to the touch, humming faintly, like a living thing. "This is impressive. Your people are adapting quickly, bridging worlds in ways I hadn't expected." Her tone held respect, crimson eyes tracing the weapon's lines, the runes on her axe flaring in sync, casting violet light across her green knuckles, her cape swaying as she tested the pistol's weight, a warrior recognizing craftsmanship.

"We have to," Carter said, jaw tightening a hair, her cap's shadow deepening the lines on her face. "The creatures out there are evolving stronger, smarter, some armored like tanks, others slipping through shadows like smoke. The convergence is accelerating, portals opening faster, bleeding Ashvalen deeper into our world. We can't afford to fall behind." Her voice hardened, a soldier's resolve forged in blood, her eyes flicking to a mage reinforcing a Humvee's hood, its steel plates pulsing with glowing metal veins, warm and humming like a heartbeat.

I nodded, running a hand over the Humvee's hood, its surface etched with runes that shimmered blue, the metal vibrating faintly under my palm, alive with magic, its olive drab paint chipped but reinforced with plates that gleamed like polished silver. "This might actually work," I said, voice rough, hope flickering stubborn under the weight of the road, the checkpoint's betrayal still burning in my gut, Sara's scream pulling north, the curse clawing low, every hope will crumble.

Carter turned to us, brown eyes serious, her cap casting a shadow across her brow, her armor's runes pulsing steadily, a quiet promise of power. "We could use people like you, travelers with experience, willing to fight, who've faced the convergence and lived. If you're interested, we could enhance your gear, give you the tools to survive out there, maybe even thrive." Her tone was direct, soldier to soldier, no sugarcoating, her gaze holding mine, steady and searching.

I glanced at Mithis, her nod quick, crimson eyes steadying me, her green fingers tightening on the sidearm, runes flaring briefly. "What's the catch?" I asked, crossing my arms, my rifle thudding against my chest, its scratched stock grounding me, the ache in my leg a dull pulse beneath damp bandages.

"No catch," Carter said, tone flat, practical, her gloved hand resting on her sidearm's grip, runes glowing green under her fingers. "Just that you remember where you got the upgrades and maybe help us out if you're ever nearby, or any intel you might find, a hand in a fight, whatever you can spare. We're building something here, but we can't do it alone." Her gaze held mine, brown eyes steady, no bullshit behind them, a soldier's honesty carved in every line of her face.

I considered the weight of Sara pulling north, her scream a beacon I couldn't ignore, the curse whispering low, but Haven's strength, the dome, the mages, the enhanced gear felt like a lifeline, a way to keep fighting. "Alright," I said, nodding firmly, my voice rough but sure. "Let's see what you've got."

Over the next few hours, the warehouse buzzed around us, mages and techs swarming our gear with deft, practiced hands, their tools clattering, chants weaving through the air like a low hum. My rifle came back etched with runes along the barrel, glowing blue, the metal warm to the touch, its bullets now infused with magic to shred enchanted hides, their casings pulsing faintly, humming in their magazine. A mage tested it, firing a round into a steel plate, the projectile streaking blue, punching clean through with a crack, the plate buckling, sparks flying. Mithis's axe was reinforced, its blade honed razor-keen, the purple glow blazing brighter, runes pulsing hot along the haft, casting stark violet shadows as she swung it, the air whistling sharply. They even warded the Jeep, carving symbols into the frame with glowing chisels, protective sigils to repel lesser anomalies, the olive drab paint shimmering with blue and gold veins, the engine humming smoother, its growl deeper, like a beast waking up.

When it was done, Carter approached, boots scuffing the concrete floor, a smirk tugging her lips, her armor's runes pulsing steadily, reflecting off her cap's brim. "You're ready," she said, handing me my rifle, its weight heavier with purpose, the blue glow casting faint shadows across my torn jacket, its cuffs frayed and crusted with blood. "But be careful. The convergence is unpredictable portals shift, creatures adapt. Even with these enhancements, the road ahead won't be easy." Her tone was firm, a warning etched in grit, her brown eyes searching mine, soldier to soldier.

"We'll manage," I said, shouldering the rifle, its glow warm against my chest, the enhanced stock fitting snugly, grounding me against the ache in my ribs, Sara's scream pulling north, relentless.

Mithis smiled, crimson eyes glinting warm, her axe gleaming in her grip, its blade catching the warehouse's dim light with a shimmer of purple. "This will help. Thank you."

As we prepped to roll out, Carter handed me a small device, a portable radio, scratched and dented, its plastic casing etched with runes that pulsed faintly blue, a leather strap dangling from its side. "If you need help, tune into this frequency," she said, voice low, firm, her gloved hand steady as she passed it over. "We'll do what we can, intel, coordinates, maybe a mage or two if you're close enough." Her eyes held mine, a spark of camaraderie breaking through her command, her cap's shadow softening the lines on her face.

I nodded, tucking it into my pack, the canvas crinkling under my fingers, the radio's weight a small comfort against the road's uncertainty. "Appreciate it, I considered staying here. Haven's is something worth protecting." My voice was rough, sincere, the town's pulse a spark of hope against the convergence's shadow.

The Jeep rumbled alive, engine growling low, deeper now with the wards' enhancement, as we pulled out of Haven, tires crunching gravel, the warehouse's steel walls fading behind us, the dome's golden glow shrinking in the rearview, barricades shrinking to jagged silhouettes against the dusk. The enhanced gear hummed with my upgraded rifle, axe, Jeep, its runes pulsing in rhythm with the road, a quiet promise of strength. The convergence still clawed at the world, Ashvalen's bleed deepening with every portal, but with Haven's tools, we had teeth to bite back, a chance to carve a path north. Sara burned relentlessly, her scream a beacon, the curse whispering low, every life you touch will rot, but Mithis's steel beside me held it at bay.

The sun sank low as we drove, a bloody orange smear across the horizon, casting long shadows over buckled asphalt, the Jeep humming steadily, its runes catching the fading light in streaks of blue and gold, shimmering like veins of magic woven into the steel. Mithis sat shotgun, her glowing axe propped at her feet, its blade casting purple shadows across her mud-caked boots, crimson eyes fixed on the darkening road ahead, her cape pooling dark against the torn vinyl seat.

The silence stretched comfortably, a rare pause after days of chaos, gunfire, portals, and enforcers until the radio in my pack crackled, Carter's voice slicing through static like a blade, sharp and urgent. "McAllister, do you copy? This is Carter from Haven." The words jolted me, my pulse spiking, the Jeep's growl a steady counterpoint beneath the static's hiss.

I glanced at Mithis, her brow lifting a hair, crimson eyes narrowing as she leaned forward, her axe haft creaking in her grip. I fished the radio out, its runes pulsing blue under my thumb, the plastic warm to the touch, its strap dangling as I pressed the button. "We're here, Carter. What's going on?" My voice scraped rough, the road blurring under the tires, a faded signpost leaning crooked in the headlights' wash, "Marquette 25 MI" barely legible under rust.

A pause stretched, static hissing like distant rain, then her voice returned, strained, tighter than before, a soldier's calm fraying at the edges. "I need to ask you something, and I hope you'll be honest. Did you or your companion take one of the pistols from the armory? One of the experimental models?" Her words were clipped, urgency cutting through, the dome's hum faint in the background, drowned by the clatter of Haven's warehouse.

I frowned, confusion knotting my gut, my eyes flicking to Mithis, her expression unreadable, crimson gaze fixed on the radio, her green fingers resting on her axe. "No, we didn't. Everything we took was authorized rifle runes, axe upgrades, and Jeep wards. Why?" My fingers tightened on the radio, its edges digging into my palm, the Jeep's runes pulsing faintly, casting blue light across the dash.

Mithis shifted, her cape rustling against the torn seat, her shoulders easing as she sighed, leaning forward, green hands resting on her knees, her voice calm but firm, cutting the cab's quiet like a stone through still water. "I did." The admission landed heavy, her crimson eyes meeting mine, steady as steel, no trace of guilt, just fact, her gloves creaking as she flexed her fingers.

I turned to her, surprise jarring me straight, the Jeep's tires humming steadily beneath us, a pothole jarring my ribs, the pain sharp but fleeting. "You what?" My tone spiked, keener than I meant, irritation flaring hot, my grip tightening on the wheel, chipped paint flaking under my thumbs.

She crossed her arms, crimson eyes unflinching, her tone even, unapologetic. "I didn't think it would matter. It was just sitting there, collecting dust, one of those glowing ones, half buried under rags in a crate. I thought it might be useful, something to give us an edge." Her voice stayed steady, her gaze holding mine, green skin stark in the cab's dim light, the pistol at her side gleaming faintly, its runes pulsing green against the leather holster she'd rigged from Haven's scraps, its strap knotted tight.

Carter's voice crackled back, clipped but edged with urgency, the static buzzing like a swarm. "Well, it matters. That pistol wasn't just any weapon; it was one of our experimental prototypes, magically attuned to its wielder. Its loss could compromise our operations if it falls into the wrong hands or if it's misused." Her tone hardened, a soldier's discipline cutting through, the clatter of Haven's warehouse louder now, tools ringing in the background.

Mithis looked down, a flicker of guilt easing her green brow, her hand brushing the pistol at her side, its runes shimmering brighter as her fingers grazed the grip, a soft hum vibrating the air. "I didn't realize. I didn't mean to cause trouble." Her voice dipped, softer now, the warrior's steel giving way to sincerity, her cape pooling dark around her shoulders, wolf pelts shedding ash onto the seat.

I sighed, gripping the wheel tighter, the road blurring under the headlights, my irritation cooling to frustration, the soldier in me knowing intent mattered more than the act. "Carter, listen. We'll bring it back if you need it. It's not like we're planning on using it for anything shady." My tone steadied, calm kicking in, though the sting of Mithis not telling me lingered, a burr in my trust, Sara's scream pulling north, relentless.

Another pause, static buzzing, then Carter's voice eased, calmer but firm, the urgency softening, a soldier weighing options. "No need to bring it back, but I need to make sure you understand what you're carrying. That pistol was designed to bond with the first person who wields it. If Mithis has used it or even handled it with intent, it's hers now, and no one else can use it effectively. It's keyed to her energy, her will." Her words carried weight, a mix of warning and trust, the dome's hum fading in the background, replaced by the clink of tools.

Mithis raised an eyebrow, intrigued, pulling the pistol free, its sleek barrel gleaming in the cab's dim light, runes glowing brighter as her fingers curled around the grip, a low hum vibrating the air, the green light washing her green skin, casting stark shadows across her sharp features. "It's bonded to me?" Her voice lifted, curiosity threading through, her crimson eyes tracing the weapon's lines, the runes pulsing in time with her heartbeat, a warrior sensing power.

"Yes," Carter replied, static crackling faintly, her tone warming, a teacher now, guiding. "It'll adapt to your skills, your strength, your magic, your intent, and grow stronger the more you use it, like an extension of your will. But it also means you're responsible for it. If you lose it or it's stolen, it could be dangerous in the wrong hands, unstable, even catastrophic if someone tries to force its power." Her voice steadied, firm but not accusing, the clatter of Haven's warehouse softening behind her.

Mithis nodded, holstering the pistol with care, the runes dimming as it settled against her thigh, the leather creaking faintly, her green fingers lingering on the grip, a promise etched in her touch. "Understood. I'll take care of it keep it safe, use it right." Her tone hardened, resolute, a vow, her crimson eyes glinting fierce, steadying me, the guilt fading from her brow.

Carter's voice warmed further, a smile breaking through the static, a spark of camaraderie. "I'm not angry, Mithis. I just need to make sure you realize the importance of that weapon. Use it wisely, and if you ever need advice on how to unlock its full potential, new runes, techniques, anything, call me. We're in this together." Her words carried a soldier's bond, forged in shared fights, the dome's hum returning faintly, a pulse of Haven's strength.

"Thank you," Mithis said, sincere, her gloved hand resting on the pistol's grip, cape rustling as she settled back, wolf pelts shedding ash onto the seat, her crimson eyes softening, a rare warmth cutting her steel.

I chuckled, shaking my head, stubble rasping my palm as I rubbed my jaw, the knot in my chest easing, the Jeep's growl a steady hum beneath us. "Next time, maybe mention when you're borrowing experimental weapons, alright?" My tone teased, a half-smile tugging my lips, the irritation fading to trust, Mithis's steel grounding me against the road's chaos.

She smirked, crimson eyes glinting warm, a rare flash of mischief cutting her warrior's edge. "Noted." Her lips tugged wider, the pistol's runes pulsing faintly at her side, her cape brushing the seat with a quiet scrape, her green skin stark in the headlights' wash.

The radio crackled one last time, Carter's voice firm again, a soldier's farewell. "Stay safe out there, both of you. And keep an eye on that pistol, it's more valuable than you know. Haven out." The static cut off, the device thudding into my pack as I switched it off, its runes dimming, the leather strap coiling in the canvas.

As the Jeep rolled on, I shot Mithis a sidelong glance, the road blurring under the headlights, buckled asphalt streaked with glowing vines, their leaves shimmering blue in the dusk. She studied the pistol thoughtfully, turning it in her gloved hands, its runes pulsing in time with her movements, the green glow washing her green skin, casting stark shadows across her sharp features, her crimson eyes glinting with a mix of curiosity and resolve. "Why didn't you think to tell me?" I asked, half-joking, my tone light, tires crunching gravel as we hit a rough patch, the Jeep's wards flaring briefly blue.

She shrugged, a small smile playing at her lips, her cape brushing the seat. "I didn't think it was a big deal. Besides, it seems to like me." Her voice lilted, teasing, as she tested the pistol's weight with a quick flick, the glow flaring brighter, a hum vibrating the air, her crimson eyes glinting with mischief.

I couldn't help but laugh, rough and dry, the sound bouncing off the Jeep's steel walls, easing the weight of the road. "Fair enough. Just try not to surprise me, alright?" My eyes flicked back to the highway, the weight of her beside me steadying the chaos, Sara's scream pulling north, the curse whispering low, but hope burning brighter, fueled by Haven's gifts.

"No promises," she said, smirk widening, crimson eyes glinting keen in the cab's dimness, the pistol settling back at her side, its runes dimming to a soft pulse, her axe propped at her feet, casting purple shadows across her boots.

Shaking my head, I refocused on the highway stretching west, asphalt buckling under encroaching vines, their thorns sharp in the headlights, glowing faintly blue, a mark of Ashvalen's bleed. The pistol was an unexpected twist, another piece of Ashvalen stitched into our fight, but if it gave us an edge bonded to Mithis, growing with her strength, I wasn't complaining.

Sara burned north, relentless, her scream a beacon I'd chase until it broke me; the road ahead loomed wild, Haven's glow a fading memory in the rearview, its dome a golden smudge against the bruised sky.

The silence settled again, the Jeep humming steadily, wards pulsing faintly, casting blue and gold streaks across the dash, the enhanced engine growling deeper, smoother, a beast tamed by magic. Supplies rattled in the back ammo cans, clinking, MREs shifting, jerry cans sloshing a lifeline. The air thickened outside, a tang of ozone mixing with pine and damp earth, the convergence's fingerprints creeping closer with every mile, the horizon darkening as the sun sank fully, stars piercing the bruised sky, unnatural violet streaks threading through them.

Then, cresting a low rise, a faded green sign came into view, half-swallowed by vines twisting thick and thorny, their leaves shimmering blue in the headlights' wash, pulsing faintly like a heartbeat. "REST AREA – 1 MILE" stood out in peeling white letters, legible, the metal pole bent at an angle, rust streaking red down its length like old blood, pooling in cracks at its base. A chipped arrow pointed right, toward a shadowed turnoff swallowed by dense pines, their needles glinting wet under the rising moon, branches twisting faintly, unnatural in the silver light.

"Rest area," I said, easing off the gas, tires crunching gravel as the Jeep slowed, engine's growl dropping to a low rumble, the wards flaring briefly blue, casting stark shadows across the dash. "Might be worth a stop to stretch our legs, check for anything useful, maybe a map or supplies." My voice was rough, my leg throbbing faintly under damp bandages, the ache in my ribs a dull pulse, but the soldier in me knew pauses were rare, opportunities fleeting.

Mithis nodded, her eyes narrowing as she scanned the sign, her axe haft creaking in her grip, the pistol's runes pulsing green at her side, casting a faint glow across her green knuckles. "Could be a trap or a resource. Hard to tell out here." Her tone stayed cautious, cape rustling as she leaned forward, senses attuned to the convergence's pulse, her gaze flicking to the shadowed turnoff, the pines looming like sentinels.

"Yeah," I muttered, gripping the wheel tighter, chipped paint flaking under my palms, my rifle slung low, its blue runes pulsing faintly, warm against my torn jacket. "Either way, we go in carefully, eyes open, weapons ready." A faint hum vibrating the ground, barely perceptible – setting my nerves on edge, the convergence's shadow creeping closer.

23 REST AREA RESPITE

I glanced at Mithis, her profile sharp against the Jeep's streaked window, crimson eyes glowing faintly in the cab's dimness, their light catching the dust motes swirling in the air. Her green skin stood stark against the drab olive interior, her cape of wolf pelts pooling over the torn vinyl seat, the axe across her back casting a soft purple glow from its pulsing runes. "We could use a break. What do you think?" My voice scraped rough, the road's endless hum wearing thin on my nerves, each mile a grind against the ache in my ribs and the claw slash on my leg, Sara's scream flickering north like a burr under my skull, relentless, the curse whispering low: every life you touch will rot.

She nodded, her gaze flicking toward the horizon where the sun bled a fiery orange into a bruised, violet-streaked sky, clouds rippling unnaturally, as if Ashvalen's touch warped them too. "Might as well. Better to rest now than push too hard and regret it later." Her tone was steady, practical, a warrior's pragmatism honed by battles I could only imagine, her cape rustling as she shifted, the axe's glow flaring briefly, casting stark purple shadows across the cracked dashboard, where the fuel gauge hovered just above a quarter tank.

The Jeep rumbled off the highway, tires crunching onto the cracked asphalt of the rest area's parking lot, weeds clawing through fissures like skeletal fingers, their tips glistening with dew in the headlights' wash. The lot stretched desolate, littered with faded detritus, a crumpled soda can, a shredded tire tread, a plastic bag caught in a gust, skittering across the pavement like a ghost. A dilapidated building squatted at the center, its peeling paint once white, now a sickly gray with grime, sagging under a rusted metal roof, corrugated panels warped and streaked with red oxide, creaking faintly in the breeze. A faded sign above the entrance read "Rest Stop 47," half the letters chipped away, leaving "Re t S p 4" in peeling red, a relic of a world that no longer existed.

A few picnic tables dotted the perimeter, their wood weathered to a splintered silver, warped from neglect, one missing a bench entirely, its rusted bolts jutting up like broken teeth, glinting in the dusk's dying light. Another table lay overturned, its legs bent, half-buried in overgrown grass that shimmered faintly blue, Ashvalen's blood seeping into the earth. Surrounding it all, dense pines swayed in a gentle wind, their branches whispering low, needles glinting wet under the rising moon, the air thick with the sharp tang of sap, damp rot, and a faint ozone hum, the convergence's fingerprint lingering like a storm about to break.

I parked near the building, cutting the engine, the sudden silence slamming down heavy, almost jarring after hours of the Jeep's guttural growl, the only sound now the faint tick of cooling metal and the pines' soft hiss. Grabbing my rifle, its blue runes pulsing faintly, warm against my palm, I stepped out, boots thudding gravel, the crunch loud in the quiet. I stretched, muscles protesting with a dull ache, stiff from gripping the wheel too long, my torn jacket creaking as I rolled my shoulders, the fabric crusted with dried blood and ichor, frayed cuffs brushing my split knuckles. The cool dusk bit at my exposed skin, carrying a whiff of rust from the Jeep's chipped frame, mingling with pine and the sour decay of abandoned places, my leg throbbing faintly under damp bandages, the claw slash a constant reminder of the road's cost.

Mithis climbed out beside me, her glowing axe slung over her back, its purple runes pulsing bright against her green skin, casting violet light across her sharp features, her crimson eyes scanning the lot with a predator's caution. Her cape swayed with each step, wolf pelts brushing her calves, shedding faint ash and singed hairs, her boots scuffing softly, deliberate, as she moved, the experimental pistol at her thigh gleaming with green runes, humming faintly in its leather holster. "Doesn't look like anyone's been here in a while," she said, voice low, cutting the quiet, her crimson eyes tracing the shadows between the pines, the empty lot stretching desolate, its asphalt cracked and buckled, weeds clawing for dominance.

"Good," I said, snagging a canteen from the Jeep's cluttered back, its aluminum dented and scratched, the metal cold and heavy, sloshing as I hefted it, the weight grounding me against the weariness clawing at my bones. Supplies rattled behind it, ammo cans clinking, MREs shifting, jerry cans thudding against dented steel. "I could use some peace and quiet for a bit." My fingers brushed the canteen's scratched surface, the cold metal steadying me, Sara's scream looping north, the curse a shadow I couldn't outrun.

We walked toward the building, its windows shattered into jagged mosaics, glass glinting dull in the rusted frames, reflecting the moon's silver light in fractured shards. The door hung crooked on rusted hinges, groaning mournfully in the breeze, its faded green paint peeling in strips, revealing warped wood beneath, a faint "Push" sticker curling at the edges. Inside, the air hung stale and heavy, thick with dust that swirled in our flashlight beams, a sour hint of mildew creeping from cracked walls, their beige plaster sagging, stained with water streaks like old tears. The floor was littered with debris, faded candy wrappers crinkling underfoot, a torn road map curling at the edges, its Ohio counties smudged and illegible, a busted plastic chair splintered in a corner, its legs twisted like a broken insect. A row of vending machines leaned against one wall, their glass fronts cracked but intact, labels peeling "C Cola," "Choco Crunch," "Zesty Chips" faded ghosts of a world long gone, their coin slots rusted shut, buttons worn smooth from forgotten hands. At the far end, restrooms loomed, their signs faded to illegible smears, doors ajar with shadows pooling dark inside, a faint drip echoing from within, steady as a heartbeat.

Mithis drifted to one of the vending machines, peering through the fractured glass, her reflection warping on the surface, crimson eyes glinting curious in the dimness. "What's this?" Her tone lilted, a mix of intrigue and amusement, green fingers brushing the rusted coin slot, runes on her axe flaring purple, casting violet light across the machine's faded logos, her cape rustling as she leaned closer.

"Snacks," I said, smirking despite the ache in my chest, leaning against the doorframe, rifle resting easily against my thigh, its blue runes pulsing faintly, warm in the cool air. "Or it used to be. Bet it's all gone bad by now, stale as hell, probably crawling with ants or worse." My voice was rough, the memory of gas station runs Zeppelin blaring, a cold soda in hand stinging sharply, a life before dragons, portals, and Ashvalen's bleed tore it all apart.

She tilted her head, crimson eyes narrowing as she studied the machine, her green brow arching, cape rustling as she tapped the glass with a gloved knuckle, the clink echoing in the quiet. "Your world is strange. You keep food in machines, locked away like treasure?" Her voice held disbelief, a warrior from Ashvalen grappling with Earth's quirks, amusement curling her lips, her green fingers tracing the machine's rusted edge, runes flaring brighter.

"Convenient," I said with a shrug, smirk tugging wider, the absurdity of explaining vending machines to an orc easing the road's weight for a moment. "At least it was, back when the world made sense. Grab a soda, a bag of chips, and keep moving. Now it's just junk, like most everything else." My voice dipped, the sting of lost normalcy hitting harder than I expected, my eyes flicking to the torn map on the floor, its faded highways a mockery of the world we navigated now.

As Mithis poked around, prying at the machine's coin slot with a gloved finger, I sank onto a metal bench near the entrance, its frame cold through my jeans, rust flaking under my weight, creaking faintly as I settled. Unscrewing the canteen's cap, I took a long drink, cool water hitting my throat, crisp and clean, washing down the dust and weariness clinging to me like road grime, the taste faintly metallic from the canteen's battered interior. I exhaled, letting the moment settle, the quiet a rare balm against Sara's scream looping north, the curse clawing low, its whisper a cold burr: every hope will crumble. The pines outside swayed, their whispers blending with the building's creaks, the moon's silver light spilling through the shattered windows, casting jagged shadows across the debris-strewn floor.

Mithis joined me a beat later, clutching a dusty bag of chips she'd pried from the machine's guts, its plastic crinkling loudly, the label half-torn, "Salt & Vinegar" legible under a layer of grime, the expiration date long faded. She ripped it open with a sharp tug, the tang of vinegar cutting through the stale air, sharp and pungent, and sniffed cautiously, her green nose wrinkling slightly before she popped one in her mouth. Her expression turned thoughtful, crunching echoing off the walls, green lips pursing as she chewed, crimson eyes glinting with approval as she savored the unfamiliar taste, crumbs dusting her gloves, catching the axe's purple glow.

"Not bad," she said, voice muffled mid-crunch, swallowing with a faint nod, her crimson eyes bright with a spark of delight, a warrior finding joy in the mundane, offering me the bag, the plastic crinkling in her grip, crumbs scattering onto her cape, clinging to the wolf pelts.

I laughed, rough and dry, the sound scraping my throat, bouncing off the walls, easing the weight for a fleeting second. "Glad to know our snacks get your approval." I waved it off, taking another swig from the canteen, the cold water grounding me, the absurdity of it, Mithis, an orc from Ashvalen, munching chips like we were on some warped road trip, lightening the ache in my chest, her presence a quiet anchor against the chaos.

The calm shattered fast. A rustling slipped from the pines edging the rest area, quiet at first, barely audible over the breeze, then a twig snapped, crisp and deliberate, cutting the dusk's hush like a blade. I stiffened, canteen thudding the bench as I grabbed my rifle, barrel snapping up, muscles tensing hard, adrenaline spiking hot, my pulse a drumbeat in my ears. The air shifted, heavier now, laced with a whiff of something sour-sweet, like rotting fruit or clotted blood, faint but wrong, curling my gut, the convergence's shadow creeping closer.

"You hear that?" I whispered, voice low, eyes locked on the treeline where shadows stretched long and jagged under the pines, their branches trembling faintly, unnaturally, the moon's light glinting off wet needles, a faint blue shimmer flickering deep within, barely visible but unmistakable, a portal's echo, or something worse.

Mithis nodded, already on her feet, axe in hand, its glow flaring brighter, casting stark purple light across her green face, illuminating the sharp lines of her jaw, her crimson eyes glowing fierce, piercing the dimness like embers. "We're not alone." Her tone hardened, cape swaying as she stepped beside me, boots silent on the cracked pavement, the pistol at her thigh humming faintly, its green runes pulsing in rhythm with her axe, a warrior braced for blood.

The rustling swelled, branches trembling harder, needles shaking loose, pattering to the ground like rain, and a shadow flickered among the trees, quick and fluid, too big for wind, too deliberate for an animal. My finger hovered over the trigger, heart kicking hard against my ribs as I stood, sweeping the treeline with the rifle's glowing barrel, its blue runes flaring brighter, warm in my grip. Mithis flanked me, axe raised, her movements smooth, predatory, her boots scuffing softly, cape bunching as she braced, runes pulsing steadily along her arm, casting violet light across the gravel, her crimson gaze locked on the shadows.

"Come out," I called, voice steady, cutting the quiet like a blade, carrying across the lot with a soldier's authority. "We're not looking for trouble, but we're ready for it." My pulse thrummed, adrenaline honing the world to the rustle of leaves, the creak of the building's rusted roof behind us, the weight of the rifle cold and sure in my grip, its runes humming faintly, ready to shred whatever emerged.

Silence stretched taut, heavy as the dusk, the air thick with ozone and rot, the pines' whispers falling still, as if the forest held its breath. Then, slow and deliberate, a figure peeled from the trees, stepping into the moonlight's silver wash, their silhouette lean and ragged against the pines' dark wall. A young man, no older than twenty, his clothes torn denim and a faded flannel, streaked with dirt and dark smears that glinted wet blood, maybe, or ichor, his boots caked with mud, laces frayed to threads. His face was pale, gaunt under a mop of matted brown hair, eyes wide and hollow with desperation, sunken deep in shadowed sockets, darting wildly between us and the trees. He stumbled forward, hands raised high, palms trembling, empty, no weapon, just raw fear etched deep in his hunched shoulders, his breath fogging in short, ragged bursts, steaming in the chill.

"Please," he said, voice shaking, cracking on the edge of a sob, barely audible over the breeze, his boots scuffing gravel as he edged closer, his skinny frame swaying like he might collapse any second. "I'm not armed. I just... I need help." His words tumbled out, desperate, raw, his hands trembling harder, fingers twitching like he expected us to shoot, his flannel torn at the shoulder, revealing a jagged scratch, crusted with blood, fresh enough to gleam faintly.

Mithis and I exchanged a glance, her crimson eyes narrowing, wary, axe still raised, its glow flaring purple, casting stark shadows across her green face, her posture tense, a warrior weighing threat against pity. My eyes flicked back to him, reading the panic in his hunched shoulders, the way his knees buckled faintly, the hollow exhaustion in his gaunt face, no deception there, just a kid pushed past his breaking point. I lowered my rifle a hair, barrel dipping toward the gravel but ready, finger off the trigger, my voice steady, soldier's calm holding the line. "Who are you? And what's got you running like that?" Suspicion gnawed low, the road's lessons burned deep trust was a gamble, but he looked beat to hell, no threat in his trembling frame.

"My name's David," he said, stepping fully into the lot's light, the Jeep's headlights washing his pale skin, highlighting the dirt smudged across his cheek, the blood crusted in his hairline, his hands still raised, shaking harder now, his breath fogging in short bursts. "I've been out here for days, three, maybe four, lost track. Got separated from my group north of Cincinnati. I thought I heard something chasing me, rustling, growling, but I couldn't see it, just shadows moving too fast." His voice cracked again, eyes darting wildly to the treeline, where the pines stood still, their branches unmoving now, the blue shimmer gone, or hidden, his words spilling faster, panic driving them. "I swear I'm not trouble. I just need food, water, anything. I won't bother you after that, I swear." His plea hung desperate, raw and unfiltered, his hands dropping to clutch his torn flannel, fingers trembling against the frayed fabric.

Mithis frowned, her gaze snapping back to the treeline, axe haft creaking in her gloved grip, runes flaring brighter, casting violet light across the gravel, her cape swaying as a gust rustled the pines, carrying that sour-sweet rot again, fainter now but unmistakable. "You might have been followed," she said, voice low, certain, her crimson eyes narrowing, scanning the shadows, her boots shifting silently, ready to spring, the pistol at her thigh humming louder, its green runes pulsing in warning.

David's face crumpled, fear spiking clear, his knees buckling a hair before he caught himself against a picnic table, its wood groaning under his weight, lichen flaking onto his torn jeans. "I don't know, I didn't see anything clear, just heard it, felt it, like eyes on my back. Please, don't leave me out here." His voice broke, a sob swallowing the last word, his eyes glistening wet in the headlights' glare, hands clutching the table's edge, splinters digging into his palms, desperation carved in every line of his gaunt frame.

I hesitated, jaw tightening, weighing him against the road's brutal lessons, trust could kill, but so could abandoning someone who might know something, might lead us closer to Sara, to Marquette, to answers. His hollow eyes held no lie, just fear and exhaustion, a kid no match for the convergence's claws. "Alright," I said, voice firm, jerking my chin to the picnic table a few feet off, its wood sagging under lichen and rot, keeping him in sight but out of reach. "Sit down over there. We'll get you something, but you stay where I can see you."

David nodded fast, gratitude flashing in his sunken eyes, a shaky breath escaping as he collapsed onto the bench, its frame groaning louder under his slight weight, his lanky frame hunching forward, elbows on his knees, breathing ragged like he'd been running for miles. Mithis kept watch, crimson eyes locked on him, axe loose but ready, her shadow stretching long across the pavement in the Jeep's headlight spill, her green fingers tightening on the haft, runes pulsing steadily, her cape swaying faintly, a warrior's vigilance unyielding.

I grabbed a plastic bottle of water and an MRE from the Jeep's cluttered back, the canvas crinkling as I rummaged, "Beef Stew" scratched into the faded pack, its corners torn but intact, the bottle's label peeling, "Purified" barely legible under grime. I handed them over, crouching nearby, rifle within arm's reach on the gravel, its blue runes pulsing faintly, warm in the cool air. David tore into the food with shaking hands, ripping the MRE open with a soft tearing noise, the smell of reconstituted meat mixing with the rest area's damp rot, sharp and heavy, as he shoved it in, barely chewing, crumbs sticking to his cracked lips, water sloshing as he gulped half the bottle in one go, rivulets running down his chin, soaking his torn flannel.

"Where was your group headed?" I asked, voice low, watching his frantic bites, the way his eyes flickered nervously to the treeline every few seconds, his shoulders twitching at every rustle of the pines, the moon's light glinting off the bottle's plastic, casting faint shadows across his gaunt face.

"North, near Cincinnati," he said between mouthfuls, his voice muffled, swallowing hard, crumbs scattering onto his jeans, the MRE pack crinkling in his grip. "We were aiming for a safe zone, some small town, Eversville, I think, heard it had a military outpost, food, walls. Been moving for eight days, scavenged what we could, canned beans, rainwater, and a few granola bars from a gas station. Slept in shifts, kept watch, thought we'd make it by dawn." His voice dipped, eyes dropping to the table, fingers clutching the MRE pack like a lifeline, nails digging into the plastic. "Then we got ambushed, middle of the night, out of nowhere. Mutants, maybe, or something worse. Came out of the trees fast, too fast, like people, but wrong. Skin gray, eyes glowing yellow, claws tearing through us like paper. I saw Jen, my cousin, go down first, screaming 'til her voice cut off, blood everywhere. I ran, didn't think, just bolted, heard the others yelling, then nothing, just silence. Kept running 'til my lungs burned, hid in a ditch 'til morning, covered in mud, shaking. Been stumbling ever since, dodging shadows, eating berries, a stale granola bar from a wrecked car, drinking from puddles when I had to." His breath hitched, rubbing his face with a shaky hand, smearing dirt and blood across his brow, his eyes glistening wet, guilt and fear tangled tight, the kind that sticks like damp rot.

My jaw tightened, grip whitening on the rifle's stock, its blue runes pulsing warm under my palm, the weight grounding me against the anger flaring hot. Mutant wraiths, enforcers, or some new horror, Ashvalen's blood tore lives apart, same as it had Sara's call, Mom's blood soaking the linoleum back home, the memory stabbing sharply. "Sounds like hell," I said, voice rough, Sara's scream looping north, the curse clawing low, every life you touch will rot. "You're tougher than you look, making it through that, keeping your head."

He shrugged, a twitch of his lips, not quite a smile, his eyes dropping to the MRE pack, fingers fidgeting with a torn corner. "Didn't feel tough just scared shitless. Still am, every noise, every shadow." His voice trembled, eyes flicking to the treeline, where the pines stood still, their branches unmoving now, the blue shimmer gone, or hidden. "You're the first people I've seen in days. Thank you for stopping, most wouldn't have, not out here." Gratitude flashed in his sunken eyes, raw and fragile, his hands shaking as he wiped his mouth with a filthy sleeve, smearing crumbs and dirt, the scratch on his shoulder glinting faintly, crusted but fresh.

Mithis, still posted up, glanced at me, her expression tight, crimson eyes narrowing, axe haft creaking in her grip, the pistol at her thigh humming faintly, its green runes pulsing in warning. "What now? We can't stay here long if he's was followed by those things, don't give up easily." Her tone cut practical, her green brow furrowing, cape swaying as a gust rustled the pines, carrying that sour-sweet rot again, fainter but lingering, a warning she didn't ignore.

David's face crumpled, fear spiking clear, his hands clutching the water bottle, plastic crinkling in his grip, his eyes darting between us, pleading. "Please, don't leave me. I'll do whatever you say, just don't." His voice broke, a sob swallowing the rest, his skinny frame trembling, the picnic table creaking as he leaned forward, desperation carved in every line.

I stood, rifle in hand, gravel crunching under my boots, my jaw tightening as I weighed the options, just survival's raw edge. "Alright," I said, voice firm, meeting his gaze, gray to brown, soldier's calm holding the line. "We'll take you with us for now, at least until we find somewhere more secure, a town, a camp, something with walls. But you listen, you move when we say, and you don't touch anything unless we tell you. Clear?"

David nodded fast, relief washing over his gaunt features, a shaky grin breaking through, his eyes glistening wet in the headlights' glare. "Yes, yeah, I get it. Thank you, I won't slow you down, I promise." He scrambled to his feet, clutching the water bottle and MRE wrapper, stuffing them into a torn pocket, the plastic crinkling loudly, his boots scuffing gravel as he stood, his lanky frame swaying but steadier now, gratitude fueling him.

Mithis didn't look thrilled, her green brow furrowing deeper, crimson eyes flicking to David, assessing, wary, but she nodded curtly, axe shifting in her grip, its glow dimming slightly, the pistol's runes pulsing steadily at her thigh. "Fine. But we keep moving the road waits for no one, and neither do those creatures." Her tone hardened, a warrior's warning threaded through, her cape rustling as she stepped toward the Jeep, her crimson gaze lingering on David, promising she'd watch him closely, trust earned in inches, not given.

We packed up fast, the canteen clicking as I tossed it into the Jeep's back, its aluminum thudding against an ammo can, the sound sharp in the quiet. David climbed into the rear, his lanky frame folding awkwardly between ammo cans and jerry cans, their metal surfaces scratched and dented, thudding as he settled, his torn flannel bunching at the elbows, his pale skin stark against the Jeep's drab olive, the water bottle clutched tight in his lap. Mithis took the shotgun seat, axe propped against the door, its purple runes casting faint shadows across her boots, the pistol at her thigh gleaming green, her cape pooling dark over the torn vinyl, shedding ash and singed hairs. I slid into the driver's seat, key turning with a scrape, the engine coughing alive, a low growl vibrating the cracked dash, the fuel gauge twitching faintly, still above a quarter tank, enough for now.

The rest area faded in the rearview, its busted building swallowed by dusk, the picnic tables shrinking to splintered silhouettes, the pines' shadows stretching long and jagged with every mile, their branches twisting faintly, unnatural in the moonlight, the highway stretching dark ahead, buckled asphalt streaked with glowing vines, their blue shimmer a warning of Ashvalen's bleed. The Jeep rolled on, engine humming under the bruised sky, headlights cutting swaths through the gloom, glinting off rusted car husks littering the shoulder sedans and pickups, doors ajar, windshields spiderwebbed with cracks, tires sunken into cracked asphalt, their rubber cracked and peeling, abandoned relics of a world unraveling.

David sat hunched in the back, arms wrapped tight around himself, his torn flannel bunching at the elbows, his pale skin almost glowing in the cab's dimness, eyes darting nervously to the windows every bump we hit, the Jeep's wards flaring briefly blue, casting stark shadows across his gaunt face. Mithis sat beside me, glowing axe propped against the door, its purple runes pulsing steady, her crimson gaze fixed forward, steady as steel, the pistol at her thigh humming faintly, its green runes a quiet promise of power, her cape pooling dark, wolf pelts shedding ash onto the seat, the air in the cab thick with dust, oil, and a tang of David's sweat, sharp against the pine filtering through the cracked window.

For a stretch, no one spoke, the silence heavy, thick with the road's weight, broken only by the Jeep's tires thumping over potholes, gravel spitting beneath us, the wards humming faintly, their blue and gold veins shimmering across the dash. The highway rolled on, desolate, the glowing vines creeping thicker along the edges, their thorns glinting sharp in the headlights, a reminder of the convergence's grip. Eventually, I glanced at the rearview, catching David's pale face in the mirror, sunken cheeks twitching as he chewed his lip, his eyes wide, glistening with exhaustion and fear, his fingers fidgeting with a frayed thread on his flannel, twisting it tight.

"How are you holding up, back there?" I asked, keeping my tone casual, eyes flicking back to the road, where a rusted pickup loomed, half-swallowed by overgrown grass that shimmered blue, its hood popped open like a gutted carcass, a faded "For Sale" sign taped to its cracked windshield, fluttering in the breeze.

David jolted, startled, his head snapping up like I'd caught him mid-thought, his breath fogging in the cab's chill. "Yeah, I'm okay. Just... tired, I guess." His voice came out quiet, frayed, hands tightening around his knees, nails digging into the torn denim, leaving crescents, his boots scuffing the Jeep's floor, kicking up dust that swirled in the headlights' spill through the rear window.

"You've been on your own a while, huh?" I pressed, voice low, steering around the pickup, its rusted frame groaning as the wind rocked it, the Jeep's wards flaring briefly, casting blue light across the cab, illuminating David's hollow eyes, the scratch on his shoulder glinting faintly, crusted but raw.

He nodded, slow and heavy, his breath hitching, fogging the air in short bursts. "Yeah, three days, maybe four, lost track after the ambush. Thought I could make it to a safe zone, but everything went wrong." He swallowed hard, eyes dropping to his lap, fingers fidgeting faster, tearing the thread loose, his voice cracking as he spoke, raw with the memory. "We'd been moving north for eight days, a group of ten, scavenged what we could, canned beans, rainwater caught in tarps, a few granola bars from a gas station, even some wild apples, sour but edible. Slept in shifts, kept watch with a couple of hunting rifles, a machete, whatever we had. Thought we'd hit Eversville by dawn. Then they came out of the trees middle of the night, no warning, just screams and claws." His voice broke, hands trembling as he rubbed his face, smearing dirt and blood across his brow, his eyes glistening wet, reflecting from the moonlight.

"Go on," I said, voice steady, my grip tightening on the wheel, chipped paint flaking under my thumbs, the road blurring under the headlights, Sara's scream looping north, the curse clawing low, David's story too close to the chaos that took her.

My jaw tightened, anger flaring hot, the rifle's stock warm under my palm, its blue runes pulsing faintly, grounding me against the memory of Sara's call Jake, something's wrong the same chaos, the same claws, Ashvalen's bleed tearing lives apart, Mom's blood soaking the linoleum, the scream that drove me north. "Sounds like hell," I said, voice rough, eyes flicking to the rearview, catching his hollow gaze, the weight of his story settling heavy, hope flickering stubborn under the curse's shadow. "You're tougher than you look, making it through that, keeping your head. Most would've broken."

He shrugged, a twitch of his lips, not quite a smile, his eyes dropping to the MRE wrapper in his pocket, fingers fidgeting with its torn edge, crumbs scattering onto his jeans. "Didn't feel tough just scared shitless, running on empty. Still am, every noise, every shadow, feels like it's coming for me." His voice trembled, eyes flicking to the window, the dark beyond streaked with glowing vines, their thorns glinting sharp in the headlights, then back to me, gratitude flickering in the hollows, fragile but real. "Thanks for picking me up. Don't know how much longer I'd have lasted out there, alone, with nothing but a stick I sharpened for a weapon."

Mithis shifted, cape rustling, her crimson gaze sliding to me, then back to David, axe haft creaking in her gloved grip, the pistol's green runes pulsing at her thigh, a quiet warning. "Luck's a thin shield out here," she said, voice low, cutting the cab's quiet like a blade, her green brow furrowing slightly, her posture tense, still wary. "You've got grit, surviving that will do that, sharpen it, or it won't last." Her tone stayed flat, practical, a warrior's advice, but her crimson eyes lingered on him, assessing, measuring his resolve, trust earned in inches, her axe's glow dimming slightly, casting faint purple shadows across her boots.

David nodded, swallowing hard, his hands tightening around the water bottle, plastic crinkling in the quiet, his eyes flicking to Mithis, a spark of determination breaking through the fear, her words sinking in, a lifeline he could grasp. "I'll try," he said, voice quiet but steadier, his skinny frame straightening a hair, the Jeep's rumble a steady pulse beneath him, the wards flaring briefly blue, casting stark light across his gaunt face, illuminating the scratch on his shoulder, crusted but raw, a reminder of how close he'd come to breaking.

24 NEON AND NIGHTMARES

Mithis turned sharply, her crimson eyes narrowing to slits as she studied David, the glow of her axe casting jagged purple shadows across her green face, the light catching the sharp angles of her jaw, her expression taut with suspicion. Her gloved hand rested lightly on the machete at her hip, its runes pulsing green, a quiet warning that hummed in the Jeep's dim cab, her cape of wolf pelts rustling faintly. "You're lucky to have survived. Most wouldn't." Her voice cut low, steady but edged with steel, searching for cracks in his fragile facade, runes flaring brighter along her arm, casting violet streaks across her green knuckles.

David managed a weak smile, lips twitching but not reaching his hollow eyes, sunken deep in shadowed sockets, glinting with a mix of fear and exhaustion under the cab's faint light. "Yeah. Lucky." His voice rasped thin, brittle as cracked glass, the word hollow, forced, carrying a weight that didn't match his trembling frame. He shifted on the back seat, the torn vinyl creaking under his bony frame, his lanky form hunching tighter, shoulders curling inward like he could shrink into the shadows, his torn flannel bunching at the elbows, streaked with mud and dark smears of blood or ichor, hard to tell in the dimness.

Something about his tone gnawed at me, too hollow, too rehearsed, an itch under my skin that wouldn't shake loose. I glanced at him in the rearview, catching the way his hands fidgeted with his sleeve, tugging it down over his wrist with short, nervous jerks, fingers trembling against the frayed fabric, like he was hiding something beneath the grime-streaked flannel, his knuckles pale, nails bitten to jagged stubs. The Jeep's headlights washed the road ahead in a blue glow, vines twisting along the edges, their shimmering blue veins reflecting off the cracked dashboard, pulsing faintly like a heartbeat, but my focus stayed on him, his shoulders tense, his jaw twitching under a sparse layer of stubble, sweat beading on his brow despite the chill seeping through the cracked window.

"David," I said slowly, keeping my voice steady, a soldier's calm drilled into me from years of chaos, checkpoints, ambushes, and now portals tearing the world apart. "You didn't mention anything about getting hurt back there. Are you injured?" My grip tightened on the wheel, chipped paint flaking under my thumbs, the ache in my ribs a dull pulse beneath my torn jacket, Sara's scream flickering north like a burr in my skull, relentless, the curse whispering low: every life you touch will rot.

He froze, hand still mid-tug on his sleeve, fingers trembling against the frayed fabric, his breath hitching audibly in the cab's quiet, fogging in short bursts. "What? No, I'm fine. Just scratches, that's all." His voice pitched higher, cracking on the edges, a nervous edge that didn't match his earlier exhaustion, his eyes darting between me and the window, where the dark loomed thick, pulsing with the blue veins of Ashvalen's blood, vines curling tighter along the asphalt's cracked edges, their thorns glinting sharp in the headlights.

Mithis tilted her head, her crimson gaze honing to slits, flaring brighter as she leaned forward, cape rustling against the torn seat, the axe haft creaking in her gloved grip, its purple runes glowing keen along the blade, casting stark violet light across her green face. "Then let us see." Her tone sliced cold, a command wrapped in quiet steel, no room for evasion, her posture tense, muscles coiled under her patched leather tunic, the pistol at her thigh humming faintly, its green runes pulsing in sync with her axe, a warrior's warning etched in every line of her frame.

David's eyes flicked between us, wild and glassy, his face draining paler under the cab's dim light, sweat streaking dirt down his gaunt cheeks, glistening in the headlights' spill through the windshield. "It's nothing. Really. Just scratches from running through the woods' branches, thorns, you know." His words tumbled fast, tripping over themselves, his hands jerking back to clutch his knees, nails digging into the torn denim, leaving crescents, his breath fogging faster, sharp and ragged, like a cornered animal's.

"David," I said firmly, pulling the Jeep to a stop with a crunch of gravel under the tires, the engine's growl fading to a low hum as I killed it, the sudden silence heavy, broken only by the faint tick of cooling metal and the pines' soft hiss outside. "Let's not make this harder than it needs to be. Show us." My voice stayed even, but my gut twisted tight, suspicion coiling hot, too many lies started with shaky hands and darting eyes, too many lives lost to trust misplaced Mom's blank eyes staring up from the linoleum, the crack of my rifle as I ended those red-eyed things, the curse clawing low, a shadow I couldn't outrun.

He hesitated, breath hitching, a ragged sound that shook his thin frame, his eyes glistening wet, reflecting the Jeep's dashboard glow, his lips trembling as he pressed them tight. Then, with a shaky sigh, he relented, rolling up his sleeve, the flannel peeling back reluctantly, stiff with dried mud, sweat, and something darker, crusted in the folds. My stomach tightened at what I saw: a jagged bite mark gouged into his forearm, the skin around it red and swollen, puckered and angry at the edges, streaks of purple threading outward like poison creeping under the surface, pulsing faintly, unnaturally, like the vines outside. Teeth marks stood out stark, too big for human, too deep for a glancing scrape, each puncture crusted with dark blood that flaked as he moved, the wound oozing a thin, blackish fluid, its sour-sweet stench cutting through the cab's dusty air, curling my gut.

"Damn it," I muttered, shoving the driver's door open with a creak of rusted hinges, stepping out onto the gravel, the crunch loud in the quiet, my boots scuffing as I yanked the back door wide, its wards flaring blue briefly, Haven's magic humming in the steel. The cool night air bit, laced with pine, damp earth, and that sour tang of rot, sharper now, clinging to David's wound, the Jeep's headlights cutting long shadows across the cracked pavement, glinting off scattered glass and twisted vines.

"When did this happen?" My voice scraped rough, hands flexing against my rifle's stock, its glowing barrel cool under my palm, the blue runes pulsing faintly, warm with power, grounding me against the anger flaring hot, the road's lessons burning deep bites like that weren't just injuries, they were countdowns.

David shrank back against the seat, his lanky frame curling tight, his voice trembling as he stammered, "I don't know, maybe a day ago? Two? It was dark, chaotic, I didn't see what got me, just felt it, sharp, then burning. I thought it wasn't that bad, thought it'd heal." His eyes darted wildly, pleading, hands clutching his arm like he could hide it again, the water bottle tumbling forgotten to the floor with a clatter, rolling against an ammo can, its plastic glinting in the headlights' spill.

Mithis climbed out beside me, her expression dark as storm clouds, crimson eyes glinting hard in the headlight spill, cape swaying as she squared up, her boots scuffing gravel with deliberate weight. "That's not just a scratch. You've been bitten by something from the convergence, something cursed." Her voice dropped low, cold as forged steel, axe gleaming purple in her grip, runes flaring bright along her arm, casting jagged violet light across her green knuckles, her posture rigid, a warrior braced for blood, the pistol at her thigh humming louder, its green runes pulsing in warning.

"I didn't want to say anything," David blurted, words spilling fast and frantic, his breath fogging in the chill, steaming in short bursts. "I thought you'd leave me behind or worse, kill me! But I'm fine, I swear! It's not infected or anything, it's just... sore!" His voice cracked high, desperate, hands shaking harder as he pressed the bitten arm against his chest, the sleeve slipping back to expose the wound's raw edges again, the purple streaks pulsing faintly, like a heartbeat, the blackish ooze glistening wet in the light, its stench sharper, curling my gut tighter.

I exchanged a look with Mithis, her crimson eyes hard as flint, her stance tense, muscles coiled under her patched leather tunic, axe held loose but ready, its glow casting stark shadows across the gravel. "You know what this means," she said, her voice low, the edge keen enough to cut through the night's quiet, her gaze flicking to me with a weight that said we can't risk this, her green brow furrowing, the pistol's runes pulsing in sync with her axe, a quiet promise of power and judgment.

I nodded grimly, turning back to David, my jaw locking tight enough to ache, the rifle's weight grounding me against the adrenaline spiking hot. "If you're bitten, there's a good chance you're infected with something. And if that's the case..." I let it hang, the unspoken heavy Mom's blank eyes staring up from the linoleum, her blood soaking my boots, the crack of my rifle as I ended those red-eyed things, their claws slashing air, Sara's scream cut off by static, the curse clawing low, every life you touch will rot. "We just don't know what's going to happen."

"I'm not infected!" he shouted, voice cracking, echoing off the pines lining the road, sharp and shrill, his hands flailing wildly as he leaned forward, sweat streaking dirt down his gaunt cheeks, his eyes wide and wet, reflecting the Jeep's headlights like a cornered animal's. "I swear! It doesn't even hurt anymore; it just stings a little. That's all! I'm not turning, I'd know if I was!" His plea broke raw, trembling on the edge of tears, his skinny frame shaking, the flannel tearing slightly at the shoulder, revealing another scratch, smaller but fresh, crusted with blood.

"That's not how this works," Mithis said coldly, stepping closer, axe haft creaking in her grip, its glow flaring purple, casting her green face in stark relief, lips pressed thin, crimson eyes unyielding like twin embers burning through the dark, her cape snapping as a gust rustled through, carrying the hum of something alive in the vines twisting along the road, their blue veins pulsing faster, like they sensed the tension. "Bites like that don't wait for permission. They take you, slow or fast, and you won't know until it's too late."

"Hold on," I said, raising a hand, palm rough with scabs, cutting the air between them, my voice steady, trying to anchor the moment against the chaos threatening to spiral. "David, you said you've had this for a day or two. Have you felt anything? Fevers? Hallucinations? Weird cravings, blood, meat, anything?" I drilled into him, searching his face for the tells: sweat too heavy, eyes too glassy, the fevered flush of infection, the twitching madness.

He shook his head frantically, matted hair flopping across his brow, hands clutching his arm tighter, nails digging into the swollen skin until a bead of blood welled up, mixing with the blackish ooze, the stench sharper now, sour-sweet and wrong. "No! Nothing like that! I feel fine, tired, yeah, hungry, but that's it! Please, I just need a chance to prove I'm okay!" His voice trembled, raw and desperate, eyes glistening wet, pleading, his skinny frame curling tighter, like he could will the bite away.

Mithis's gaze didn't waver, crimson boring into him, her stance rigid as stone, axe haft creaking in her grip, runes pulsing hot, casting violet light across the gravel, her green brow furrowing deeper. "And what happens if he's lying? Or if he turns while we're driving, rips out your throat, tears me apart before we blink? That bite's not human, not animal. It's convergence, and I don't even know what dose." Her voice stayed low, but the threat coiled tight, her cape snapping again as another gust rustled through, carrying the vines' hum, louder now, a low buzz that vibrated my teeth, the air thickening with ozone and rot.

I took a deep breath, the cold air stinging my lungs, trying to think through the haze, the weight of the road's lessons, trust could kill, hesitation could kill, but so could abandoning someone who might still be human. David's fear was palpable, soaking the cab with a sour tang, his eyes holding no fevered flush, no twitching madness, just exhaustion and terror, but the bite's purple streaks pulsed like a countdown, a ticking clock we couldn't ignore. Mom's blood on my hands, Sara's scream cut off by static, the crack of my rifle as I ended those things I couldn't lose more, not to hesitation, not to mercy gone wrong. "Alright," I said finally, keeping my tone firm, locking eyes with him, gray to brown, soldier's calm holding the line. "Here's what we're going to do. We'll keep an eye on you for the next day or two. If you show any signs of turning fever, shakes, cravings, anything, we'll deal with it fast. Until then, you stay in the back, you don't touch anything, and you tell us if you feel even a hint of something wrong. Got it?"

David nodded fast, relief flooding his face like a tide, washing out the panic for a shaky second, his lips twitching into a ghost of a grin, eyes glistening wet in the headlights' glare. "Thank you. I won't let you down, I promise I'll tell you if anything changes, I swear." His voice trembled still, hands easing off his arm, the sleeve sliding back to cover the bite, the purple streaks hidden but not forgotten, his skinny frame slumping against the seat, breath fogging fast in the chill, the water bottle rolling under his foot, crinkling faintly.

Mithis didn't look convinced, her green brow furrowing deeper, crimson eyes glinting hard as she shot me a look, your call, your risk, but she nodded reluctantly, a curt dip of her chin, axe shifting in her grip, its glow dimming slightly, casting faint purple shadows across her boots. "One mistake, and he's out, human or not." Her tone sliced final, the pistol at her thigh humming faintly, its green runes pulsing steadily, her cape brushing the Jeep's door frame with a scrape as she turned back to the passenger seat, her posture still tense, a warrior's vigilance unyielding.

"Understood," I said, climbing back into the driver's seat, the cracked vinyl creaking under me as I turned the key, the engine coughing alive with a rough growl that vibrated the dash, the wards flaring blue briefly, casting stark light across the cab. The Jeep rolled back onto the road, tires humming over buckled asphalt, the tension inside thick enough to choke on David's ragged breathing, Mithis's silent watch, my pulse thudding steadily but warily, the rifle propped against my seat, its blue runes pulsing faintly, warm and ready. I kept one eye on the rearview mirror, catching David huddled in the back, bitten arm cradled tight against his chest, his gaunt face half-shadowed, eyes darting nervously to the windows where the vines pulsed blue in the dark, their thorns glinting sharp, a reminder of the convergence's grip.

We'd given him a chance, a thin thread of trust stretched taut, but the weight sinking in my gut wouldn't ease. We might regret this, might pay for it in blood if that bite turned sour, if those purple streaks spread, if David's humanity peeled away under Ashvalen's curse. For now, we could only keep moving, the road stretching west into the unknown, Sara's scream pulling north, relentless, the curse whispering low, hope flickering stubborn but fragile against the dark.

The night settled quietly at first, almost unnervingly so, the Jeep parked crooked under a flickering neon sign "Motel 6," half the letters burned out, buzzing fitfully and casting jagged red streaks across the lot's cracked pavement, the asphalt buckled and streaked with glowing vines, their blue veins pulsing faintly, like a heartbeat beneath the surface. We'd holed up in a room on the ground floor, its door chipped and peeling, green paint flaking to reveal warped wood beneath, the lock busted but barricaded with a dented dresser shoved hard against it, its splintered edge groaning under the weight. Inside, the air hung stale, thick with dust and the musk of mildew seeping from stained carpet, its brown fibers matted and curling at the edges, the walls yellowed and peeling, water stains blooming like bruises under cracked plaster, a faded "No Smoking" sign dangling crooked above the bed.

Mithis stood by the window, her glowing axe resting against her leg, its purple runes pulsing steadily, throwing violet light across her green skin, illuminating the sharp lines of her face, her crimson eyes scanning the dark beyond the grimy glass, cape swaying in the draft from a busted seal. Her patched leather tunic creaked faintly as she shifted, the pistol at her thigh humming softly, its green runes casting a faint glow across her wolf-pelt cape, shedding ash and singed hairs onto the carpet. I sat near the door, rifle in my lap, barrel cool against my jeans, finger off the trigger but ready, the dresser's splintered edge digging into my back, its chipped veneer flaking under my weight, the ache in my ribs a dull pulse beneath my torn jacket, crusted with blood and ichor.

David had dozed off on the sagging bed, its springs creaking with every shift, the mattress dipping under his bony frame, his breathing shallow and uneven, bitten arm tucked tight against his chest under a threadbare blanket patched with stains, its edges frayed, reeking faintly of sweat and mold. His gaunt face twitched in sleep, sweat beading on his brow, matted hair sticking to his skin, the bite hidden but its purple streaks burned into my memory, a countdown we couldn't ignore, the curse whispering low, every life you touch will rot.

The first sign of trouble came as a low, rhythmic thumping, distant but swelling, steady, rolling through the dark like a heartbeat waking up angry, vibrating the floorboards with a low buzz that set my teeth on edge. I froze, hand tightening around my rifle's scratched stock, its blue runes shimmering brighter from Haven's touch, casting faint light across my split knuckles. The sound burrowed into my skull, a dull thud-thud-thud that rattled a cracked coffee mug forgotten on the nightstand, its "World's Best Dad" logo chipped and faded, the ceramic clinking faintly against the wood.

"You hear that?" I whispered to Mithis, voice low, cutting the room's heavy quiet, my breath fogging in the chill seeping through the window's busted seal, carrying a whiff of pine and that sour-sweet rot, sharper now, curling my gut.

She nodded, eyes narrowing to slits as she leaned closer to the glass, her axe haft creaking in her grip, runes flaring brighter, casting stark purple shadows across her taut face, her green brow furrowing as she peered into the darkness beyond the neon's weak glow. "Something's coming big, and not alone." Her tone stayed steady, but the edge honed sharp, her cape snapping as she shifted, the pistol at her thigh humming louder, its green runes pulsing in warning, her boots scuffing the carpet with deliberate weight.

The sound grew closer, louder, a deep, resonant thudding now, paired with a tremor shaking the floor, dust sifting down from the ceiling's cracked plaster in thin, gray wisps, coating my tongue with a gritty tang. I stood, boots scuffing the matted carpet, and moved to the window beside Mithis, rifle up, barrel brushing the frame as I squinted into the night, the glass smeared with grime, streaked with old rain, reflecting the neon's red in jagged pulses.

The motel parking lot sprawled empty, bathed in the flickering red of the neon sign, its buzz a low drone against the quiet, rusted cars slumped at the edges: sedans, pickups, a van with a shattered windshield, tires flat, doors ajar, their interiors gutted, upholstery torn and spilling foam. A dumpster lay tipped over, spilling trash, soda cans, fast-food wrappers, a child's shoe that skittered in the breeze, catching the neon's glow. Beyond the lot, the road and surrounding pines loomed cloaked in shadow, their branches swaying uneasily, tips glinting blue like the vines we'd passed, their veins pulsing faster, the air thick with a sour tang of rot and ozone, the convergence's fingerprint tightening its grip.

Then, out of the darkness, shapes began to peel free slowly at first, indistinct, humanoid but wrong, their movements jerky and unnatural, like puppets cut loose from strings, their silhouettes jagged against the pines' dark wall. As they lurched closer, the neon's red wash caught them, revealing grotesque details: pale, translucent skin stretched tight over skeletal frames, veins pulsing black beneath, glowing like worms under glass, writhing with unnatural life. Their eyes burned dull yellow in hollow sockets, glinting sickly in the dark, heads twitching with insect-like precision, mouths gaping wide to show jagged teeth dripping black ichor onto the pavement, steaming faintly in the chill. Each step cracked the asphalt, bony limbs too long, too thin, ending in claws that scraped sparks as they moved, their bodies emaciated but powerful, muscles rippling under taut skin, spreading out to circle the motel with a predator's patience, their screeches low and guttural, a chorus of hunger that clawed at my skull.

"Mutants," Mithis hissed, gripping her axe tightly, its glow flaring hot purple, runes blazing along the blade as she squared up, cape rustling against her boots, her green knuckles whitening around the haft, the pistol at her thigh humming louder, its green runes pulsing in sync. "Ten, maybe twelve organized, hunting as a pack." Her voice stayed low, but the tension coiled tight, her crimson eyes glinting fierce, a warrior braced for blood, her posture rigid, muscles coiled under her patched leather tunic.

David stirred on the bed, groaning, a ragged sound that broke the quiet as his eyes fluttered open, blinking groggily through the haze, matted hair sticking to his sweat-slick brow, his gaunt face twitching with confusion. "What's going on?" His voice rasped, thick with sleep, bitten arm shifting under the blanket as he rubbed his face with a shaky hand, the purple streaks hidden but their stench lingering, sour-sweet and wrong, curling my gut tighter.

"Trouble," I said, moving to the door, checking the dresser barricade, its chipped edge held firm, but the wood creaked as I pressed against it, splinters flaking onto the carpet. "We've got company mutants, like the ones that hit your group. Stay put and keep quiet." My tone snapped, rifle slung over my shoulder as I scanned the room, the neon's red flickering through the window in jagged pulses, casting stark shadows across the yellowed walls, the air thickening with dust and the copper tang of fear.

David's gaze darted to the glass, catching the mutants' yellow eyes glowing through the dark, and his face drained white, a sickly pallor washing out the grime, his breath hitching audibly, fogging in short bursts. "Oh God... I've seen those before. They tore my group apart, Jen, Mark, all of them, ripped to pieces, blood everywhere." His voice cracked high, trembling as he scrambled back on the bed, the springs squealing under his bony frame, blanket tangling around his legs as he clutched his bitten arm tighter, the purple streaks pulsing faintly, visible through the flannel's torn edge, his eyes wide and wet, reflecting the neon's red like blood.

"Stay calm," Mithis said, her voice steady as steel, crimson eyes flicking to him for a beat before snapping back to the window, her axe raised, its glow cutting through the room's dimness, casting violet light across her green face. "Panic won't help you, won't help any of us. Focus, or you're dead." Her cape swayed as she shifted, boots scuffing the carpet, the pistol at her thigh humming faintly, its green runes pulsing steadily, her posture rigid, a warrior's discipline holding the line.

The mutants hit the edge of the parking lot, their movements slowing as they fanned out, circling the motel with eerie precision, claws scraping pavement in a staccato rhythm that clawed at my skull, their yellow eyes glinting like sick fireflies, heads jerking with unnatural twitches. One stepped closer, its skeletal frame lurching forward, translucent skin rippling over bone, and let out a low, guttural screech, a sound like metal grinding bone, piercing the night and sending a cold jolt down my spine, the neon sign flickering faster as if in response, its buzz a frantic drone against the quiet.

"They know we're here," I said grimly, jaw tightening as I gripped my rifle, its weight grounding me against the adrenaline spiking hot, the blue runes pulsing brighter, warm in my grip, Haven's magic humming in the steel. The room felt smaller, walls pressing in, the air thickening with dust, mildew, and the sour tang of David's fear, his bitten arm a ticking clock we couldn't ignore.

Mithis nodded, her expression unyielding, crimson eyes blazing fiercely, her green brow furrowing as she adjusted her grip on the axe, its runes pulsing hot, casting violet light across her boots. "We need to move. Staying here will get us cornered, trapped like rats in a cage." Her voice cut practical, a warrior's pragmatism honed by Ashvalen's chaos, her cape snapping as she turned, scanning the room for an exit, the pistol at her thigh humming louder, its green runes pulsing in warning.

David stumbled off the bed, his bitten arm cradled tight against his chest, hands shaking hard enough to rattle the loose change in his torn pocket, his boots scuffing the carpet as he backed toward the wall, his face pale as death under the neon's red wash. "What do we do? They'll tear us apart if we go out there just like before, claws everywhere, blood " His voice pitched shrill, cracking on the edges, eyes darting wild between us and the window, the mutants' screeches swelling shrill, a chorus of hunger rattling the frame, his breath fogging fast, steaming in the chill.

"We fight our way out," Mithis said, her tone cold and certain, crimson eyes flaring brighter as she shot him a look with no room for weakness, her axe raised, its glow cutting a path through the dusk, runes blazing hot purple. "Unless you'd rather wait for them to come in and rip you apart here, limb by limb." Her cape snapped as she turned, boots thudding carpet, the pistol at her thigh humming faintly, its green runes pulsing steadily, her green knuckles whitening around the axe haft, a warrior braced for blood.

A crash exploded from the room next door, the wall shuddering, hardwood splintering with a sharp crack, plaster cracking as the mutants pounded against it, their screeches swelling shrill and deafening, a chorus of hunger that clawed at my skull, rattling the frame. Dust and debris rained from the ceiling in a gritty haze, coating my tongue with a chalky tang, the building groaning under the assault, the neon outside flickering wildly, throwing jagged red streaks across the chaos, the coffee mug toppling from the nightstand, shattering on the carpet with a dull crunch, shards glinting in the axe's purple glow.

"Alright," I said, slinging my rifle over my shoulder and grabbing the pack, its canvas rough against my palm as I yanked it up, extra magazines clinking inside, the weight grounding me against the adrenaline spiking hot. "We're going out the back. There's a fire escape window in the bathroom. Move, now!" My voice snapped, cutting through the din as I pointed to the far end of the room, the bathroom door ajar, shadows pooling dark inside, a faint drip echoing from within, steady as a heartbeat.

Mithis bolted to the bathroom, her boots thudding carpet then tile, shoving the window open with a grunt, the rusted frame screeching as it gave, glass smeared with grime swinging wide, the night air rushing in cold, sharp with pine and that sour-sweet rot, curling my gut tighter. She peered out, axe up, its glow washing the cracked pavement below in purple, casting stark shadows across the gravel. "It's clear for now, no eyes back here, but they're close." Her voice came quick, clipped, cape brushing the sill as she leaned out, her crimson eyes scanning the dark, the pistol at her thigh humming faintly, its green runes pulsing steadily.

David hesitated, his hands shaking so hard the blanket slipped to the floor, pooling at his feet in a stained heap, reeking of sweat and mold, his bitten arm clutched tight, the swollen skin glinting purple

Jacob Salvia

in the axe's light, pulsing faintly, like a heartbeat. "I don't think I can I can't face them again." His voice broke, eyes darting wild between us and the window, his skinny frame trembling, boots scuffing the carpet as he backed toward the wall, his breath fogging fast, steaming in the chill.

"You don't have a choice," Mithis snapped, grabbing his good arm with an iron grip, yanking him toward the window with a tug that made him stumble, his boots catching the carpet's edge, nearly tripping him. "Move now, or I'll drag you!" Her tone sliced harsh, crimson eyes blazing as she shoved him forward, her strength brooking no argument, her cape snapping as she turned, axe raised, its glow cutting through the bathroom's dimness, casting violet light across the cracked tiles, the sink's rusted faucet dripping steadily, the sound sharp in the quiet.

One by one, we climbed out. I went first, boots hitting the cracked pavement behind the motel with a dull thud, the gravel crunching loud in the quiet, rifle up as I swept the shadows, the air biting cold against my face, thick with the sour stench of decay drifting from the pines, their branches twisting faintly, unnatural in the moonlight, their tips glinting blue, pulsing like the vines. Mithis followed, landing silently beside me, axe gleaming, cape swaying as she scanned the dark, runes pulsing steadily along her arm, casting violet light across the gravel, her crimson eyes glinting fiercely, the pistol at her thigh humming faintly, its green runes pulsing in warning. David came last, tumbling clumsily out the window, his lanky frame catching the sill with a grunt, bitten arm smacking the frame hard, the swollen skin splitting slightly, oozing blackish fluid that glistened wet, he winced, stifling a yelp, and hit the ground awkwardly, gravel crunching under his worn soles, his breath fogging fast, steaming in the chill. The mutants hadn't reached this side yet, their screeches echoing shrill from the front, the pounding growing louder, the motel's walls trembling behind us, plaster dust sifting down in thin, gray wisps.

"We need to get to the Jeep," I said, scanning the lot for a clear path, the neon's red flickering weak across the rusted husks of abandoned cars sedans, pickups, a station wagon with a shattered windshield, their tires flat, doors ajar, interiors gutted, upholstery torn and spilling foam, a child's car seat tangled in weeds, its plastic cracked and faded. The Jeep sat parked crooked at the lot's edge, its olive drab frame glinting under the flickering sign, runes etched into its steel shimmering blue, Haven's wards still holding, for now.

Mithis pointed to a gap between the circling mutants, their yellow eyes glinting through the dark like sick fireflies, claws scraping pavement as they tightened the noose, their translucent skin rippling over bone, veins pulsing black beneath, glowing like worms under glass. "There it is narrow, but open. If we're fast, we can make it." Her voice stayed steady, axe raised, its glow cutting a path through the dusk as she took point, her boots scuffing gravel with deliberate weight, cape snapping fiercely in the wind, the pistol at her thigh humming louder, its green runes pulsing in sync with her axe.

We ran, keeping low as we darted across the lot, gravel crunching under my boots, breath fogging quick in the chill, rifle slung tight against my chest, its weight bouncing with every step, the blue runes pulsing brighter, warm in my grip, Haven's magic humming in the steel. The mutants caught sight of us almost instantly, their glowing eyes snapping toward us with a jerky twitch, heads tilting unnaturally as they let out piercing howls high and shrill, clawing at my skull like shards of glass, rattling the air, the neon sign flickering wildly, its buzz a frantic drone against the chaos. Their skeletal frames surged forward, claws sparking against the pavement, translucent skin rippling over bone as they closed fast, their screeches swelling shrill, a chorus of hunger that vibrated my teeth, the air thickening with ozone and rot, the vines along the lot's edge pulsing faster, their blue veins glowing brighter, like they fed on the chaos.

"Go!" I shouted, swinging my rifle up and firing a burst, glowing bullets streaking blue from the barrel, Haven's runes flaring as they punched into the nearest mutant's chest, black ichor spraying hot and steaming onto the asphalt, the stench sour-sweet and choking, the creature staggering, screeching wild, its yellow eyes dimming for a beat as it clawed at the wounds, translucent skin splitting, veins pulsing black beneath, glowing like worms under glass.

Mithis swung her axe as one lunged from the side, its claws slashing air inches from her cape, the blade cutting clean through its torso with a wet crunch, parting translucent flesh and bone like paper, black ichor gushing thick and splattering her boots, steaming in the cold air, the stench curling my gut tighter. The mutant collapsed, writhing on the ground, its severed halves twitching grotesquely, yellow eyes dimming as it clawed at the pavement, leaving gouges in the cracked surface, its screeches fading to a gurgling rasp, the vines nearby pulsing faster, their blue veins glowing brighter, like they drank the ichor's spill.

David stumbled beside me, his breath hitching, boots skidding gravel as he struggled to keep up, his face pale as death under the neon's red wash, sweat streaking dirt down his gaunt cheeks, bitten arm flailing as he nearly tripped over a rusted hubcap, catching himself against a car husk with a dull clang, the metal groaning under his weight, his voice breaking shrill, cracking with terror. "They're everywhere, God, they're gonna kill us!" His eyes darted wildly, reflecting the mutants' yellow glow, his skinny frame trembling, the bite's purple streaks pulsing faintly, visible through the flannel's torn edge, oozing blackish fluid that glistened wet, its stench sharper, curling my gut tighter.

"Just keep moving!" I yelled, firing another burst, bullets sparking off a mutant's bony shoulder, ricocheting with a whine into the dark as it spun toward us, claws slashing wild, missing my jacket by a hair, the air hissing past my ear, the creature's screech piercing my skull, rattling my teeth. I ducked, rolling gravel under my boots, and fired again, bullets streaking blue, punching through its translucent chest, black ichor spraying hot, steaming onto the pavement, the mutant staggering, claws scraping air as it fell, yellow eyes dimming, its skeletal frame twitching grotesquely, the vines nearby pulsing faster, their blue veins glowing brighter, like they fed on the chaos.

We hit the Jeep, Mithis swinging the passenger door open with a creak of rusted hinges, its wards flaring blue as she braced it wide, her axe raised in her other hand, runes blazing hot purple as she scanned the closing circle, cape snapping fiercely in the wind, the pistol at her thigh humming louder, its green runes pulsing in sync. "Get in!" Her voice snapped, cutting over the engine's roar and the mutants' screeches, her crimson eyes glinting fiercely, a warrior braced for blood, her boots scuffing gravel with deliberate weight.

David scrambled into the backseat, his lanky frame tumbling over the gear, ammo cans clattering, a jerry can thudding against the floor as he curled tight, bitten arm clutched against his chest, the purple streaks pulsing faintly, oozing blackish fluid that glistened wet, its stench sharp in the cab's close air, his breath fogging fast, steaming in the chill, his eyes wide and wet, reflecting the mutants' yellow glow through the windows. I slid into the driver's seat, key turning with a rough scrape, the engine roaring alive, a guttural growl vibrating the cracked dash, headlights flaring bright and washing the mutants in stark blue, their translucent skin glinting wet as they surged closer, claws sparking against the pavement, screeches swelling shrill, a chorus of hunger that clawed at my skull.

Mithis leapt into the passenger seat, slamming the door hard just as one lunged, its claws raking the window with a screech of metal on glass, leaving deep gouges in the reinforced pane, wards sparking blue as they held, the mutant's yellow eyes glaring through, inches from her face, its jagged teeth dripping black ichor, steaming faintly in the chill, its screech piercing my skull, rattling my teeth. "Drive!" she shouted, voice cutting over the engine's roar, axe braced across her lap, runes pulsing fiercely, her cape snapping as she braced, the pistol at her thigh humming louder, its green runes pulsing in warning.

I floored it, tires squealing on the pavement, gravel spitting wild as we peeled out, the mutant sliding off with a howl, claws scraping the hood, leaving scratches in the warded steel, sparks flying as we broke free, the motel shrinking fast in the rearview, neon flickering weak behind a swarm of glowing eyes and shrieking shadows, their skeletal frames lurching after us, claws sparking against the pavement, screeches fading as the Jeep's wards flared blue, casting stark light across the cab, the vines along the road pulsing faster, their blue veins glowing brighter, like they fed on the chaos. The highway stretched dark ahead, buckled asphalt streaked with glowing vines, their thorns glinting sharp, Sara's scream pulling north, relentless, the curse whispering low, hope flickering stubborn but fragile against the dark.

25 FUR AND FURY

A trio of mutants clung to the Jeep's sides, their translucent skin glinting wet under the headlights' stark blue wash, yellow eyes blazing with feral fury. Their bony limbs jerked unnaturally, claws raking the reinforced frame with screeches of metal on steel, sparks flaring hot in the dark, showering the pavement like dying fireflies. One mutant's skeletal hand gouged a deep scratch across the driver's side door, wards flaring blue in protest, magic humming in the steel, holding firm but strained, the stench of their black ichor sharp and choking, curling my gut.

Mithis leaned out the passenger window, her cape of wolf pelts snapping wildly in the wind, ash and singed hairs scattering into the night. She swung her axe in tight, brutal arcs, its purple runes blazing hot, casting violet light across her green face, her crimson eyes glinting fiercely. The blade cleaved through a mutant's shoulder with a wet crunch, bone and flesh parting like paper, black ichor spraying thick and steaming onto the asphalt, splattering her boots and cape, the creature tumbling loose with a shrill, piercing howl that clawed at my skull. Another lunged from the hood, claws gouging the doorframe, leaving deep gashes in the warded steel; Mithis caught it mid-air, her axe slicing clean through its torso, the halves flopping grotesquely to the ground, twitching in a pool of steaming ichor, yellow eyes dimming as its screeches faded to a gurgling rasp, the vines along the lot's edge pulsing faster, their blue veins glowing brighter, like they fed on the chaos.

The Jeep shuddered as I swerved around a rusted car husk, its windshield spiderwebbed and glinting in the neon's dying flicker, a faded "For Sale" sticker curling at the edges, the mutants' screeches fading into the distance, swallowed by the night's heavy quiet, the pines' whispers threading through the dark. My heart pounded against my ribs, a staccato thud echoing in my skull, hands gripping the wheel tight enough to ache, chipped paint flaking under my palms, dusting my torn jeans. The ache in my ribs pulsed beneath my jacket, crusted with blood and ichor, the claw slash on my leg throbbing faintly under damp bandages, a constant reminder of the road's cost. The highway stretched dark ahead, buckled asphalt streaked with glowing vines, their thorns curling tighter around twisted guardrails, pulsing blue like veins under the earth, Ashvalen's blood creeping closer.

"That was too close," I muttered, voice scraped rough, glancing in the rearview, catching nothing but shadows and the motel's receding silhouette, its neon buzzing lonely, a pinprick of red against the bruised sky. The air in the cab smelled of dust, oil, and the sour tang of fear, sharp against the pine filtering through the cracked window, the wards humming faintly, their blue and gold veins shimmering across the dash.

David sat huddled in the backseat, his bitten arm cradled tight against his chest, the sleeve of his torn flannel slipping to expose the healed bite, now a scar puckered pale against his gaunt skin, the purple streaks gone, the wound closed unnaturally fast, a faint shimmer lingering under the surface, like Ashvalen's magic hadn't fully released him. "They followed me," he said, voice trembling, cracking on the edges as his gaunt face twitched in the mirror's dim wash, sweat beading thick on his brow, streaking dirt down his hollow cheeks. "They must have followed me from the woods, those things, their eyes, they never stopped hunting. I'm sorry, I'm so sorry." His breath fogged quick, steaming in the cab's chill, hands shaking as he rubbed his face, smearing dirt and sweat, his eyes wide and glistening with guilt, reflecting the dashboard's faint glow, the scar glinting faintly, a reminder of the bite's shadow.

Mithis glanced at me, her expression grim, crimson eyes glinting hard in the cab's gloom, axe resting across her lap, its glow dimming to a soft shimmer, runes pulsing faintly along the blade. "He's a liability. We can't keep running from his mistakes, first the bite, now this, drawing them right to us." Her voice cut low, practical but edged with frustration, cape rustling as she shifted, her green fingers tightening on the haft, the pistol at her thigh humming faintly, its green runes pulsing in sync, casting faint light across her wolf-pelt cape, her posture tense, a warrior's vigilance unyielding.

I nodded, jaw tightening, but said nothing, eyes locked on the road ahead, cracked asphalt blurring under the headlights, vines shimmering blue in the corners, their thorns glinting sharp, the air thickening with pine, damp earth, and the faint ozone hum of the convergence. The motel faded to a pinprick in the rearview, its danger behind us, but the weight of the night pressed heavier with every mile. David's scar, the mutants' howls, the curse clawing low: every life you touch will rot. My grip whitened on the wheel, chipped paint flaking under my thumbs, the ache in my ribs a dull pulse, Sara's scream flickering north, relentless, pulling me forward.

The Jeep rumbled down the cracked highway as the sun climbed higher, a pale gold disc breaking through a sky streaked with unnatural violet, clouds rippling like oil on water, Ashvalen's touch warping the heavens. Long shadows stretched from overgrown trees, their branches twisted and heavy with glowing vines, blue tips glinting wet in the light, and rusted car husks littered the ditches sedans, pickups, a school bus tilted on its side, doors ajar, tires sunken into moss, metal flaking red under the sun's glare, windows shattered into jagged mosaics, reflecting the sky's violet streaks.

Exhaustion gnawed at my focus, a dull ache spreading behind my eyes, my shoulders stiff from hours gripping the wheel, muscles protesting with every turn, my torn jacket creaking as I shifted, the fabric crusted with blood, ichor, and road grime, frayed cuffs brushing my split knuckles. The claw slash on my leg throbbed under damp bandages, the pain a constant burr, but we hadn't found a safe place to stop; every turnout looked too exposed, every shadow too deep, hiding claws or worse. The air filtering through the cracked window smelled of damp earth, pine, and ozone, the convergence's fingerprint tightening its grip, the vines along the road pulsing faster, their blue veins glowing brighter, like a heartbeat beneath the asphalt.

Mithis sat in the passenger seat, axe resting against her leg, its purple runes pulsing steadily, casting faint violet light across her green skin, illuminating the sharp lines of her jaw, her crimson eyes scanning the road ahead with a predator's keenness. Her cape pooled dark over the torn vinyl seat, wolf pelts shedding ash and singed hairs, the pistol at her thigh humming faintly, its green runes pulsing in sync with her axe, her patched leather tunic creaking faintly as she shifted, her posture tense. David slumped in the back, pale and silent, his bitten arm hidden under his tattered flannel, patched with sweat and grime, the scar glinting faintly in the sunlight spilling through the window, his head lolling against the seat, eyes half-closed, as if sleep tugged at him but couldn't take hold, his gaunt face twitching faintly, sweat beading thick on his brow, streaking dirt down his hollow cheeks.

I was about to suggest pulling over any ditch would do for a breather, just five minutes to figure out our next move, when Mithis tensed, her hand snapping to her axe, runes flaring brighter, casting stark violet light across the cab, her green knuckles whitening around the haft. "Stop the Jeep," she said, voice cutting the cab's quiet like a blade, her crimson gaze locked forward, piercing the road ahead.

"What is it?" I asked, already easing off the gas, tires crunching gravel as the Jeep slowed, engine growling low, vibrating the dash, the wards humming faintly, their blue and gold veins shimmering across the steel, magic holding steady but strained.

She pointed ahead, her gloved finger steady, unwavering. "There's something on the road, I can feel it." Her tone hardened, crimson eyes narrowing to slits as she leaned forward, cape brushing the dash, the pistol at her thigh humming louder, its green runes pulsing in warning, her green brow furrowing as she scanned the trees flanking the road, their branches swaying, glinting blue at the tips, pulsing like the vines.

I squinted, spotting a broken-down car sitting sideways across the highway, its hood crumpled like a fist had punched it, metal twisted inward, tires flattened and sagging into the asphalt, rubber cracked and peeling, rust streaking red down its faded blue frame, pooling in the cracks like dried blood. A makeshift barricade of debris and scrap metal sprawled around it splintered planks, a busted tire, a dented gas can, shards of shattered glass glinting in the sunlight, and a rusted refrigerator door leaning crooked, its handle snapped off, blocking the road, leaving a narrow gap just wide enough for the Jeep to squeeze through if I angled it right, the edges jagged. The sun glinted off the metal, blinding, the air still but heavy with a tang of oil, rust, and that sour-sweet rot drifting from the wreck, curling my gut tighter, the vines along the road pulsing faster, their blue veins glowing brighter, like they sensed the trap.

"Looks like trouble," I muttered, pulling the Jeep to a stop a safe distance back, gravel spitting under the tires as the engine idled low, vibrating the cracked dash, the wards humming faintly, their blue and gold veins shimmering across the steel. My gut twisted, a setup screamed loud in the stillness, the quiet too perfect, too staged, the pines' whispers threading through the dark, carrying a low buzz that vibrated my teeth.

Mithis nodded, her expression hard as forged steel, axe gleaming purple in her grip, runes pulsing brighter along the blade. "It's an ambush. The air's wrong, too thick, too still, like it's holding its breath." Her voice stayed low, certain, runes flaring brighter along her arm as she scanned the trees flanking the road, their branches twisting faintly, unnatural in the sunlight, their tips glinting blue, pulsing like the vines, the pistol at her thigh humming louder, its green runes pulsing in sync.

David sat up, his voice trembling, cracking high as he leaned forward, hands clutching the seat's edge, knuckles whitening through the grime, his gaunt face paling further, sweat beading thick on his brow, streaking dirt down his hollow cheeks, eyes darting wild to the barricade, the scar on his arm glinting faintly, shimmering under the sunlight. "What do we do? That's a trap, isn't it? They're waiting for us!" His breath fogged quickly, steaming in the cab's chill, his flannel bunching at the elbows, patched with sweat and grime, the scar pulsing faintly, a reminder of the bite's shadow.

"Stay in the Jeep," I said, grabbing my rifle and stepping out cautiously, boots thudding gravel, the crunch loud in the quiet, the cool air biting my face with a mix of pine, rust, and that sour-sweet rot, sharper now, curling my gut tighter. "Keep low, don't touch anything, and keep your head down." My tone snapped firm, rifle up as I swept the road, finger resting lightly on the trigger, its glowing barrel shimmering blue, Haven's runes pulsing warmly in my grip, grounding me against the adrenaline spiking hot.

Mithis followed, axe in hand, its glow cutting through the daylight, casting violet light across the gravel, cape swaying as she flanked me, her boots silent on the asphalt, her crimson eyes scanning the trees with a predator's keenness, the pistol at her thigh humming faintly, its green runes pulsing steady, her patched leather tunic creaking faintly as she moved, her posture tense, a warrior braced for blood.

The highway stretched eerily quiet, the wind rustling through the trees the only sound. I scanned the area rusted cars slumped in the ditch, their tires sunken into moss, windows shattered into jagged mosaics, a faded billboard leaning crooked overhead, its writing in an alien script peeling to gray tatters, the words unreadable but heavy with menace, the silence pressing heavy against my skull, the vines along the road pulsing faster, their blue veins glowing brighter, like they fed on the tension.

Then, a voice slithered out from behind the barricade, smooth and oily, cutting the quiet like a knife, dripping with false charm. "Easy there, friend! No need to get trigger-happy!" A man stepped into view, hands raised in a show of mock surrender, palms calloused and streaked with grime, fingers twitching faintly, betraying his calm.

He was tall and wiry, his frame lean under a tattered leather jacket patched with duct tape, the seams fraying, a smug grin splitting his stubbled face, teeth yellowed and uneven, one chipped at the corner, glinting in the sunlight. A shotgun hung slung across his back, barrel scratched but gleaming dull, its stock wrapped in frayed electrical tape, and a knife rested on his belt, its handle wrapped in frayed cord, the blade glinting sharp, stained with dark streaks of blood or ichor, hard to tell. His boots were scuffed, caked with mud and ash, laces frayed to threads, and a faded bandana hung loose around his neck, stained with sweat and grime, his dark eyes glinting hungry under the sunlight, sizing us up like meat.

"You've wandered into our little toll road," he said, voice smooth but laced with menace, lowering his hands slowly, thumbs hooking casually into his belt, fingers brushing the knife's handle, a subtle threat. "If you want to pass, it'll cost you supplies, gear, whatever you've got worth a damn in that Jeep." His grin widened, not reaching his cold eyes, his stubble rasping as he scratched his jaw, the sound sharp in the quiet, the vines along the road pulsing faster, their blue veins glowing brighter, like they sensed the standoff.

"Not interested," I said flatly, keeping my rifle trained on his chest, its glowing barrel steady, blue runes flaring under my grip as I squared up, boots planted wide on the cracked asphalt, the wards humming faintly, Haven's magic holding steady but strained, the air buzzing electric.

The man chuckled, a low, rasping sound that scraped the air, his grin widening but not reaching his cold eyes, glinting dark under the sunlight. "Oh, I think you'll reconsider. You see, my friends and I don't take kindly to freeloaders. It takes a lot to keep this road safe, mutants, wraiths, and worse things crawling out of the woods." He tilted his head, a predator sizing meat, his bandana fluttering faintly in the breeze, his fingers twitching toward his knife, the vines along the road pulsing faster, their blue veins glowing brighter, like they fed on his words.

As if on cue, more figures peeled from the trees and abandoned vehicles flanking the road, at least seven, shadows resolving into men and women, all armed, rifles and pistols glinting in scarred hands, blades gleaming at their hips, their gear a patchwork of scavenged junk torn jackets patched with canvas, a dented helmet strapped to a man's head, its visor cracked, a machete strapped to a woman's thigh with electrical tape, its blade notched but sharp. They moved slowly, spreading out to circle us, boots scuffing gravel and asphalt, their faces weathered, eyes glinting hungry under patchy sunlight, the air thickening with sweat, gun oil, and the sour tang of greed, the vines along the road pulsing faster, their blue veins glowing brighter, like they sensed the trap closing.

Mithis stepped closer to me, her axe glowing, runes pulsing steadily along the blade, casting violet light across the gravel, her crimson eyes flicking across them like a hawk tracking prey, her cape rustling as she squared her shoulders, the pistol at her thigh humming louder, its green runes pulsing in sync. "Bandits," she said coldly, voice low and certain, her green brow furrowing, her posture tense, a warrior braced for blood, her boots scuffing gravel with deliberate weight.

"Yeah," I muttered, grip tightening on my rifle, the stock cool against my palm, blue runes pulsing warmly in my grip, grounding me against the adrenaline spiking hot. "Figures the world goes to hell, and the roaches crawl out, picking bones clean." My voice stayed low, but the anger flared hot, the road's lessons burning deep trust was a gamble, and these scavengers played for blood.

The leader's grin widened as his gaze slid to Mithis, lingering on her axe, its purple glow reflecting in his dark eyes, glinting with greed. "Interesting weapon you've got there, missy. Bet that'd fetch a nice price, magic like that's rare salvage, could trade it for a month's worth of food, ammo, maybe even a safe bed." His tone lilted greedily, hand twitching toward his knife, fingers brushing the frayed cord, his boots shifting faintly, betraying his calm, the vines along the road pulsing faster, their blue veins glowing brighter, like they fed on his hunger.

"Try and take it," Mithis said, voice low and dangerous, stepping forward, axe haft creaking as her green knuckles whitened, runes flaring brighter, casting stark violet shadows across her taut face, her crimson eyes blazing fierce, daring him to move, the pistol at her thigh humming louder, its green runes pulsing in sync, a quiet promise of power and judgment.

The man's grin faltered, a flicker of unease crossing his stubbled face, his eyes darting to her axe, the runes' glow reflecting in his pupils, but he recovered fast, chuckling, keener this time, a nervous edge threading through. "Look, no need to get violent. Just hand over your supplies, ammo, food, whatever's in that Jeep, and we'll let you go, no blood spilled, no trouble." His hands spread wide, mock-reasonable, but his crew tightened their circle, weapons glinting as they shifted stance, rifles cocking with sharp clicks, a pistol glinting dull in a woman's scarred hand, her lips curling into a sneer, the air buzzing electric with the standoff, the vines along the road pulsing faster, their blue veins glowing brighter, like they sensed the trap closing.

"Not happening," I said, voice hard, rifle steady on his chest, finger itching on the trigger, blue runes flaring brighter under my grip, the wards humming faintly, the magic holding steady but strained, my pulse thudding steadily but warily, the ache in my ribs a dull pulse, the claw slash on my leg throbbing faintly, a gentle reminder.

The man sighed, shaking his head, a theatrical slump to his shoulders, his bandana fluttering faintly in the breeze. "Shame. I was hoping we could do this the easy way, guess you folks need a lesson in generosity." He nodded to his crew, a flick of his chin, and they raised their weapons, a pistol and rifles glinting dull as they fanned out, boots grinding gravel, the air thickening with gunpowder and the sour tang of greed, the vines along the road pulsing faster, their blue veins glowing brighter, like they fed on the tension.

Mithis didn't wait; she surged forward with a fierce cry, axe swinging wide in a brutal arc, its glow blazing hot purple as runes flared like forge fire, casting violet light across the gravel. The leader ducked fast, the blade whistling inches over his head, cleaving through the barricade behind him with a splintering crack wood and metal burst apart, debris flying fast, a jagged plank spinning past his ear, grazing his stubble with a thin red line as he stumbled back, cursing, his boots skidding gravel, his knife slipping from his belt to clatter on the asphalt.

The bandits opened fire, bullets zipping past with whines, pinging off the Jeep's warded frame in bursts of blue sparks, Haven's magic flaring bright, holding firm but strained, the steel groaning under the assault. I dropped to one knee, ducking behind the Jeep's hood, returning fire with controlled bursts, glowing rounds streaking blue from my rifle, punching through a bandit's shoulder with a wet pop, blood spraying red as he spun howling to the ground, his rifle clattering uselessly, snapping in half under his weight. The crack of gunfire echoed across the highway, ricocheting off rusted cars and twisted trees, the air thick with gunpowder, dust, and the sour tang of blood kicked up from the asphalt.

Mithis was a whirlwind of destruction, her axe glowing brighter with each swing, cutting through the chaos with terrifying precision, her cape snapping wildly behind her, wolf pelts streaked with dust and sweat, boots grinding gravel as she danced through them, runes pulsing hot along her arm. She deflected a bullet mid-flight with a flick of her blade, the slug sparking orange as it whined harmlessly into the dirt, kicking up a puff of dust, then cleaved a bandit's rifle in half, metal parting with a high whine, the man staggering back with a yelp as she drove her elbow into his jaw, a sharp crack echoing as he dropped cold, blood trickling dark from his nose, pooling on the asphalt. Another lunged with a machete, its blade notched but sharp; Mithis parried with her axe, sparks flying as metal clashed, then spun, slamming the flat of her blade into his temple, dropping him silent to the dirt, his machete clattering across the pavement.

Behind me, David crouched low in the backseat, his bitten arm clutching the seat's edge, knuckles whitening through the grime, his gaunt face paling further, sweat beading thick on his brow, streaking dirt down his hollow cheeks, eyes darting wild between the gunfire and the window, the scar glinting faintly, shimmering under the sunlight, like Ashvalen's magic lingered still. "I can't just sit here!" he stammered, voice cracking high, his breath hitching, fogging fast in the cab's chill, his flannel bunching at the elbows, patched with sweat and grime, the scar pulsing faintly.

"Stay down!" I shouted, slamming a fresh mag into my rifle with a click, the clatter of brass hitting the pavement as I fired again, pinning a bandit behind a rusted truck, bullets sparking off its frame, forcing him low, his curses muffled by the gunfire's crack, the air thick with gunpowder and dust. "We've got this, don't move, don't make it worse!" My voice snapped, cutting through the din, the ache in my ribs a dull pulse, the claw slash on my leg throbbing faintly,

But David wasn't listening. His breath hitched, a low, guttural growl rumbling from his chest, shaking the Jeep's frame as his body trembled hard, hands clawing at his flannel, ripping the fabric at the seams. His eyes flickered, glowing amber in the cab's dimness, pupils dilating wide, swallowing the light, his breathing growing heavy, ragged gasps fogging the air, steaming in the chill, his gaunt face twisting with pain, sweat streaking dirt down his hollow cheeks, the scar on his arm pulsing faster, shimmering under the sunlight, like Ashvalen's magic woke something deep within.

"David?" I called, glancing back, voice tight with alarm as I popped another shot, a bandit's pistol spinning from his hand, clattering across the asphalt with a dull clang, the man cursing as he ducked behind a rusted sedan, bullets sparking off its frame, the air thick with gunpowder and dust, the vines along the road pulsing faster.

He clutched his bitten arm, teeth gritted in pain, the scar pulsing under his sleeve as if alive, shimmering with a faint blue glow, like the vines outside. "I don't know what's happening, but I can feel it, it's burning!" His voice broke, half-scream, half-roar, shaking the cab as his frame shuddered violently, muscles bulging under his torn flannel, seams ripping with sharp pops, his breath steaming hot, fogging the windows, his eyes glowing brighter, amber and fierce, but holding a strange, human clarity.

Before I could react, David let out a roar that shook the ground, a deep, primal bellow rattling the Jeep's windows, vibrating through my boots as I braced against the hood, the sound clawing the air, shaking leaves loose from the trees, scattering them across the pavement. His body twisted, expanding bones cracked like dry branches, skin stretching taut as fur sprouted thick and coarse across his arms, chest, face, brown and matted, glinting wet in the sunlight, rippling with muscle. His frame swelled, towering, muscles rippling under the pelt, his features warping into a powerful, bear-like visage, jaws wide with fangs glinting sharp, eyes burning amber but holding David's fear, his humanity, in their depths. His clothes tore apart, flannel and denim shredding to rags that fluttered to the pavement, his massive paws slamming the asphalt with a thud that cracked it, sending gravel flying, the vines nearby pulsing faster, their blue veins glowing brighter, like they fed on his transformation.

"David?" I said again, voice tinged with shock and awe, rifle dipping a hair as I stared the kid I'd pulled from the woods now loomed eight feet tall, hunched and hulking, a werebear of raw power, claws flexing long and black at his sides, fur bristling as he shook off the last of his human frailty, his breath steaming hot in the cool air, fogging in thick clouds, the scar on his arm now a faint shimmer under the fur, pulsing faintly.

The creature he'd become turned to me, head tilting, amber eyes locking mine, glinting with a strange, human clarity, his massive chest heaving as he took a shuddering breath. "I'm still here," he rumbled, voice deep and resonant, gravel grinding under thunder, but unmistakably David's, his fear threading through the growl, his humanity holding against the beast within. "And I'm going to help, can't let you fight alone." His fangs glinted, breath steaming hot as he straightened, fur rippling with muscle, claws flexing long and black, the ground trembling faintly under his weight.

I had no time to process it before the werebear charged, a blur of muscle and fury barreling into the fray, the ground trembling under his weight, asphalt cracking with each step, gravel flying in wild sprays. The bandits froze, faces twisting from smug to sheer terror as he roared again, a sound that clawed the air, rattling the Jeep's windows, shaking leaves loose from the trees, scattering them across the pavement, the vines along the road pulsing faster, their blue veins glowing brighter, like they fed on his fury. One bandit fired a panicked shot, the bullet whining, its slug glancing off David's thick fur with a dull thud, flattening harmless to the dirt, kicking up a puff of dust as he surged forward undeterred, his amber eyes blazing fierce, locked on his prey.

With a swipe of his massive claws, David sent two bandits flying bodies spinning through the air, crashing into a rusted sedan with a crunch of metal and bone, the car's frame buckling under the impact, glass shattering into jagged shards, their rifles clattering uselessly to the pavement, one snapping in half with a sharp crack, the men lying limp, blood trickling dark from their noses, pooling on the asphalt. Another swung a bat at him, a desperate arc, the wood cracking as David caught it mid-swing, splintering it in his grip like dry twigs, shards flying fast, then backhanded the man sprawling, his jaw cracking with a sickening pop as he hit the asphalt limp, his bat rolling uselessly across the pavement.

"Fall back!" the leader shouted, bravado gone, voice pitching shrill as he stumbled away, boots skidding gravel, shotgun slipping loose to clang against the barricade, its barrel glinting dull in the sunlight, his knife trembling in his grip, useless against the beast before him. "What the hell is that thing?" His eyes widened, glassy with panic, sweat streaking down his stubbled face, his bandana fluttering faintly as he backed toward the trees, branches snapping in his wake.

"It's our friend," Mithis said coldly, axe slicing clean through another bandit's rifle, metal parting with a high whine, the man staggering as she spun, slamming the flat of her blade into his temple, dropping him silent to the dirt, blood trickling dark from his nose, pooling on the asphalt, her cape snapping wildly behind her, wolf pelts streaked with dust and sweat, boots grinding gravel as she moved, runes pulsing hot along her arm, the pistol at her thigh humming louder, its green runes pulsing in sync, a quiet promise of power and judgment.

The remaining bandits broke, scattering fast into the trees and abandoned vehicles, boots pounding frantically as they vanished into the shadows, leaving gear and curses behind rifles dropped in the dirt, a pistol clattering across the pavement, a dented helmet rolling to a stop against a rusted tire, the air thick with gunpowder, dust, and the sour tang of fear.

The leader tried to bolt, his boots skidding gravel as he turned, but

Jacob Salvia

David cut him off, lumbering swiftly despite his bulk, planting himself in the man's path with a ground-shaking thud, towering over him, fur bristling as he roared, the Jeep's windows buzzing, the sound clawing the air, shaking leaves loose from the trees, scattering them across the pavement. The man froze, shotgun slipping from his hands to clatter on the asphalt, its barrel glinting dull in the sunlight, his knife trembling uselessly in his grip, his face draining white, sweat streaking dust down his stubbled face, his bandana fluttering faintly, his dark eyes wide and glassy, reflecting David's amber glow.

David stepped closer, claws flexing long and black, his massive chest heaving as he loomed, amber eyes burning down at the bandit, glinting with a strange, human clarity, his breath steaming hot in the cool air, fogging in thick clouds, fur rippling with muscle. "Leave," he growled, voice rumbling like thunder rolling, each word a hammer strike shaking the air, vibrating my teeth, the ground trembling faintly under his weight. "And don't come back or I'll find you." His fangs glinted sharply, jaws wide as he leaned in, the leader's knife trembling uselessly in his grip, his boots scuffing gravel as he backed away, branches snapping in his wake, the vines along the road pulsing faster.

The man didn't need telling twice; he turned and bolted, boots pounding frantic across the pavement, disappearing into the dark tangle of pines shimmering blue, branches snapping in his wake as he vanished, his curses fading into the trees' whispers. David stood tall, his massive frame silhouetted against the violet-streaked sky, fur bristling as he let out a final, rumbling growl, the sound fading into the quiet, the highway stretching eerily still, the air thick with gunpowder, dust, and the sour tang of victory, fragile but hard-won.

26 PRAYER ON THE PAVEMENT

The fight ended as abruptly as it began, the highway falling into an eerie silence, broken only by the heavy breathing of Mithis, David, and me, our breaths fogging in the cool air, mingling with the acrid stench of gunpowder, dust, and the copper tang of blood splattered across the cracked asphalt. Shattered gear littered the road, splintered wood, a dented rifle barrel, a bandit's dropped knife glinting dull in the sunlight, its handle wrapped in frayed cord, now smeared with dirt and blood. The vines along the road pulsed faintly, their blue veins glowing softer now, as if sated by the chaos, their thorns curling tighter around rusted guardrails, glinting sharp in the dying light.

David stood hulking in the road's center, an eight-foot tower of muscle and fur, his massive chest heaving, amber eyes blinking slowly as he looked down at his clawed hands, black and glistening, flexing with uncertainty, each claw as long as a dagger, etched with faint blue veins shimmering under the fur. His brown pelt was matted with sweat, dirt, and streaks of bandit blood, rippling as he shifted weight, his paws scraping the asphalt with a low grind, leaving shallow gouges in the cracked surface. "I didn't hurt you, did I?" he asked, voice trembling under the deep growl, his bear-like head tilting toward us, pointed ears twitching as if testing the quiet, amber eyes glinting wet with a mix of relief and fear, reflecting the violet-streaked sky.

"No," I said, lowering my rifle, its glowing barrel dipping to rest against my thigh, the blue runes dimming as my pulse steadied, the ache in my ribs a dull pulse beneath my torn jacket, crusted with blood and ichor. "You saved us, David turned the tide single-handedly, tore through them like they were nothing." My voice scraped rough, awe threading through as I stepped closer, boots scuffing gravel, the crunch loud in the quiet, the curse clawing low but quieter now, *every life you touch will rot*, its whisper drowned by the weight of his strength. I studied his massive form, the way his fur rippled with muscle, his amber eyes holding a human clarity, a stark contrast to the feral power radiating from him.

Mithis approached cautiously, her axe resting against her shoulder, its purple runes fading to a soft shimmer, casting faint violet light across her green skin, illuminating the sharp lines of her jaw, her crimson eyes narrowing thoughtfully as she studied him, cape of wolf pelts swaying in the breeze, shedding ash and singed hairs onto the asphalt. "This is what the bite did to you?" Her tone eased a hair, less sharp but still probing, her gloved hand tightening briefly on the axe haft, the pistol at her thigh humming faintly, its green runes pulsing in sync, a quiet promise of power. She circled him slowly, boots silent on the gravel, her crimson gaze sweeping his towering frame, noting the blue-veined claws, the scar on his arm now hidden under fur but pulsing faintly, shimmering with Ashvalen's magic.

David nodded, his massive shoulders slumping, fur rippling as he shifted weight, his paws scraping the asphalt again, sending a faint tremor through the ground. "I think so. I thought it would turn me into something horrible, those mutants with their yellow eyes, or worse, something mindless, ripping everything apart. But I can still think, still feel. I'm still me." His voice rumbled deep, uncertain, amber eyes glinting wet with relief and fear, his bear-like head dipping as if ashamed of his bulk, his breath steaming hot in the cool air, fogging in thick clouds, the scar's faint shimmer pulsing under his fur, a reminder of the bite's shadow.

Mithis tilted her head, her crimson gaze boring into him for a long beat, her green brow furrowing as she processed his words, then nodded curtly, a flicker of respect crossing her taut face. "You're a werebear, a creature of immense strength and resilience, rare even among the Gin in my world, where such transformations are revered, not cursed. They're warriors, protectors, noble when they rise. It seems the convergence has awakened something in you, twisted the bite into this, a gift, not a curse." Her tone steadied, analytical but warm with a warrior's admiration, her cape rustling as she stepped back, axe haft creaking in her grip, runes pulsing purple against her green skin, casting stark violet shadows across the gravel, the pistol at her thigh humming faintly, its green runes pulsing steadily.

David looked at her, amber eyes wide, then down at his paws again, claws flexing slowly, black and glistening, the blue veins shimmering faintly, as if testing their reality. "I don't know how to control it. It just happened, like a fire inside, burning until I couldn't hold it back. What if I lose myself, turn into something I can't stop, hurt someone I don't mean to?" His growl eased, trembling again, his massive frame shrinking slightly as his breath hitched, fur receding like a tide pulling back, revealing patches of pale skin slick with sweat, the scar glinting faintly, shimmering with Ashvalen's magic.

"You won't," I said firmly, stepping up, voice cutting through his doubt, steady as a soldier's command, my boots grinding gravel as I clapped his shoulder, still broad even as he shrank, the fur warm and coarse under my palm, grounding him like he'd grounded us in the fight. "You didn't just keep your head; you fought for us and chose to protect us when you could've run or lost control. That's not something you lose, David. We'll figure this out together, step by step, make sure you master it." My voice stayed steady, gray eyes locking with his amber ones.

He gave a hesitant nod, his form collapsing inward, bones cracking softly now, quieter than the violent shift before, fur melting back to pale skin slick with sweat, muscles shrinking until he was lanky, human, shivering in the torn rags of his flannel and denim, the fabric hanging loose over his bony frame, visibly exhausted, his breath fogging fast in the cool air. He slumped against the Jeep's side, the warded steel creaking under his weight, hands trembling as he rubbed his healed arm, the scar glinting under the sun's dying light, puckered pale but shimmering faintly. "Thanks," he rasped, voice raw, leaning heavy against the olive drab frame, the wards flaring blue briefly.

"Let's get out of here," I said, helping him into the backseat, his weight sagging against me, boots dragging gravel as I eased him in, the torn vinyl creaking under his bony frame, the cab smelling of dust, oil, and the sour tang of his sweat, sharp against the pine filtering through the cracked window. "We've had enough excitement for one day, and we need distance from this mess bandits, mutants, all of it." My voice stayed steady.

Mithis nodded, climbing into the passenger seat, axe propped against the door, its glow dimming to a soft shimmer, runes pulsing faintly along the blade, her cape pooling dark on the floor, wolf pelts streaked with dust and sweat, shedding ash onto the torn vinyl. "Agreed. But this changes things. David's strength may be exactly what we need in the fights ahead, mutants, wraiths, whatever the convergence throws at us. If he can harness it, master the shift." Her voice stayed low, crimson eyes flicking to him in the rearview, then forward, thoughtful but firm, her green fingers tightening briefly on the axe haft, the pistol at her thigh humming faintly, its green runes pulsing steadily, a quiet promise of power.

I started the Jeep, the key scraping rough in the ignition, the engine growling alive with a guttural roar, vibrating the cracked dashboard, the wards flaring blue briefly, casting stark light across the cab, their blue and gold veins shimmering across the steel, Haven's magic holding steady but strained. Glancing in the rearview, I caught David's tired face pale but relieved, his gaunt features softened by exhaustion, his healed arm resting limp in his lap, no trace of the bite's swelling now, just a puckered scar glinting faintly, shimmering with Ashvalen's magic. "You did good back there," I said, voice steady, meeting his amber eyes in the mirror, their glow dimming but still fierce.

He managed a small smile, lips twitching, exhaustion etching deeper lines into his gaunt face, his matted hair sticking to his sweat-slick brow, the rags of his flannel hanging loose over his bony frame. "Thanks. I just hope I can keep it under control, not be a liability again, not drag you into more trouble." His voice rasped thin, hands fidgeting with the frayed fabric, eyes dropping to his lap, the scar glinting faintly, a reminder of the bite's shadow, but also his strength.

"We'll figure it out," I assured him, steering the Jeep back onto the road, tires humming over buckled asphalt as the barricade shrank in the rearview, splintered wood, scattered gear, and bloodstains fading to a blur, the vines along the road pulsing faintly, their blue veins glowing softer now, as if sated by the chaos. "You're with us now, and we are going to need you too." My voice stayed steady, gray eyes flicking to the road ahead, the ache in my ribs a dull pulse, the claw slash on my leg throbbing faintly, a reminder of the road's cost, but David's strength a new light against the darkness.

A renewed sense of purpose filled the cab as we drove away, the air buzzing with it, electric and sharp, David's transformation a wild card, unpredictable but powerful, Mithis's resolve unyielding as forged steel, her crimson eyes glinting fierce, my own drive burning north for Sara, relentless, her scream flickering in my skull like a beacon. The world was still a chaotic hellscape, the convergence bleeding deeper every mile, vines pulsing blue along the road, their thorns glinting sharp, but with David's strength and our grit, we had a keener edge, a sharper blade against whatever waited ahead mutants, bandits, or the curse clawing low, every life you touch will rot.

The road stretched on for miles, desolate and unbroken, fields of overgrown grass swaying gold and blue under a patchy sun, their stalks heavy with glowing vines, their blue veins pulsing faintly, like a heartbeat beneath the earth. Rusted car husks littered the ditches: sedans, pickups, a delivery van tilted on its side, its faded logo peeling to gray tatters, doors ajar, tires sunken into moss, metal flaking red under the sunlight, windows shattered into jagged mosaics, reflecting the violet-streaked sky. Crumbling billboards leaned crookedly along the highway, their faded promises "Visit Marquette!" "Cold Beer Ahead!" peeling to gray, the words barely legible under a film of grime and ash, their steel frames twisted, glinting blue at the edges, as if the convergence had claimed them too. The fight with the bandits and David's shift weighed heavily.

The sun dipped low, a bloody orange smear igniting the horizon, casting long shadows across the asphalt, the sky bruising purple and violet, clouds rippling like oil on water. A cluster of buildings resolved into view, a small town, mostly intact but eerily still, its edges blurring into the dusk's bruise, the air thick with pine, damp earth, and the faint ozone hum of the convergence. As we rolled closer, it took shape: modest homes with sagging porches and peeling paint, their clapboard siding faded to gray, windows boarded with splintered planks, a commercial strip of brick storefronts standing defiant but worn, their signs "Betty's Eats," "Miller's General Store," "Gulf Gas" glinting under cracked neon and rust, flickering weakly in the dusk. Cars parked haphazardly along streets and driveways, doors ajar, tires flat, looked abandoned mid-flight, their owners either gone or holed up, hoods popped, interiors gutted, upholstery torn and spilling foam, a child's backpack tangled in weeds, its straps frayed to threads. The quiet pressed thick against the Jeep's rumble, broken only by the wind rustling through skeletal trees lining the street, their branches glinting blue at the edges, pulsing faintly, like the vines.

"This place doesn't look abandoned," Mithis said, crimson eyes scanning the streets as we slowed, her axe haft creaking in her grip, runes pulsing purple against her green skin, casting faint violet light across her taut face, her cape of wolf pelts rustling as she leaned forward, peering through the streaked windshield. "But it doesn't look alive, either too still, too hollow, like it's holding its breath." Her voice stayed low, wary, the pistol at her thigh humming faintly, its green runes pulsing in sync, a quiet promise of power, her patched leather tunic creaking faintly as she shifted, her posture tense, a warrior braced for blood.

"Only one way to find out," I said, easing the Jeep to a crawl, tires crunching gravel and broken glass as we hit the outskirts, the engine growling low, vibrating the cracked dashboard, the wards humming faintly, their blue and gold veins shimmering across the steel, Haven's magic holding steady but strained. My gut twisted at the thought that this meant traps or ghosts, and neither boded well, the silence too perfect, too staged, the pines' whispers threading through the dark, carrying a low buzz that vibrated my teeth, Sara's scream flickering north in my skull, relentless.

David sat up in the backseat, his voice hesitant, cracking as he rubbed his healed arm, the scar glinting faintly, shimmering with Ashvalen's magic, his gaunt face twitching with unease, sweat streaking dirt down his neck despite the chill, the rags of his flannel hanging loose over his bony frame. "Do you think anyone's here? Survivors, maybe?" His amber eyes darted nervously to the empty streets, reflecting the flickering neon, his hands fidgeting with his torn sleeve, the scar pulsing faintly, a reminder of his transformation, his strength, but also his fear.

"I don't know," I said, scanning the stillness boarded windows, a tipped-over trash can rolling in the breeze, its dented lid clattering faintly, a faded "Welcome to Pine Hollow" banner flapping torn from a lamppost, its edges frayed to threads, fluttering in the dusk. "But it's worth checking out. If there are survivors, they might know something about the convergence, the roads, and Marquette. Or they

Jacob Salvia

might need help." My voice stayed steady, rifle resting against my thigh, its glowing barrel cool in my hands, the blue runes pulsing warmly, grounding me against the adrenaline spiking hot, Sara's scream flickering north, relentless, pulling me forward, hope flickering stubborn but fragile against the dark.

Mithis nodded, her expression honing, crimson eyes glinting hard as she adjusted her grip on the axe, its runes flaring brighter, casting stark violet light across the cab. "Stay alert. This could be a trap bandits, mutants, or worse, something the convergence spit out." Her tone cut practical, her cape brushing the dash with a scrape, the pistol at her thigh humming louder, its green runes pulsing in sync, her green knuckles whitening around the axe haft, a warrior braced for blood.

I parked the Jeep near the diner, a squat brick box with a cracked neon sign buzzing, "Betty's Eats" flickering red over a busted door hanging ajar, its hinges rusted and groaning in the breeze, the windows smeared with grime, streaked with old rain, reflecting the dusk's bruise. I cut the engine, the silence slamming down heavy, broken only by the wind rustling through skeletal trees, their branches glinting blue at the edges, pulsing faintly, like the vines, and the faint creak of a shop sign swinging crooked across the street, its faded "Open" peeling to gray. I grabbed my rifle, its glowing barrel cool in my hands, the blue runes pulsing warmly, grounding me against the adrenaline spiking hot. Mithis hefted her axe, its purple runes flaring, casting violet light across her green skin, her cape swaying as she stepped out, boots silent on the gravel. David followed cautiously, his steps scuffing gravel, hands flexing uneasily at his sides, amber eyes darting wild in the dusk, the rags of his flannel hanging loose, the scar glinting faintly.

We moved through the town, checking buildings one by one, boots thudding on warped porches, their splintered boards creaking under our weight, doors groaning open to stale air thick with dust, mildew, and the sour tang of rot, the silence buzzing with echoes of haste. The diner stood empty, but signs of life lingered half-eaten meals on plastic tables, congealed gravy pooling beside cracked plates, a fork stuck upright in a mound of cold mashed potatoes, a coffee mug tipped over, its "World's Best Mom" logo chipped and faded, spilling grounds across the chipped counter. Blankets piled in corners of a hardware store beside a tipped-over rack of rusted tools, hammers, screwdrivers, a crowbar glinting dull under a film of dust, suggested someone had slept there recently, the fabric reeking of sweat and fear. In the general store, scattered cans of tuna, beans, and peaches rolled loose in the aisles, their labels peeling under a film of grime, dented and stacked hasty, a shopping basket tipped over, spilling a child's stuffed bear, its fur matted and missing an eye, staring blankly at the ceiling. The air smelled of mildew, sweat, and the faint copper tang of blood, the quiet pressing heavy against my skull, the vines outside pulsing faintly, their blue veins glowing softer now, as if sated by the town's despair.

"This place was lived in," Mithis said, running gloved fingers over a stack of canned food on the diner counter dented tins of peaches, spam, and creamed corn, their labels curling at the edges, stacked hasty against a busted coffee maker, its glass pot cracked, spilling grounds across the chipped plastic, the air thick with the sour tang of rot. "Recently days, maybe less. They didn't leave willingly." Her voice stayed low, crimson eyes flicking to the shadows pooling in the corners, axe gleaming in her grip, runes pulsing purple against her green skin, the pistol at her thigh humming faintly, its green runes pulsing steadily, a quiet promise of power.

"But where is everyone?" David asked, voice tinged with unease, cracking as he stepped closer, peering through the diner's grimy window at the empty street, the neon's red flickering weakly, casting jagged streaks across the pavement. His amber eyes glinted nervously in the dimness, hands fidgeting with his torn sleeve, the scar pulsing faintly, shimmering with Ashvalen's magic, his gaunt face twitching with unease, sweat streaking dirt down his neck despite the chill, the rags of his flannel hanging loose over his bony frame.

As we stepped outside, a sound snagged my ear, distant, like murmuring voices, too quiet to parse, threading through the wind's rustle and the creak of a swinging shop sign, its faded "Open" peeling to gray, swaying crooked across the street. I froze, rifle up, ears straining against the dusk's heavy quiet, my pulse kicking up, the ache in my ribs a dull pulse, the claw slash on my leg throbbing faintly under damp bandages. "You hear that?" I asked, glancing at Mithis, my voice low, barely above a whisper, the air buzzing with the convergence's faint ozone hum, the vines outside pulsing faintly, their blue veins glowing softer now, as if listening.

She nodded, her expression honing, crimson eyes narrowing to slits as she tilted her head, axe haft creaking in her grip, runes flaring brighter, casting stark violet light across her green face, her cape rustling as she scanned the street. "It's coming from that building, the church, end of the street." She pointed with a gloved finger, steady and unwavering, to a squat brick structure with cracked stained glass, its tall steeple silhouetted black against the darkening sky, a rusted cross leaning crooked at the tip, swaying in the breeze, casting jagged shadows across the pavement, the vines along the road pulsing faintly, their blue veins glowing softer now, as if sated by the town's despair.

We approached cautiously, boots scuffing gravel and broken

Jacob Salvia

pavement, the murmuring swelling louder, overlapping whispers, a hum of fear or prayer buzzing through the air as we neared, the sound vibrating my teeth, curling my gut tighter. The church's heavy wooden doors hung slightly ajar, warped and splintered at the edges, their green paint peeling to reveal gray wood beneath, candlelight flickering from within, casting jagged gold streaks across the cracked steps littered with pine needles, ash, and a scattering of broken glass, glinting in the dusk. A faded "Pine Hollow Community Church" sign leaned crooked beside the entrance, its letters chipped and fading, swaying in the breeze, creaking faintly, the vines along the steps pulsing faintly, their blue veins glowing softer now, as if listening.

I pushed the door open with my rifle's barrel, the wood groaning on rusted hinges, the sound echoing in the quiet, revealing a group huddled near the altar two dozen or so, men, women, children, packed tight on pews and the floor, their faces pale and gaunt under flickering shadows, eyes glinting wet in the candle glow, reflecting the flames' dance. Blankets draped thin over shoulders, patched and frayed, hands clutched tight around makeshift weapons kitchen knives with chipped blades, a crowbar glinting dull, a splintered broom handle sharpened to a point, clothes patched and filthy, reeking of sweat and fear, the air thick with wax, mildew, and the copper tang of desperation. A child clutched a ragged doll, its stuffing leaking from a torn seam, staring blankly at the floor, while an old man muttered under his breath, hands twisting a rosary of chipped wooden beads, the sound a faint clack in the quiet.

An older man stood as we entered, rising from a pew near the front, his thick gray beard matted with grime, face lined deep with weariness, eyes keen but sunken under heavy brows, glinting with a mix of wariness and resolve in the candle glow. He held up a hand, palm calloused and trembling faintly, his voice steady but wary, cutting the murmurs to a hush, the sound fading like a held breath released. "That's close enough. Who are you, and what do you want?" His tone carried weight, worn but firm, a faded plaid shirt hanging loose over his broad frame, its cuffs frayed to threads, a hunting knife sheathed at his hip glinting dull in the candlelight, its handle wrapped in frayed cord, stained with dark streaks blood or ichor, hard to tell, his boots scuffed, caked with mud and ash, creaking faintly on the worn floorboards as he shifted weight.

"Travelers," I said, lowering my rifle barrel, dipping but ready, its blue runes pulsing warmly in my grip, my voice steady as I met his gaze, gray to brown, soldier's calm holding the line. "We're just passing through, saw the town, thought there might be survivors. We're not here for trouble, not bandits, not scavengers." My boots scuffed the worn floorboards, dust swirling in the candle glow, the air thick with wax, mildew, and the copper tang of fear, Sara's scream flickering north in my skull, relentless, pulling me forward, hope flickering stubborn but fragile against the dark.

The man studied us for a long beat, his eyes flicking from my rifle to Mithis's glowing axe, its purple runes pulsing against her green skin, then to David's hunched frame, his amber eyes glinting nervously in the dimness, the rags of his flannel hanging loose, the scar pulsing faintly. His jaw tightened, lips pressing thin under his matted beard, then he nodded, a curt dip of his chin, his shoulders slumping slightly as he rubbed his beard, stubble rasping in the quiet, the sound sharp against the murmurs swelling again. "You're not the first to come looking. But you might be the first not to bring trouble. Bandits hit last week, took half our food, beat two of our men bloody, left 'em for dead in the street." His voice rasped, heavy with exhaustion, his hands clenching into fists at his sides, knuckles whitening through the grime, the group shifting uneasily behind him, a child whimpering softly, muffled by a parent's shush.

"What happened here?" Mithis asked, her crimson gaze sweeping the group kids clutching parents, their faces pale and gaunt, a woman rocking with a toddler asleep in her lap, his tiny hands curled around a patched blanket, an old woman muttering under her breath, hands twisting a rosary of chipped wooden beads, the sound a faint clack in the quiet. Her axe rested easily in her grip, runes pulsing purple, casting faint violet light across her green skin, her cape swaying as she stepped closer, boots silent on the worn floorboards, the pistol at her thigh humming faintly, its green runes pulsing steadily.

The man sighed, a heavy sound that shook his broad frame, his eyes dropping to the floor, scarred with scuff marks, candle drips, and faint bloodstains, barely visible under a film of dust and soot. "We've been holding out as best we can, but now the world is hell. gone mad out there, tearing itself apart. Creatures come through the woods at night, mutants, fast ones with claws and yellow eyes, tearing through anything in their path, picking us off when we scavenge for food or fuel. Lost too many trying to fight 'em, my boy, Thomas, three days back, torn apart by the river, nothing left but his jacket, shredded and soaked in blood." His voice cracked, raw and jagged, hands clenching tighter, knuckles whitening through the grime, his eyes glistening wet in the candle glow, the group shifting uneasily behind him, murmurs swelling again, threaded with fear and grief, a child whimpering softly, muffled by a parent's shush. "We've gathered here for safety, boarded the windows, set traps, tripwires, sharpened stakes, anything we could rig, but it's not enough, just a roof and prayers now, waiting for the end."

"Why don't you leave?" I asked, voice steady, one leader to another. "There's a safe zone west of here, Haven, military and mages holding it, warded against the convergence. Might be better than staying here, waiting to die." My boots scuffed the worn floorboards, dust swirling in the candle glow.

A woman near the back, thin and wiry, her hair a greasy tangle under a knit cap, shook her head, cradling a sleeping kid tighter, his tiny hands curled around a patched blanket, his face pale and gaunt even in sleep. Her voice trembled but held firm, cutting through the murmurs, her eyes glistening wet in the candle glow, reflecting the flames' dance. "The roads are too dangerous, mutants, bandits, portals spitting God-knows-what, tearing through anything that moves. We don't have enough weapons or supplies to make it that far. Tried two weeks ago, took a truck, loaded it with what we had, five dead before we turned back, ripped apart by those things, their screams still in my head." Her hands clutched the kid's patched jacket, knuckles whitening through the grime, her voice breaking on the edges, the group nodding agreement, fear threading through their silence, a child whimpering softly, muffled by a parent's shush, the vines outside pulsing faintly, their blue veins glowing softer now, as if sated by their despair.

Mithis crossed her arms, axe haft resting against her shoulder, its runes pulsing purple, casting faint violet light across her green skin, her expression unreadable but her crimson eyes hard, glinting fiercely in the candle glow. "You can't stay here forever, hiding behind prayers and boarded windows, it won't save you. Eventually, those creatures will overwhelm you, break through these walls, candles or not. You're not fighting, you're delaying." Her tone stayed flat, practical, her cape rustling as she shifted weight, boots silent on the worn floorboards.

"We know," the man said grimly, his jaw tightening as he met her gaze, a flicker of defiance under the weariness, his eyes glistening wet in the candle glow, reflecting the flames' dance. "But what choice do we have? Run and die out there, torn apart by claws or bullets, or stay and fight 'til we can't, there's no good options left when the world's tearing itself apart, when the sky's wrong and the ground's alive." His voice rasped, heavy with exhaustion, his hands clenching tighter, knuckles whitening through the grime, the group shifting uneasily behind him, murmurs swelling again, threaded with fear and resignation, a child whimpering softly, muffled by a parent's shush.

I glanced at Mithis, her crimson eyes steadying me, glinting fierce in the candle glow, then at David, his amber eyes wide with a mix of pity and unease, the scar pulsing faintly, shimmering with Ashvalen's magic, his gaunt face twitching with exhaustion, the rags of his flannel hanging loose over his bony frame. "We could help them," I said, voice steady, the weight of it settling fast, a soldier's resolve holding the line, Sara's scream burning north in my skull, relentless, but these people, their fragility, tugged too, a flicker of Mom's blank eyes flashing in my skull, her blood soaking my boots, the crack of my rifle as I ended those red-eyed things. "Not just pass through, help them fight, get them ready, maybe get them heading to Haven."

David's amber eyes widened further, darting between me and the group, his hands flexing nervously at his sides, the scar pulsing faintly, shimmering, his voice cracking with unease, trembling on the edges. "Help them? How? We're barely holding it together ourselves, mutants, bandits, the convergence, and me... I don't even know what I am, not fully, what if I lose control again?" His gaunt face twitched, sweat streaking dirt down his neck despite the chill, his amber eyes glinting nervously in the candle glow, reflecting the flames' dance, the rags of his flannel hanging loose, the weight of his transformation heavy in his words, but also his strength, a spark of hope flickering stubborn but fragile against the dark.

27 CURSE IN THE CANDLELIGHT

"We clear out the immediate area," I said, my voice cutting through the church's heavy quiet, firm despite the ache gnawing at my bones. "Take care of whatever's threatening them, so they can have a chance to regroup and plan their next move." My hands flexed on my rifle's scratched stock, its runes etched by Haven's mages shimmering blue in the candlelight, a reminder of the fight still ahead.

The man, Samuel, frowned, his thick gray beard shifting with the motion, deep lines carving his weathered face as he studied me. His plaid shirt hung loose over broad shoulders slumped with exhaustion, the faded fabric patched with dirt and sweat. "You'd do that? For strangers?" His tone wavered between hope and suspicion, his calloused hand tightening on the hunting knife at his hip, its leather sheath cracked from use.

I nodded, meeting his sunken eyes, keen despite the weariness, glinting like dulled steel under heavy brows. "If we can help, we will. But you'll need to be ready to leave once it's safe. Staying here isn't an option, not with the convergence tightening its grip." My gaze flicked to the boarded windows, the creak of warped wood underscoring my words, a reminder of the chaos clawing closer every night.

The group exchanged uncertain glances, hushed whispers rippling through the pews, a mother pulling her toddler tighter against her patched coat, an old man's rosary beads clicking as his hands twisted them. Samuel stepped forward, extending his hand deliberately, the tremor in his fingers betraying the weight he carried. "If you're willing to take that risk, we'll do our part. I'm Samuel, by the way."

"McAllister," I said, shaking his hand, his grip firm, rough as sandpaper, warm from the tension he couldn't shake. "Jake McAllister."

Mithis hefted her axe from where she'd propped it, the purple runes along its blade flaring as she swung it onto her shoulder, crimson eyes glinting fiercely in the flickering glow. Her cape of wolf pelts rustled against her patched leather tunic, the green of her skin stark against the church's muted tones. "Let's get to work," she said, her voice low and clipped, carrying the weight of a warrior who'd seen too many battles to hesitate.

I sat at the edge of the altar, the cold wood creaking under me as I pulled out the map Carter had given me back at Haven, a crumpled sheet of paper, edges frayed, marked with routes in smudged ink. My rifle rested across my lap, its barrel cool against my jeans, the runes shimmering as I traced the jagged lines we'd traveled: Florida's sagging bungalow, Jacksonville's burning skyline, the motel's mutant swarm, and now this quiet, dying town. Each mark a scar, each mile a fight, all leading north to Sara, her scream still echoing in my skull, primal.

Samuel approached, his boots scuffing the dusty floorboards, his thick beard shifting as he frowned down at me. "You seem to have seen your share of trouble out there," he said, his voice gravelly, worn thin by nights of watching shadows creep closer.

I glanced up, nodding as I folded a corner of the map under my thumb. "Trouble's everywhere these days. Dragons over New York, mutants tearing up motels, bandits on the highways, name it, we've fought it. But this..." I gestured toward the town, the motion taking in the boarded windows, the huddled survivors, the air thick with wax and fear. "This is different. It feels like everything's closing in, like the convergence is getting worse, faster."

Samuel sighed, sinking onto the edge of a nearby pew with a groan of old wood, his hands resting heavy on his knees. "You're not wrong. We've noticed it too. At first, it was just strange creatures, things we'd never seen before, skittering out of the woods with claws and eyes that glowed wrong. Then the portals started opening closer to town, blue orbs flickering in the dark, spitting out horrors. And now..." He paused, his gaze dropping to the floor, scarred with scuff marks and candle drips. "It's like the land itself is turning against us, grass cutting like knives, trees twisting overnight, the air buzzing with something alive."

"What about the people who were here before?" I asked, leaning forward, elbows on my knees, the map crinkling in my grip. "The ones who didn't stay?"

"Most of them fled," Samuel said, his voice dropping low, heavy with regret. "Headed for the safe zones, Haven, maybe, or wherever they thought they'd find walls and guns. Some didn't make it, found their trucks overturned a mile out, blood and bones scattered in the ditches. Others... I don't know. We stayed because we thought we could hold out, keep our homes, our lives. But every night, it feels more hopeless. Every scream, every lost soul chips away at what we've got left."

Mithis, who'd been sharpening her axe nearby, its blade scraping rhythmically against a whetstone, spoke up, her voice cutting through the quiet like a blade. "The convergence isn't random. Something is driving it, pushing it to spread, stitching worlds together like thread through flesh. If you stay in one place too long, it will find you." She didn't look up, her green fingers steady on the haft, runes pulsing as sparks flicked from the steel.

Samuel gave her a weary look, his brow furrowing deeper, unease flickering in his keen eyes. "And you know this because...?"

"Because I've seen it before," she said simply, her tone flat but carrying the weight of memory, her tribe, the Gin, battling necromancers and dragons, their lands warped by Ashvalen's bleed long before it hit Earth. She met his gaze then, crimson eyes unyielding, and he didn't press further, though the unease in his expression deepened, his hand brushing the knife at his hip like a reflex.

I folded the map with a crease and stood, slinging my rifle over my shoulder, its weight grounding me. "We'll deal with whatever's out there tonight, but after that, you need to start thinking about moving. The longer you stay, the more dangerous it'll get, portals, mutants, whatever's twisting the woods. This town's a trap waiting to snap shut."

Samuel nodded reluctantly, his jaw tightening as he rose, the pew creaking under his shifting weight. "I understand. Thank you for giving us a shot at something better." His voice rasped gratitude, real, his hand flexing as if itching to do more than wait.

The tension in the air thickened as night fell, a heavy blanket settling over the church. The survivors stirred, preparing for another attack, men checking the barricades at the doors, women stacking what little ammo remained beside a crate of dented cans, kids clutching blankets patched with faded cartoon characters.

I found a quiet corner near the back, my back pressed against the cold stone wall, its rough surface biting through my faded army tee. David sat across from me on the floor, his head resting on his hands, amber eyes half-lidded under matted hair, his breath fogging in the chill seeping through the cracked windows.

"How are you holding up?" I asked, keeping my voice low, the rifle resting beside me, its barrel within reach.

He looked up, uncertainty clouding his gaze, his gaunt face twitching as he rubbed his healed arm through the rags of his sleeve. "I don't know. This thing inside me, it's like it's always there now, just beneath the surface, growling, waiting. I'm scared of what might happen if I lose control, if it takes over and I'm not me anymore." His voice cracked, hands trembling as they pressed harder against his scar, the puckered skin glinting in the candlelight.

"You didn't lose control back there," I said, leaning forward, elbows on my knees, my tone steady to anchor him. "Against the bandits, you turned, fought, and saved us. Kept your head when it mattered most. That has to mean something, you're stronger than you think."

He nodded, a small, shaky motion, but the doubt lingered in his hunched shoulders, his fingers tracing the scar like it might flare up again. "Maybe. I just don't want to hurt anyone I care about."

Mithis approached, her crimson eyes glowing in the dimness, boots silent on the worn floorboards. She stopped beside us, her axe resting in her grip, its purple runes pulsing like a dying ember. "He needs rest," she said, her tone firm but not unkind, her green face softened by the candle glow. "We all do if we're fighting tonight, we can't be half-dead ourselves."

"Agreed," I said, meeting her gaze, the weight of the day pressing heavy on my chest. "But we can't all sleep at once, not with mutants prowling out there."

"I'll take first watch," Mithis said, her voice brooking no argument as she straightened, cape rustling against her patched tunic. "You and David get some rest. I'll wake you if anything happens, screeches, claws, portals, you'll hear me." Her crimson eyes flicked to the door, alert and unyielding.

I hesitated, instinct warring with exhaustion, Sara's scream, Mom's blood on my hands, the dragon's roar all clawing at me to keep moving, but I nodded. "Alright. Wake me in a few hours."

Mithis gave a curt nod and moved to stand by the door, her axe gleaming in the candlelight, a sentinel against the night. I leaned back against the wall, the stone's chill seeping into my spine, my rifle within reach, its runes a comfort. Sleep didn't come easily; my mind churned with thoughts of the convergence, the survivors huddled around me, the portal Samuel feared, and whatever waited in the woods. Sara burned north, relentless, her voice a tether I couldn't shake.

But eventually, exhaustion won out, a tide pulling me under. The world faded to darkness, the church's murmurs and creaks blurring into nothing, and for a moment, I let myself rest. When I opened my eyes, the first light of dawn filtered through the shattered stained glass windows, casting colorful patterns of reds, blues, and golds across the dusty floor, a fragile beauty against the bleakness lingering in the air. My back ached stiff from the stone, a dull throb radiating up my spine as I sat up, rubbing grit from my eyes.

Mithis stood by the door, still alert, though her posture had eased, shoulders less rigid, axe propped against the frame, its runes pulsing. David was curled up on a pew, snoring, his lanky frame tucked tight under a threadbare blanket, his bitten arm no longer a concern, just a scar glinting pale in the dawn glow.

"Morning," I said, standing and stretching, joints popping in the quiet as I slung my rifle over my shoulder, its weight settling familiar against my chest.

She nodded, crimson eyes flicking to me, then back to the windows.

"You needed the rest. It's quiet outside, too quiet, maybe, but I doubt it'll stay that way for long. Something's brewing out there." Her voice stayed low, wary, her green hand tightening on her axe haft.

I grabbed my pack, the canvas rough against my palm, and adjusted the straps. "Let's see what this town is up against. Daylight's our best shot to scout it out."

Mithis followed me as we stepped outside into the crisp morning air, the chill biting my face with a mix of pine and rust, the town sprawling, deceptive in its peace. The kind of stillness that makes your skin crawl, empty streets, boarded windows, a faded "Welcome" banner flapping torn from a lamppost. Survivors from the church were starting to stir, their faces weary but determined as they emerged into the gray dawn, clutching blankets and makeshift weapons.

Samuel met us in the town square, a cracked patch of pavement ringed by sagging storefronts where a few others were organizing supplies: dented cans of beans, a crate of ammo with peeling labels, a rusted gas can leaking fumes. "You're up early," he said, his voice rasping as he wiped his hands on his plaid shirt, leaving streaks of grime across the faded colors.

"Figured I'd take a look around," I replied, scanning the square, a tipped-over trash can rolled in the breeze, a diner's neon sign buzzing weakly overhead. "Get a better sense of what we're dealing with before night falls again."

Samuel nodded grimly, his jaw tightening as he gestured for us to follow. "We can show you. It's not pretty, but you need to see it, see what's killing us slowly."

Samuel led us through the narrow streets, his boots scuffing over broken pavement littered with pine needles and ash. The first stop was the perimeter crude barricades of scrap metal and furniture, jagged edges of bedframes and rusted car doors lashed together with frayed rope and bent nails, holding against the night's assaults. A splintered dining table leaned crookedly atop a pile of cinder blocks, its chipped varnish glinting dull in the dawn light.

"This is the main line of defense," he said, gesturing to the patchwork wall, his voice heavy with frustration. "We reinforce it every day, drag whatever we can find from the houses, the stores, but it's not enough. The creatures come at night, clawing, pounding, and every time, we lose a little more ground, another board, another life."

Mithis ran her gloved fingers along the edge of a rusted fender, her crimson eyes narrowing thoughtfully as she tested its weight, the metal creaking under her touch. "These won't hold against anything serious, mutants with claws, anything organized. You're lucky the attacks haven't been worse, coordinated, with numbers." Her voice stayed practical, her cape swaying as she straightened, axe resting in her other hand.

Samuel winced, his beard shifting as he nodded, a flicker of shame crossing his weathered face. "We know. We just don't have the resources for anything better, no steel, no tools, just what's left lying around. Scavenging's too risky now, lost three last week to a pack of those yellow-eyed things."

Next, we visited the outskirts, where the town dipped into a forested area, a tangle of pines and oaks warped by the convergence, their trunks glistening wet and black, branches gnarled like claws reaching for the sky, tips glinting blue with Ashvalen's touch. The air thickened here, heavy with rot and ozone, the ground soft underfoot, carpeted with brittle leaves that crunched like glass.

"This is where they come from," Samuel said, gesturing to the woods, his hand trembling as it swept the treeline. "Every night, they pour out of their creatures I can't even begin to describe. Some fast, all claws and teeth, glowing eyes like sick fireflies; others slow, shambling, rotting but relentless. We've tried setting traps, snares, pits with sharpened stakes, but they're smart, smarter than they should be, dodging or breaking through."

Mithis crouched, her cape pooling dark on the damp earth as she examined the ground scuff marks, claw gouges, and a smear of black ichor staining a root. "The convergence is strong here," she said, her voice low, certain, her runes pulsing brighter along her arm as if sensing the pulse beneath the soil. "There may be a portal nearby, a tear bleeding Ashvalen into this place."

"A portal?" Samuel asked, his face paling under the grime, his hand brushing his knife again like a talisman.

"A tear between worlds," I explained, my voice steady as I scanned the woods, rifle up, its barrel cool against my cheek. "It's how the creatures are getting through blue orbs, pulsing like the one I saw back in Florida, spitting out dragons, mutants, whatever's merging with Earth. If there's one nearby, we need to find it and shut it down, cut the thread before it unravels you completely."

Samuel shook his head, his breath fogging in the chill, eyes darting to the twisted trees. "No one who's gone into those woods has come back, not my boy Thomas, not the scouts we sent. We don't even know how deep they go, how far the convergence has spread."

"We'll find it," Mithis said firmly, standing with a rustle of her cape, her axe gleaming purple in her grip. "If we don't, this town won't last another week, the portal will keep vomiting death until there's nothing left to take."

The last stop was the center of the town, where the survivors had set up their supplies, a makeshift camp in the square, ringed by sagging storefronts. A small group of women and children huddled near a cooking station a dented propane stove flickering weak under a pot of watery soup, steam curling into the crisp air while a few men sorted through what little remained: a crate of ammo, half-empty, bullets rattling loose in their trays; dented cans of tuna and peaches, labels curling under grime; a pile of threadbare blankets smelling of mildew.

"This is all we've got," Samuel said, his voice heavy with regret, his hands flexing helplessly at his sides. "We've been scavenging from nearby towns, hardware stores, and gas stations, but the roads are too dangerous now, swarming with bandits and worse. We're running out of everything: food, bullets, hope."

I crouched beside the ammo crate, inspecting the contents, mostly 9mm and buckshot, scratched and tarnished, a handful of .223 rounds that'd fit my rifle but not much else. "You've got enough to hold off a small attack," I said, flipping a dented bullet between my fingers, its brass glinting dull in the dawn light. "But not much more, not against a swarm or anything big."

Samuel sighed, a heavy sound that shook his frame, his eyes dropping to the cracked pavement. "That's what I'm afraid of, every night's a gamble, and we're losing chips fast."

As we walked back toward the church, the town's stillness pressing heavier with every step, I turned to Mithis, her crimson eyes steady beside me. "What do you think?"

She didn't hesitate, her voice cutting through the morning chill. "We need to find the portal, track it to its source in those woods. The creatures won't stop until it's closed; they'll keep coming, smarter, stronger, until this place is a graveyard." Her axe haft creaked in her grip, runes pulsing as she scanned the treeline, her cape swaying against her patched pants.

Samuel looked between us, his expression uncertain, his beard shifting as he rubbed his jaw, stubble rasping in the quiet. "You'd do that? For us? Go into those woods, risk your lives for people you don't even know?"

I nodded, meeting his gaze, the weight of it settling fast. Sara burned north, her scream a relentless pull, but these people, this fragility, tugged too, a flicker of Mom's blank eyes flashing in my skull, her blood still warm on my hands in memory. "We've seen what happens to places like this if the convergence isn't dealt with: towns swallowed, people torn apart, nothing left but bones and ash. If we can stop it here, maybe you'll have a chance to get out, get to Haven, or somewhere safe."

"And if we can't?" he asked quietly, his voice a whisper, his keen eyes searching mine for something, hope, maybe, or a lie to cling to. His hands clenched into fists at his sides, knuckles whitening through the grime, the weight of his son's loss, Thomas, torn apart by the river, etching deeper into his weathered face.

I took a breath, the cold air stinging my lungs, and glanced at Mithis, her crimson eyes unyielding, a rock in the storm, then back to him. "If we can't, then we'll buy you as much time as we can. Clear the area, thin the threats, and give you a window to run. But it won't be pretty portals don't close easily, and whatever's guarding it will fight like hell. We've seen necromancers raise the dead, dragons burn cities, mutants swarm motels, this'll be no different." My voice stayed steady, but the truth hung heavy: the castle witch's skeletal grin, Gorzod's blood on my knife, the mutants' claws gouging the Jeep all proof of how deep this mess ran.

Samuel swallowed hard, his Adam's apple bobbing as he nodded, a flicker of resolve hardening his sunken eyes. "Alright. If you're going in, we'll start packing what we can, get the kids ready, and get the supplies. We won't waste whatever chance you give us." His tone rasped gratitude, but fear threaded through it, his hand brushing his knife again like a prayer.

Mithis shifted, her axe gleaming as she squared her shoulders. "We move at dusk, daylight's wasting, and night's when they're active. We'll scout first, find the portal, then hit it hard." Her voice cut practically, her runes pulsing brighter, a promise of the fight ahead.

I slung my rifle tightly against my chest, its runes flaring as I nodded. "Dusk it is. Let's get ready, check gear, rest up. We're not losing anyone else if I can help it." Sara flickered north, Mom's blank stare lingered, but this town, this fight was here, now, and I'd be damned if I walked away.

28 THE BLEEDING VEIL

The sun hung low, a bloody orange smear igniting the horizon as we approached the forest's edge, its twisted pines casting long, jagged shadows across the cracked earth. The air grew colder with every step, laced with a sour tang of rot and ozone that made my skin crawl, an unnatural stillness settling heavy, the kind that whispers trouble before it strikes. The trees loomed warped and gnarled, their branches intertwining overhead into a skeletal canopy, black bark glistening wet with Ashvalen's touch, blotting out much of the fading light.

Samuel had insisted on coming with us, despite his lack of training, and said he couldn't sit back while we risked our lives for his people. He carried an old hunting rifle, its wooden stock scratched and weathered, gripping it tight enough that his knuckles whitened through the grime coating his hands. His plaid shirt flapped quietly in the breeze as he followed me and Mithis into the woods, his breath fogging quickly in the chill.

David stayed behind in the town with the survivors, still recovering from his werebear transformation. His amber eyes had been wide with exhaustion when I'd told him to rest, his lanky frame slumping against the church pew as if the fight with the bandits had drained him hollow.

"This place feels... wrong," Samuel muttered, his voice trembling slightly as he glanced around, sharp eyes darting to the twisted trunks, the faint blue glint tipping their branches like veins pulsing under the earth.

"It is," Mithis said bluntly, her glowing axe resting easily on her shoulder, its purple runes casting jagged light across her green face. Her cape swayed as she moved, boots silent on the yielding ground. "The convergence is strong here, thicker than the campsite, heavier than the castle. The portal must be closed, bleeding Ashvalen into this world." Her tone carried the weight of experience, echoes of her tribe's battles against realm-warping forces.

I raised my rifle, its barrel cool against my cheek, runes shimmering subtly blue as I scanned the underbrush dense with blackened thorns and glowing vines curling tight around roots.

"Keep your eyes open," I said, my voice low, steadying Samuel's nerves as much as my own. "Whatever's coming through that portal might not wait until nightfall to find us, mutants don't sleep, and necromancers don't rest." Mom's blood flashed in my mind, warm and slick on my hands, the crack of my rifle as I'd ended those red-eyed things, instinct kept me sharp, even as exhaustion gnawed at my edges.

The deeper we went, the stranger the woods became, a labyrinth of warped nature stitched with Ashvalen's fingerprints. The trees twisted into unnatural shapes, trunks bent at sharp angles, some split halfway as if clawed apart, others fused like melted wax, their bark marked with glowing runes that pulsed dimly green, a sickly heartbeat under the surface.

The ground was uneven and spongy, sinking gently under my boots, patches of blackened moss spreading across the earth like a disease, its edges curling up to reveal glistening tendrils that twitched when we passed.

Mithis crouched near one of the runes etched into a gnarled oak, her gloved fingers brushing the glowing lines, jagged, spiraling symbols that wriggled lightly under her touch, like worms burrowing through flesh.

"These marks aren't random," she said, her voice low, analytical, runes on her own arm flaring purple in response. "They're amplifying the portal's power, spreading its influence across the forest, anchoring it, feeding it energy from this world and the other." She straightened, her cape pooling dark as she wiped her hand on her patched pants, eyes narrowing at the treeline.

Samuel frowned, stepping closer, his rifle trembling slightly in his grip as he peered at the rune, its glow reflected in his sunken eyes. "Can we destroy them, break 'em up, stop the spread?"

Mithis shook her head, her crimson gaze flicking to him, steady and unyielding. "Not yet. If we disrupt these without closing the portal first, it could destabilize the entire area, rip the woods apart, and bring everything crashing down on us. Back in the Gin lands, I saw a shaman try it once, tore a valley in half, buried half the tribe under stone and roots." Her tone stayed flat, but the memory darkened her expression, a flicker of old grief threading through.

"Great," I muttered, keeping my rifle aimed ahead, its runes flaring briefly as I swept the shadows, half-expecting yellow-eyed mutants or skeletal scouts to lurch out like they had at the motel or the castle. "Let's just hope nothing notices us before we find the damn thing. The last thing we need is another dragon or a swarm piling out early."

As we pressed on, the air grew heavier, charged with a strange energy that prickled my skin, raising the hairs on my arms. The subtle hum of the runes swelled louder, a low buzz vibrating through my boots into my chest, mingling with an otherworldly whisper, guttural, overlapping voices that seemed to drift from everywhere and nowhere at once, clawing at the edges of my mind like the witch's chant back in the castle chamber.

"Do you hear that?" Samuel asked, his voice trembling sharper now, his rifle jerking slightly as he scanned the trees, breath fogging quick in the deepening chill.

"Yeah," I said, my grip tightening on my rifle, ears straining against the whispers, too indistinct to parse, too alive to ignore. "It's coming from up ahead, closer than I'd like." My pulse kicked up, Sara's scream flickering north, Mom's blank eyes staring from memory, I didn't have time to dwell on this, Jake, focus, I thought.

We pushed through a dense thicket of thorns snagging at my jeans, glowing vines snapping brittle underfoot, and emerged into a small clearing, the air thick with the scent of scorched earth and ozone. At its center, the ground lay blackened, a jagged circle of charred soil radiating outward like a blast scar, and a subtle shimmering light hovered a foot above it. It wasn't much yet, just a flicker of energy, barely visible against the forest's gloom, a distortion warping the air like heat off asphalt, but it pulsed with unmistakable power, a slow heartbeat that shook the dirt barely beneath my boots.

"The portal," Mithis said, her voice low and grim, stepping forward with her axe raised, its glow washing the clearing in purple streaks. Her runes flared brighter, sensing the tear's energy, her cape swaying as she squared her shoulders.

It wasn't fully open, not like the castle's gaping maw or the blue orb I'd seen in Florida, but it was growing, its edges flickering wider with each pulse. The runes we'd seen along the way were feeding it, anchoring it to the forest, funneling Ashvalen's chaos into Earth's bones. I could feel it in my gut, a wrongness pressing heavier every second, the same dread I'd felt when dragons wheeled over New York or when Gorzod's tribe roared around that campsite fire.

"What now?" Samuel asked, gripping his rifle tighter, his knuckles whitening through the grime as he stared at the shimmer, its light glinting dimly in his wide eyes.

"We prepare," Mithis said, stepping into the clearing, her boots crunching charred earth as she scanned its edges. "If we destroy the portal before it stabilizes, we can cut off whatever's coming through, sever the link, choke the convergence here. But it won't go quietly. Be ready, anything could spill out when we strike." Her voice stayed steady, a warrior's calm forged in battles against her world's horrors.

I followed her in, my rifle aimed at the subtle shimmer, its runes flaring blue as I took position near a jagged stump, its roots twisted black and glistening. "What kind of resistance are we talking about, mutants, skeletons, something worse?"

"Anything and everything," Mithis replied, her crimson eyes narrowing as she tested the ground with her boot, kicking up a puff of ash. "Creatures, mutants with claws, undead scouts like the castle's guards. Anomalies, energy bursts, shifting terrain. Maybe even the portal itself is alive in its way, a wound that fights to stay open. Back in the Gin lands, I saw one lash out tendrils of light that burned through steel, dragged a warrior("Creatures, mutants with claws, undead scouts like the castle's guards. Anomalies, energy bursts, shifting terrain. Maybe even the portal itself is alive in its way, a wound that fights to stay open. Back in the Gin lands, I saw one lash out tendrils of light that burned through steel, dragged a warrior into the void." Her tone stayed matter-of-fact, but her grip tightened on her axe, runes pulsing fiercely.

Samuel hesitated at the clearing's edge, his hands shaking harder now, the rifle's barrel dipping as he swallowed hard, his Adam's apple bobbing beneath his beard. "Are you sure we can do this? I mean... three of us against that?" His voice cracked, fear threading through as he glanced at the shimmering tear, its pulse quickening faintly like it sensed us.

"No," I admitted, meeting his gaze, my jaw tightening as Mom's blood flashed warm in my memory, the crack of my shot echoing off the bungalow's peeling wallpaper. "But we're doing it anyway, seen too many die waiting for 'sure.' Sara's out there, your people are counting on us, this portal's not taking anyone else if I can stop it." My voice rasped resolve, steadying him as much as myself.

Mithis began examining the clearing's edges, her axe glowing brightly as she searched for traps or hidden dangers, her boots kicked through ash, testing roots and vines that pulsed gently blue, her cape swaying with each deliberate step.

I set up a defensive position near a large rock, its surface slick with moss and cold against my shoulder, using it for cover while keeping my rifle trained on the portal, its shimmer flickering faster now, edges stretching wider.

Samuel knelt beside me, his breathing shaky but steadying, the hunting rifle trembling slightly in his grip as he mirrored my stance.

"If anything comes through, aim for the head," I told him, my voice low, cutting through the whispers swelling around us. "Most things don't like that, no matter where they're from; mutants, undead, even dragons drop faster with a skull shot." I checked my mag, the click of brass sharp in the quiet, runes flaring blue along the barrel as I chambered a round.

He nodded, his grip tightening, the rifle steadying a hair as he exhaled slowly, fogging the chill air. "Understood, headshots. I can do that." His tone hardened subtly, a flicker of the man who'd held this town together through nights of terror.

Mithis returned, her axe glowing brighter now, its purple light washing her green face in stark relief as she crouched beside us. "The runes around the clearing are feeding the portal, six of them, carved into the trees at the edges, pulsing in sync with that thing," she said, nodding at the shimmer. "We'll need to destroy them first, break their hold, then focus on the portal itself. Smash the anchors, and it'll weaken enough for us to close it."

"Great," I said, checking my ammo again, half a mag left, spares clinking in my pack, enough to hold a line but not a swarm. "Let's hope whatever's on the other side doesn't notice us until it's too late, last thing we need is a necromancer or worse stepping through mid-fight."

As we prepared to move, the whispering around us grew louder, a guttural chant rolling through the trees, the subtle shimmer of the portal pulsing faster, its edges stretching wider with a low hum that vibrated my teeth. The air felt charged, electric against my skin, as if the forest itself was holding its breath, waiting for us to strike or for something to strike back.

"It knows we're here," Mithis said quietly, her crimson eyes narrowing as she rose, axe gleaming, fierce in her grip, runes flaring hot along her arm.

"Then let's not keep it waiting," I said, my rifle at the ready, its runes glowing steady as I stepped into the clearing beside her, Samuel flanking me with his shaky resolve.

The clearing pulsed with energy, the subtle shimmer of the portal growing brighter and more unstable with each passing second, its edges flickering like a flame caught in a draft. The runes etched into the surrounding trees glowed fiercely, green light bleeding into the charred earth, feeding the tear's power with a relentless heartbeat that shook the ground barely under my boots.

The forest's unnatural whispers swelled louder, shifting into a low, menacing chant, guttural words I couldn't parse, clawing at my skull like the witch's ritual back in the castle, her skeletal grin still burned into my memory.

Samuel's grip on his rifle tightened, his sharp eyes darting nervously between the portal and the dark woods, sweat beading on his brow despite the chill. "Something's wrong, more wrong than it was," he muttered, his voice trembling sharper as he shifted his weight, boots crunching ash.

"You don't say," I replied, my voice grim, rifle steady as I swept the clearing's edges, half-expecting skeletal scouts or yellow-eyed mutants to peel from the shadows like they had at the motel, claws sparking against pavement.

Mithis stepped forward, her glowing axe at the ready, its purple light cutting sharply through the gloom as she squared her shoulders.

"The portal isn't acting on its own," she said, her tone low, certain, her runes flaring brighter as she scanned the shimmer. "Someone or something is controlling it, guiding the convergence, pulling the strings. This isn't a wild tear, it's deliberate, shaped." Her cape rustled as she shifted, a predator sensing prey beyond the veil.

Before I could respond, the shadows around the clearing deepened unnaturally, the light from the portal dimming as if being swallowed by a thicker darkness. The air thickened, heavy with a sour tang of decay and burnt wire, the chant swelling into a chorus of throats gargling blood. From the blackness at the clearing's edge, a figure emerged, cloaked in black robes that rippled like liquid tar, edges fraying into wisps of shadow that trailed behind.

Their face hid beneath a deep hood, but glowing red eyes pierced through the gloom, twin embers burning with malice, sharper than the red-eyed things I'd dropped back at the bungalow.

"So," the figure said, their voice cold and echoing with unnatural power, a jagged resonance that clawed at my ears like breaking glass. "You've come to interfere, pathetic ants scurrying to delay the inevitable." They stepped closer, robes swirling as if alive, the ground beneath them blackening further, ash curling up in tendrils at their feet.

"Who are you?" I demanded, raising my rifle, its barrel locking on their chest, runes flaring blue as my finger rested lightly on the trigger. My pulse hammered, Mom's blood warm in memory, Sara's scream sharp focus, damn it.

The figure chuckled darkly, a low, rasping sound that scraped the air, their red eyes glinting with amusement as they tilted their head, shadows shifting under the hood. "You may call me Malakar," they said, the name dripping venom, each syllable a blade twisting in the air. "Not that it matters, you'll be dead soon enough, your bones ground to dust beneath the new world's weight." Their hand rose slowly, skeletal fingers emerging from the robe's sleeve, pale, elongated, tipped with black nails that gleamed wet, trailing subtle green sparks as they gestured at the portal.

Mithis's grip on her axe tightened, her green knuckles whitening around the haft, runes blazing hot purple as she stepped beside me, cape snapping sharply in the charged air. "You're the one controlling this portal," she said, her voice low and dangerous, crimson eyes locked on Malakar. "Why? What are you trying to accomplish, power, destruction, some twisted throne over the ashes?"

Malakar's red eyes gleamed brighter, malice curling their unseen lips as they laughed again, sharper, colder, a sound that rattled my ribs. "This world is weak," they spat, the word laced with disgust, their hand sweeping wide to take in the warped forest, the trembling earth. "Fractured, fragile humans squabbling over scraps, hiding in churches while their cities burn. The convergence is simply a means to an end, a tool to reshape it into something stronger, something worth ruling.

Ashvalen might fuse with Earth's bones, a crucible to forge order from chaos. You're too small to see it, ants clawing at a god's shadow." Their voice swelled, the chant around us pulsing in sync, the portal flaring brighter behind them.

I aimed my rifle squarely at their chest, its runes glowing fiercely as I squared my stance, boots grinding ash into the charred earth. "Not on our watch," I said, my voice hard, cutting through the chant's drone. Sara flickered north, Mom's blank eyes stared, the dragon's ichor still stained my Jeep's bumper.

This bastard wasn't taking anything else, not this town, not these people. My finger tightened lightly on the trigger, the air buzzing electric with the standoff, Samuel's shaky breath fogging beside me, Mithis's axe gleaming like a forge fire ready to strike.

29 MALAKAR'S MANTLE

Malakar raised a hand, skeletal fingers gleaming pale under the black robe's sleeve, and the portal behind him flared violently, a burst of sickly green light ripping through the clearing, its edges pulsing wildly like a wound tearing wider. A guttural roar echoed from its depths, deep and resonant, shaking the charred earth beneath my boots as the first creature emerged.

It was a massive, spider-like abomination, eight jagged, chitinous legs clawing the ground, each tipped with barbs that glinted wet in the portal's glow, its bulbous body armored in black plates that shimmered like oil slicks. Glowing blue eyes, six of them, clustered like a nightmare's crown locked on us, pulsing with cold hunger as it scuttled forward, mandibles snapping loud enough to echo off the warped trees.

Samuel let out a curse, "Jesus fuckin' Christ!" stumbling back, his hunting rifle jerking in his trembling grip as he tripped over a root, ash puffing around his boots. His weathered face drained pale under the grime, keen eyes wide with terror. "What the hell is that thing?"

"Just the beginning," Malakar said, his voice dripping with cruel delight, a dark smile splitting the shadows beneath his hood as his red eyes flared brighter. His hand stayed raised, black nails trailing green sparks that danced in the charged air.

More creatures poured from the portal, a flood of twisted chaos spilling into the clearing. Humanoids with elongated limbs loped forward, skin gray and stretched tight over jagged bones, mouths gaping wide with razor-sharp teeth that gleamed wet, their eyes hollow pits glowing yellow like the mutants at the motel. Winged beasts followed, their leathery skin taut over skeletal frames, red eyes burning like embers as they screeched high and shrill, claws slashing the air as they took flight. The forest trembled under their weight, the runes on the trees pulsing faster, feeding the portal's frenzy.

"Take them!" Malakar commanded, his voice reverberating through the clearing, a jagged edge cutting through the chant swelling around us. The creatures lunged, their movements unnaturally fast blurs of chitin, teeth, and claws surging toward us like a tide.

I fired the first shot, my rifle's enhanced rounds etched with

Haven's blue runes streaking bright as they slammed into the spider-like abomination's glowing eye. The impact burst the orb in a spray of black ichor, thick and steaming, and the creature screeched a high, grating wail that clawed at my skull as it stumbled back, legs thrashing wildly. But it recovered fast, too fast, mandibles snapping as it scuttled sideways, blue eyes refocusing with cold fury. My pulse hammered, Mom's blood flashing warm in my hands, focus, Jake, focus.

Mithis charged forward, her glowing axe a blur of purple light as she swung it in a brutal arc, cleaving clean through one of the humanoid creatures. Its torso parted with a wet crunch, black ichor spraying hot across the charred earth, splattering her patched leather tunic and streaking her green face. The thing collapsed, twitching grotesque as its severed limbs clawed at the dirt, yellow eyes dimming. Her cape of wolf pelts snapped behind her, runes along her arm blazing hot as she pivoted, ready for the next.

Samuel scrambled for cover behind a gnarled tree, its bark glistening black, his rifle shaking in his hands as he fired at one of the winged beasts circling overhead. The shot cracked, clipping its leathery wing, a tear ripped through the membrane, sending it spiraling down with a shriek that pierced the air, crashing into the underbrush in a tangle of claws and dust.

"Keep shooting!" I barked, reloading my rifle with a click, brass clinking at my feet.

"Mithis!" I shouted, slamming a fresh mag home, the runes flaring blue as I swung the barrel up. "We need to take out those runes and starve the portal!"

She nodded, her crimson eyes glinting fiercely as she swung her axe in a wide arc, the glowing blade slicing air to keep the creatures at bay. Another humanoid lunged, teeth snapping inches from her arm, and she drove the haft into its jaw, shattering bone before finishing it with a downward chop.

"Cover me!" she called, voice steady despite the chaos, boots grinding ash as she broke toward the nearest tree.

I turned my focus to the runes etched into the warped trunks, their green glow pulsing like a heartbeat feeding the portal's rage. Aimed at one jagged line spiraling tight and squeezed the trigger. The bullet struck true, a blue streak punching through the bark, and the rune flickered, crackling like a dying ember before going dark. The portal shuddered, its glow dimming, edges wavering as if gasping for breath, but not enough.

Malakar's red eyes flared with anger, a snarl twisting the shadows beneath his hood. "You dare defy me? Fools!" He raised both hands, dark tendrils of energy snaking from his fingers, black and glistening, trailing green sparks as they slammed into the ground. The earth cracked, fissures spiderwebbing through the ash, and more creatures emerged from the shadows, skeletal scouts clad in rusted chainmail, their eyeless sockets glowing green like the castle guards, and twisted things with too many limbs, eyes burning hatred as they surged toward us.

Samuel let out a panicked yell, "Oh God, no!" as one of the humanoids lunged at him, its claws raking across the tree he hid behind, shredding bark in a spray of splinters. Before it could strike again, a massive, clawed hand grabbed it from behind, yanking it back with a wet snap. The creature's spine cracked as it was torn apart, black ichor splattering the dirt. It was David.

The werebear roared, his amber eyes blazing fierce in the clearing's gloom, towering eight feet of muscle and fur, brown and matted, rippling as he shook off the kill. His massive paws flexed, claws glinting black and long, his bear-like jaws wide with fangs that dripped saliva onto the ash.

"I couldn't just sit there!" he growled, his voice deep and rumbling, threaded with determination as he squared up, chest heaving from the run through the woods.

"Good timing!" I shouted, firing at another rune, blue streaked through the air, shattering the mark with a burst of sparks, the portal flickering again, weaker now. My heart pounded, Sara's scream keen in my skull. This kid, this werebear, was saving us again.

David charged into the fray, his massive form barreling through the spider-like abomination, claws raking its chitin, cracking plates as he sent it crashing into a tree with a splintering thud, the trunk snapping halfway as the creature screeched, legs thrashing uselessly.

Mithis moved with deadly precision, her axe cleaving through another humanoid, its head parted clean, rolling into the ash as black ichor gushed before she reached the next rune, destroying it with a single swing, the purple glow flaring hot as the mark went dark.

The portal flickered again, its edges wavering wildly, a high whine cutting through the chant, but it wasn't enough, not yet. Malakar snarled, his hands glowing with dark energy, green sparks crackling as he raised them toward us.

"You will not ruin my work!" he roared, his voice a thunderclap shaking the clearing, sending a wave of black energy surging forward rippling like tar, burning the air with a stench of sulfur and rot.

Mithis planted her axe in the ground, blade sinking deep into the ash as it glowed brighter. A shimmering barrier erupted around us, purple light flaring hot from her runes, forming a dome just as the wave slammed into it. The impact shattered the shield in a burst of sparks, the force rattling my teeth, but it held long enough, leaving us unharmed, ash swirling thick around our feet.

"We need to take him down," she said, her voice steely, yanking her axe free with a grunt, runes pulsing fierce along her arm as she squared up, cape snapping in the charged wind.

I nodded, aiming my rifle at Malakar, his red eyes burning through the haze. "Samuel, focus on the creatures, keep 'em off us! Mithis, David, with me!" My tone snapped, cutting through the chaos as I stepped forward, boots grinding ash.

The three of us charged toward Malakar as Samuel provided cover, his rifle cracked, shots taking down the winged beasts circling overhead, one spiraling into the dirt with a torn wing, shrieking as it clawed the ground. Malakar summoned more dark tendrils black and writhing, lashing out like whips but David plowed through them, his massive claws slicing the energy apart, shredding it into fading wisps as he roared, fangs glinting wet. The tendrils recoiled, useless against his bulk.

Mithis closed the distance, her axe glowing like a beacon as she swung it at Malakar, a brutal arc aimed for his chest. He blocked with a shield of dark magic, green light flaring as the blade met it, sparks bursting hot, but the force sent him stumbling back, robes rippling as he grunted, red eyes narrowing. "You think you can stop me?" he spat, venom lacing his voice, hands clawing the air as his shield wavered.

"We don't think," I said, pulling the trigger, a blue round streaked from my rifle, punching through his chest with a wet thud, black blood spraying as his shield faltered, green light flickering out. Malakar staggered, a gasp rasping from beneath his hood, his skeletal hand clutching the wound.

Mithis seized the opening, her axe cleaving through his staff, a twisted rod of black metal topped with a pulsing green gem. The blade shattered it in a burst of blinding light, shards flying wild as the gem cracked, its energy exploding outward in a shockwave that rattled the trees.

"No!" Malakar screamed, his voice cracking shrill as the portal behind him began to collapse its edges folding inward, a high whine tearing through the air as the green light dimmed fast.

The creatures still pouring through howled in agony, humanoids dissolving into ash mid-step, winged beasts dropping from the sky in heaps of crumbling bone, the spider abomination collapsing with a final screech, its legs curling inward as its blue eyes went dark. The portal's energy destabilized, a vortex of fading light sucking inward, pulling at the air with a force that tugged my jacket.

With one final, desperate roar, raw and guttural, shaking the clearing, Malakar vanished in a burst of black smoke, the shadows swallowing him whole, leaving only a scorch mark where he'd stood and the fading shimmer of the portal behind.

The clearing fell silent, save for the crackling energy of the collapsing portal, a low hum fading to nothing as its light winked out.

Ash swirled thick in the air, settling over the charred ground, the stench of sulfur and ichor heavy against the forest's rot.

Mithis stepped forward, her axe glowing as she swung it one last time, a precise strike at the portal's center, severing its last tether to the runes. The shimmer flickered, pulsed once, and vanished, leaving behind only a blackened scar in the earth, cracked and still.

David shifted back into his human form, collapsing to his knees with a heavy thud, his lanky frame trembling as sweat streaked his gaunt face. His torn flannel hung in rags, amber eyes half-lidded with exhaustion, breath fogging fast in the chill as he rubbed his healed arm its scar glinting pale under the dimming light.

Samuel emerged from behind the tree, his rifle hanging loosely at his side, barrel smoking as he stared at the piles of ash and bone, the spider's cracked shell, the silence pressing heavy after the chaos. "We did it," he said, his voice shaking, keen eyes wide with disbelief as he stepped into the clearing, boots scuffing ash. His beard shifted as he exhaled hard, relief and fear threading through his slumped shoulders.

"For you and for now," Mithis replied, her gaze scanning the forest, warped trees still loomed, their runes dark but ominous, the air thick with unease. Her eyes glinted hard, axe resting in her grip, its glow dimming as she squared her cape, a warrior braced for the next fight.

I nodded, gripping my rifle tightly, its runes cooling against my palm as the adrenaline ebbed, leaving a hollow ache in its wake. "We gave you a reprieve, so use it. Make sure your people get somewhere safe." Sara burned north, Mom's blood lingered warm, and the dragon's roar echoed. This wasn't over, not by a long shot, but we gave these people hope.

The walk back was quiet, save for the occasional rustle of the warped forest's twisted branches swaying, their blue-tipped leaves whispering secrets we couldn't parse. The portal was gone, its destruction leaving a scar in the air, a shimmer that faded with each step, but the woods still felt heavy, alive with the convergence's pulse. Mithis's warning echoed in my mind: this was just the beginning, Malakar was one puppet, and the strings stretched further, deeper.

David walked beside me, his steps heavy and uneven, boots dragging through the soft earth. His transformation had taken a toll muscles, trembling under his torn flannel, sweat streaking dirt down his hollow cheeks, but he carried himself with a quiet determination, amber eyes glinting fiercely despite the exhaustion. Samuel followed close behind, gripping his rifle like it was the only thing anchoring him to reality, his breath fogging as he scanned the treeline, still jumpy from the battle.

"You think he's gone?" Samuel asked, breaking the silence, his voice rasping as he rubbed his beard, stubble rasping in the quiet.

"Malakar?" I replied, glancing back at him, my rifle resting against my shoulder, its weight grounding me. "For now, yeah, he took a round to the chest and vanished in smoke. But people like him, necromancers, mages, whatever he was, they don't stay gone for long. Seen it before: the castle witch, Gorzod's fight, power like that clings, finds a way back." My tone stayed grim, Mom's blank eyes flashing, the crack of my shot ringing in memory.

Mithis glanced back, her crimson eyes glinting in the dim light filtering through the thinning canopy, axe haft creaking in her grip. "He was powerful, but reckless. His portal was unstable because he underestimated us, rushed the weave. Next time, whoever we face will be smarter, more patient, someone who's watched this fail and learned." Her voice stayed low, analytical, green skin stark against the dusk's bruise as her cape rustled, a warrior weighing the war ahead.

Samuel sighed, his shoulders slumping heavier, the rifle dipping in his hands. "Great. Something to look forward to, more bastards like him, more nightmares crawling out of nowhere." His tone carried bitterness, but a flicker of resolve hardened his keen eyes, the man who'd held his town together surfacing through the fear.

The forest began to thin, twisted trees giving way to more familiar pines still warped, still touched by Ashvalen, but less oppressive, their branches swaying in a breeze carrying pine and rust instead of rot. The edge of the town came into view, a small cluster of buildings, battered but standing, sagging porches and boarded windows bathed in the last smear of orange light from the sinking sun.

Survivors peeked out from doorways and cracked windows as we approached, their wary eyes scanning us, some wide with hope, others narrowed with skepticism, hands clutching makeshift weapons tight.

The church's heavy wooden doors swung open with a groan as we neared, and a few of the braver townsfolk stepped out onto the ash-dusted steps to meet us. A young woman, twenty, her dark hair tied back under a frayed knit cap, ran up to Samuel, a makeshift spear clutched in her hands, its tip a sharpened broom handle wrapped in duct tape. Her face pale, streaked with grime, lit with concern as she threw her arms around him, nearly dropping the weapon in her haste.

"Dad! Are you okay?" she asked, her voice trembling as she hugged him tight, patched jacket rustling against his plaid shirt.

"I'm fine, Alix," Samuel said, patting her back with a calloused hand, his tone easing as he pulled her close, relief washing out some of the weariness in his slumped frame. "Thanks to them, I wouldn't be standing here without 'em." He nodded toward us, keen eyes glinting gratitude under heavy brows.

The crowd's attention turned to us, two dozen faces, gaunt and hollowed by nights of terror, flickering candlelight from the church casting jagged shadows across their patched clothes and weary stares. Some gripped kitchen knives or splintered planks, others held kids tight, their small hands clutching blankets patched with faded cartoon characters.

I stepped forward, resting my rifle against my shoulder, its runes dimmed but ready, the weight steadying me as I faced them. "The portal's gone," I said simply, my voice cutting through the murmurs, steady despite the ache gnawing my bones. "Whatever was driving the creatures, mutants, winged bastards, that spider thing, it's shut down, won't be coming back. At least not for a while, not through that tear." My boots scuffed the cracked pavement, ash swirling around my feet, Sara's scream flickering north in my skull.

Murmurs rippled through the group, a mix of relief and disbelief, whispers threading through the quiet. An older man stepped forward, stooped, his gray hair thinning under a stained baseball cap, hands trembling as he clutched a crowbar. "You mean... we're safe?" His voice shook, hope warring with doubt, eyes glistening wet in the dusk light.

"For now," Mithis said, her tone keen, cutting through the fragile optimism like a blade. She stood beside me, axe resting in her grip, its purple glow dimming as she scanned the crowd, crimson eyes unyielding. "But the convergence isn't over. Malakar was one thread, one puppet. There are others out there, portals deeper, forces stronger. You'll need to decide: stay here and fortify what you can, or pack up and move before the next threat finds you, because it will." Her cape rustled as she shifted, green skin stark against the church's faded brick, a warrior's warning etched in her stance.

Samuel raised his hand, palm calloused and steady now, quieting the crowd as murmurs swelled keener. "They're right," he said, his voice rasping firm, carrying the weight of a man who'd buried his son and held this town together through hell. "We've been hanging on by a thread, hoping things would get better, praying in that church, patching barricades with junk. But this town isn't defensible, not against what's coming next, and we don't have the resources to stay forever, not with food running low and ammo down to scraps. It's time to start planning for what's next, Haven, somewhere safe, anywhere but here."

A woman holding a small child stepped forward, thin, her brown hair a greasy tangle under a patched scarf, her arms trembling as she clutched the kid tighter, his small face buried in her shoulder, her patched jacket stained with grime. "How do we even begin?" Her voice trembled, cracking on the edges, eyes wide and wet with fear as she rocked the child. "The roads are dangerous, mutants, bandits, those portals spitting God-knows-what every mile. We don't know where to go, don't have enough weapons or supplies to make it anywhere, lost a truck two weeks back, five dead before we turned around, blood all over the asphalt." Her words broke raw, the crowd shifting uneasily behind her, nods and whispers threading through their ranks.

I glanced at Mithis, her crimson eyes steady, a rock in the storm, then at David, his amber gaze softening with pity as he rubbed his healed arm through the rags of his sleeve. "You start small," I said, my voice steady, cutting through the rising panic. "Pack what you can carry: food, blankets, whatever ammo's left. Strip those barricades for anything useful: metal, rope, spare parts. We've cleared a path, get you moving toward Haven, west of here. Military's there, mages too, walls, guns, people who've held the line against this mess." My tone hardened, Mom's blood warm in memory, the dragon's ichor on my bumper. This wasn't just their fight, but we needed to keep moving. "It won't be easy, but sitting here waiting to die's not an option. You've seen what that gets you."

Samuel nodded, stepping beside me, his beard shifting as he squared his shoulders, a flicker of resolve hardening his sunken eyes. "He's right, we've lost too much to keep pretending this'll fix itself. Thomas, the others, they're gone because we stayed too long. We move, or we're next." His voice rasped conviction, Alix clinging tighter to his arm, her spear trembling in her grip.

The woman with the child swallowed hard, her breath hitching as she nodded, tears streaking grime down her cheeks. "Okay... okay, we'll try. For them." She hugged the kid closer, his small hands clutching her scarf, the crowd murmuring in agreement, fearful, but alive with a spark of purpose.

Mithis hefted her axe, its glow flaring as she scanned the darkening streets, the warped woods looming beyond. "We'll rest tonight, regroup, and plan. Dawn comes, and we start moving. The convergence doesn't sleep, and neither should we." Her tone stayed practical, crimson eyes glinting fiercely, a warrior ready for the road ahead.

I slung my rifle tighter, its runes cooling against my chest as the weight of the day settled heavy, Malakar's scream, the portal's collapse, the survivors' fragile hope. Sara burned north, relentless, but this town, these people, they were a fight I could win, a step toward clawing something back from the chaos.

"Let's get to work," I said, nodding toward the church, the first stars piercing the violet sky above.

30 AXEL'S AWAKENING

I looked back at Samuel, his weathered silhouette framed by the church's open doors, the first light of dawn painting his gray beard in gold. "Gather your supplies, keep everyone together, and leave at first light," I said, my voice steady despite the ache settling deep in my bones, rifle slung tight against my chest. "The roads aren't safe, mutants, bandits, portals spitting hell every mile, but staying here is worse, a death sentence written in ash. Head west toward Haven, and don't stop until you find a place you can call home: walls, guns, people who've held the line." My boots scuffed the cracked pavement, ash swirling around me, Sara's scream flickering north in my skull.

Samuel nodded, his expression resolute, keen eyes glinting fiercely under heavy brows as he squared his slumped shoulders. His plaid shirt hung loose, streaked with grime and sweat, the hunting knife at his hip a dull promise of fight left in him. "We'll do it," he rasped, voice threading with gratitude and steel. "And if we cross paths again, I'll make sure we're still standing. I owe you that much for giving us this shot." He clapped Alix's shoulder, her makeshift spear trembling in her grip as the crowd murmured behind him, a mix of shaky hope and resolve rippling through their patched ranks.

Mithis, David, and I exchanged a glance, her crimson eyes steady, his amber glinting tired but firm, before turning to leave. As we walked back to the Jeep, parked crooked under a sagging pine at the town's edge, the weight of what we'd accomplished and what still lay ahead pressed heavily on my shoulders, a dull throb radiating from my stiff spine. The portal's collapse, Malakar's scream, and the creatures dissolving into ash felt like a fleeting win, a single thread snipped from a tapestry still weaving chaos across the world.

"They'll make it," Mithis said quietly, her voice low as she fell into step beside me, axe resting in her grip, its purple runes pulsing against her green skin. Her cape of wolf pelts rustled in the morning breeze, a warrior's calm threading through her words.

"I hope so," I replied, sliding into the driver's seat, the cracked vinyl creaking under me as I slung my rifle beside the dash. "But we've got a lot more work to do. Malakar wasn't the endgame." My hands flexed on the wheel, chipped paint flaking into my lap, Mom's blood warm in memory.

Jacob Salvia

David climbed into the back, his lanky frame folding awkward into the torn seat, voice steady despite the exhaustion etching his gaunt face sweat streaking dirt down his hollow cheeks, amber eyes half-lidded but keen. "Where to next?" he asked, leaning forward, arms resting on the front seatbacks, his rifle clattering against the floor as he shifted.

I turned the key, the engine roaring to life with a guttural hum that broke the dawn's quiet, vibrating the cracked dash under my palms. "North," I said, eyes scanning the horizon, twisted trees fading into haze, the sun climbing higher over a patchwork of Earth and Ashvalen. "We're still finding my family."

With that, we left the town behind, its people standing in the glow of the rising sun, Samuel barking orders, his daughter hefting a crate, the woman with the child clutching her patched scarf tight. They were ready to face whatever came next, a fragile spark of purpose flickering in their weary ranks.

The road ahead stretched endlessly, a surreal blend of cracked highways buckling under glowing vines and impossible landscapes, fields of razor-edged grass swaying blue, trees punching through asphalt with bark glistening wet and black, the convergence's fingerprints smearing reality into a fever dream.

Mithis sat in the passenger seat, her crimson eyes scanning the horizon, keen and unyielding, her hand resting on her axe, its haft propped against the door, runes pulsing like a heartbeat. I kept one hand on the wheel, the other brushing my rifle, eyes darting across the shifting terrain, half-expecting dragons to wheel overhead or mutants to peel from the shadows like they had at the motel.

David leaned forward in the back, his arms draped over the seatbacks, rifle across his lap, green eyes amber now only when the werebear stirred, darting between Mithis and the ever-shifting road ahead. "Does anyone else feel like things are getting... weirder?" he asked, breaking the tense silence, his voice cracking with a mix of awe and unease.

Mithis gave him a side glance, her green brow arching, crimson eyes glinting dry amusement. "Define 'weirder.' You're riding in a machine with two people from different worlds, one's an orc who fought a necromancer, the other's a former soldier who's seen dragons burn cities. Oh, and you turn into a werebear when the mood strikes. When exactly did things get weird for you?" Her tone stayed flat, but a rare smirk tugged her lips, softening the warrior's edge for a heartbeat.

David smirked back, a ghost of a grin cracking his tired face as he rubbed his healed arm, its scar puckered pale under the torn flannel sleeve. "Fair point. I guess I'm just late to the party. Still feels like the world's spinning faster than I can keep up."

As the morning wore on, the eerie silence that had cloaked us since leaving the town broke a subtle shift at first, a low hum threading through the air, pervasive, coming from everywhere and nowhere at once. I glanced at Mithis, her posture snapping upright, body tensing like a coiled spring, her axe haft creaking in her grip as her runes flared brighter. "Do you hear that?" I asked, voice low, ears straining against the hum, a buzz that prickled my skin like the castle's chanting, alive and wrong.

"Yes," she replied, her voice laced with unease, crimson eyes narrowing as she leaned forward, cape rustling against the torn seat. "But it feels... different, not the portal's pulse, not necromancy. Something new, woven into the air itself." Her green fingers tightened on her axe, runes glowing fiercely, a warrior sensing a threat she couldn't name.

Suddenly, the Jeep's dashboard lights flickered green gauges blinking wildly, a chaotic dance I hadn't seen since the radio died back in Florida, drowned in static over Zeppelin's riffs. The radio crackled to life, its dead silence shattering with a burst of white noise that filled the cab, grating. Then a voice, calm, measured, laced with a smug edge, cut through, clear as if someone sat beside me. "Finally! Someone drives me who isn't clueless."

I slammed on the brakes, tires screeching as the Jeep lurched to a halt, gravel spitting wildly beneath us. Mithis grabbed her axe, swinging it up in a blur of purple light, her crimson eyes darting around the cab and out the streaked windows, expecting an ambush, a figure peeling from the vines like Malakar's shadow. David's head shot forward between the front seats, his rifle clattering to the floor with a dull thud as he flailed, amber flickering in his wide eyes before fading back to green. "What the hell was that?" he yelped, scrambling to recover his dignity, hands fumbling for the gun.

"I... I think it came from the car," I said, hesitating as I turned to the dashboard, its cracked plastic glinting in the morning sun, gauges still twitching like a pulse. "Uh... hello?" My voice cracked, absurd as it felt, hand hovering over the wheel.

The voice chuckled low, amused, rolling through the cab like a friend sharing a private joke. "Hello to you, too, human. Took you long enough to notice, thought I'd have to start honking to get your attention. Do you always ignore your car?" The tone was smug, warm, a hint of gravel threading through like an old mechanic chewing a cigar.

I blinked, utterly baffled, staring at the radio's dead dial, its needle frozen since the convergence hit, now alive with a glow. "Wait... are you saying you're... the Jeep?" My brain stalled, gears grinding as I tried to process this latest twist in a world already gone sideways.

"That's correct," the voice replied, smugness peaking as the dashboard lights pulsed once, synced to its words. "Name's Axel, been hauling your sorry ass around for years, but I wasn't awake until your worlds decided to throw a magical blender party. Guess I'm the lucky rig who got a soul in the mix."

Mithis stared at the dashboard, her crimson eyes narrowing to slits, axe still raised as her runes flared hot, casting purple streaks across her taut face. "This is not normal," she muttered, voice low and clipped, a warrior sizing up a threat or a trick she couldn't place. "Machines don't speak, not in the Gin lands, not anywhere I've fought."

"No kidding," I said, leaning back against the seat, the cracked vinyl creaking as I rubbed my temples, a dull ache blooming behind my eyes. "Okay, Axel... why are you talking? And more importantly, how? Last I checked, Jeeps don't wake up with opinions, magic or not."

"Magic, obviously," Axel said, tone casual as if explaining the weather, a hum vibrating the dash like a laugh. "When your world collided with Ashvalen, I got... let's say, 'upgraded.' One minute I'm a regular ol' vehicle, rattling you through Florida's potholes, the next I'm self-aware, soaking up whatever juice this convergence is pumping out. Been waiting for you to notice me ever since figured you'd catch on after I tanked that dragon hit back in Jacksonville." The smugness softened, a hint of pride threading through, like a partner claiming his due.

I rubbed my temples harder, the absurdity piling onto a day already heavy with Malakar's blood and the portal's collapse. "Great. Now my car has a personality. First mutants, then werebears, now a talking Jeep. What's next, a chatty fridge?"

"Correction: I am your car, and you're lucky to have me," Axel shot back, voice rising with mock offense, the radio crackling. "I've got access to all sorts of new features thanks to this magic nonsense, like, for instance, I can detect movement up to two miles away. Speaking of which, you've got company heading this way closing fast." The tone shifted, all business, the dash lights pulsing red in warning.

Mithis and I exchanged a glance her crimson eyes flaring fierce, my gut twisting tight as adrenaline spiked hot. "What kind of company?" I asked, gripping the wheel again, chipped paint flaking under my palms as I scanned the road, vines pulsing blue along the edges, trees swaying with unnatural life.

"Looks like... humanoid shapes, about a dozen of them," Axel replied, voice steady but urgent, the hum beneath it tightening. "They're moving too fast to be human, too smooth for regular undead. Two miles north, cutting through the woods, ETA maybe five minutes if you sit here gawking."

"Undead?" Mithis guessed, her hand tightening on her axe, runes blazing hot as she leaned forward, cape snapping against the seat. Her green knuckles whitened, a warrior braced for the fight she knew too well: skeletons in the castle, mutants at the motel, the convergence's endless spawn.

"Most likely," Axel confirmed, dash lights flickering red in sync with his words. "But these are... different, more coordinated, less shambling mess, more pack hunters. You're not gonna want to stick around to find out what's steering them, not with just three of you and me still figuring out my glowy bits."

I didn't need to be told twice. "Hold on!" I shouted, slamming the gas pedal to the floor, tires squealing as the Jeep roared forward, gravel spitting wildly behind us. The landscape blurred vines streaking blue, trees melting into green haze as we sped down the buckling highway. Behind us, I caught glimpses in the rearview mirror of shadowy, humanoid shapes peeling from the woods, sprinting with unsettling precision. They didn't stumble like the zombies I'd dropped back in days past; they ran, legs pumping smooth and synchronized, eyes glinting yellow in the dawn light, a pack closing distance with chilling intent.

"They're gaining," Mithis warned, her voice keen, crimson eyes flicking to the mirror as she braced her axe across her lap, runes pulsing fiercely.

David fumbled his rifle, trying to line up a shot through the back window, barrel swaying wild as the Jeep rocked, his lanky frame jostling against the seat. "Damn, I can't get a bead on 'em!" he growled, frustration cracking his voice as the gun slipped again, clattering against the floorboards.

"Not for long," Axel said confidently, a smug edge cutting through the tension. "Time to see what this baby can do, hold tight!" The engine roared louder, a guttural growl vibrating the dash, and I felt a jolt as the Jeep surged forward with a burst of speed I didn't know it had magic-fueled, unnatural, the needle on the speedometer spinning past its limit. Trees blurred into streaks of green and black, vines whipping past like veins under the earth, and the figures in the mirror shrank fast, falling behind as the distance stretched.

"Whoa! When did you get nitro?" I asked, gripping the wheel tight, chipped paint digging into my palms as I fought to keep us steady, adrenaline spiking hot through my chest.

"Magic upgrade," Axel replied, smugness peaking as the dash lights pulsed gold, synced to his laugh. "Told you I've got tricks up my sleeve or, uh, my chassis. Convergence juiced me up better than any V8 overhaul you ever half-assed in that garage." His tone was grinning, a partner reveling in the chaos.

The road ahead curved, a jagged bend buckling under glowing roots, and I wrestled the wheel, tires screeching as we rounded it. Then a massive fallen tree loomed dead ahead, trunk thick as a house, bark glistening wet and black, sprawled across the asphalt with no way around, its branches spiked with blue-tipped thorns. My heart sank, a cold jolt cutting through the adrenaline. "Axel, we've got a problem!" I shouted, voice tight as I braced for impact.

"Relax," Axel said, tone casual, almost playful, the hum beneath it steadying. "Just hang on, trust your ride." Before I could argue, the Jeep lifted off the ground, tires glowing with a golden light, a shimmer rippling over the olive drab frame like Haven's wards flaring hot. We soared over the tree, chassis clearing the thorns by inches, the air rushing past the windows as my stomach dropped weightless, surreal before landing smoothly on the other side, tires thudding against the cracked pavement, suspension absorbing the hit like it was nothing.

Mithis let out a breath she'd been holding, her green knuckles easing on her axe as the purple glow dimmed, cape settling against the seat. "What in the name of the gods was that?" she asked, voice low, a rare edge of awe threading through her warrior's calm as she stared at the dash.

"Enhanced suspension," Axel said, clearly enjoying himself, the radio crackling with his grin. "Magic's got perks, call it Ashvalen's gift to a beat-up old rig. You're welcome, by the way saved your asses from a real messy pile-up." His smugness rolled thick, a partner claiming his spotlight.

The figures chasing us stopped at the tree, their yellow eyes glinting through the haze, motionless, a dozen shadows halted by the barrier, unable to follow. They watched us for a heartbeat, heads tilting with that eerie precision, before retreating into the woods, melting into the twisted pines like ghosts fading at dawn. My pulse steadied, the adrenaline fading to a dull buzz as I slumped back in the seat, hands still gripping the wheel tight enough to ache.

"Okay, Axel," I said, voice shaking as I exhaled hard, "you've officially earned your spot on the team talking or not, you're in."

"Damn right I have," Axel shot back, dash lights pulsing gold once in smug approval. "Now, where to next, more portals to smash, more freaks to outrun?"

Mithis leaned back, her crimson eyes fixed on the horizon, vines curling tighter along the road, the sun climbing higher over a world stitched with chaos. "Wherever it takes to find your family," she said, voice steady, a rock anchoring us as her axe rested across her lap. "Sara's north Michigan's still out there, and we're not stopping 'til we've got her."

"And maybe figure out why the world's gone to hell," I added, glancing at the road ahead, cracked asphalt buckling under Ashvalen's grip, a highway twisting into the unknown. "Portals, necromancers, talking cars someone's pulling strings, and I'm damn tired of running blind."

Axel chuckled, a low rumble vibrating the cab. "One thing's for sure, you're in for one hell of a ride with me on board. Buckle up, meatbags, this world's only getting weirder." The Jeep roared forward, engine echoing through the surreal landscape as we plunged deeper into the chaos, tires humming over a road that wasn't Earth's anymore.

The Jeep roared on, its engine humming steadily as we sped away from the undead pack, the tension in the cab thick but easing as the chase faded behind us. The dense forest thinned abruptly, trees parting to reveal a wide clearing bathed in the late morning sun, a surreal sight that yanked my focus from the road.

Nestled in the shadow of a towering stone castle sat a medieval village, ripped straight from a fantasy novel and dropped into this fractured world. Timber-framed houses with thatched roofs huddled in a tight circle, their walls weathered gray, some patched with mud and straw, smoke curling from crooked chimneys. A crumbling stone wall ringed the settlement, moss-slick and cracked, chest-high in places, its jagged edges glinting with shards of embedded metal, a hasty defense against whatever prowled beyond.

Beyond the wall, the castle loomed dark and foreboding, its jagged spires clawing the violet-streaked sky like skeletal fingers, weathered granite blocks stacked unevenly, pulsing with green light through cracks in the stone. It echoed the castle we'd fought in Malakar's witch-haunted lair, but older, heavier, its shadow stretching long across the village like a predator waiting to strike.

"Now that looks like trouble," David muttered from the back seat, leaning forward to peer through the windshield, his lanky frame jostling the seatbacks as his green eyes narrowed at the sight, amber flickering, a werebear's instinct stirring under his exhaustion.

Mithis nodded, her crimson eyes narrowing as she studied the scene, axe haft creaking in her grip as her runes pulsed, sensing the air. "There's something wrong here," she said, voice low and certain, green skin taut across her brow. "The air feels... oppressive, thick with intent like the castle witch's chamber, but colder, older. This isn't just convergence bleed, it's controlled." Her cape swayed as she shifted, a warrior braced for a threat she couldn't yet name.

Axel's voice cut through the tension, keen and dry from the dash. "You're telling me I'm picking up vibes I don't like, and I don't even have a gut to twist. I'm staying put right here, but don't expect me to roll in there if things go south, castles and I don't mix, and I'm not keen on testing my glowy tires against whatever's brooding in that heap." The radio crackled, his smug edge tempered by a rare wariness vibrating the cab.

I eased the Jeep to a stop just outside the village gates, tucking it under the shade of a massive oak, its trunk warped, branches sagging heavy with blue-tipped leaves that shimmered in the breeze, roots buckling the earth like skeletal hands. "Let's leave Axel here," I said, grabbing my rifle from beside the dash, its runes cool against my palm as I slung it over my shoulder. "If this place is hostile, I don't want to give 'em more reason to freak out by rolling up in a talking Jeep, already got enough weird on our plate without a chatty rig spooking 'em."

David snorted, a tired grin cracking his gaunt face as he hefted his rifle, its barrel scratched but steady in his grip. "Yeah, 'cause we don't look suspicious at all, two disheveled men and an orc strolling in like it's Sunday market day. Real subtle." His tone was dry, but his green eyes glinted keenly, exhaustion giving way to a flicker of fight as he climbed out, boots thudding gravel.

I ignored him, slinging my pack over my shoulder, canvas rough against my faded army tee, ammo cans clinking inside. Mithis adjusted her axe, its purple glow dimming as she stepped out, her expression wary, crimson eyes sweeping the gates like a hawk tracking prey. "Let's move," she said, voice clipped, cape rustling against her patched cargo pants. "Stay sharp, this isn't a village, it's a cage waiting to snap shut."

We approached the gates cautiously, boots crunching over cracked earth littered with pine needles and ash, the air thickening with a tang of smoke and rot as we neared. Two guards stood watch, lanky figures in mismatched armor dented breastplates strapped over patched tunics, their halberds leaning lazily against the crumbling wall, blades rusted but keen. The taller one, face gaunt, stubble patchy across a sunken jaw, stepped forward, his brown eyes narrowing under a dented helm as he gripped his weapon, knuckles whitening through grime. "Halt," he barked, voice rough with a quiver he couldn't hide, halberd jerking up to bar our path. "State your business now."

"We're travelers," I said calmly, hands raised slightly to ease the tension, rifle slung easily but ready across my chest. "Looking for supplies and information, roads ahead, what's coming through the convergence. Not here to stir anything up." My tone stayed steady, eyes locked on his, reading the nerves twitching beneath his scowl of fear, not fight, driving him.

The guard's gaze flicked to Mithis, narrowing as recognition flared, his lips curling, a sneer threading through his fear. "An orc," he muttered, voice dropping low, grip tightening on his halberd as the second guard, a shorter man, beard patchy and gray, shifted uneasily behind him, hand brushing a dagger at his belt. "What's your kind doing here raiding, scouting for your tribe?" Suspicion dripped thick, his eyes tracing her axe, its runes pulsing purple in the morning light.

Mithis bristled green shoulders squaring, crimson eyes flaring hot as her hand flexed on her axe haft, a warrior's pride clawing up, but she stayed silent, jaw tight, letting me handle it. I stepped forward, cutting the air between them, voice firm. "She's not what you think, not a raider, not a threat. She's with us, and we're not here to cause trouble. Fought worse than you can imagine to keep places like this standing." My tone hardened, Mom's blood flashing warm, the dragon's ichor still staining the Jeep's bumper; this wasn't the time for their small-world fears.

The guard hesitated, his halberd dipping as his keen eyes flicked over me, my scratched rifle, my patched jeans, then David, his lanky frame and steady grip, before settling back on Mithis, her unyielding stare. He exhaled hard, a grunt of reluctant concession, then nodded toward the village, weapon lowering slowly. "You can enter," he said, voice gruff but unsteady, "but don't cause problems. Keep that axe sheathed, orc. The Elder'll want to see you, and he doesn't take kindly to strangers stirring shit." He stepped aside, the second guard mirroring him, their armor clanking as the gate creaked wider.

As we stepped through, the village unfolded a tight ring of houses hunched around a muddy square, their thatched roofs sagging under moss and time, windows boarded or shuttered with splintered planks. The air hung heavy with smoke from smoldering hearths, mingling with a sour tang of sweat and decay drifting from the shadowed alleys. Villagers moved quickly through the square, pale faces drawn tight, eyes downcast, avoiding ours as they hurried past, clutching patched cloaks or baskets of meager roots and grain. A woman in a frayed skirt darted across our path, her arms laden with firewood, head ducked low, her steps faltered as she glimpsed Mithis, then sped up, disappearing behind a crooked wall. A man hauling a dented bucket of water froze mid-stride near a well, his gaunt face twitching before he turned away, water sloshing over the rim.

"This place feels... wrong," David muttered, voice low as he shifted closer, hand resting on his rifle, green eyes darting over the villagers' hurried movements, their ragged clothes hanging loose on bony frames, their silence louder than shouts. "They're not just scared they're hollowed out, like something's sucked 'em dry."

Mithis nodded, her crimson gaze sweeping the square past a rickety cart tipped against a wall, its wheel missing, to the castle's shadow stretching cold over the rooftops. "They're terrified," she said, voice steady but threaded with a warrior's certainty, axe haft creaking in her grip. "Something's keeping them in line, fear, yes, but deeper, like a leash they can't see. This isn't survival, it's submission, stitched into their bones." Her runes pulsed, sensing the air's weight, her cape swaying as she scanned the looming spires, a predator sniffing a trap.

I nodded, gut twisting as the castle's green-lit cracks pulsed in the distance the Witch's lair had felt alive too, its walls breathing with intent. "Whatever's up there," I said, voice low, rifle steady in my hands, "it's not letting go easy. Let's find this Elder and figure out what we're walking into." Sara burned north, relentless, but this village its quiet dread, its shadowed master was a thread we couldn't leave dangling.

31 SCREAM IN THE STONE

We were guided through the muddy square to the largest building in the village, a modest hall of weathered timber and stone, its peaked roof sagging under moss and time. A golden sun emblem was carved deep into the heavy oak door, its edges worn smooth but glinting in the morning light, a faded promise of something brighter than the gloom clinging to this place. The guards, their mismatched armor clanking, pushed the door open with a groan, ushering us inside, their halberds now gripped tight, eyes darting nervously as they flanked the entrance.

The interior smelled of damp wood and old wax, a warmth cutting through the chill from a single hearth flickering in the corner, its embers casting long, wavering shadows across the rough-hewn walls. At the far end stood the Elder, a tall, gaunt man with deep-set eyes sunken beneath heavy brows, his long gray beard spilling over a simple robe of undyed wool, clean and stark against the ragged villagers we'd passed outside. His hands rested on a gnarled staff, topped with a dull iron cap, fingers bony but steady, his presence commanding despite the frailty etching his frame. The hall was sparse, wooden benches pushed against the walls, a cracked table littered with maps and candle stubs, but his gaze pinned us like a blade, keen and unyielding.

"You're outsiders," he said, his voice deep and measured, rolling through the quiet like distant thunder, each word deliberate as he studied us from beneath hooded lids. "What brings you to our village, what stirs you to cross this forsaken ground?"

I stepped forward, boots scuffing the uneven floorboards, rifle slung easily but ready across my chest. "We're looking for my sister and her family, Sara, her husband Mark, their kid Lily," I said, voice steady despite the ache clawing my gut, her scream echoing keen from that panicked call back in Florida. "They were in Michigan when this chaos started portals, creatures, the whole damn world unraveling. The trail led us here, and we're not leaving 'til we know where they are." My hands flexed at my sides, chipped paint from the Jeep's wheel still dusting my palms, Sara burned north, relentless.

The Elder's eyes flickered a heartbeat, a twitch beneath his calm mask, before he schooled his expression, deep-set gaze locking mine.

"I see," he said, tone flat, giving nothing away as he leaned on his staff, knuckles whitening against the wood. "Many have passed through here, travelers, scavengers, lost souls seeking refuge. Few remain, fewer still leave at their own accord."

"What do you mean by that?" Mithis asked, her tone keen as a blade, cutting through the heavy air. She stepped beside me, axe resting in her grip, its purple runes pulsing, crimson eyes narrowing at the Elder, her green skin stark against the hall's muted tones, cape swaying as she squared her shoulders, a warrior sensing a lie.

The Elder's gaze shifted to her, a flicker of unease threading through his calm as he gestured toward the castle looming beyond the hall's small, shuttered window, its dark spires piercing the violet sky, green light pulsing through cracked stone. "That place is cursed," he said, voice dropping low, heavy with a weight he didn't explain. "Those who disappear are often taken there, some say it's the castle that calls to them, a whisper in their dreams, dragging them into the dark. Others believe they're snatched by creatures in the night, claws and shadows that leave no trace but screams." His staff tapped against the floor, a hollow thud underscoring his words.

I clenched my fists, nails biting my palms, Sara's voice tight, frayed, "Jake, something's wrong" ringing loud in my skull. "Do you know if a young woman, her husband, and their child were taken there?" I asked, stepping closer, voice hardening as Mom's blood flashed warm in my memory. I wouldn't lose her, too, not to this place, not to anything.

The Elder hesitated, his gaze shifting left, toward the flickering hearth, a dodge so subtle I nearly missed it before settling back on me, too steady now, too practiced. "It is possible," he said, words careful, measured like stones dropped into still water. "We do not keep track of... all who vanish. The castle takes what it will, and we endure what remains."

I wasn't buying it his pause, that flicker, stank of something hidden. David leaned in beside me, his green eyes narrowing keenly under matted hair, voice low and edged. "You're lying," he said, hand resting on his rifle, exhaustion giving way to a flicker of steel honed by the bandits, the werebear's roar. "You know something, spit it out, old man."

The Elder stiffened, his gaunt frame drawing taut, hands tightening on his staff 'til the wood creaked, deep-set eyes flashing cold under heavy brows. "I advise you to leave this village," he said, voice dropping to a hiss, "before you attract... unnecessary attention. There are forces here beyond your grasp, boy." His tone cut keenly, a warning laced with something darker, something scared.

"Not until we get answers," I said firmly, planting my boots wide, rifle steady in my grip, Sara's scream, Lily's giggles over FaceTime,

Mark's steady calm all burned too bright to back down. "You're hiding something, and I'll tear this place apart if I have to."

Before the Elder could respond, the door creaked open with a groan of rusted hinges, a slow, deliberate sound that snapped the tension taut. Two guards stepped inside, their mismatched armor clanking in the quiet, halberds no longer resting casually against the wall but aimed square at us, blades glinting dull, tips trembling in their grips. Their faces gaunt, pale, eyes hollowed by fear, locked on us, a silent threat closing the trap.

"You should have left when you had the chance," the Elder said, his voice cold now, stripped of its measured calm, deep-set eyes glinting malice as he straightened, staff thudding hard against the floor.

Mithis moved first, axe swinging up in a blur of purple light, runes flaring hot as she dropped into a defensive stance, cape snapping fiercely behind her. "Try it," she growled, crimson eyes blazing at the guards, green knuckles whitening around the haft, a warrior born of the Gin, unbowed by threats.

David cursed under his breath "Shit, here we go" raising his rifle quick, barrel steady despite the exhaustion etching his lanky frame, green eyes darting between the guards. "What the hell is going on here? Why's this turning into a damn standoff?"

I grabbed my rifle, backing toward the door, its splintered wood cool against my shoulder, voice keen as I locked eyes with the Elder. "Why are you trying to stop us? What are you hiding, spit it out, now!" My pulse hammered, Mom's blank stare flashing, the crack of my shot echoing off the bungalow's walls, I wouldn't let this bastard bury Sara too.

"You don't understand," the Elder hissed, his gaunt face twisting, a smile curling his lips grim, hollow, like a man resigned to a deal he loathed. "The castle demands tribute, and newcomers always bring... the best results, fresh blood, strong souls, untainted by this place's rot." His staff tapped again, a slow rhythm matching the dread sinking in my gut.

It clicked that the villagers weren't just scared, they were complicit, feeding the castle's hunger to save their skins. The hurried glances, the hollowed faces, the guards' twitchy grips, they weren't surviving, they were sacrificing. "Where's my sister?" I shouted, voice echoing raw in the hall, rifle swinging up to aim square at the Elder's chest, runes flaring blue, Sara's scream clawing loud.

His smile widened, grim and cold, deep-set eyes glinting like wet stone. "Alive," he said, voice low, deliberate, savoring the cut. "For now, how long she stays that way depends on the castle's whims, not mine."

That was all I needed. Rage flared hot, drowning the ache, Sara alive, trapped in that cursed heap. "Move!" I barked, shoving the door open with my shoulder, wood splintering under the force as I burst into the square. Mithis swung her axe, a brutal arc blocking the guards' path, its glowing edge clashing against a halberd with a spark of purple light, metal screeching as she held them back. David fired a warning shot, crackling loud, bullet punching the ceiling, dust raining down, scattering the villagers outside into panicked yelps, their ragged forms darting for cover behind carts and walls.

We bolted for the gate, boots pounding mud, but more guards closed in six now, peeling from alleys and doorways, their weapons gleaming dull in the morning light, swords, spears, a crossbow twanging an arrow that grazed my pack, tearing canvas. "This way!" Mithis shouted, veering toward an alley between two houses, narrow, shadowed, its walls slick with moss and rot.

We ducked in, shouts echoing behind us harsh, frantic, "Stop 'em!" The alley's stink of mildew and stagnant water choked the air as we sprinted, boots slipping on slick stone. The passage twisted, dumping us out near the oak where the Jeep waited, its olive drab frame glinting under blue-tipped branches. "Axel, get ready!" I yelled, voice raw as we broke into the open.

The Jeep's headlights flashed on, gold, cutting the morning haze, and its engine roared to life, a guttural growl vibrating the ground. "About time thought you'd gotten cozy in there!" Axel's voice crackled smugly through the dash, lights pulsing once as the doors swung open on their own. "Hop in, company's getting pissy!"

We piled in, me diving into the driver's seat, Mithis slamming the passenger door, David tumbling into the back as arrows clattered against the metal exterior, thuds keen, one splintering against the reinforced window, wards sparking blue. "Punch it!" David shouted, voice cracking high as he yanked his door shut, rifle clattering against the floorboards.

Axel didn't need telling twice. The Jeep tore out, tires squealing on the gravel, skidding through the open gate as guards scrambled after us, their shouts fading fast. The village shrank in the rearview, huddled houses, the hall's sun emblem glinting, villagers peering from shadows as we sped down the buckling road, dust swirling thick behind us. My heart pounded, Sara alive, trapped in that cursed castle looming ahead, its spires piercing the sky, green light pulsing like a heartbeat through cracked stone.

"We're going back," I said, gripping the wheel tight 'til my knuckles ached, chipped paint flaking into my lap, Sara's scream, Lily's pigtails, Mark's voice all burning bright.

Mithis nodded, her crimson eyes blazing fiercely, axe resting across her lap, runes glowing hot. "Of course, we are no castle, no curse keeps what's yours." Her voice cut steady, green skin taut with a warrior's resolve forged in the Gin's battles.

David reloaded his rifle, bolt sliding smoothly, a metallic click keen in the cab, his gaunt face set with a determination honed by the werebear's roar, the bandits' blood. "Let's gear up," he said, green eyes glinting hard. "If that castle thinks it can keep your sister, it's in for a rude awakening."

Axel chuckled, a low rumble vibrating the dash, lights pulsing gold in smug approval. "You three are insane, charging a cursed heap after pissing off a whole village? I like it got balls, I'll give ya that." His tone grinned, the Jeep's hum syncing with our drive as we sped away, the castle's shadow stretching ominously in the distance.

"We need a plan," Mithis said, her voice cutting through the cab's tension as the road blurred beneath us, vines curling tighter, asphalt cracking under Ashvalen's grip. "That castle isn't just a fortress, it's a nexus of dark magic, alive with intent like the witch's lair. We go in blind, we're dead." Her runes pulsed, crimson eyes scanning the horizon, a warrior weighing the fight ahead.

David, still catching his breath, chest heaving from the sprint, leaned forward, arms braced on the seatbacks, voice steady despite the sweat streaking his hollow cheeks. "We can't just storm the place, not after that welcome. We need to know what we're dealing with, layout, guards, whatever's holding Sara." His green eyes flicked to me, a flicker of pity threading through his resolve, Michigan a world away, now so close.

I nodded, mind racing, Sara alive, the Elder's grim smile, the castle's green pulse, all churning hot with Mom's blood, every fight that'd brought us here. "We'll scout first, then strike," I said, voice firm as I gripped the wheel, eyes locked on the road twisting toward that cursed heap. "Need the layout, the defenses, whatever creatures are guarding it, assume the village is in on it, every bastard there feeding that thing. We're on our own with no backup."

Axel's voice crackled through, smug but keen. "I can scout the perimeter sensors, they're juiced up from this magic mess. Can pick up anomalies, traps, heat signatures, give you the lay of the land without tipping 'em off." The dash lights pulsed once, gold flaring, a partner flexing his newfound tricks.

"Good," I replied, easing the Jeep off the road into a shadowed copse of twisted pines cloaking us, their blue-tipped branches swaying as we cut the engine. "We'll use the cover of night, fewer eyes, more shadows. David, you and I approach from the eastern terrain rougher there, might hide us better. Mithis, take the west, your stealth's our edge. We meet at the back, where defenses might be weaker, sync watches, we move at 2 AM." My tone snapped precisely, muscle memory from army drrills kicking in as I checked my gear belt secure, chest rig stocked with glowing mags, backpack heavy with MREs and med kits, the scratched AR-15 humming with Haven's runes.

David nodded, checking his rifle bolt sliding smoothly, brass glinting as he chambered a round, green eyes steady despite the exhaustion etching his frame. "Got it east it is. I'll keep low, watch the patterns." His hands moved quickly, practiced now, the kid from the woods hardening into something keener.

Mithis sharpened her axe, steel scraping rhythmically against a whetstone pulled from her pack, its edge glowing purple as runes flared with each stroke. "West's mine silent 'til it's time to strike," she said, voice low, crimson eyes glinting fiercely, a warrior born for this, her cape pooling dark as she prepped.

At 2 AM, we split Axel rolling silently with lights off, his frame shimmering as he dialed down his magic, a ghost in the shadows navigating the warped terrain. His reports crackled through our comms, crisp and clipped:

Perimeter Security: "Magical wards ringing the castle, nasty ones, set to detect life forms, heat, breathing. I can slip 'em if I keep my emissions low, metal and magic don't ping the same as you meatbags."

Guard Patrols: "Skeletal warriors chainmail clanking, green eyes glowing like the castle scouts mixed with living guards, red-eyed bastards in dark armor. They circle every 15 minutes, clockwork front's heavy, back's lighter."

Entry Points: "Main gate's a fortress iron bars, wards pulsing green, guards thick as flies. Back's got a servant's door, small, rusted, hidden under ivy. Thermal's faint, but it's there, less watched, your best shot."

Mithis moved like a shadow through the western woods, boots silent on damp earth, cape blending with the twisted pines as she flanked the castle's stone walls. Her voice crackled low through the comms: "Dropped two patrols skeletons, too focused on the front to hear me coming. There's a window near the back door, narrow, high, no bars. Ventilation or escape could be a fallback if we need it."

David and I approached from the east, rough terrain, jagged rocks, and gnarled roots cloaking our steps as we crept low, rifles up. The castle loomed closer, spires clawing the night sky, green light pulsing sickly through cracks, its shadow cold against the warped forest. Patrols moved predictable skeletons rattling every 15 minutes, red-eyed guards sweeping torches in lazy arcs. We timed our advance, sliding forward when they turned, freezing when their lights swung near, breath fogging in the chill, Sara's scream driving me step by step.

We met Mithis at the castle's back, its stone wall slick with moss and damp, the hidden door Axel spotted cloaked in overgrown ivy pulsing blue. I pulled the vines aside, thorns snagging my gloves, revealing a rusted iron slab, its ancient lock pitted but intact, hinges groaning as the wind brushed it. "David, can you pick this?" I asked, voice low, hoping we could slip in quiet blasting it'd wake the whole damn place, and Sara didn't have time for that.

He nodded, dropping to a knee, pulling a small leather pouch from his pack, lockpicks glinting dull as he worked, fingers steady despite the adrenaline twitching his gaunt frame. "Got it from a scavenger back when they ambushed us, figured it'd come in handy," he muttered, probing the lock with a thin pick, feeling for the tumblers. Minutes stretched, tense skeletons clanked in the distance, a torch flickered beyond the wall, then a click broke the quiet, his lips curling into a slight, tired smile as the door eased open an inch. "We're in," he whispered, pocketing the tools.

Mithis stepped up, axe at the ready, runes glowing purple as she squared her shoulders. "I'll go first if there's anything magical, I'll sense it before it senses us," she said, voice low, crimson eyes glinting fiercely, a warrior's instinct leading her. She pushed the door, hinges creaking, revealing a dimly lit corridor, its air heavy with damp stone, mildew, and an acrid tang of dark magic curling up my spine.

We slipped in, boots near-silent on flagstones slick with condensation, walls lined with flickering torches casting long, dancing shadows that stretched grotesque across the rough-hewn stone. Mithis led, axe up, her cape swaying as she scanned the gloom runes pulsing steadily, a lantern against the dark. David followed, rifle raised, green eyes darting keenly, while I flanked them, rifle steady, every echo of Sara's scream "Jake, something's wrong!" pushing me deeper.

The corridor was narrow, shoulders brushing damp walls, air thick with rot and ozone, then widened as shadows shifted ahead. Skeletons emerged, five of them, bones clattering, chainmail rattling as they lunged with unnatural speed, green eyes glowing sickly like the castle's cracks, swords pitted but keen. "Stay behind me," Mithis whispered, voice low but commanding, swinging her axe in a wide arc, purple light flaring hot as it sliced through the first wave, shattering ribs and skulls with a crunch like dry leaves, dust billowing thick.

David aimed, firing precise shots, his bolt-action cracking, glowing bullets streaking blue as they punched through bone, disrupting the dark magic animating them. One skeleton staggered, skull exploding in a spray of ash, collapsing as its legs twitched uselessly. "I've got your back," he said, reloading quickly, bolt sliding smoothly, brass clinking as he dropped another, flanking Mithis, its spine snapping under the hit. I fired too, semi-auto barking, rounds tearing through chainmail and bone, spraying dust as I swept the corridor, Mom's blood, the dragon's ichor fueling each shot.

The corridor opened into a larger hall, vaulted ceiling lost in shadow, stone walls slick with green slime pulsing in sync with the castle's heartbeat, air colder, heavier with magic's weight. The fight swelled skeletons joined by living guards, dark-armored figures with red eyes glowing fiercely under dented helms, swords absorbing torchlight as they swung with brutal intent. Mithis clashed steel-on-steel, sparks flying as her axe met a blade, runes blazing as she parried, driving a guard back with a grunt. David's aim faltered, panic twitching his hands, shots going erratic, grazing armor instead of piercing, until one lunged at Mithis's side.

"Watch out!" he shouted, voice cracking high as he snapped a wild shot. The bullet clipped the guard's shoulder, staggering him. I dropped my rifle too close now drawing the enchanted sword from the castle rack, its gold runes flaring as I swung, slashing a guard's arm clean off, black blood spraying hot, his scream cut short as Mithis finished him with an axe chop to the chest, armor crumpling like foil.

Room after room, each a gauntlet of dark magic and steel. A mage in one chamber, robes tattered, staff crackling green, unleashed a wave of energy, shadows writhing as it surged. Mithis charged, axe glowing brighter, absorbing the backlash as she leaped, blade slicing through his arcane shield in a burst of light, staggering him. I fired cover, blue rounds sparking off stone while David's shot punched his chest, light magic flaring as the mage screamed, collapsing in a heap of smoke and shattered staff.

"We need to keep moving," I urged, voice raw, Sara's scream clawing louder as we pushed into a vast hall ceiling swallowed by shadow, colossal columns carved with grotesque, fanged figures looming over us, air cold enough to fog my breath, dark magic thick as tar against my skin.

The ground trembled, a low rumble shaking dust from the columns as a behemoth emerged from the shadows. A nightmare of scales and muscle, ten feet tall, humanoid but twisted, its body dripping venomous ooze that hissed against the stone, eyes glowing malevolent red, claws long as my forearm, gleaming wet. It roared deep, guttural, echoing off the walls, a sound that rattled my teeth and froze my blood.

Mithis took a stance, axe pulsing with her heartbeat, runes flaring hot as she squared her green shoulders. "This one's mine," she declared, voice steady, crimson eyes locked on the beast, a warrior claiming her ground, forged by Gorzod's blood and the Gin's trials.

David and I circled, rifle up, sword drawn, searching for weakness. "Left side, under the arm soft spot!" David shouted, firing a blue round, scales cracking, but the beast roared louder, enraged, swinging a massive arm that Mithis ducked, her axe slashing its leg, green blood spraying as it bellowed, stumbling. I darted around, boots slipping on ooze, leaping onto its back, sword glowing fierce as I stabbed its neck scales thinner there, blade sinking deep. It thrashed wildly, bucking claws raking air as I held tight, driving deeper, venom stinging my hands. Mithis swung low, axe cleaving its other leg, a wet crunch dropping it to its knees with a ground-shaking thud. Together we finished it, my sword twisting, her axe slashing its last roar fading to a gurgle as it collapsed, lifeless, ooze pooling black beneath.

Breathing heavy, lungs burning, hands slick with venom and blood, we regrouped, adrenaline ebbing. "That was the guardian," I rasped, wiping my blade on my jeans, Sara's scream keen as ever. Then a slow, deliberate clap cut the quiet, each sound keen, reverberating off unseen walls, a voice slithering from the shadows ahead.

"Well done," it said, youthful yet ancient, silk over gravel, warped by time as a robed figure stepped into the torchlight, clapping slow, deliberate, each echo a drop in a vast, empty cavern. Tall, lean, his black robe trailed like liquid shadow, edges fraying into wisps that danced in the still air. His face pale, keen, unnaturally smooth, tilted as he studied us, eyes narrowing under a deep hood, glinting obsidian-black with a cold, piercing depth that rifled through me, peeling back skin to bone. I tightened my grip on my sword, gold runes flaring, sweat beading, cold despite the ache in my arms, Sara alive driving me steady.

"You're a curious lot," he mused, pacing a slow circle, boots silent on flagstones, robe whispering like a serpent's coil, his gaze darting between us, assessing, dissecting. "Not Blackfang too sloppy, too raw for their disciplined venom. Nor Shadow Dominion, those dogs cloak themselves in darkness, strike from voids, not stumble in like pups lost in my lair." His long, bony finger tapped his chin, nails black, gleaming wet, mocking smile curling thin lips, though his eyes stayed cold, unblinking.

"The Voidwalkers, perhaps?" He paused, head tilting, unnatural neck bending too far, a crack as his gaze bored deeper. "No... no runes of the abyss, no whispers tainting your breath, you're clean of their curse." His smile widened, cruel, torchlight glinting off teeth too keen. "And yet, here you stand breathless, bold, seeking something. Not me, though I'm not your prize, am I?"

I glanced at David, his nod subtle, jaw set, knuckles whitening around his rifle as green eyes locked the figure, steady despite the panic from the hall. Mithis tensed beside me, axe glinting, green hand hovering near the pistol strapped to her thigh, runes pulsing, a warrior braced, sensing evil older than Malakar, patient as stone. The air crackled with his presence, ancient, malevolent, a predator savoring the hunt's slow unwind.

"The Silver Vanguard, then?" His tone keened, impatient, hand flicking dismissive at my scratched gear. "No, you lack their sanctimonious gleam, their polished platitudes." His gaze snapped to Mithis, a dry laugh rasping out. "The Order of the Whispering Grove?

Hah, they'd burn an orc before marching beside one, and you " he jabbed a finger at me "reek of dirt and blood, not their incense." His head tilted further, impossible, grotesque eyes rifling through us, a cold weight pressing my skull like the witch's grin back in the castle.

"Wait..." he muttered, voice dipping low, incredulous, as confusion crept into his smug mask, brow furrowing, robe stilling. "No sigils, no banners, no grand purpose radiating from you, not legion, not order, not even some petty warlord's errand boys. You're not... anyone, are you?" His laughter started dry, brittle, then swelled jagged, unhinged, bouncing off the hall's unseen walls. "Oh, this is rich. I thought you were a threat, a challenge! But you're nothing nobodies, lost in my castle with no one to mourn you!"

The mockery stung "nobodies," but Sara's scream burned too bright to falter. I squared my stance, sword up, boots planted as his laughter tapered, his pale hand wiping an invisible tear, composure chilling back to calm. "Well, then," he said, voice smooth, menacing, "if you're no one... perhaps I'll make use of you." He raised a hand, bony fingers crackling, green air thickening with dread, and I braced, blade glowing fierce, ready for whatever hell he'd unleash.

32 BLOOD ON THE BLADE

The wizard's hand hung in the air, bony fingers twitching like a spider testing its web, black nails gleaming wet, green sparks crackling at their tips. His mocking laughter still echoed in my skull, a jagged loop that clawed at my sanity, but now it was drowned by a low hum, deep, resonant, like the earth itself groaned under the castle's weight.

The shadows around us thickened, pooling into something solid, something alive, dark tendrils curling up from the flagstones, coiling like smoke given form. I tightened my grip on the sword, its gold runes flickering, pulsing erratically as if it sensed the storm breaking loose, my knuckles whitening through the grime and venom streaking my hands, Sara's scream driving me steady.

"You think you're someone?" he said, his voice sliding from amusement to a cold, serrated edge, obsidian eyes glinting with a predator's glee beneath his hood. "Let's see what someone can do against this, what your hollow shell withstands when it's cracked open." He snapped his fingers, a whip-crack splitting the air, and reality tore apart not a portal like Malakar's, not the blue orbs I'd seen in Florida, but a raw crack, jagged, red-veined, bleeding darkness into the hall.

Out of it crawled a shape I knew too well, even before it fully formed my face staring back, twisted and hollow, eyes black as tar, skin pale and stretched tight over a grin that wasn't mine. It was me, but not me, the me I'd buried under years of guilt and cheap whiskey, the me who'd frozen when Mom's blood pooled on the linoleum, the me who'd choked when it mattered most.

"Shit," I muttered, stepping back involuntarily, boots scuffing the slick stone, my chest tightening as the shadow-me straightened, its grin widening, teeth wrong, too long, glinting wet in the torchlight. It lunged, a blur of malice, and I raised the sword in time, steel clashing against a knife it held, my old army blade, chipped and rusted, lost in a ditch after the discharge, now gleaming cruel in its grip.

Mithis moved like lightning, axe swinging to intercept, purple runes blazing as she aimed for its neck, but the wizard flicked his wrist, a lazy gesture dripping with power. A wave of shadow-beasts erupted from the walls, half-wolf, half-smoke, their forms

Jacob Salvia

shimmering fluid, claws of black mist slashing air as they poured toward her, cutting her off. "Deal with those," he sneered, his voice a blade twisting in the chaos, obsidian eyes locked on me, mocking, daring. David roared, bones cracking as he shifted, amber eyes flaring in his werebear form, claws slashing through the first beast that lunged too close, shredding it into wisps of dark vapor that hissed against the stone. The hall turned into a maelstrom of snarls, steel, and the wet crunch of bone and ichor echoing off the vaulted ceiling.

 The shadow-me didn't wait, came at me fast, knife flashing in a jab, I knew too well my moves mirrored back. "You couldn't save her," it hissed, voice dripping with my own self-loathing, gravelly, raw, every word a punch to the gut I'd thrown at myself in sleepless nights. "You won't save her either, Sara's next, bleeding out while you choke again." My chest tightened, grief and rage tangling hot, but I swung the sword anyway, gold runes sparking as it clashed against the knife, the impact jarring my arm, lighting up its dead eyes with a hollow gleam.

 Behind me, Mithis shouted over the chaos, voice cutting through the snarls, "Don't listen to it! It's feeding off you, your doubt, your pain!" Her axe cleaved through a shadow-beast, purple light flaring as its misty form split, black ichor splashing the stone floor, steaming where it hit. David roared again, massive paws slamming a beast into a column, stone cracking under the impact, dust raining down as he tore through another, fur matted with vapor and blood. They were holding, outnumbered, but this thing, this shadow of me, was mine to face, a reckoning I couldn't dodge.

 The wizard paced, robe trailing like spilled ink across the flagstones, his slow steps a taunt, a predator circling prey too stubborn to die. "You want answers, boy?" he said, voice rising, brittle with glee. "Here's one: your sister's alive because I let her live fuel for the convergence, a sweet little ember to stoke the fire. Every scream, every drop of blood is opening the door wider, tearing the worlds apart 'til they kneel to me." He laughed, jagged, a sound that clawed my ears. "And you? You're just the spark to light it pathetic, broken, dragging your guilt right to my altar."

 The shadow-me slashed, knife catching my arm, a hot line of pain searing through my sleeve, blood welling dark against the faded army star logo. I didn't drop the sword, gritted my teeth, swung back. "Shut up!" Voice growling low, blade arcing hard. It dodged too fast, too much like me at my peak, lean and keen from army days before the bottle dulled me. "You're not real," I snarled, but it felt real, every jab, every taunt sinking deep. "You killed her," it whispered, circling me, knife glinting as it feinted left. "Mom's blood's on you froze when she needed you, choked 'til she was gone. And the funniest part if you acted quicker, you could have saved her," it said, laughing at me.

I swung again, desperate, the sword glowing brighter, gold flaring hot against the gloom. That glow it hit me, the same as in the forest, the same as when I'd prayed over Mom's shallow grave, clawing dirt with split nails 'til my hands bled red with hers. This wasn't just a fight; it was a reckoning, a mirror I'd dodged too long. "Yeah, I screwed up," I said, voice steadying, raw but solid as I faced it. "I failed her stood there while she bled out, too slow, too weak. But I'm not failing them." Sara's scream, "Jake, something's wrong!" Lily's giggles over FaceTime, Mark's steady calm, they burned bright, tethering me. Mithis's axe flashing purple, David's roar tearing through monsters they fought for me, and I'd be damned if I let this shadow win.

Its grin slipped, faltered, black eyes narrowing as I pressed forward, sword humming in my hands, gold turning white-hot. "You're not me," I snarled, stepping in close. "You're just what I let myself believe guilt I carried too long." I drove the blade into its chest, no dodge this time, the glow flaring, blinding, a burst of light that swallowed the hall. It screamed glass shattering, a wail of breaking reality before dissolving into ash, swirling thick at my boots, the knife clattering uselessly to the stone.

The wizard stopped pacing, his smug mask cracking, pale face twisting as obsidian eyes widened. "Impossible," he spat, voice shaking, raising both hands, green sparks crackling wild. Dark tendrils lashed out thinner now, fraying at the edges, weaker than before I'd rattled him, cracked his game.

Mithis broke through her fight, axe dripping black ichor, cape streaked with vapor, charging the wizard with a warrior's cry, "Now!" David followed, a blur of fur and fury slamming a shadow-beast aside, claws slashing mist as he cleared her path. I ran too, sword raised, blood pounding in my ears, Sara alive fueling every step through the haze.

The wizard flung a wall of dark energy, black and rippling, surging toward us, but Mithis met it head-on, axe blazing purple as she carved through, runes flaring, splitting the wave in a burst of sparks that singed the air. David leaped over her, eight feet of muscle and rage, tackling the wizard, claws raking his robe, tearing fabric and drawing black blood that smoked where it hit stone. I got there a heartbeat later, sword swinging at his chest, he twisted, dodging narrowly, but the blade caught his arm, slicing deep, a line of black blood hissing as it burned the floor.

"You're nothing!" he shrieked, staggering back, robe frayed, smugness gone, voice raw with desperation. "You can't stop this, the convergence is mine!" The hum swelled, frantic, the crack pulsing red and wild behind him, a wound tearing wider. Whatever he was planning, it was close, and Sara was in its jaws.

"Watch me," I said, voice low, cold, charging again, boots pounding stone, sword glowing fierce as guilt and rage forged into something harder.

He snarled, throwing up a shield of shadow, a shimmering wall that stopped my swing cold, steel clashing with a dull thud that jarred my arms. Mithis flanked him, axe biting into the barrier, cracks spiderwebbing fast as purple light flared, her green face taut with focus, cape snapping fiercely. David roared, slamming his full weight into the wizard's side, a freight train of fur and claws sending him stumbling, shield shattering in a burst of dark mist. I drove the sword forward, aiming for his heart, gold runes blazing white, he caught the blade bare-handed, black blood oozing between bony fingers, his grin twisting sick and triumphant despite the pain.

"You're too late," he rasped, voice a wet hiss, grip tightening 'til the steel groaned, snapping his other hand toward the crack. It flared red, light flooding the hall, a searing glow that burned my eyes, and a scream tore through the noise, raw, piercing, not mine, not Mithis's, not David's.

I knew that voice knew it from late-night calls, from Michigan winters, from a life before this hell.

"Sara!" I yelled, spinning toward the sound, heart lurching as the red light dimmed enough to see. Through the pulsing haze, there she was, my sister, dragged from the shadows by chains of dark energy coiling around her wrists and throat, her dark hair matted with sweat and blood, her face pale but alive, eyes wide with terror. Beside her, Mark, her husband, battered, his steady frame slumped, brown eyes glassy but fighting, hands clawing at the chains binding him. No Lily, no pigtails, no giggles, thank God for that small mercy, but the wizard wasn't done.

"You want them?" he hissed, grip tightening on my sword, black blood dripping hot, his obsidian eyes glinting cruel as he jerked his free hand. "Then watch your spark burn out." The chains tightened, lifting Sara and Mark off the ground, her scream choking off as dark energy surged, coiling around them like snakes, pulsing red against their skin. Mark grunted, voice breaking, his hands spasming uselessly as the chains squeezed.

A wet, tearing sound, bone snapping, flesh giving way filled the air, final. Their bodies went limp, Sara's head lolling at an impossible angle, eyes blank, Mark's chest caving as the chains crushed him, then dropped, lifeless heaps crumpling to the stone, blood pooling dark beneath them, spreading across the flagstones. The red crack pulsed once, twice, then stabilized a full-blown portal roaring with power, its edges solidifying, a gateway wide and alive.

"No!" I screamed, the word ripping out like a gunshot, raw and ragged, tearing my throat as my knees hit the floor, sword clattering beside me, gold runes flickering. Everything stopped: the fight, the noise, the world. Sara's face, still, empty, her keen cheekbones slack, stared back, unseeing. Mark's hand twitched once, fingers curling, then stilled, blood seeping from his cracked lips. I'd failed again. Mom's blood warm in my hands, Sara's scream cut off by static, now this hole where my family used to be. My chest caved, breath gone, grief drowning me, numbness swallowing the edges.

The wizard laughed jaggedly, victorious, a sound that stabbed through the fog. "There's your prize, hero," he spat, stepping back toward the portal, robe swirling as shadows coiled around him. "The convergence thanks them for their deaths, finished it, ripped the seam wide. You're welcome to die with the rest. Your 'nothing' meant something after all." He raised his arms, green light flaring wild, ready to vanish into his triumph.

Mithis grabbed my shoulder, green hand iron-tight, yanking me up. "He's not done!" her voice cutting through the haze, crimson eyes blazing fierce as she hauled me to my feet. David roared, charging the wizard, claws slashing air, but a blast of dark energy threw him back, slamming him into a column with a sickening crunch, stone splintering as he slumped, groaning, fur matted with blood, shrinking to human, amber fading to green.

I couldn't breathe, couldn't think lungs burning, vision blurring but my hands found the sword, fingers closing numb around the hilt, its glow flickering like it was pissed too, like it felt her loss. "You're dead," I said, words a whisper, flat and cold, carrying everything rage, grief, the last shred of me that still gave a damn. I stood, legs shaking, boots slick with their blood, pointing the blade at him, gold runes flaring against the red portal's glare.

He smirked, half in the portal, shadows swallowing his legs. "Try it, boy, your spark's snuffed out." His voice dripped smug, certain I was broken, Mom's blood, Sara's scream, he thought he'd won.

I didn't charge, didn't scream, just moved, mechanical, army drills kicking in, muscle memory overriding the hole in my chest. The sword glowed brighter, gold turning white-hot, humming. I threw it not at him, but at the portal's edge, where it anchored into the stone. It struck true, embedding deep with a crack of light, gold runes flaring, blinding cracks splintering outward, white webbing through the red glow. The portal shuddered, a whine piercing the air, edges buckling inward.

The wizard's smirk vanished. "What " voice breaking as the portal screeched, collapsing, sucking at him like a vacuum, shadows flailing as he clawed the air, robe whipping wild. "No, no!" he shrieked, green light sparking, useless dragged in, his last scream cut off as the crack sealed shut, stone floor trembling, a scorch mark all that remained, the sword glowing steady where it stuck.

Mithis ran to David, boots pounding stone, helping him up, her green hands steady as she braced his lanky frame. He was breathing, groaning low, blood streaking his torn flannel, green eyes half-lidded as he clutched his ribs. I didn't move, couldn't eyes locked on Sara and Mark, their bodies still warm, still, blood pooling wider, dark against the gray flagstones, her hair fanned out like she was sleeping, his hand open like he'd reached for her 'til the end. Lily, wherever she was, pigtails and giggles, she was all I had left, a spark in the ash.

"We have to go," Mithis said, voice urgent, crimson eyes flicking up as the hall trembled, stones cracking overhead, dust raining thick, the castle groaning like it felt his loss too. "It's coming down now!" Her cape swayed as she hauled David higher, his arm slung over her shoulder, green skin stark against his pale face.

I nodded, numb, mechanical, stumbling to the sword, yanking it free with a scrape of steel on stone. The glow faded, just cold metal now, Sara's blood streaking its edge as I gripped it tight, knuckles aching. I looked at her, one last time, her face still, Mark beside her, the life I'd fought for snuffed out, then turned away, boots heavy on the trembling floor. "Let's find her kid," I said, voice flat, hollow. "Then we burn this place to the ground, every stone, every shadow."

The hall shook harder, columns cracking, chunks of ceiling crashing down in bursts of dust and rubble, torchlight flickering wild as the castle buckled. We moved Mithis, dragging David, his groans faint, my steps slow but steady.

33 SCREAM THROUGH THE STONES

The castle groaned like a dying beast, stone grinding against stone, a deep, guttural roar shaking the air as slabs cracked and tumbled from the vaulted ceiling overhead. Dust choked the hall thick, acrid, stinging my eyes as it swirled in the flickering torchlight each crash a thunderclap rattling my bones.

My boots hit the flagstones hard, dull thuds swallowed by the chaos, every step driving me forward, away from the bodies I'd left behind. Sara and Mark were swallowed by shadows and rubble now, their blood pooling dark where I couldn't look back, not yet, not while Lily was still in here somewhere. Four years old, all giggles and messy brown curls, she had to be alive. She had to be.

Mithis dragged David upright, her green arm iron-steady under his slumped weight, his lanky frame swaying, blood matting his sweaty hair, human again after the werebear's strength burned out from that last brutal hit. His torn flannel hung in rags, crimson streaking his pale face, green eyes half-lidded with pain. "Move!" she barked, voice sharp, cutting through the ringing in my ears, crimson eyes blazing fierce as her cape snapped behind her, streaked with ichor and dust.

The sword hung heavy in my hand its gold runes faded, just cold steel now, streaked with Sara's blood and the wizard's black ichor my knuckles aching as I gripped it tight, throat so tight I could barely breathe. I nodded, Sara's scream echoing in my skull, Mom's blank eyes staring and pointed down the hall where the wizard had slithered from, shadows pooling thick beyond the crumbling arch.

"She's that way," I said, more to myself than to them, voice cracking raw, a plea to the universe as much as a plan "He kept them alive for his damn ritual Sara, Mark. Lily's gotta be close, a spare for his twisted game." My chest heaved grief and rage, tangling hot, but I didn't wait, didn't think, just ran, boots pounding stone, Mithis and David staggering behind me, their breaths ragged in the dust-choked air.

The corridor twisted, walls buckling, fissures spiderwebbing through damp stone as the castle tore itself apart, a beast thrashing in its death throes. Torches flickered out one by one, plunging us into near darkness, flames snuffed by falling debris, leaving only slivers of moonlight stabbing through cracked gaps above.

The wizard was gone, sucked into his own collapsing portal, his scream cut off but his stench lingered, decay and dark magic clinging to the air like damp rot. If he'd kept Sara and Mark as fuel for the convergence, he'd have kept Lily too, a bargaining chip, a spare battery, a child's fear to stoke his fire. She wasn't dead, I'd feel it, a hole deeper than the one already tearing me apart, I'd know if she was gone.

A slab of stone crashed down ahead, jagged, massive, blocking half the path, dust exploding thick as it hit. I vaulted it, knee scraping, bloody on the edge, pain flaring hot but ignored, landing hard, boots slipping on slick flagstones as I kept going, sword swinging loose in my grip. Mithis cursed behind me "Damn it!" her voice sharp as she hauled David over, his groan faint, her green hands steady against his faltering steps. "This place won't hold much longer!" she yelled, crimson eyes glinting fiercely through the haze. "We need an exit now!"

"After we find her," I snapped, voice breaking harsh, not breaking stride, lungs burning as the hall stretched on, shadows clawing at my vision. It opened suddenly into a circular chamber, ceiling half-caved, jagged stone gaping to a bruised sky, moonlight spilling cold through the ruin, silver washing the cracked floor. In the center stood an iron cage, rusted, its bars glowing dimly with runes like the ones we'd shattered at the portal, pulsing, sickly green, a cage for a child. Inside, curled tight in a ball, knees to her chest, small hands clutching a torn blanket, was Lily.

"Lily!" I shouted voice raw, sprinting across the chamber, boots pounding echoes off the shattered walls. She flinched, tiny body jerking, her little face streaked with dirt and tears, brown curls matted with grime, but those big brown eyes, Sara's eyes locked onto me, wide and trembling. "Uncle?" she whimpered, voice small, shaky, barely a whisper over the castle's groans, hands clutching the blanket tighter, knuckles pale under the filth.

"Yeah, kid, it's me, Uncle Jake," I said, dropping to my knees hard enough to bruise, the sword clattering beside me as I reached through the bars. Her huge, wet eyes searched mine, a flicker of hope breaking through the fear. The cage door was locked, a heavy padlock pulsing with that same dark energy, runes etched deep into the iron, alive with the wizard's taint. I grabbed it, yanking hard, desperate, shock biting cold into my palms, a jolt that numbed my fingers, sharp and bitter. "Son of a... " I growled, pulling back, hands shaking as the energy pulsed stronger.

Mithis shoved past me, green shoulder brushing mine, axe raised, runes flaring purple as she squared up. "Stand back," she ordered, voice clipped, a warrior's command swinging the blade in a brutal arc. It hit the lock, purple light flaring hot, sparks bursting wild as metal screeched the runes flickered, crackled, then died, the padlock shattering into blackened shards that clinked against the stone. I ripped the door open, hinges groaning, scooping Lily into my arms, her small weight crashing into me like a lifeline. She clung tight, tiny hands fisting my faded army tee, face burying into my chest, sobbing soft and ragged against my shoulder.

"I've got you," I whispered, voice breaking, holding her close, her warmth grounding me, pulling me back from the edge I'd teetered on since Sara's neck snapped. "I've got you, Lil, I'm here." Her curls tickled my chin, her hiccups shaking her small frame, and I pressed my cheek against her head, grime and all, breathing her in, the only part of the old world still left.

David coughed, leaning heavily against the chamber wall, cracked stone crumbling under his weight, his face pale as death, blood streaking from a gash above his brow, green eyes glinting tired but warm.

"Good to see you, kid," he rasped, managing a weak grin, teeth gritted against the pain. "Now let's get the hell out, don't wanna test this heap's hospitality any longer." His torn flannel hung loose, one hand clutching his ribs, the other bracing his rifle's stock against the floor.

The chamber shook with a deep rumble rolling through the stone, dust raining thick as a column groaned overhead, splintering quietly. Mithis scanned the room, crimson eyes narrowing, cape swaying as she pointed to a side passage, half-blocked by debris, moonlight glinting dimly through its crumbled end. "The ritual's gone, but the castle's tied to it, bound to his power," she said, voice steady despite the chaos. "It's collapsing faster now, that's our way out." Her green hand flexed on her axe, runes pulsing slowly, a warrior mapping escape through ruin.

I shifted Lily to one arm, her small legs dangling, arms locked tight around my neck, grabbing the sword with the other, its weight cold and steadying. "Lead on," I said, voice rough, eyes locked on Mithis as she kicked rubble aside, stone clattering loudly, David limping behind her, his breaths shallow and sharp. Lily's sobs quieted to hiccups, her face buried deeper into my shoulder, blanket trailing loose. "Where's Mommy?" she mumbled, voice muffled, small and searching, each word a knife twisting deeper.

My gut clenched, Sara's blank eyes flashing, Mark's limp hand twitching, swallowing hard against the lump choking my throat. "She... she's not coming, kid," I said, voice rough, barely holding. "Mommy and Daddy... they're gone. But I'm here, I won't let anything happen to you, swear it." It was a lie I'd told myself too many times: Mom bleeding out, Sara's scream cut off, but I'd make it true for Lily, carve it into reality with my bare hands if I had to. Her hiccups stilled, breath hitching faintly, and I gripped her tighter, her warmth a tether through the haze.

The passage sloped down, air growing damp and stale, thick with mildew and the sour tang of crumbling stone walls closing tight, brushing my shoulders as we moved. Footsteps echoed, too many, too fast, clattering sharply behind us. I froze sword up, Lily clutched close as shapes peeled from the dark ahead: skeletal warriors, bones rattling loudly, chainmail glinting dull under red-glowing eyes, leftovers from the wizard's army, animated husks too stubborn to die with him.

"Behind me!" I yelled, setting Lily down quickly beside David, her small hands clutching his leg as he straightened, gripping his rifle despite the tremble shaking his blood-streaked hands. Mithis stepped up beside me, axe ready, green jaw set, crimson eyes blazing fiercely, a warrior unbowed by the odds.

The skeletons charged, no finesse, just relentless, hungry swords pitted but sharp, bones clattering as they surged. I swung the sword, biting through a ribcage, shattering it into dust that swirled thick at my boots, the clang of steel on bone jarring my arm. Mithis took two at once, her axe a blur of purple light, runes flaring as she cleaved skulls with a wet crunch, dust and chainmail raining down.

David fired. bolt-action cracking slow but dead-on each glowing round punching through bone, dropping skeletons where they stood, brass clinking faint as he reloaded with shaky fingers.

"There are too many," he grunted, voice tight, a shot grazing a skeleton's arm as it lunged its blade slashing air inches from Lily's curls. I tackled it, shoulder slamming bone, sword driving through its spine with a snap, it crumbled, dust choking my throat, but more poured in a tide of death that didn't care about odds, red eyes glowing relentlessly through the haze.

Mithis grabbed my arm, green hand iron-tight. "We can't fight them all, the exit's close!" pointing ahead, where moonlight glinted through a crumbled wall, a jagged gap spilling cold night air into the passage. I scooped Lily up, her arms locking around my neck, blanket trailing as she pressed tight, and we ran boots pounding stone, breath fogging fast. The skeletons chased, clattering louder, bones scraping the wall, but the passage narrowed, slowing them, their chainmail catching on jagged stone as we burst through the gap.

We hit the night, cold air slapping my face, sharp with pine and ash, the castle looming behind us, spires toppling slowly, a roar of stone and dust swallowing the chamber we'd left. Lily clung tighter, small body trembling, her breath hitching against my neck.

"Axel!" I shouted, voice raw, spotting the Jeep a hundred yards out, headlights flashing gold through the warped woods, its engine roaring alive, rolling toward us fast, skidding to a stop in a spray of gravel and dirt.

"Get in, now!" Axel's voice crackled smugly even through the chaos, doors swinging open as the dash lights pulsed urgently. I threw the back door wide, sliding Lily inside, her small frame tumbling onto the torn seat, David climbing in after, wincing sharply as he gripped his ribs, blood streaking the vinyl. I jumped in front with Mithis, her axe clattering against the floorboards, slamming the door as the castle's collapse shook the ground, a thunderous wave rattling the Jeep's frame.

"Go!" I yelled, voice breaking Axel peeling out, tires kicking dirt and roots as we tore away, the castle shrinking in the rearview, spires crashing, walls folding inward, dust billowing thick into the violet sky. Lily clung to me from the back, small hand gripping mine through the gap, fingers cold and trembling, her curls brushing my arm as she pressed close, a lifeline in the dark.

"Where's Mommy?" she asked again, quieter now, voice small against the engine's hum, brown eyes searching mine, wet with tears she didn't understand yet.

I swallowed hard, throat burning, Sara's blank stare flashing, Mark's hand still staring out the windshield as the castle faded to a smoldering ruin in the mirror. "She's gone, Lil," I said, voice barely holding, cracking on her name "Mommy and Daddy... they're not coming back. But you're with me now, we're family, you and me."

Her fingers tightened small, fierce, and I squeezed back, the weight of that promise crushing my chest, a vow I'd die to keep this time.

Mithis glanced over, crimson eyes softening, fierce but steady, green hand resting lightly on her axe, runes dimming slowly. "We'll keep her safe," she said, a vow as much as a fact, voice low, threaded with the warrior's grit that'd carried us through Malakar, the bandits, and all the other nightmares we faced. David nodded from the back, silent but solid, green eyes glinting through the pain, blood streaking his gaunt face as he braced Lily's shoulder, a brother-in-arms forged in fire.

Axel broke the tension, voice crackling smug through the dash, lights pulsing gold, "Well, that was a shitshow, castle down, wizard toast, and we're rolling with a new passenger. Where to now, boss, more heroics, or you finally gonna let me rest these glowy tires?" His tone was grinning, a partner reveling in the chaos, but the hum beneath it steadied us, a lifeline through the wreck.

"West," I said, voice steadying, cold steel threading through the grief. "Safe zone, we've got one more to protect, Lily's all that's left." The road stretched ahead, dark, buckled under glowing vines, uncertain as hell, but her hand in mine kept me moving, small and warm against the hole Sara, mom, and Mark left.

The wizard was gone sucked into his ruin but the convergence wasn't over, still pulsed somewhere, chaos still bled. I'd lost too much; Mom's blood on my hands, Sara's scream silenced, but I wasn't losing her. Not Lily. Not ever.

34 THE GLOW AGAINST THE HOLLOW

Axel rumbled down the cracked highway, engine growling low, as weary as we were after the castle's fall. Dust swirled behind us, swallowing the ruin's smoldering wreckage against the violet-streaked dusk. In the back, Lily slept curled against David, her small chest rising beneath my frayed army jacket, its olive drab patches a thin shield over her fragile frame. Her dirt-smudged face, streaked with dried tears, looked peaceful, brown curls spilling over David's arm--her makeshift pillow. He slumped beside her, breathing shallow, blood crusting his matted hair, torn flannel hanging off a frame too stubborn to quit, his bruises a reminder of the wizard's blast. I gripped the wheel, Sara's scream echoing in my skull, Mark's limp hand twitching in memory. I'd bleed out to keep her safe.

Up front, Mithis sat shotgun, axe across her lap, purple runes pulsing gently in the dimming light. Her crimson eyes scanned the road, unyielding, green skin stark against the Jeep's cracked interior, a warrior guarding us since Gorzod's camp. Her ichor-streaked cape hung limp, but her steady presence anchored me, a rock against the hollow grief threatening to swallow us all.

Axel kept us rolling, headlights cutting twin gold beams through the gathering twilight, his voice quieter than usual, smug edge softened by the weight of what we'd lost. "Safe zone's twenty miles out," he said, dash lights pulsing faint gold in sync. "Military checkpoint, a safe zone outer ring. Looks like it's still standing, walls up, guns hot."

"Good," I muttered, voice rough, gripping the wheel 'til my knuckles ached, split skin cracking under the strain, blood smearing the chipped paint I hadn't noticed 'til now. My hands throbbed, a dull pulse I barely felt, drowned by the faces flashing behind my eyes every blink: Sara's blank stare, Mark's broken body, Mom's blood pooling on the linoleum. I'd gotten Lily out, small, warm, alive in my arms, but it didn't fill the hole they'd left, didn't quiet the screams looping relentlessly in the silence. Nothing would, grief was a weight I'd carry 'til it crushed me, but Lily's breath, soft and steady, kept me driving.

The landscape shifted as we rolled on highways buckling under glowing vines from Ashvalen, asphalt fracturing into dirt tracks overgrown with razor-edged grass that shimmered faint blue in the dusk. Twisted pines loomed on either side, trunks glistening wet and black, branches tipped with unnatural light while dragons circled distant peaks, their silhouettes stark against the bruised sky, roars rolling faint but real across the miles. The convergence hadn't stopped the wizard's portal was just one thread in its weave, one crack sealed while others pulsed out there, bleeding chaos into Earth's bones. I tightened my grip, jaw set, teeth grinding, west was our shot, a safe zone with walls and guns, a place to breathe, to hold what I had left.

We hit the checkpoint at twilight, a sprawl of barbed wire curling sharply over concrete barriers, floodlights glaring harsh white across the cracked road, casting jagged shadows that danced in the cooling air. Soldiers in mismatched gear waved us down, fatigues patched with duct tape, helmets dented but steady, rifles up but not aimed, barrels glinting dull under the lights. "State your business," one barked, a sergeant by the faded stripes on his sleeve, face weathered hard under a week's stubble, brown eyes narrowing as he stepped closer, hand resting lightly on his holstered sidearm.

"Survivors," I said, leaning out the window, cold air biting my face. "Got a kid with us, four years old, pulled her from hell back there. Looking for shelter, a spot to rest." My voice rasped, throat raw from shouting, from grief, eyes flicking to Lily through the streaked glass, her small form huddled under the jacket, a flicker of hope in this mess.

The sergeant peered past me, softening a hair as it landed on Lily's sleeping face, then nodded, a curt dip of his chin. "Roll in, camp's half a mile up the track. Keep your weapons holstered, lest we say otherwise, don't care who you are, rules hold here." His eyes lingered on Mithis' green skin stark against the dusk, crimson glare unyielding, axe gleaming faint purple across her lap, but he didn't comment, just stepped back, waving us through with a gloved hand. A smart man sees enough weird to know when to shut up.

Axel rolled through the gates, tires crunching gravel, engine humming steadily past rows of tents flapping quietly in the breeze, makeshift barricades of scrap metal and sandbags ringing the perimeter. People milled in the glow of campfires, families huddled close, loners sharpening blades by lantern light, a few Ashvalen folk like Mithis scattered among them, elves with bone-white hair, an orc in dented armor glinting dull by a fire, survivors stitched together from two worlds. It wasn't home, not yet, not with Sara's scream still clawing my skull, but it was solid: walls standing tall, guns manned, a chance to stop running for a damn minute.

We parked near a cluster of tents at the camp's edge, canvas patched and faded, stakes driven deep into the hard-packed dirt, Axel's engine ticking softly as it cooled, headlights dimming to a faint gold glow. I climbed out boots, thudding gravel, lifting Lily from the back, her small weight steady against my chest, warm through the jacket's worn fabric. She stirred, mumbling softly, "Uncle?" Brown eyes fluttering, half-open, voice sleepy and searching as she reached for me, small hand brushing my stubbled jaw. I brushed her curls back, grime-streaked, soft under my calloused fingers. "Right here, kid, we're safe now." She nodded, trusting, clinging tight, and I held her close, her breath a quiet anchor against the storm in my head.

Mithis hopped out, stretching slowly, green shoulders rolling as her cape rustled, faint axe still close, its haft creaking in her grip as she scanned the defenses: watchtowers looming dark, soldiers pacing the wire, campfires flickering steadily. "This place will hold," she said, voice low, certain eyes tracing the perimeter, "For now, walls are thick, guns are loaded. Good ground to stand on." David climbed out slowly, wincing sharply, one hand braced on the Jeep's frame, his torn flannel streaked with blood and dust, green eyes glinting tired but alive. "Better than the castle," he grunted, managing a half-smile, teeth gritted against the ache. "No wizards, no collapsing ceilings, hell, I'll take it."

A woman approached, faded army jacket hanging loose over a wiry frame, clipboard clutched in one hand, short brown hair tucked under a cap, voice clipped but not cold, worn smooth by nights of triage and lists. "New arrivals?" she asked, eyes flicking over us, sharp but weary. "Names and skills, we assign tents based on what you can do, to keep this place running." Her pen hovered over the paper, ready to scratch us into our home, fragile order.

I set Lily down, keeping her small hand tight in mine, her blanket trailing in the dirt. "I'm... call me Jake," I said, voice steadying. Ex-military army grunt, ten years in. Good with a gun, decent at fixing shit vehicles, barricades, whatever breaks." I nodded to Lily, her curls bouncing as she swayed sleepily against my leg. "This is Lily, my niece, four, no skills yet 'cept staying tough." I jerked my head to the others "Mithis fighter, knows magic, damn near unstoppable with that axe. David same, plus he's a werebear when it counts, claws and all. And Axel's the Jeep, talks, drives himself, a magic upgrade from the convergence."

She blinked, pen pausing at that last one, brown eyes flicking to Axel's glowing dash, then scribbled it down, a faint smirk tugging her lips. "Alright, Jake, you're on patrol rotation, walls need eyes, and you've got the aim. Mithis, training detail, folks here could use your edge, teach 'em to fight like you. David, rest up tonight, then repair crew, we've got roofs leaking and traps to rig. Lily, the kids' tent's got food, beds, and someone to watch her. Axel, uh, stay useful, keep rolling." She tore off a tag scratched with 47 in black ink, handing it to me, canvas crinkling in my grip. "Number 47 settle in, work starts tomorrow dawn, bell's your wake-up."

Jacob Salvia

We found Tent 47 near the camp's edge, canvas worn thin, patched with gray tape, stakes driven deep into the rocky dirt, a squat shelter under a twisted pine spilling blue-tipped needles in the breeze. Inside was sparse but dry, three cots lined up, springs creaking quietly under faded blankets, a lantern flickering warm yellow on a crate, a stack of wool covers smelling of a hint of mildew, but cozy. I set Lily on the nearest cot, her small frame sinking into the thin mattress, tucking a blanket around her, its rough weave catching on her curls. She grabbed my hand before I could pull away, fingers small, fierce. "Don't go," she whispered, brown eyes wide, wet with sleep and fear, Sara's echo staring up at me.

"Not going anywhere," I said, sitting beside her, the cot creaking under my weight. "Sleep, Lil, I'll be right here, promise." My voice softened rough edges smoothed for her, and I brushed her hair back, thumb tracing the dirt, smudge on her cheek 'til her eyes fluttered shut, breathing evening out slow and steady. I stayed hand in hers 'til her grip slackened, her small snores a lifeline in the quiet.

Mithis dropped her gear by the tent flap, axe clanking softly against her pack, sitting cross-legged on the dirt floor to sharpen her blade, whetstone scraping rhythmically against steel, purple runes flaring softly with each stroke. David collapsed on the far cot, springs groaning loudly, already snoring, blood-crusted hair spilling over the pillow, exhaustion claiming him fast. I stepped outside, boots scuffing gravel, leaning against Axel's hood, its metal cool under my palms, engine ticking quietly as it settled. The camp hummed with quiet voices murmuring by fires, clinking tools as a mechanic hammered a generator, a kid's laugh piercing the dusk, normal sounds in a world gone sideways, fragile but real.

"Think this'll last?" I asked, half to Axel, half to the night, voice low, eyes tracing the floodlights glinting off barbed wire, the dark beyond pulsing with unseen threats.

"Long as you make it," Axel replied, headlights dimming to a soft gold glow, voice steady through the dash "You've got a knack for beating odds: castle's dust, wizard's toast, and you're still rolling with me. That's somethin'." His smug edge softened, a partner's faith threading through.

I pulled out my father's flask from a pocket in my pack, something else thought lost through everything that happened, but it stuck with me, scratched steel cool against my thumb, a relic from days gone by. I took a swig of water, not whiskey, sharp and clean, steadying the tremor in my hands, the ache in my chest.

Mithis stepped out, boots silent on the gravel, standing close, her green shoulder brushing mine, warm through her patched tunic. "She's strong," she said nodding toward Lily's cot, crimson eyes

288

softening faint "Like you, stubborn as hell, still fighting." Her voice carried a warrior's weight forged in the Gin's battles, tempered by our own, but a quiet thread ran beneath, steady and sure.

"Not strong enough," I muttered, Sara's blank eyes flashing, Mark's crushed frame, Mom's blood warm on my hands, voice rough, staring at the flask as guilt clawed up. "Lost too much, couldn't save 'em, couldn't stop it."

She turned, crimson locking mine, fierce but warm, green hand resting firm on my arm, grounding me. "You didn't lose her or us," she said, voice low, cutting through the haze. "That's what matters now, Lily's here, breathing, because you didn't quit. We build here a home, for her, for what's left." Her lips curled a small smile breaking through, rare and real, and I looked at her, not just the warrior who'd cleaved through necromancers and beasts, but the woman who'd stuck with me through hell, green skin and red eyes a constant in the dark. "Yeah," I said, voice low, steadying, "For her and us." She nodded, smiling, holding, and something shifted, grief didn't fade, didn't shrink, but it made room for this, a fragile spark beside the hole.

Days blurred into weeks, safe zone rhythm settling over us, a fragile pulse in the convergence's shadow. I patrolled the walls, rifle steady in my hands, runes glowing faint blue as I paced the wire, eyes tracing the warped woods for undead shambles or worse, portals flickering faint on the horizon, dragons wheeling silent in the dusk. The air carried rot and ozone, Ashvalen's bleed, but the camp held, its floodlights a stubborn glare against the dark.

Mithis trained the camp's scrappers, turning scared kids and shaky loners into fighters, her axe flashing purple as she barked orders in the dirt ring, green skin stark against their pale faces, teaching them to stand, to swing, to live. David patched roofs and rigged traps, hammer pounding stakes, hands steady despite the bruises fading slowly, his werebear side, a quiet trump card he kept holstered, green eyes glinting calm as he hauled wire and wood.

Lily started talking again, small words at first, "Uncle" and "safe," then more, her laugh breaking free as she played with other kids by the fire pits, chasing sticks in the dirt, pigtails bouncing wild. That sounds bright, and cuts through the grief, a light I'd kill to protect. Axel ran supply hauls, rolling out with soldiers to scavenge gas and cans, griping loudly through the dash "These potholes'll dent my soul!" but grinning smugly when he pulled back, headlights flaring gold, a guard dog with wheels.

We built not just tents, but a real spot. Tent 47 gave way to a wooden shack, rough-hewn logs hauled from the woods, nails pounded 'til my hands blistered, its slanted roof patched with scavenged tin, a porch jutting crooked where Lily knelt to draw pictures in the dirt with a stick. Sunflowers, a Jeep with googly eyes.

Mithis carved runes into the frame, purple lines pulsing softly along the door, warding off magic, she said, it still lingered out there. "Convergence is not dead yet," she'd mutter, axe close, her green hands steady as she etched protection into our walls. David hauled logs, grunting through the ache, ribs still tender, while I nailed boards, sweat stinging my eyes, Axel parked beside us like a sentinel, engine humming low as night fell.

One night, weeks deep, the safe zone glows steadily. I sat on that porch, Lily asleep inside on a cot piled with blankets, her soft snores drifting through the plank walls. Mithis sat beside me close, her axe resting against her knee, runes dim under the lantern's flicker, green shoulder brushing mine, warm and solid.

The sky glowed faint portals pulsing distant on the horizon, stars swallowed by violet haze, the convergence creeping closer, its threads still weaving chaos beyond our walls. I held my father's flask, a tiny reminder of a world that will never be again. "This won't hold forever," I said low voice, eyes tracing the floodlights' edge. "Portals, monsters, it's coming, isn't it?"

"No," Mithis agreed, crimson eyes steady, meeting mine "Not forever, nothing does in this mess. But it holds tonight. That's enough for now." Her voice carried a warrior's calm honed by Gorzod's blood, the castle's ruin but softened faint, a thread of hope she'd forged with us. She rested her hand on mine, green fingers warm, calloused squeezing light, grounding me.

David joined us, leaning on the porch railing, wood creaking under his weight, green eyes calm, blood long washed from his hair, a faint grin tugging his gaunt face. "We've got a home," he said, voice quiet, steady. "First one I've had in a while, beats motels and woods, even with the damn vines creeping closer." His flannel was new, patched but clean, rustled softly as he crossed his arms, a man rebuilt from the kid I'd pulled from that rest area.

"Me too," I admitted, voice rough, Lily's snores a soft hum behind me, squeezing Mithis's hand tighter, her warmth a lifeline through the ache. "Lost everything, Mom, Sara, Mark, but this..." I glanced at the shack, rune-carved, log-stacked, Lily's dirt drawings smudged by the door. "This is ours, small, scarred, but mine." My chest tightened, grief still there, a weight I'd carry, but it sat beside this now, a fragile light stitched into the dark.

The camp slept, a bubble of quiet in a broken world, fires crackling low, a guard's boots crunching gravel on the wire, a kid's murmur fading into the night. Axel sat parked beside the shack, headlights off, engine silent, dash lights pulsing faint gold as he dozed, a smug sentinel watching our patch. I stood, boots scuffing the porch, pulling the flask for one last swig, water sharp against my tongue, steadying the tremor that never quite left. Mithis rose too, axe in hand, cape swaying softly, standing close, her presence a rock I'd leaned on too long to count. David stayed railing, creaking as he leaned back, green eyes tracing the sky, calm in a way I hadn't seen before.

"We keep it," I said, voice low, firm, looking at them both, "Whatever comes: portals, curses, dragons, we hold this. For her, for us." My hand rested on the shack's frame, wood rough under my palm, runes warm where Mithis had carved them, a promise etched into this scrap of earth.

Mithis nodded, crimson eyes glinting fiercely, a small smile curling her lips. "For her, for us," she echoed, green hand squeezing mine once more, a vow sealed between us. David tipped his head "Damn right," he said, voice steady "Got somethin' worth fighting for ain't letting it go." His grin widened, a flicker of the kid who'd roared through bandits, solid now, rooted here.

I stepped inside, Lily's snores soft, steady, kneeling by her cot, brushing a curl from her dirt-smudged face. She stirred, mumbling sleepily, "Uncle?" brown eyes fluttering faint, Sara's echo alive in her small frame. "Right here, Lil," I whispered, voice breaking softly, "Always." She sighed, settling deeper, small hand finding mine, gripping tight as sleep took her again. I stayed watching her breathe, grief a shadow beside this light, a home built from ash and blood.

Outside, the convergence waited, portals pulsing faint, dragons circling silent, curses and monsters stirring beyond safe zone walls, but here, with Lily's hand in mine, Mithis's steady watch, David's quiet strength, and Axel's smug hum, I had something worth fighting for.

A home, small, scarred, stitched together from ruin, but ours. The road had ended not with peace, not with victory, but with this, a fragile stand against the dark. And that was enough.

ABOUT THE AUTHOR

Jacob Salvia is an American author whose storytelling bridges ancient cultures, military tradition, and mythic imagination. Born and raised in Central Florida, Jacob is a proud member of the Little Traverse Bay Bands of Odawa Indians, drawing on his Native American heritage, particularly the lore of beings like the Wendigo, to breathe life into modern and otherworldly legends.

Beyond Native traditions, Jacob finds inspiration in the sweeping epics of fantasy literature and the timeless archetypes of Greek mythology. An avid historical reenactor, he brings a deep respect and firsthand understanding of military history, strategy, and world cultures into his world-building, creating layered, authentic narratives where history and myth intertwine.

Through his work, Jacob explores the blurred boundaries between Earth and hidden realms, reminding readers that the ancient powers of the world — and beyond — are never truly asleep.

www.ingramcontent.com/pod-product-compliance
Lightning Source LLC
LaVergne TN
LVHW041727160825
818627LV00001B/29